Murder By Quill

by

Michael Phillips

Michael Phillips is the author of many popular fiction books and series, including:

The Sword, the Garden, and the King
Angel Harp
Heather Song

The Green Hills of Snowdonia
From Across the Ancient Waters
Treasure of the Celtic Triangle

The Secret of the Rose
The Eleventh Hour
A Rose Remembered
Escape to Freedom
Dawn of Liberty

American Dreams
Dream of Freedom
Dream of Life
Dream of Love

The Livingstone Chronicles
Rift in Time
Hidden in Time

Shenandoah Sisers and Carolina Cousins
Angels Watching Over Me
A Day to Pick your Own Cotton
...and six more titles

The Journals of Corrie Belle Hollister
My Father's World (with Judith Pella)
Daughter of Grace (with Judith Pella)
...and nine more titles

The Secrets of Heathersleigh Hall
Wild Grows the Heather in Devon
Wayward Winds
Heathersleigh Homecoming
A New Dawn Over Devon

The Destiny Chronicles
Destiny Junction
Kings Crossroads

Murder By Quill
Copyright © 2013 by Michael Phillips

Cover photograph of Cullen House with quill by Fiona Simpson.

Published 2013 by Yellowood House, an imprint of Sunrise Books

ISBN: 978-0940652682

A Cast of ~~Characters~~ *Suspects*

The Town

JOHN THOMPSON—owner of local Abra Bits & Collectables specializing in books, pens, and writing paraphernalia

ALAN AND KEARA LONG—owners of local Paper Shoppe on Cullen square

RICHARD RIGGS—Detective Chief Inspector of Buckie Police Dept., detective division

MARGARET WESTBROOK—Detective Sergeant, assistant to Riggs

Cullen House

HUGH BARRIBAULT—64, owner of Cullen House. Old-school, committed to preserving traditional values and the craft of bookmaking in publishing. Recently established Barribault Foundation and new publishing venture Barribault House to keep excellence in publishing and bookmaking alive.

MISS CYNTHIA GORDON—Barribault's personal secretary and assistant and overseer of staff of Barribault House and Barribault Foundation.

REGINALD COOMBES—Cullen House butler, lives on premesis.

CONSTANCE FOTHERINGAY—Cullen House cook.

MRS. MERIDETH WALTON—Cullen House housekeeper and overseer of domestic day staff. She and husband live on premesis.

The Eight

MIKE ST. JOHN—36, Aberdonian Congregationalist minister, though disdains the use of "Rev." A friendly and outgoing klutz with active sense of humor. He has written a clever and ingenious whodunit, with Scottish sleuth modeled after Father Brown.

SHELBY FITZPATRICK—34, unmarried California psychologist with a passion for history. Her sweeping 700 page "family saga" which chronicles the history of Wales—inspired by her own family roots through her grandfather who immigrated to U.S.—is reminiscent of her favorite author James Michener.

MELINDA FRANKS—29, Vivacious, pretty, outgoing graduate student at Cambridge studying English Literature specializing in poetry.

DAME JENNIFER MEYERSON—57, stately Englishwoman, known and revered throughout Britain, married to British diplomat, friend of Queen Mum.

GRAHAM WHITAKER—49, American professor of economics, former editorial assistant for NY publisher. His witty yet thoughtful imagination has produced an engaging and poignant writing style. His short story collection is as varied as the selections are thought-provoking and compelling, though the one humorous piece, "The Importance of Love, a Brief History," a spoof of his favorite author P.G. Wodehouse, is pure farcical fun.

FATHER DUGAN SMYTHE—56, Anglican priest from London, predisposed against Scotland and Scots in general, though fond of their whisky. Notwithstanding that his is the only so-called "religious" work under consideration, his beliefs appear ambiguous.

DR. BRISCOE COBB—53, confirmed bachelor, academician, and skeptic. Shakespearean expert and intellectual snob, Professor of English Literature of the 16th and 17th centuries at Oxford, he despises the lingering reputation of C.S. Lewis who wrote and taught in the same field. Agnostic and antagonistic toward all religion, especially Christianity.

JESSICA STOKES—42, unmarried hopeful authoress of eight unpublished books of "intellectually challenging" fiction, reader of Spinoza, Voltaire, Shaw types, single and feminist, teaches introductory philosophy at Manchester. Openly critical of men, she carries herself with a condescendingly superior air.

The Winning Entries

Conundrum at Craigievar Castle by Mike St. John

Song of the Western Mountains by Shelby Fitzpatrick

Journeys Inward, Journeys Outward, Poems by Melinda Franks

Civilization in the Third Millennium: Globalization and the Future of Western Politics, Religion, Culture, and Art by Dame Jennifer Meyerson

Snowflakes on the Thames, and Other Stories by Graham Whitaker

The God Delusion, the Atheism Myth: Toward a Reconciliation of Opposites by Father Dugan Smythe

New Perspectives on Shakespeare by Dr. Briscoe Cobb

Ratchett, by Jessica Stokes

CONTENTS

PROLOGUE

Sons and daughters choose neither parents, station, nor surroundings where the roots of their lives are destined to grow. Fiona Kilcardy would certainly not have chosen the concrete streets and stone jungles of Belfast as the ideal garden in which to nurture her secret longings.

With gunfire and car-bombs as background music to her youth, Fiona's thoughts often filled with peaceful seashores, lonely mountains, and protected glens of streams, green grass, deer, and rabbits, where silence reigned in place of strife. She dreamed of cottages where mothers and fathers could raise children and grow flowers and laugh and be happy together.

The diary was a gift on her sixteenth birthday.

The inscription inside from her mother was as simple as profound:

> *My dear Fiona,*
> *This is the story of your life. It has yet*
> *to be written...and you will write it.*
> *Love always,*
> *Mummy.*

Fiona's first entries were not as philosophical as her mother's sentiments. She spoke of school, daily routines, and the fear that gripped her when the fighting came close. As her father grew into prominence in the protestant Ulster Brigade, then her brothers with him, gradually the pages of Fiona's diary filled with increasing hatred for what they called "the cause." By the time she turned twenty, the fancies of childhood seemed far away. Soldiers from England were everywhere, a constant reminder that she lived in no serene highland glen, but in nothing less than a war zone. Guns not flowers dictated the rhythms of life. By then the diary lay abandoned in a drawer beneath ragged dresses and worn out shoes, untouched sometimes for a year at a time.

At twenty-four, her mother dead, Fiona's life had become a drudgery of cooking, cleaning, and keeping house for her father and two brothers. All their talk was of plots to drive the IRA from the north. Her father was by then a leader among protestant militants. To escape Belfast became Fiona's consuming passion.

She had accepted the advances of a newcomer to Belfast whom she convinced herself was sincere. She doubted that she loved Fingall Hainn. But in war ravaged Belfast, what right did she have to be choosy. If she did not marry soon, she would probably eventually be raped, or find herself in a marriage arranged by her father for the political expediency of his plans.

She tried to convince herself that Fingall would make a decent marriage. He read books, which was more than she could say for her brothers and their acquaintances, whose literary prowess extended no farther than being able to read a Guiness label. Fingall was also religious in his own way. She suspected that he might be from Eire, though he did not speak of his past. He quoted Yeats and spoke of becoming a mystic-poet in the same tradition, even perhaps a clergyman, though how poetry and religion mixed was beyond her. She cared nothing for religion. But it was a relief to meet a young man who was not obsessed with the Ulster wars. If religion was the reason, that was fine with her.

Fiona vaguely knew of the Phoenix Park murders in Dublin. What she did not know was that Selwyn Kilcardy had led a retaliatory attack in Belfast in which several IRA leaders were killed. Immediately afterward her father disappeared, his life a target, to a safehouse in the country. Neither he nor her brothers knew that the IRA had plans to abduct Fiona for ransom until Kilcardy came out of hiding.

Suddenly one afternoon, three hooded IRA terrorists burst into the Kilcardy house on Shankhill Road. A deafening round of automatic shots exploded the place apart.

A block away, two British soldiers heard the gunfire. Sprinting toward the scene, they saw terrorists dragging a screaming girl from the building. The older of the two dropped to his belly and yanked the pistol from his side. Thirty seconds later, three IRA terrorists lay dead on the ground and the corporeal was carrying the girl to safety.

"What is your name?" he asked as he set her down on a patch of brown grass.

"Fiona," she sobbed, clinging to his neck as he tried to stand. "Fiona Kilcardy...please help me—don't leave me!"

"You are safe now," he replied, trying to calm her. "No harm will come to you."

More help arrived shortly. The girl was obviously in shock, deepened the more when she learned of the death of her two brothers. An aunt from a nearby house took charge of her.

Concerned for her recovery, the older of the soldiers returned the following day to the house of Fiona's aunt, and the day after that. By week's end the girl was out of bed, back on her feet, and soon able to return and put her own home back in order. By then, an occasional smile returning to her eyes, the corporeal realized that he had saved the life of what was surely the most beautiful girl in all Belfast.

He came to the funeral for her two brothers later in the week. As she stood beside him in his dress uniform, the shy glances up at his face made it obvious that Fiona was gazing upon the handsome soldier with something more than passing gratitude.

Alone in the world, her father still gone, and having been rescued from probable death by a dashing and heroic Englishman, what could Fiona Kilcardy do but fall in love? The diary in her drawer, so long neglected, now filled with a torrent of love-thoughts. But it was a dangerous affair. The whirlwind romance that followed was intensified by peril. Every waking moment when he was not on duty the young soldier spent at the run-down house on Shankhill Road. Fiona's dreams of happiness away from this dreadful city sprouted anew.

But the corporeal cherished a secret which he must tell before long. He knew well enough how things stood. He had known it when he came. He was Catholic. Eventually it would come out. He must tell Fiona and her relatives, and somehow hope to find a way to convince them he was no enemy.

But Fiona, too, possessed a secret. His name was Fingall Hainn.

As fate would have it, Fingall was away in Cork during the events that were destined to alter Fiona's life forever. Everyone in the neighborhood knew about the visits of the young English corporeal and what they portended. Fingall would know how things stood within hours of his return to Belfast.

Fiona's soldier-lover came to call one evening. Fearing that their time together may soon be troubled by Fingall's return, and anxious to make the evening memorable, she prepared a lavish meal, ending her *preparations by dashing perfume on face and neck, perhaps too liberally. He came with flowers. The wine flowed. They laughed and talked freely. When they awoke the next morning in one another's arms, she knew she could never be the wife of Fingall Hainn.*

Returning to Belfast after a long absence, Fingall Hainn divined immediately that a change had come to the girl he assumed was his. Learning of the attempted abduction and rescue, he suspected the cause. It did not take the powers of a Sherlock Holmes for him to discover the identity of the English soldier involved in the incident. But he would make no accusation without proof.

That proof, it turned out, came from the quarter he least expected — from his rival for Fiona's heart.

The night spent under Fiona's roof proved more emotionally unsettling for the young Englishman even than for the Irish maiden who found herself involved with two men. He had never considered himself unusually devout. Yet the day after their tryst, his conscience, untroubled by the killing of terrorists, suddenly growled to life. Accusations seared his brain. He had forsaken the teaching of the Church. He had dishonored the only girl he had ever loved. How could he expect her to marry him when he had been so careless of her purity. He had sacrificed sexual fidelity on the altar of his own desire. His love for Fiona, till then pure, had become sin in the eyes of his church.

In despair, he sought the confessional, never suspecting that his every move was being watched by his jealous rival.

He left his barracks one afternoon, taking care, he thought, not to be seen. Following circuitous byways and back streets and lanes, he made his way to the nationalist sector of West Belfast. There he found a church and went in search of the priest, asking if he would hear his confession. Seeing his uniform, and realizing from his tongue that he was no Irishman, the priest hesitated.

"Are you Catholic, young man?" he asked warily.

"I am, Father."

"Very well," nodded the priest. "Let me put a thing or two in order and I will see you in the confessional in five minutes."

He showed him the way, then briefly left him.

When the black-robed man entered the confessional a few minutes later, the young soldier was too consumed by his own thoughts to realize that it was not the same man he had spoken with in the churchyard.

Tearfully he poured out to a stranger a detailed account of the facts that haunted him like a black cloud.

Knowing that he must see Fiona again, he scribbled a brief note, walked to Shankhill Road and the familiar house, and put it through the letter slot before making a hasty retreat.

Fiona found the note, and hurried outside, searching in every direction. Seeing no sign of the messenger, she opened the single sheet of paper.

> My dear Fiona, she read.
>
> Forgive my absence these recent days. I have been busy with my duties. I want very much to talk to you. Please meet me at the park where you first showed me your favorite roses, tomorrow at noon.

Fate, however, continued to spin webs of evil fortune for these two lovers. A car bomb exploded that night outside the young soldier's barracks. Though rendered unconscious for several days with extensive chest wounds and a broken leg, his life was spared. When consciousness returned, he found himself in a military hospital in Birmingham. Beside himself to contact Fiona, he wrote every day. But never a word came in reply.

Fiona, meanwhile, waited in the park by the roses, the note crumpled in her hand, till darkness at last made the streets unsafe. Weeping, she made her way home.

The following weeks faded into a blur of tearful uncertainty. Not knowing of the car bomb, she alternated between fits of fear for the corporeal's life, and what was worse, that for reasons she could not fathom he had deserted her.

Recouperating in England, her soldier-hero never knew that Fiona was pregnant with his child.

The entries in Fiona's diary turned dark. The dreadful, hopeless early weeks of her pregnancy progressed. In her despair, she allowed Fingall to take advantage of her. Eventually she could hide the fact of her pregnancy no longer. Fingall mistakenly thought the child his. Fiona laughed bitterly at the suggestion, and finally told him the truth.

Her serene young man of poetic and religious bent went wild with rage. Terrified for her life, Fiona fled. Safe in her aunt's home that night and unable to sleep, Fiona pulled out her diary to write of the horrible

5

day. With tears dripping onto the page, she recorded Fingall's last words before he had flown into the rage that had driven her away:

> Weep for him now while you can. He will
> die before you lay eyes on him again. He
> will die at my hand.

She remained haunted by his threats. However, Fingall Hainn soon also disappeared.

As her baby grew within her, Fiona's despondency deepened. More attacks and several devastating car bombs in the neighborhood drove them all from their homes. Her life completely disrupted. Fiona despaired of being able to give her baby a life of happiness. Her writings took a morbid turn. The only hope a son or daughter had would be to escape this hell…without her. She was not so far gone as to think of taking two lives. If blood was to be on her hands, it would be only her own.

Suicide, however, was spared her when she died in childbirth.

The moment the English corporeal recovered sufficiently to be released, he returned to Belfast. Months had passed. A bombed out shell was all that remained of the house on Shankhill Road where he had discovered a fleeting interlude of happiness.

Searching records and newspapers and interrogating scores of people over the course of the following months turned up not a single trace of Fiona or her family.

ONE

The Shop

The Scottish coastal village of Cullen along the temperate Moray Firth offered the ideal seaside holiday.

The town and its environs was a relaxed old-fashioned place where visitors came to forget the pace of modern life. Its three busiest shops sold ice cream, fish and chips, and antiques. The setting hardly seemed likely for murder.

It might have been different centuries ago perhaps, during days of swords and ghosts and the betrayal of ever-shifting clan loyalties. Macbeth, after all, was a Scot, and had carried out his mischief only sixty miles from there.

Murder made sense back in Scotland's glory days when, if you didn't kill someone every year or two, you were hardly worthy of being called a man.

But surely not in this civilized age. Not in Cullen.

A tall and imposing figure strode briskly between rows of gray stone houses.

The buildings among which he walked were gray, the street and sidewalk were gray, the roof slates were gray. Once leaving the greenery of the surrounding countryside and entering its cities and towns, gray became the predominant feature of the northern Scottish landscape.

Mercifully on this day, that gray was overspread by a cheery blue reflecting off the azure-green of the sea. The brilliance above was broken here and there by tufts of woolly white that added just the right touch to the chilly morning.

The walker had made his way from Cullen House along a half-mile spectacular wooded drive into the village proper. The great mansion had been home and private retreat to author and philanthropist Hugh Barribault for twenty years. He was never seen without his tightly-rolled dark blue umbrella. His full head of distinguished graying black hair, covered by neither hat nor cap, accentuated ruggedly handsome features and gave him an air of erudition and authority.

Barribault was of the old school in every way. Though he usually dined alone, he dressed formally every evening for dinner, and never so much as left his private apartment without a tie.

With the crisp gait of the Germanic branch of his ancient Celtic ancestry, he turned into a narrow lane and made his way toward the noisy main thoroughfare through town.

A moment later he entered the cramped quarters of Abra Bits & Collectables.

"Good morning, John!" he said, greeting the proprietor. "How goes the trade?"

"Lots of tourists, but no one's buying," replied the shopkeeper. "And you, Hugh—golden words spilling onto the page?"

"The creative sap was flowing this morning. But an accident put a stop to it."

"Run out of ink?"

"A writer's dream! Sadly, nothing so easily solved. I finally had a morning without interruptions. Nothing to do but await my guests...and then catastrophe. I broke the nib of my pen."

"That is a disaster! Which one?"

"That 1940s Duofold I bought from you years ago...still the best pen in my collection. I dropped it on the tile floor. Broke my heart!"

"Bring it in, Hugh. I'll outfit it with a new nib. No bother."

"Ah, but such a nib it was! I had to do something to take my mind off the tragedy, so I came out for a walk. No doubt I'm restless to get the thing underway. Have you made any progress with that old key you were trying to duplicate for me?"

"It's nearly filed down to match the broken one you brought me. I'll be up to check on it soon."

"Good. I'd rather not change that outside lock to the supply room.—By the way, I've also been looking for a new clock," Barribault added. "Not actually *new*, of course…Victorian probably, perhaps Edwardian—American or French… Westminster chimes."

"I may have one coming in that will fit the bill. Didn't you once write a story in which a clock figured into your crime?"

Barribault nodded. "But it was destroyed at the time of the murder. A terrible thing to do, but sometimes one has to make sacrifices for a story. There was also a hypodermic needle that came into it as I recall, filled with some exotic poison…I've forgotten the details. The plots run together after a while."

Barribault's attention was drawn outside where a professionally dressed young woman in her late twenties walked by along the sidewalk.

"Who's that?" he asked. "Seems I recognize her."

Thompson stepped to the window.

"Maggie Westbrook…*Detective Sergeant* Westbrook. Her father's a friend of mine."

"I'll call her next time I need a member of the constabulary," chuckled Barribault. "I don't much care for Chief Inspector Riggs. Bit of a pompous blowhard if you ask me."

The author turned back into the shop. "Well today's the big day!" he said.

"The arrival of your new colleagues, eh?" rejoined Thompson. "It's all anyone around here's talking about. You and your famous eight are on the front pages of every newspaper in Scotland."

"Impossible to keep something this big secret, I suppose."

"A juicy setup," Thompson went on, "—famous author sponsors writer's contest…finalists secluded away in a castle. It's straight out of Agatha Christie."

Barribault roared. "Hardly so sinister as what would interest Hercule Poirot or Miss Marple! I only wish you were one of them, John."

A momentary flash flared from the shopkeeper's eyes. But he quickly suppressed it.

"In any event, they will be here this evening," added Barribault. "Perhaps then the hubbub will quiet down. With that in mind, I suppose I should finish my therapeutic walk and get back to the House."

"Before you go," said the shopkeeper, "I've something to show you." He disappeared into a small alcove yet deeper in the hidden recesses of his shop where a small work desk crammed into a corner was piled with assorted tools. Not only was John Thompson an antique dealer, he specialized in pens and nibs and ink wells and stands and blotters and hand-made feather quills and traveling letter boxes—any and all paraphernalia connected to the writer's craft.

For a man who made his living writing books like Thompson's most regular customer, and doing so the old fashioned way, by hand with vintage fountain pens, the place was a veritable candy store of treasures. Adding to the intrigue of the place, the shelves of several small rooms were piled from floor to ceiling with antiquarian books. The mere sight of the spines and their fusty fragrance were enchantment to the imagination and perfume to the nostrils of the book lover. Barribault often lost himself for hours among them. He always came away from the shop reinvigorated to resume his own literary efforts.

"Finished it last night," said Thompson, returning a moment later and handing his creation to his visitor. "The feather slips off the end, just there—" he added, pointing. "Underneath is a Sheaffer snorkel mechanism. It's a quill with fillable chamber. No redipping! Looks like an ordinary quill, but you can write for eight pages uninterrupted!"

"The snorkel bit actually works?" asked the author.

"Just look." Thompson took the quill back, slipped the feather from the end, then slowly turned the top of the cylinder as out from beneath the nib came protruding the sharp snorkel tip designed to draw ink into the pen from an inkwell like a tiny syringe.

"Genius, John," said Barribault. "You designed this yourself?"

"Made it from spare parts of several old pens I had. Want to take it up to the House for a test drive and let me know how it works?"

"I'm afraid I might break it. I'm not quite so archaic that I want to go back to feather quills! Even one that requires no dipping. To be honest, John," Barribault added after a moment, I'd rather you spent your time writing. I've told you—I'm convinced there's a best-seller in you!"

Thompson nodded, a peculiar smile crossing his lips.

After a few more minutes of conversation that ranged from Henry the Navigator to the Knights Templar to Thompson's theory of the site of the battle of Mons Graupius between the Picts and Romans, the author turned to leave the shop.

As the echo from the bell fell silent, the shopkeeper opened the bottom drawer of the desk beside him. From it he removed a two-inch stack of paper. Methodically he turned over its sheets, glancing through the familiar pages as he fell to brooding about many things.

Meanwhile, Hugh Barribault continued to the square at the center of town. He stopped briefly at The Paper Shoppe for the day's *Telegraph, Times,* and *Press and Journal* from Alan Long. Finally he completed the circle he had begun earlier, walking up Grant Street and again through the gate into the grounds of Cullen House.

TWO

The Eight

The first of The Eight arrived by taxi and was altogether a disappointment.

Word had leaked out the day before that Cullen Taxis had been hired to collect Dame Jennifer Meyerson at the Aberdeen airport at 12:30. Village watchers began clustering in the square long before that. Though the taxi wouldn't be due until at least 1:45, one of the others *might* arrive in the meantime.

No one did.

At 1:47, punctual as fate, the familiar green taxi rounded the bend at the top of the street and sped toward them. Shouts and exclamations went up. Everyone edged close to the street for a look as the carroty-orange mop of their own Spunky Cruickshank behind the wheel came into view.

But Spunky wheeled onto Grant and up toward Cullen House almost without slowing, and disappeared through the gate into the trees without fanfare. The middle of town fell silent and that was that. Other than a passing glimpse of the elegant lady's gray hair where she sat erect in the back seat, there hadn't been much to see.

"Bit o' a damp fuse, that," remarked Alan Long as he turned back into his Paper Shoppe at the corner.

Ten minutes later, Spunky guided his taxi slowly out through the gate, then crept right onto South Deskford. He didn't dare drive empty back through the middle of town where he knew he would be mobbed by questions. He had been paid double the going airport rate to keep his mouth shut.

On the second floor of the north wing of Cullen House, Barribault's butler Reginald Coombes was just leading their first guest to her room.

* * *

The crowd in Cullen's village square did not have long to wait for the second of Barribault's guests. This time their patience was rewarded with something to talk about.

A bright yellow Mini convertible came into sight moving down the hill in the wake of Spunky's taxi. At the wheel sat an uncommonly beautiful young woman in her late twenties, auburn-red hair flying in the breeze. The moment she became visible, shouts and waves went up. The young men who had been following the photographs in the news all knew who *this* was.

The car slowed. Unable to help herself as she made her way through the boisterous crowd, the driver eased her sporty Mini to a stop.

Immediately two dozen eager gawkers swarmed forward. She flashed a bewitching smile.

"Would this by any chance..." she began with feigned innocence, making no attempt to disguise her American accent, "be *Cullen*?"

"That it is, ma'am!" replied a young man in his early twenties. He pushed his way to the driver's side of the car and leaned down. "Anything you need, ma'am...the name's George Hay."

"Get back, Geordie!' shouted a voice behind him. "She ain't aboot t' luik at the likes o' yersel'."

The young woman, however, leaned forward, then stared straight up into young Hay's face.

"And who are you, George," she said with a flirtatious gleam in her deep blue eyes, " — the mayor?"

She reached up, to the delight of the onlookers, grabbed the bill of his cap and yanked it over his eyes. A good-natured laugh followed as she shoved him back, opened the door of the car she had driven up from Cambridge, and stepped out.

The crowd was instantly in the palm of her hand. Anyone who could best Geordie Hay was all right in their book. For an enchantress like this to put him in his place—they would be talking about this all day!

The girl was of short stature, probably five foot three, her face round, her skin creamy white, her mouth small, her blue eyes wide set. Expressive lips ever hinting at mischief, and brilliant white teeth, were enough to mesmerize any red-blooded man with an enigmatic air of mystery. Her accent, seemingly American at first, the more one listened, morphed into an enigmatic uncertainty. Words fell from her lips like subtle notes of a fine wine, hinting at influences from across ancient waters. To the perceptive observer, she might be more than she appeared...even perhaps more than she herself realized.

Her eyes scanned the crowd. They came to rest on a tall slender man on the steps of the shop opposite her car. That he seemed more detached than the town's young bucks made him a perfect target for her flirtatious wiles.

She made her way through the crowd straight toward him.

"Hello there," she purred. "My name is Melinda Franks. From your distinguished look, it would not surprise me if *you* were the mayor."

"No, ma'am," the man replied. "Cullen's got nae mayor, ye ken. I'm jist a shopkeeper. This is my place here," he said, nodding behind him. "I'm Alan Long, ma'am."

"Well, then, Mr. Long," said the girl, "mayor or not, I have the feeling you could tell me the way to Cullen House."

"Ye're on the richt street already, ma'am. Jist keep as ye're boun'. The gate's jist up there ahead."

The enlivened crowd noisily clustered up for a closer look. Continuing to work it like a skilled politician, young Miss Franks now turned and slowly made the way back to her car and climbed in. As she inched forward, the crowd parted like the Red Sea. Gently she accelerated, then, when the way was clear, sped away up Grant Street, casting one last wave behind her, followed by a peel of happy laughter echoing in the breeze.

* * *

After the vivacious Melinda Franks, the arrival of Father Dugan Smythe in a hired Mercedes twenty minutes later again proved a disappointment.

The fifty-six year old Anglican priest had flown from London to Edinburgh. He had driven up this morning, lunching in Aberdeen, before continuing into the wilds of Morayshire. Well traveled, he yet looked on Scots beyond the Forth as uncivilized descendents of the Picts. The whisky of the region, of course, was an undeniable contribution to the world. But why anyone would come here on a holiday, much less actually *live* here, was beyond him.

The familiar Mercedes insignia on the hood attracted the immediate attention of the onlookers. The moment it turned up Grant Street, they knew it must contain the third of The Eight. Hoping for better luck this time, Geordie Hay and a few of his cohorts crept off the sidewalk into the street for a closer look.

But though Smythe slowed as he made his way to keep from hitting any of the rowdy blackguards, the tinted windows kept them from getting a clear glimpse of him inside.

* * *

Fifty-one year old Graham Whitaker, American university professor of economics and onetime editorial assistant for a small New York publishing house, drove into town with something else on his mind than finding the way to Cullen House.

He had come up Scotland's west coast from Glasgow, overnighting in Oban. Continuing today, he had stopped for a snack and tea at Inverness, and had enjoyed a full pot. He had not been out of the car since.

His internal plumbing had reached the bursting point as he drove beneath the viaduct and into town.

He pulled into the square and stopped in front of a small stone building marked "Toilets," jumped out, and hurried inside.

"That is a profound relief," he sighed to himself as he walked back into the sunlight a minute later.

He paused in surprise. Spread around his car were a hundred people staring straight at him.

He broke into a confused grin. "What is this?" he laughed. "Did I do something wrong?"

"Naethin' like that, sir?" said an elderly man in front.

"What then?" chuckled Whitaker. "Are all the town's visitors scrutinized when they make use of these facilities?"

"Meanin' no disrespect, sir...we was jist wantin' t' ken if ye was ane o' the eight, an' was on yer way t' the Muckle Hoose."

"Sorry, I don't think I understand...what is a *muckle hoose*?"

"The big hoose, laddie—Cullen House."

"Oh...Cullen House...yes, that is exactly where I am going. Perhaps you can point me on my way."

"Jist ahind us there," said the man pointing behind him, "past the Market Cross, ken, an' up the street."

"Ah, yes, I see... Market Snodsberry's Victory Monument."

"What's that ye say, laddie?"

"Nothing," replied Whitaker, smiling to himself. "Just a bad Wodehouse joke."

* * *

The Cullen House to which these first four of the famous "Eight" were bound was the home and private estate of the wealthy Scottish author who was at the center of the day's hullabaloo. Many in the publishing establishment called its present owner eccentric. Barribault didn't mind. His aim had been to restore the great mansion as much as possible to its former glory. In that objective he had been largely successful.

Unmarried, he employed, in addition to Coombes, a secretary, a cook, a full time housekeeper with several day assistants, a maintenance man, and a full time landscape professional to keep the grounds immaculate. Three of his staff lived at the House in very nice quarters. Others had residences in town. His secretary lived in Keith. The head housekeeper and her retired husband had their own apartments on the second floor of the south wing above the kitchen. He paid them all well and they were content.

Though he had been born into money, Barribault had accumulated as much with his own pen as had come from his father. An award winning novelist of the first rank, with sales to match the literary accolades, as well as noted playwright and historian, Barribault's writing style, temperament, and lifestyle were notably of the old school. It had often been said of him that he was born in the wrong century, following more in the tradition of Dickens and George MacDonald than the likes of Clancy, Grisham, and King. The advent and explosion of Kindle books were but more salt in the wound of his traditionalism.

Hollywood once held fascination for him, but no longer. He had not been to a movie in fifteen years. There were some things it was simply best to forget. He wrote by hand and only occasionally employed a typewriter, leaving transcriptions to his personal secretary, the efficient Miss Cynthia Gordon. He had never so much as set his fingers to a computer, and had only a disinterested awareness that such things as blackberries and ipods existed. He was shrewd enough, however, to appreciate Miss Gordon's skill with the computer in her office. He could not deny that it streamlined the composition of his manuscripts. Of what she did for him on the internet by way of research, he wanted to know as few details as possible. He had a personal aversion to the entire premise on which the internet was based, though he marveled at the results. He had not, however, given sanction to the entire new world of digital media—he allowed no iphones or other mobile devives on the premises, and his arriving guests had been instructed to bring none.

Those who knew Hugh Barribault well, and such were few indeed, might have wondered at the apparent dichotomy between certain details of his hidden biography and the traditional values he so openly espoused. But even his closest associates knew little of that past. And none knew of the conflicted burdens he bore as a result of it.

Though still studied in colleges and universities as representative of a small neo-Victorian school of late twentieth-century authors, the sales of his books had for some time been in decline. The result was personal. He found it increasingly difficult to pour his heart and soul into writings the public was no longer interested in. He did not want to lapse into that pathetic prerogative of the aged—writing critiques against modernism nobody heeded. His contribution to posterity had to be more positive, practical, and enduring.

In Barribault's view, no one was encouraging excellence. Not only were ebooks shrinking the demand for what he called *real* books to unheard of levels, those books that were being produced were of inferior quality. To make matters worse, the editors in most publishing houses hadn't a clue what comprised writing excellence. The lust for thrill-driven sex and horror and the occult ruled acquisitions departments without care for theme and structure of plot and depth of characterization. Justifying such trends because the public must be given what it wants, most publishing houses, in Barribault's opinion, had sold out what should be their foundational mission—to publish lasting books of physical quality and beauty, whose contents reflected integrity, truth, substance, excellence, and virtue.

Hugh Barribault had recognized several years before that he was aging. He was alone in the world. He had therefore devoted much thought to what ought to become of the estate and his fortune when he was gone. How, he wondered, might he exercise an impact among future generations? What could he do to stem the tide of modernistic drivel? How might his influence invigorate books of the future with a reassertion of classic literary principles?

In short: What lasting legacy could he leave the literary world?

The four men and four women arriving in Cullen on this day represented the cornerstone of his plan.

For the past two years Hugh Barribault had been engaged in the legalities of setting up a literary foundation—to which Cullen House and the Barribault estate would be given at his death. At the same time he had begun the establishment of a for-profit publishing company dedicated to the principles of excellence and quality he revered.

Upon this venture, he had determined to expend his fortune. He would lay out whatever it took in however many years were left him to insure that the publications of the new Barribault House received the acclaim they deserved. The company would be respected in the publishing world, and attract the best and brightest of future generations of writers.

To this end he had committed himself to hire the best editors, designers, research and production staff, publicists—all individuals who shared his vision of what publishing should be.

Every book produced by Barribault House would be cloth bound by printeries dedicated to the craft of the bookmaking art. Attention would be given to detail and old-world quality at every level. He envisioned an impact such that, in time, Barribault House would have the stature and a coterie of prestigious authors to enable it to compete with the largest firms in New York and London. He would not even try to compete with the ebook world. Even if it was a shrinking audience, he would target his efforts toward traditional lovers of real *books*.

Barribault had also been hard at work on a new, he hoped, blockbuster novel of his own, with which, in conjunction with eight original works, the inaugural Barribault House line would be launched.

It was his method of selecting those eight new works that had caused such a national stir and led to this exciting day in the Scottish village of Cullen.

It was his intent for Barribault House to continue publishing more new authors yearly subsequent to this initial highly publicized launch, along with veteran authors who brought him their works. Each year's unpublished writers would be selected from among entries in a massively publicized writing contest, not the least of whose details included an advance cheque in the amount of £100,000. Their publications might include fiction, poetry, drama, non-fiction, and literary criticism. The winners would be invited to Cullen House every September, all expenses paid, to discuss with Barribault and one another the future of English literature. As but one of the fringe benefits of selection, they would be entitled to visit Cullen House any time—to cloister away to write, to discuss his or her work with Barribault or his staff, or merely to inject the creative juices with a dose of inspiration from the surrounding Scottish countryside. And from his growing stable of authors, Barribault would select men and women who shared his values and perspectives to sit on the board of his foundation and be given rotating management positions in the publishing company, thus insuring a constant infusion of new creative blood at the highest levels. Whether he would allow his publications eventually into Kindle editions, that was a bridge he was not yet prepared to cross in his mind.

Work had begun not long thereafter to convert half of the second floor of the south wing of Cullen House into editorial offices and headquarters for the foundation and publishing house. Rumors had, of course, immediately begun circulating through the community, for a dozen or more local tradesmen had been hired for the work. Speculation ranged between many possibilities: That Barribault was marrying a Spanish heiress whom he was bringing to Cullen House, and that he was updating the place in order to sell it, that he was redecorating the wing to appease a ghost who had appeared to him in the middle of the night.

The mystery of the remodeling did not last long. Barribault went public with his plans soon enough. That had been two years ago.

To signal the formation of Barribault House, and to announce the guidelines for the first year's contest, Barribault took out full page ads in both the *London Times* and the *New York Times*, and sent press releases to another hundred newspapers on both sides of the Atlantic.

Within days, hopeful authors and authoresses by the thousands were scurrying to their word processors with dreams of fame and fortune dancing in their heads.

* * *

One of these had been Jessica Stokes, forty-two, who fancied herself more than a *hopeful* authoress, but the genuine article who had simply not been discovered yet. She wrote what she called "intellectually challenging" fiction, which might have given more than a little insight into the fact that none of her eight novels were published. That her bedtime reading consisted of the likes of Spinoza, Bacon, Voltaire, George Bernard Shaw, and some of the twentieth century's most obscure feminist authors, indicated in no small measure the nature of the highbrow content with which she had loaded down her previous "works," as she called them.

One of her favorites was the Australian feminist author of *My Brilliant Career*. There were rumors on the campus where she taught three classes of introductory philosophy that she was modernist in more ways than philosophically. Nothing, however, was known for certain.

One thing Jessica Stokes was not was a fool. She desperately wanted to be published. In the announcement of Barribault's contest she saw her chance.

Casting aside everything she thought she knew about writing, she undertook a complete renovation of her style, including her perspectives on interweaving the elements of plot and sophisticated content. The result had been successful, and here she was stepping off the westbound Bluebird Coach in Cullen's town square a little after three.

No one expected any of The Eight to come by bus. Stokes' arrival went completely unnoticed.

She was obviously a stranger come for a visit, thought one or two as they observed her standing alone as the bus left town. When she began walking up Grant Street pulling a single midsize suitcase clattering on wheels behind her, most assumed her bound for the Grant Arms or the self-catering cottage two blocks further up at Number 9. They were astonished, however, to see her continue straight past the Co-op, past Number 9, and on through the black iron gates into the precincts of Cullen House.

One of The Eight on foot!

By tomorrow she would be able to afford a taxi or hire a car. But her expenses had not yet been reimbursed. She was dressed in the most expensive outfit she owned. Though she earnestly hoped she would not be seen until she was standing at the front door of the castle, on her half-time untenured teacher's salary, for the rest of this day at least, Jessica Stokes was nearly broke.

* * *

The twenty-four months following the Barribault announcement in the two *Times* passed as time always does, quickly for some, slowly for others, but with steady inexorability whether one was bored or busy.

Long before this eventful day, Barribault's initial staff had been installed in the newly revamped wing of Cullen House. A solicitor had been brought in to oversee the affairs of the Foundation and set in order the disposition of Barribault's vast assets. Wills and trusts and copyrights were but the tip of a complex legal iceberg, every detail of which had to be considered.

Four editors were now on hand, their efforts coordinated by Barribault himself with the assistance of Cynthia Gordon. Their work for the year after the *Times'* announcements, had been to sift through thousands of initial proposals.

The rules for the Barribault Writing Contest had been relatively straightforward:

Each submission must come from a writer previously unpublished in book form.

Submissions were allowed in five distinct literary genres:

Poetry;

Short stories, contemporary or historical;

Essays on current cultural or political topics to include at least one on the state of modern English writing and literature;

Fiction of any kind—contemporary, historical, children's, fantasy, allegory, science fiction, mystery, even love stories; and finally,

Non-fiction—philosophy, spirituality, or literary study demonstrating originality of thought.

The submissions must include a detailed synopsis, and, in the case of fiction, the first five chapters, one later chapter of the author's choosing, and a detailed outline or proposed rough draft of the final chapter, subject of course to later necessary plot adaptations. In the case of the other genres, an equivalent body of material was required.

Submissions must contain no byline or give any indication of the identity of their authors, other than the temporary use of a *male* or *female* pseudonym which must accurately represent the author's gender. This latter stipulation irritated Ms. Stokes. Had it not been an absolute rule, she would have employed a masculine pen name to heighten her chances of success. For the sake of the potential prize she knew she had better go along with it. Addresses were to be listed by post box only. There must be no means by which any submission could be judged other than purely on its own merits. An author's age, reputation, position, background, and so-called public platform would weigh nothing in the decision, only quality, content, originality, and writing craft.

Initial submissions had ended eleven months after the *Times'* advertisements with the announcement, one month later, of fifty finalists.

Those finalists were notified that they had six months to complete their various works.

Then began the most difficult work of Barribault and his team. From the completed work of the fifty, eight winners had to be chosen who would represent the first authors, along with Barribault himself, to be published in the new line.

These eight would come to Cullen for a week's literary retreat with Barribault. During that time, in conjunction with his staff, the final editorial process would begin, each author working closely with Barribault and his team of experienced experts.

The finished works would begin to be published and released to the public nine months later.

Thus, accompanied by an unprecedented promotional effort, the initial line of Barribault House would be launched into the publishing world

* * *

Briscoe Cobb, intellectual snob from Oxford, drove into Cullen in his sleek black Jaguar XG with an attitude he had been nursing for a week.

His outlook on this thing was ambivalent. Twice he had been on the verge of chucking it all and notifying Barribault that for personal reasons he found it necessary to decline the honor of his selection and withdrawing his manuscript from the much-publicized competition.

But who couldn't use the money? And having such publicity invested in a new study of Shakespeare would certainly boost his reputation in academic circles.

Yet he could not escape the feeling that the whole affair was tawdry and plebian. For a man of his stature at Oxford to secretly enter a writing *contest* of all things! It was beneath him.

He had chastised himself a dozen times in the last year for doing so. But he hadn't been able to help himself. The lure had proved too great, even for a sophisticated academic. Whether guilt over his own long hidden secret contributed to the complexity of his feelings about the thing, he himself was the least qualified to be able to say.

Then he had learned—shockingly!—that he was one of the winners. His study of Shakespeare actually had a chance to be published! His secret was out. All Oxford knew what he had kept hidden for a year.

Even then it had not been too late…if only he could summon the courage to withdraw his entry and take his study to a scholarly house such as his own Oxford University Press.

But he hadn't. And here he was, annoyed with himself, and silently a little angry at the whole world as a result.

What were his colleagues saying about his Shakespeare being published on the same initial list—he could hardly bring himself to say it!—with common *novelists*?

* * *

Perhaps the most important member of Barribault's new staff during the early formative months was in charge of publicity.

Everything depended on the first eight books.

They had not only to be good…they had to be *great*. If they bombed, the whole enterprise was down the toilet. Barribault knew that he had to publish eight books that would appeal to a broad cross-section of readers. More than that, they had to make their authors household names whose *future* books readers would keep coming back for. Long term market share and product brand were more important than one or two flash-in-the-pan best-sellers.

An initial launch to successfully ignite that momentum was a matter of publicity as much as anything—building up anticipation every step of the way.

Heightening anticipation was always a dangerous strategy. The expectations game offered no better odds than a crap shoot. But Barribault knew his only chance of success was to make every phase of the two years a media event, and then deliver the goods when the time came.

A continuous flow of press releases and photographs and news stories and updates and carefully orchestrated leaks, therefore, poured from the telephones and computers and fax machines on the second floor of the south wing of Cullen House. Several twitter, Facebook, and blog sites had been established to chronicle progress and count down each successive phase of the contest. Barribault disliked using the very social media he despised to advance his cause. But he accomodated himself to its necessity as a variation on ends justifying means in a worthy cause.

At the end of six months, each of the eight were notified by telegram delivered to their postal boxes—not email, not fax—and formally invited to Cullen House one month later for the week's retreat to inaugurate the new publication effort. Following shortly thereafter came a detailed questionairre, from which their real identities and personal details were at last made known to Barribault's team. The names of the winners were then announced in both the *Times* of London and New York.

The winners presumably celebrated each in his or her own way. Then they made plans to arrive in the little village of Cullen in northeastern Scotland thirty days hence.

Presumably none of them yet was intimately acquainted with its ice cream or its fish and chips, nor about the antique shop that was a delight to all who loved the craft of writing.

They would all discover each in its turn.

* * *

No one noticed Shelby Fitzpatrick drive into town. She came from the west, parked opposite Dinkie Corner, and walked up past Puddleduck toward the square. Curious and thrilled just to be in Scotland, she wanted to have a look around before completing the final leg of her long journey.

Seeing the crowds, she wondered what all the excitement was about. She had done enough preliminary homework via the internet to know about Cullen's famed ice cream. She decided to get an ice cream cone now in case the opportunity didn't come again.

She spotted the shop, crossed the street, and joined the queue stretching out the door onto the sidewalk.

"Is it always so busy in Cullen?" she asked when she reached the counter.

"Oh, no, Miss, today's a special day," replied a girl as she scooped out Fitzpatrick's order.

"Why, is the queen coming?" smiled the thirty-four year old psychologist.

"Oh, no, Miss—It's Mr. Barribault's guests. The Eight they're called. They're arrivin' today. People are watchin' for them."

"All these people in town...they're waiting for Mr. Barribault's, uh...guests to arrive?"

"That's right, Miss. There's six that hae come by last count. People are keepin' track, ye ken. There's twa mair...a lady fae California an' the minister fae Aberdeen. Dinna ken why *he* isna here. It's no as gien he's got far tae come, ye ken. Gien he dinna watch himsel', he'll be last o' a'. Ye're fae America too, I take it, Miss?"

"Yes, that's right...California, actually."

"Oh, California! That is a coinci—"

Suddenly the girl stopped. Her face reddened as she took in a sharp breath of astonishment.

"But...you wouldna be hersel'—" she stammered.

"Actually, yes—I am," smiled Fitzpatrick. "My name is Shelby Fitzpatrick."

"I am pleased to meet you, Miss," said the girl, curtseying where she stood behind her ice cream counter. "I'm Sally McGregor."

"Well, Sally, I am happy to meet you too," said Fitzpatrick. "I shall consider you my first new friend in Cullen. If this ice cream is as good as they say, I am certain I shall see you again!"

* * *

From the moment of the announcements, the paparazzi had swooped down upon the winners, anxious to learn more about these individuals whom Hugh Barribault had made into celebrities overnight.

Their photographs began appearing everywhere. Within days everyone in Britain knew their names, ages, and personal histories. Barribault's publicity hounds saw to that. The Eight might as well have been rock stars.

It had been publicized from the beginning that each would be handed their £100,000 upon arriving at Cullen House. That alone was enough to fire the imaginations of the nation's scandal sheets. It was a fairy tale and lottery story rolled into one. Arrangements were well underway for the book tours through Britain and the United States.

Before that, however, Barribault planned the upcoming week as an old-fashioned excursion back into 19th century tradition. Notwithstanding the hubbub of getting his plan off the ground, once the eight writers upon whom he was gambling his future were with him, the doors of Cullen House would be closed. The hectic pace and noise would be shut out. They would gather together and step back in time. He would steep them in pride of past book-making and book-loving tradition.

Publishing their books was but one aspect of what it would take to make this thing work. He had to make every one of The Eight *believe*. They had to share his vision.

By 4:30 the cars were in their garages and the arrivals in their rooms—contemplating their extraordinary fate, looking over the material that had been left for them on each of their writing desks along with a lavish bowl of fresh fruit, biscuits, and oatcakes—with ample time to rest and dress before dinner.

The most important item on those writing tables was an envelope containing a check made out to each of the eight for the sum of £100,000.

THREE

The Dinner

A bell sounded at 5:30 to inform the guests of Cullen House that, if they had not yet begun to do so, it was high time they dressed for dinner.

They assembled in the Drawing Room at 5:58. Nods and a few superficial words went round among them. Melinda Franks and Shelby Fitzpatrick made an attempt to stir the little group toward introductions. But the silence of the three men, Jessica Stokes with her nose a little in the air, and the imposing stateliness of the older woman they assumed to be Dame Meyerson standing alone and showing no inclination to make small talk, put a damper on their efforts. All noticed that there were only seven of them in the room.

A great clock somewhere struck the hour of six. A door opened. There stood the portly butler whom each had earlier followed silently upstairs to their rooms.

"Ladies and gentlemen," said Coombes somberly. "This way please."

He led them into an exquisitely appointed Dining Room. At the head of the table, in tuxedo and tails, stood Hugh Barribault.

"Ladies and gentlemen, my new friends," he said with a warm smile, "come in, come in! Please find your places and sit down!"

They circulated about the table, locating their names, and one by one pulled back their chairs and sat down. Now first Barribault noticed a single empty place. A look of mingled concern and displeasure crossed his face. He said nothing, however, and remained standing, glancing occasionally at the clock on the wall. His seven guests waited.

At last Melinda Franks broke the silence.

"Why don't we go around the table and introduce ourselves!" she said boisterously. "All this silence makes me feel funny."

"We will become acquainted soon enough, Miss—" said Barribault, a hint of reprimand in his tone. Suddenly he stopped. An expression of disbelief seemed to unnerve him momentarily. Almost immediately he forced reason back to the throne, telling himself that he was imaging things.

"As I said, Miss Franks," he continued. "All in good time."

"How do you know who I am?" she said. "None of us have introduced ourselves."

"I know you all," rejoined their host. "Don't forget, I have read your writing, and studied it extensively. I have been informed by my staff that your photographs have been in all the papers. But as I do not read newspapers, I have seen none of them. What I know of you beyond only your names I have gleaned entirely from your writings. Nor have I looked at the biographical questionnaires you were sent upon being notified of your success. I merely asked my assistant to attach a name and occupation to each title page, nothing more—no photograph, no age, no details. I examined one thing more—that was each of your signatures at the bottom of the sheet. If I may say so, then, I already know *you* quite well, Miss, uh…Miss *Franks*."

Sensing that it would be inappropriate to reply further, the youngest member of the group said nothing more. Silence again descended. Another long minute went by.

At last, with a final glance toward the clock, which now read 6:03, Barribault turned to his right.

"I believe we shall go ahead, Coombes. You may pour each of our guests a glass of wine and tell Constance and Mrs. Walton they may begin serving."

"Very good, sir," said the expressionless butler. He turned and left the room, returning a moment later with two bottles. He opened them with a solemnity befitting a Prime Ministerial dinner. He had just begun to pour when a ghastly racket from outside interrupted the somber occasion.

Coombes set down the bottle in his hand and went to the front door. Rather than waiting for the bell, and curious about the commotion, he opened it to see a sputtering 1970s VW bug clattering and coughing toward the front of the house. A final gasp of gray exhaust shot from behind it as the engine died an inglorious and undignified death. Its driver jumped out, an unexpectedly large man considering the tiny car from which he extricated himself, and lumbered toward the door where Coombes stood silent and disapproving.

"Hi, sorry I'm late," said the newcomer. "I'm Mike St. John. Had some car trouble...afraid I got waylaid for a couple hours near Fyvie."

"You are expected, Mr. St. John," said Coombes. "I will see to your bags and...ah, hem...your, ah...automobile later. This way please."

He led the last of The Eight, who obviously had no time to dress properly, directly to the Dining Room. The butler opened the door just as Constance Fotheringay, the cook, was setting soup in front of the other seven guests.

"Excuse me, sir," he said, "the last of your guests has arrived."

"Dreadfully sorry to barge in late," said St. John. "Planned to be here hours ago, of course, but—"

Realizing that no one was saying anything, and that all eyes were staring at him, he stopped and followed Coombes toward the one empty chair at the huge table. Tripping on the edge of a Persian rug spread over the hardwood oak floor, he stumbled, nearly fell, put out a hand to steady himself on a nearby sideboard. Finally, a little clumsily, he pulled out the last empty chair, sat down heavily, and scooted himself into place.

"Good. At last, then," said Barribault, picking up the glass in front of him. "Now that we are all here, let us proceed. As the first order of business," he went on, "let me take this opportunity to welcome and toast each one of you. I am merely your host, but *you* are the guests of honor. Out of thousands of entries, you eight men and women have proven yourselves worthy of the esteem and notoriety which I believe will come to you. I salute you, each one."

He raised his glass, as did the others in turn, and led them in a drink. At last he took his seat.

"While you enjoy your soup," he said, "I will introduce you to one another. We will see if I can successfully divine your identities as I have that of Miss Franks. You, sir—" he said, glancing to the man at his right, "can be none other than Dugan Smythe. I presume I would be correct in calling you *Father* Smythe?"

Smythe nodded with a smile.

"Indeed, the collar around your neck gives you away...though not entirely. For you are not the only member of the cloth among us. But your age, coupled with various references and the general tone of your work tells me unmistakably that a man of my own generation is the author of *The God Delusion*."

"Right you are," smiled Smythe. It was a smile, however, that did not seem to contain as much humor as irony, as if there yet remained more to the story that he was not ready to divulge.

Again a peculiar expression crossed Barribault's face.

"Father Smythe, I am curious," he said. "Have we ever met?"

"I would not be likely to forget meeting you," replied Smythe.

"Hmm...I seem to know your voice. But I never forget a face, and I do not remember yours. My mind is playing tricks on me tonight.—So, everyone," he added, glancing about the table, "let me introduce you all to Father Dugan Smythe!"

Nods and a few comments followed.

"Seated beside the good father," Barribault continued fixing his gaze on a woman who appeared close to forty, "it is my guess that we have Ms. Jessica Stokes, an experienced and talented, though not yet as polished a writer as I hope she will soon become. Am I correct, Ms. Stokes?"

"You are exactly correct," replied the woman. "I have indeed written a good deal, though the circumstances have not yet been right for publication. You, of course, understand the scarcity of knowledgeable editors in the publishing houses in England, most of whom do not know worthwhile writing when they see it."

"Indeed...well we shall see if that can be changed," replied Barribault with concealed amusement. "And next to Ms. Stokes," he continued, "as we already know, is the impatient Melinda Franks, who finds silence so disquieting."

"I just saw no reason why we shouldn't get to know each other," replied the bubbly young beauty.

"Believe me," smiled Barribault, "once we are acquainted, we shall talk about many things and will get to know each other very well. But all in due course, Miss Franks."

Barribault now turned to his left, where a young woman sat across from Father Dugan. To appearances she was probably five or six years older than Melinda Franks, but in demeanor the differences in their ages could have been much greater, for she carried herself with a grace and maturity beyond her years.

"And you, I believe," Barribault said to her, "would be Shelby Fitzpatrick."

"I am," replied the American in a dignified manner. "I am very happy to meet you at last, Mr. Barribault. This is a great honor."

As she spoke, she held her hand out to their host. Barribault took it, but instead of shaking it, lifted it to his lips and lightly kissed the back of her palm.

"Charmed, Ms. Fitzpatrick. I am delighted to have you among us."

He now turned to a man approaching late middle age, perhaps in his fifties, seated beside her.

"You, sir," he said, "are the enigma of the group. I have read your writing, yet I confess myself stumped. This exercise has admittedly been something of a guessing game, and with each identification, the options ahead of me are reduced. Having come to this point, however, I have not been successful in linking you with your writings. So you will have to introduce yourself."

"I don't know whether to feel complimented or disappointed," said the man almost with the crusty sneer of a curmudgeon. "But I will take it as given, and merely comply. I am Briscoe Cobb."

"Ah, yes, Mr. Cobb! I found your study on Shakespeare the most interesting I have ever read. What you don't know about God, you seem to know about our great playwright. Your contention, however, that he was an atheist poking fun at Christianity probably reveals more about you than the bard. I find it far fetched in the extreme. But your argument that Shakespeare was an out of work hack hired by Bacon to ghostwrite the plays but who then welched on their deal by making public his own name adds an interesting twist to the legend. It may in fact hold up to critical scrutiny better than many may think. I'm sure you will have much to say about it in the years ahead. But we shall discuss all that later. I believe I am safe in stating categorically that you are *not* our second clergyman."

A few glances and smiles went around the table as gradually Barribault's guests began to feel more comfortable.

"That only leaves three of you left," said Barribault. "—Mr. St. John…" he said, now looking toward the most recent arrival. "I believe I am safe in labeling *you* thus, am I not…*Father* St. John?"

"You are," returned St. John in a thick Scottish accent. "Though being a Congregationalist minister, I do not use the *Father*, nor even a *Reverend*. I simply go by who I am. Now that you have successfully identified each of us, will you permit a question from the floor?"

"I have only identified six of you," rejoined Barribault, with a subtle smile.

"Actually, you have identified five of us. You asked Mr. Cobb to introduce himself."

"Well done, St. John!" laughed Barribault.

"And with six identifications thus made, the elementary laws of deduction lead de facto to the final two by default."

"Bravo, Mr. St. John! Shrewdly done. I see I am not the only one who enjoys games of logic. I should have seen it coming from your book. Therefore, I permit your question."

"All right then," said the Scot, "it is this: I grant that you know each of our writings—but how do you know *us*?"

"Do you doubt that one's writing contains clues to an author's identity and character?"

"Not at all. But how you could make your deductions simply by looking at our faces, I confess myself baffled."

"My conclusions are based on more than your faces," said Barribault. "Since the moment you each walked in I began looking for all manner of subtle clues. I fancy myself a sleuth, Mr. St. John—a literary sleuth. I believe writing reveals more about an author than most imagine. The pen is the revealer of the soul. Ours is the greatest profession in the world. To wield the pen is one of mankind's highest privileges and responsibilities. You see, Mr. St. John, I read each of your submissions not merely to select pieces of writing. That was secondary to my deeper motive. I read your poems, stories, and essays to select eight *individuals* upon which to found Barribault House. Only time will tell whether I have accurately read the clues each of you planted for me in your writing without even realizing you were doing so. I am more than a physiagnomist, I hope I am also a student of the soul."

It fell silent a moment as the eight reflected on his words.

"All right, then," said St. John with fun in his eyes, "would you be so good as to let me in on what particular revelation told you who *I* was?"

"You were one of the easiest of all," answered Barribault. "And not from your tardy arrival—though I gather that din I heard as you approached was caused by a Volkswagen similar to that driven by the main character in your novel. No, it was from the slant of the signature on your submission form. Even though you were signing a pseudonym, I did not think that you would also falsify your handwriting, and thus I deduced you to be left handed, a fact confirmed by the later questionnaire in your own name. That was not enough, however, for there are two other southpaws, as I believe the Americans call them, among us—Miss Franks and Father Smythe."

Heads turned toward the two, who both nodded in surprised confirmation of their host's assessment.

"Therefore, the moment Father Smythe appeared wearing his collar and I knew *his* identity, you became the only remaining left-handed suspect, as it were."

"You knew I was left-handed?"

"Look at the soup spoon in your hand, Mr. St. John."

"Ah...of course."

"But I suspected it before you picked up the spoon," added Barribault. "When you unceremoniously stumbled over the edge of the carpet and put your left hand out to steady yourself...and as we toasted one another, you lifted your wineglass with your left hand. No, Mr. St. John, I fear you were not much of a challenge."

St. John laughed with delight. Several of the others joined him.

"Now that we've had a bit of fun," said Barribault, "with six of you matched with your names, as Mr. St. John has adroitly pointed out, the final two identifications are made, I am sorry, but on the most elementary basis, that of your respective genders. At the end of the table, then, we must have none other than Dame Jennifer Meyerson and Graham Whitaker!"

The middle-aged man and stately gray-haired woman nodded and smiled.

"That reminds me of a question I wanted to raise," now said Ms. Stokes, "if you will not consider me too forward."

"I suppose that will depend on the question," rejoined Barribault. "But I fear no inquiry...go ahead, Ms. Stokes," he added with a nod.

"Why did you insist that we identify ourselves by gender orientation? I found it disconcerting, if not—"

She paused a little awkwardly and cleared her throat nervously.

"—if not culturally anachronistic," Stokes added. "I would have assumed you to be more enlightened than to allow sexual bias to enter your considerations."

"No one has ever accused me of being a modernist," said Barribault, hinting at a humorous smile.

"You justify it on that basis?"

"Let me see if I understand your question," said their host as the others listened with interest. "You are concerned that I might allow bias to enter my judgment...you assumed that I would suffer from a subtle pro-masculine, anti-female bias?"

"All men do."

Barribault chuckled, finding Ms. Stokes' prickly feminism more humorous than threatening. "I must admit that I did not expect such an intellectually prejudicial perspective from a modernist like you, Ms. Stokes," he replied. Though pointed, his tone was kindly and gracious, as one merely stating facts to one less informed than himself. "It would seem that I am the more enlightened between us, and that, without realizing it, you have fallen considerably behind the trends of current social development. I would have assumed you to be sufficiently abreast of current practice to recognize that the bias of today's society is decidedly *pro*-woman, not the other way around. That is the fatal flaw in today's feminism — it is just about eighty years behind the reality of the times. I did not detect this anti-masculine tone in your writing, which is a good thing, otherwise you and I would not be having this discussion at all. But the point is, though it is almost a joke in some circles, and not a particularly funny one — the undeniable truth happens to be that the most discriminated against minority in liberal western culture is the white straight Christian Anglo-Saxon male. However, all that as an interesting aside…the request for gender identification in the choice of your temporary pen names was my one accommodation to political correctness. Not that I care a thing for being correct by any standard but the truth. But in addition to the best and most original writing possible, I did hope it would work out to include an equal number of men and women among the Eight. In the end, Ms. Stokes, it may turn out that I am more liberated in the matter of sex and gender than yourself. As we can see, it did turn out just as I had hoped — with four men and four women."

Jessica Stokes stiffened and looked down, judging it best for once to swallow her pride and say no more.

"Why?' asked Shelby Fitzpatrick. "*Why* did you want an equal number? My concern would be exactly the opposite. I would not want to think that I received favorable treatment *because* I was a woman."

"No fear of that either, I assure you, Miss Fitzpatrick," replied Barribault. "I said *if possible* I hoped for an even split. All my initial readings were made on the basis of the writing alone. I was not aware of the pseudonyms at that point. But I wanted the information available. As to your question, we will be selling your books, as well as the new company, in a modern contemporary market. We need to be well-rounded and broad-based, I felt a thorough mix of views, perspectives, and talents, including men and women from diverse fields, would best achieve that aim. To be honest, however, I ascertained each of your genders from your writing long before your pseudonyms were made known to me. I hope that did not influence me. But none of us is as objective as we think. It is simply a fact that cannot be denied."

Barribault glanced around the table, as if in silent inquiry whether any additional questions persisted. He then grew serious again.

"So, ladies and gentlemen," he said after a moment. "You are all to be congratulated. The competition was stiff, but each of you in your own way showed me by your writings that you are prepared for publication at the highest level. You will no doubt, with the exception of Mr. St. John, all by now have discovered in your rooms your advance checks. We will discuss and finalize contractual legalities and other arrangements with my staff in the days ahead.

"You here in this room will inaugurate with me a new trend in literary excellence. Do not underestimate the significance of this moment. We will indeed get to know one another very well. Your lives will not be the same after you leave Cullen House. Your names will be recognized and your books read throughout the United States and Great Britain.

"Besides all that, what could be more stimulating than to gather with other literary individuals to discuss ideas, books, authors, and the great writing of past generations. Toward that end, I have made up a preliminary schedule for the presentation of your papers and stories. I will hand them out this evening when we gather in the Parlor for coffee.

"We will begin tomorrow morning with you, Dame Meyerson, and the extremely insightful essay with which you began your book, *Ethics vs. Modernism, A Clash to the Death.* We will then hear from you, Mr. Whitaker, and your delightful short story *Snowflakes on the Thames*, and you, Ms. Franks, and your poem reflecting modern man's plight, which I found very moving—all the more so now that I see how young you are— *Gilded Journey to Nowhere.* I mean that entirely as a compliment. It shows pathos and depth of sensitive maturity. Extremely well done.

"So now, please enjoy your dinner. I hope you will find getting to know one another as enjoyable and stimulating as I have found it getting to know each of *you* in the past six months. Afterward and in the days to come, make use of the house and grounds however and whenever you like. Please feel free to explore, and do not miss the Library on the third floor—one of the finest private libraries, in my humble opinion, in all Scotland."

FOUR

First Day

Dame Jennifer Meyerson was neither by temperament nor custom an early riser.

It was doubtful she was nervous at having been named first on the programme for the initial morning's session. At fifty-seven, she had sat opposite enough ministers and secretaries at state dinners, and mixed with enough movie stars in her day to cure her of whatever personal insecurities had unknowingly drifted into adulthood from a pampered upbringing. She had met the queen—twice, actually—and, before the dear lady's death, had been on a first name basis with the queen Mum. She had been invited to Balmoral on several occasions with the queen mother's personal party. She was therefore unlikely to be intimidated by her present surroundings at Cullen House, nor by the anticipation of having to stand before eight others to read and defend one of the essays that had helped her capture Hugh Barribault's attention.

Her sleeplessness during the night stemmed from entirely personal concerns. She knew the risk before she came. She knew the moment she entered the contest, never dreaming she might actually be one of the winners.

Now here she was. The moment of truth was nearly at hand. What would she say when it came?

She could not help wondering what he was thinking. She knew he had not forgotten. But he was certainly giving no hints.

She awoke while it was still dark and found further sleep hopeless. She lay in bed until 6:05, perhaps a respectable hour for some, but in September in northern Scotland that meant a chilly dawn outside.

Finally she rose, turned on the provided water-pot to boil in what were luxurious accommodations even by her standards, and dressed. With a cup of tea in her hand several minutes later, she sat down in the well-appointed guestroom and attempted to interest herself in a book.

Light slowly came to the windows whose curtains she had already pulled. By seven-thirty she was ready to get on with this day. Neither a big morning eater, she nevertheless decided it was time she sauntered down to the Breakfast Room and see what the others were doing.

She walked in and found the place empty. Surely at this hour she could not be the first to appear. A glance around, however, revealed that not a single plate, cup, nor bowl had been disturbed.

In keeping with that remarkable, if mysterious, old-world tradition, everything sat in silver containers on three sideboards in perfect readiness, somehow prepared by silent and unseen hands, for the *a la carte* perusal of the guests at whatever hour they chose to pick up once again the raveled sleeves of care. Covered porringers, tureens, platters, and trays, steam rising from their ornate lids, promised freshly scrambled eggs, sausage, eggs soft-boiled in the shell, kippers, bacon, fried potatoes, oatmeal, white and black pudding, possibly other meats, and, unless her olfactory senses deceived her, haggis. Slices of toast sat in several upright holders, actually for the moment still warm, beside abundantly provided crystal bowls of butter and jams, jellies, and bitter marmalade. Carafes of assorted juices, bowls of yogurt, cereals, hard-boiled eggs, a silver epergne of fruit, a pitcher of milk, and other needfuls completed the array. Coffee and tea, of course, steamed from four large pots, adding their distinctive aromas to the pleasurable morning potpourri of smells. How such a thorough menu could appear, *apparently* fresh, every morning, for the benefit of but a handful of guests at a hunting lodge or country house, and whether a day's remains were ever "recycled" into the following morning's offerings...these were but two of many mysteries associated with the *buffet*. Notwithstanding its limitations, the tradition was not one many would choose to replace with the more plebian practice of breakfast "cooked to order" by an apron-clad mistress of a modern Bed and Breakfast. This was how it had been done for generations among the elite. If one was a little late coming down and had to endure cold toast, eggs and potatoes that had been a little long in the pan, and coffee too long in the pot, one could console oneself that tradition had its compensations as well as its drawbacks.

Dame Meyerson had nearly completed her private perusal of the three sideboards. The metallic clinking of the lid as she replaced it over the tray of kippers prevented her hearing footsteps behind her entering the room.

"Good morning, Mrs. Meyerson!" came the words from a distinctly America tongue, always a little grating on British ears. In this case. However, it was polished enough with New England influences not to make her wince.

She turned to see Graham Whitaker walking toward her with a smile from the direction of the open door.

"Mr. Whitaker," she said, returning his smile and greeting.

"Find anything interesting?"

"You know, the usual," she replied. "What else can be done with breakfast?"

"True. But on the other side of it," rejoined Whitaker, "it is the one meal of the day almost impossible to spoil. Unless, of course, the coffee is bad. But we're early enough, it should be reasonably fresh. And," he added, glancing about, "judging from the looks of it, there seem an abundant variety of possibilities.— Are you going to dish up?"

"I thought I would just start with a warm cup of something. My appetite is slow to get going. I'm not big on breakfast."

"Like B. Wooster after a night at the Drones."

The lady cast an interrogative glance at Whitaker, one eyebrow arching slightly.

Whitaker took a cup placed it on a saucer, and poured into it the day's first cup of black steaming coffee. He handed it to Dame Meyerson.

"Thank you," she said. "But I prefer tea."

"Ah...then one moment."

Whitaker set down the cup, poured out a second portion, this time with tea. Then he led the way, a cup and saucer in each hand, toward a table.

"Are we late, or are we the first out of our rooms?" he said as they sat down. "I thought the place would be bustling?"

"I see no sign anyone's been here."

"We must have a houseful of late risers."

"I suppose we were up a little late last evening."

"True, and some had long trips before arriving. Where did you come from yesterday?"

"I flew into Aberdeen the day before. I spent the night before last at the Thistle. What about you?"

"I drove up from Oban."

"Ah, yes—I hear it is a nice little place. I've not been there myself."

"The drive north from there was terrific." Whitaker took a sip or two from his coffee. "What did you think," he went on, "of last evening's little tiff in the Parlor between St. John and Smythe?"

An amused smile spread over Dame Meyerson's face. "To be honest," she replied, "I rather enjoyed it. Though I would not be supposed to be a religious woman myself, I must say I think the young minister got the best of it. I thought Dr. Cobb rather made a fool of himself becoming so heated over nothing."

"That was my take," nodded Whitaker with a smile of his own.

"Mr. Barribault's good-humored dressing down of Ms. Stokes at dinner was also rather delightful."

Whitaker laughed. "I rather doubt she found it so. If looks could kill, as the saying goes. Not that they ever can, but daggers were blazing from her eyes."

"It was her own fault for asking such a moronic question."

"I try to keep my mouth shut whenever religion or politics rear their heads—politically correct or otherwise. There is never a winner. But like you, I enjoy watching to see how people comport themselves. St. John was simply making conversation, or so it seemed to me, and Cobb flew off the rails at him. St. John was perfectly justified in taking him to task."

As if on cue, into the Breakfast Room now walked Mike St. John with the jaunty air of a morning person full of buck and beans, and possibly with the caffeine of a cup or two of strong coffee already flowing in his veins.

"Good morning, good morning!" he said, greeting Meyerson and Whitaker as he cruised past them toward the steaming sideboards.

"Speak of the devil," smiled Whitaker.

St. John cocked his head in the direction of the table as he took a plate and lifted one of the lids.

"You weren't *really* talking about me?" he said good-naturedly.

"Actually, Mr. St. John," replied Dame Meyerson, "believe it or not, we were."

"Rest assured," added Whitaker, "I intended no vocational pun by mentioning the devil."

He rose and followed St. John to the side of the room and picked up a plate.

"You came up in the context of last evening's discussion," Whitaker went on as the two men worked their way along the sideboard, "when Dr. Cobb went after you. Our consensus, given the awkwardness of the situation, was that you handled yourself very well."

The echo of a silver lid clattering to the floor preempted a reply. St. John retrieved it and placed it back on its tray. A minute later, with a plate piled with eggs, potatoes, toast, and kippers in one hand, and a cup of coffee in the other, he made his way, followed by Whitaker, toward the table where Mrs. Meyerson sat awaiting them. She eyed St. John's approach with more than a little concern, for he looked dangerous. The good Mike St. John had already shown himself a little clumsy on his feet. Armed with hot food and steaming coffee, and without a free hand to catch himself should the need arise, the thirty feet between the serving sideboards and where she sat, with two empty tables and assorted chairs between, was one laden with potentialities for disaster.

With an inward sigh of relief, she watched him set down the plate, then the cup and saucer, on the table, then pull out the chair, still without incident, and ease his large frame into it. Whitaker sat down beside him.

"So you don't think I was too hard on Dr. Cobb?" said St. John as he went to work on the eggs and kippers.

"I thought he deserved it," replied Dame Meyerson. "He as good as called you a hypocrite."

"He was blunt, I'll give him that," chuckled St. John.

"Not that I agree with your religious views," the stately lady went on. "I don't know enough about them to say whether I agree or not. But every individual deserves common courtesy, and every man or woman's viewpoints, if honestly and sincerely held, deserves respect. I did not feel Dr. Cobb gave you either."

Already it was clear that Whitaker, digging into a kipper, had begun to retreat into the *rôle* of observer in which he was most comfortable.

St. John swallowed and took a thoughtful swallow of coffee.

"You're right," he said after a moment. "He was rude. At the same time I *may* have been a little hard on him. Actually...the whole thing may have been my fault."

"Why do you say that?" asked Dame Meyerson.

"I egged him on."

"How so?

"I couldn't resist. I confess, it's one of my bad habits. When I run into a stuffy dogmatist—whether a fundamentalist who goes ballistic at the mention of evolution, or an atheist like Cobb whose mind toward the supernatural you couldn't open with a crowbar—I can't help goading them. Part of it is sincerely a desire to bring the light of open-mindedness into the discussion. But I fear there is more than a little good-natured fun involved too. I can't help it—people who take themselves too seriously annoy the cassock off me. Before I know it, I am trying to add some levity to the situation. Unfortunately, Mr. Cobb didn't appreciate my humor."

"That's what I like—a minister with a sense of fun," said Melinda Franks, who had picked up the trailing fragments of St. John's comment as she walked into the room.

"A sense of humor may ordinarily be a good thing," rejoined St. John as he looked toward the twenty-nine year old graduate student. "But it is also a good way for a parson to get himself into trouble! I am in constant hot water with my parishioners!"

"Why?"

"People like their priests on the serious side. Too much humor from the pulpit and they begin questioning his spirituality. God himself is stern, they think. So too should be his spokesmen."

"Good morning, Miss Franks," said Graham Whitaker.

"Yes, yes—good morning to you all. That coffee smells wonderful!"

"I have to admit, it is quite good," said Whitaker. "For an American in Britain, one of the great trials is finding a truly excellent cup of coffee. People here are addicted to instant."

"There are Starbucks everywhere now, Mr. Whitaker. We have three in Cambridge alone."

Melinda poured out a cup from the pot, added two half slices of toast—cold by now—to a plate, and walked over to join the others.

"Personally, I'm an atheist myself," she said, taking a seat opposite Mike St. John, "but still I respect the opposite view."

"Don't you know what they say, Miss Franks," said Whitaker with a quick smiling glance toward Dame Meyerson. "There are no atheists in foxholes."

"What does that have to do with anything?" said Melinda.

"Nothing," smiled Whitaker. "I just thought I would throw it in."

"Then what do you think of the opposite truism, Miss Franks," asked the minister, "that there are nothing *but* atheists teaching in today's universities, and that, by implication, academia offers one of the *least* intellectually open-minded atmospheres in our culture for true learning? I only ask because that is the world you are in at present. I am curious to know whether you think your atheism has been arrived at with intellectual honesty, or whether you might have been influenced toward it in a multitude of ways you might not even be aware of?"

"Come, come, St. John," now put in Father Dugan Smythe, who had entered on Melinda Franks' heels and was unable to resist jumping into the fray, "that is a loaded question. You put poor Miss Franks in a Catch-22. Not that I don't believe in us men of the cloth sticking together," he added, though not in a humorous tone, "but I must take exception to the premise of your thesis."

"How so, Mr. Smythe?" asked the younger minister.

"*Father* Smythe, if you don't mind."

"Ah, of course…my apologies," said Mike.

Whitaker smiled to himself, wondering if they had yet another on their hands who took himself too seriously. Instead, for the moment, he spoke to St. John, perceiving him as a man who could take it and who, like him, enjoyed life's lighter side.

"I might have to agree with Father Smythe," laughed Whitaker. "That is a pretty heavy diet so early in the morning, St. John. What happened to your clerical sense of humor?"

"Touche!" laughed St. John. "You have skewered me with my own words!"

Before the discussion between St. John, Franks, and Smythe could progress further, inwardly disappointing to Graham Whitaker, Jessica Stokes walked in. Something about the way she carried herself, her nose still in the air, put an immediate damper on the free flow of conversation. She glanced about, went to the sideboard, dished herself out a half bowl of plain yogurt to accompany an equally sparse portion of sliced grapefruit, then went to a table at the far end of the room and sat down alone.

"Good morning, Miss Stokes," said Mike St. John, rising and walking over to greet her. "Or is it *Mrs.*? I'm sorry, I was not able to keep everyone's histories straight last evening."

"I prefer *Ms*," she answer coolly. "M-S…I am not married."

"Ah, right…I see."

St. John's ensuing attempts at small talk proved unsuccessful. When Shelby Fitzpatrick made her first appearance of the morning and walked over to join *Ms* Stokes, he turned toward her with a smile. His greeting to the southern Californian was received no more cordially than his previous one, for Miss Fitzpatrick had thoroughly taken Dr. Cobb's side in the previous night's debate. The minister's overly confident air had rankled her. Her response to his *Good morning, Miss Fitzpatrick* was icy. St John retreated a moment later to the company of Dame Meyerson and Graham Whitaker.

Melinda Franks and Father Smythe, meanwhile, had by then returned to the sideboard where they were in conversation with the last of the eight to arrive, Oxford's Dr. Briscoe Cobb. The three sat down at an empty table a minute or two later, and breakfast progressed quietly in the three small groups.

"I say," said Cobb at length, "did any of you hear that infernal ruckus last night, must have been two or three in the morning?"

"I heard nothing," said Dame Meyerson, glancing over from where she sat with St. John and Whitaker.

"Must be that ghost they talk about," Cobb went on. "What is it...some lady in a green dress? Who the devil is she, anyway? Woke me out of a sound sleep."

"I suppose you will have to ask our host," said Whitaker.

"Where is Barribault?" asked Smythe. "Did he come in earlier?"

"I was the first one down," said Dame Meyerson. "There was no sign of him."

"Mr. Barribault usually takes meals alone," said a voice behind them.

All heads jerked around to see Coombes standing at attention beside one of the doors looking as if he had been present through the entire discussion.

"Goodness, Coombes, where did you come from?" barked Cobb. "That infernal ghost could take your correspondence course!"

"Don't you know, Mr. Cobb," commented Graham Whitaker dryly, "Butlers like Coombes and Jeeves shimmer invisibly through walls and simply *appear*."

An intrigued glance shot his way from Mike St. John, but he said nothing. None of the others had an idea what Whitaker was talking about, least of all Coombes himself.

"Mr. Barribault rises early and works through tea and breakfast," Coombes went on unperturbed. "He asked me to convey that he will see you at eleven o'clock in the East Sitting

Room on the first floor, per the schedule he gave you last evening."

* * *

When the late morning's initial reading session and discussion broke up about one o'clock, most of the group made their way from the East Sitting Room along the wide first floor corridor to the Lunch Room where, according to their host, ample provision to last throughout the day until dinner would be awaiting them. Barribault himself disappeared up to his own rooms on the third floor.

As they passed the main central staircase, Cobb and Smythe turned from the others and began the circular descent to the ground floor.

"What I need before food," said Cobb in a low tone, "is a good cigar. Care to join me, Smythe?"

"A capital idea. I rather overfed at breakfast. I have been looking for a chance to escape and gulp down a couple of antacids."

They reached the front door and walked out the main entrance. Cobb produced two expensive Havanas from his vest pocket as the priest fished pills from his own jacket. Cobb handed a cigar to Father Smythe. Both men lit up, drew in several deep puffs with satisfaction, and moved in the direction of the gardens.

"A cigar won't help your digestion, Father Smythe," said a perky voice behind them. Before they could turn around, each felt a slender hand slip through his arm. Suddenly there was Melinda Franks squeezing her way between them.

"What do you know about my digestion, Miss Franks?" said the priest, turning and glancing down toward the vivacious young poet.

"Nothing more than I overheard following you down the stairs," answered Melinda.

"Not polite to eavesdrop, Miss Franks," said Briscoe Cobb.

"You were making no attempt to be secretive about wanting to get away from the others," said Franks playfully. "I think the cigar was just a ruse. Anybody else would have heard you just like I did."

"You *are* a little vixen. Do you pester everyone with such ungracious remarks?"

Franks laughed with delight. "Actually, I haven't quite decided yet. I'm still sizing everyone up...just like you, just like the others."

"You think everyone is trying to suss out everyone else?"

"Of course. That's what you do at such gatherings."

Cobb nodded, then began to chuckle as he exhaled another long draught of smoke.

Melinda turned toward the priest.

"So what do you think, Father Smythe," she said, "is Mr. Cobb too old for me?"

"I would think young St. John more your type."

"Though not yours, is he, Father?" she rejoined with a grin. "No, he's a little religious for me," Melinda went on. "And he was married before. Something about that takes the luster off the potential romance."

"You don't want an old curmudgeon like me," said Cobb, playing along. "How about that Whitaker fellow? He's an American too—you should like that?"

"He is attractive, I'll admit that," nodded Melinda thoughtfully, "—handsome, sense of humor, and very observant. Did you see him glancing about at the rest of us the whole time. He's definitely sizing everyone up."

"You said everyone was doing that."

"Only superficially. You don't really get to know anyone with surface observations. But Mr. Whitaker is different. He is looking *inside* people with those penetrating light blue eyes of his. It would make me nervous to get too close to him. I don't want anyone knowing me *that* well."

"Secrets, Miss Franks?"

"I didn't say that—only that I don't want anyone probing too deeply. Besides...he's a widower too, so that lets him out. No, I'm afraid you're stuck with me, Mr. Cobb!"

She pulled her hands out from their arms and extricated herself from the two men, then ran off.

"Where are you off to?" called Cobb after her.

"Into town," she said back over her shoulder. "I want to visit the shops and meet quaint local villagers—buxom lassies with apple cheeks and red-headed laddies with accents I can't understand. Grist for the mill, you know."

They watched her disappear along the wooded drive.

"Ah, to be young again," mused Cobb with a wistful tone.

"From the sound of it, you may not have to be," remarked Smythe.

"She was just making sport of me," said Cobb. "You mark my words, she'll play the same game on St. John and Whitaker. I see it at Oxford every year. She is one of those young women who can't be happy unless she's working her wiles on someone. I quit paying attention to all that years ago."

"I'm not sure that's her game," mused Smythe.

"What is, then?"

"I don't quite know. But I think there may have been more in that exchange than meets the eye.—Fancy a walk into town?" he added. "I think I'll see if I can find a newspaper."

"I shall pass," answered Cobb, "—conserve my energy for the ordeal ahead."

"Ah, right...your presentation is this afternoon. That should be old hat to a professor like you."

"Perhaps, but not with a critical audience as astute as Barribault. He rather grilled poor Dame Meyerson this morning like I might have one of my students who mixed up Othello and Hamlet."

"That was interesting," rejoined Smythe. "Quite unexpected, I thought."

"She proved the man's equal. Did you see that fire in her eyes? She gave it back in equal measure. I had not taken her for such a feisty lady."

"If one didn't know better, one would think the two had some animosity festering between them."

"An intriguing exchange indeed."

"Well, I am off for the village," said Father Smythe as the two men parted. "Thank you for the cigar."

* * *

Watching the display from the window of her room where she had gone after the breakup of the session, Jessica Stokes stood alone with her thoughts.

What a flirt! she mused.

She continued to observe the exchange until it broke up. In truth her annoyance with Melinda Franks' open display with two men, each old enough to be her father, masked a silent envy that she was not more forceful herself, and not actually a little more like the very thing she despised.

Jessica did not find singleness a burden. She had been aware from a young age that she was different from girls like Melinda Franks. Boys had never been drawn to her, nor she to them, though she had nursed two or three high school crushes in painful silence. Whether the feminism that had emerged as the most visible defining characteristic of her nature during her college years stemmed from true belief, or was a defense against feared rejection, would have made an intriguing query. It was an inquiry, however, into whose depths she had never ventured. Nor, had such a question occurred to her, would she have dared face it. Whatever the underlying origins of her extreme liberalism, she was a true believer now.

She turned from the window and went to the W.C. After a splash of cold water on her face, she left the room.

* * *

Meanwhile in the Lunch Room, Graham Whitaker sidled up as Mike St. John poured himself a cup of coffee at one of the sideboards.

"An interesting morning, eh, St. John, what?" he said.

"You're sounding very British today!" laughed St. John.

"I like to try it on every now and then," rejoined the American. "You Brits are always making fun of how we Yanks sound, I figure it is *de rigueur* for me occasionally to return the favor."

"Liberty granted," nodded St. John, as he loaded several slices of meat and cheese on a plate.

"You and Dr. Cobb seemed on more amiable terms this morning."

"You noted the formal niceties?"

"Everyone was watching to see if another brouhaha would break out," said Whitaker with a twinkle in his eye.

Again St. John laughed. "Not today. I don't mind the occasional wisecrack about Jonah and the whale and where Cain's wife came from. In my business you learn to expect it. I realize I must be more circumspect in my responses to Dr. Cobb in the future than I was last evening. But tell me, Dr. Whitaker...it is *Doctor*?"

"I am entitled to the appellation," nodded Whitaker as he placed a few vegetables and oatcakes on a plate, "but I never had much use for it. I'm not big on labels. My office door simply reads *Graham Whitaker, Economics*. If there is one thing I particularly dislike it's pretension. I am who I am, as I believe your Almighty once said about himself to Charlton Heston."

"Right, the famous burning bush sequence between God and Moses," smiled St. John. "Another perennial favorite for debunkers along with Cain's wife, Noah's ark, and Jonah. I may have to keep my eye on you too," chuckled the minister. "I can see that neither are you adverse to wisecracking about Christianity."

"Christianity is not a particular target," rejoined Whitaker. "I will wisecrack about anything. Not exactly an occupational hazard, as they say, but something I picked up from my father. Not always a good habit, but...well, there it is."

The two men moved toward a table and sat down.

"What I had been going to ask," said St. John, "is how an economics professor comes to be a writer...and a talented one too, I might add."

"Thank you very much," nodded Whitaker, lifting a cup of coffee to his lips. "My odyssey from economics to author is hardly as remarkable as yours from priest to mystery writer."

"Touche!" said St. John. "I suppose we both break the molds. I took my cue from Father Brown. I thought if G.K. Chesterton could make a priest the sleuth for a series of mysteries, why could I not make a minister—myself!—the *author* for my own mystery. I took time off after my wife's death, and the writing proved a great solace and tonic to my grief. It gave me something to be *about*, if you know what I mean. There was also some unpleasantness in my church that coincided with my wife's death. That too was a tremendous strain on me. Honestly, I just began writing as a diversion. I never dreamed I would be any good at it. I am more surprised than anyone at how it has turned out."

"Well Mr. Barribault obviously thinks it is better than just good. He is touting you as the next Agatha Christie of the whodunit world."

"I doubt it will come to that, but I appreciate the opportunity he has given me."

"I am sorry about your wife," said Whitaker. "What was the cause of her death?"

"Cancer."

"She was very young."

"Only thirty-two. But cancer strikes all ages. You lost your wife too, isn't that right?"

Whitaker nodded. "It has been six years. I still miss her."

"What was the cause in her case?"

"A rare form of ALS—genetic they think, but we never knew. There was some question whether she might have been saved had the research been accelerated. But funding dried up as she was reaching a critical stage."

"That's a shame. I am sorry."

Whitaker drew in a long sigh. "I began writing for much the same reason as you—to console myself."

"That explains the melancholy strains in your stories."

"Perhaps you are right. It isn't conscious, but what's inside obviously emerges onto the printed page."

"What's the connection with economics?"

"None, really," answered Whitaker. "Economics was my field of study. Almost by happenstance I was offered a job as an editorial flunky for a New York publishing house—proofreading at first. As there were no prospects on the horizon for economic professors, I took it. Before I realized it, I had spent fifteen years there, had moved up the ladder, and had become a full-fledged editor. And of course what editor doesn't dream of writing his or her *own* book, and isn't convinced he or she can do it better than the hacks they edit. I admit, I was bitten by the same bug. So I decided to leave the publishing world, return to university and finish my Ph.D. work and begin writing. My wife's death, as in your case, was the initial impetus to make the change. I did get my doctorate in time, managed to obtain a position...and, like you, am more astonished than anyone to find myself here."

"Thank you for sharing that. It must have been a great deal of work."

Whitaker nodded. "Making major changes in life usually requires hard work. But then you look back with all the more satisfaction at having accomplished something worthwhile."

Jessica Stokes entered the Lunch Room and glanced around at the two small companies that had formed in the brief time she had been in her room. Her eyes unconsciously stopped and rested on Graham Whitaker. After a second or two, she realized she was staring at him. Feeling the back of her neck warm, she quickly looked away hoping he hadn't noticed, and moved in the direction of the sideboards.

* * *

At a table across the room Shelby Fiztpatrick and Dame Meyerson were seated across from one another with cups of tea and plates of vegetables and cheese in front of them.

"I enjoyed the chapter from your book very much," Shelby said. "Mr. Barribault seemed more critical than I think you deserved. He had nothing but praise for Mr. Whitaker's story, then critiqued your piece as if we were in a high school English class."

Dame Meyerson nodded but replied only indirectly. "Mr. Whitaker's story was lovely. Who could say a word against it? Very moving, I thought."

"I have to admit being a little surprised," said Shelby, lowering her voice. "The pathos he captured in that description of the little girl walking along the river...I didn't expect it from him. I had tears in my eyes. He is obviously a likeable and witty man, but I never anticipated being so touched by his writing."

"I suspect there may be more beneath the surface of Mr. Whitaker than meets the eye."

* * *

An hour and a half later, as Melinda Franks was walking past Puddleduck on Seafield Street, she saw Father Smythe emerging from one of the adjacent shops. She quickened her pace.

"I didn't know you had come into town," she said.

Smythe turned. "Hello...uh, Miss Franks," he said, a sudden expression of discomposure flitting across his features. Flustered by the look of animation in her eyes, it took him a moment to regain his breath.

"What!" laughed Melinda as she saw his hesitation. "You look like you saw a ghost."

"Nothing. You...uh...you just caught me by surprise," said Smythe, groping for words. "You'll have to pardon an old blackcoat like me.—So you are visiting the quaint villagers, like you said. Any inspiration for a new poem?"

Melinda laughed again, and Smythe again went weak in the knees.

"It doesn't work like that, Father Smythe," she said, her tinkling voice casting a spell over him as powerful as her laugh. "A poem has to *come*. You don't force it."

"I wouldn't know about that. I was just on my way up the street to the antique shop. Care to join me?"

"Thanks, but I am worn out with local color. I think I will head back. Have fun!"

Smythe stared after her as she crossed the street, wondering if he had imagined it all.

Thirty minutes later, not forgetting the powerful interview but putting it behind him, Father Smythe was engaged in lively conversation with John Thompson at Abra Bits & Collectables. He had asked him about his assortment of vintage fountain pens, and the conversation had since moved far afield. The two men touched on the subject of Smythe's book in which Thompson showed great interest, then moved on to discuss druidic activity in Scotland past and present, the upsurge of recent interest in the Stewart dynasty as the rightful lineage to the British throne, as well as the pros and cons of Hugh Barribault's literary vision.

* * *

At five o'clock that afternoon, Hugh Barribault again greeted his guests, protégés, and future business partners, this time in the sitting area of the third floor Library. The ambiance was overpowering, books everywhere, the air pervaded with the faint fragrance of must, dust, leather, ancient paper, and old oak.

"Well, my friends," he said, easing into his own favorite chair and glancing round where the others were seated on a variety of couches and stuffed chairs, "I trust you had an enjoyable afternoon. I was quite pleased with our time together this morning."

If any lingering annoyance remained from the morning's exchange between Barribault and Dame Meyerson, the host, on his part, gave no indication of it. The lady, however, remained subdued. She contributed nothing to the discussion that followed.

"Are you ready, Dr. Cobb," Barribault went on, "to introduce your book to the others in overview?"

Cobb nodded.

"After that, we shall impose upon Miss Franks to grace us with another one or two of her lovely poems, and, Mr. St. John—perhaps you might like to read us the opening chapter of your *Conundrum at Craigievar Castle*."

* * *

Several hours later, with another lavish dinner from Constance Fotheringay's kitchen inside them, and brandy from Hugh Barribault's cellar warming the lining of their stomachs, the after-dinner discussions gradually broke up and everyone made their way to their rooms.

The great house grew quiet.

Sometime about 11:15, Briscoe Cobb heard light footsteps in the corridor. As they passed his room and receded in the distance, his curiosity got the better of him. He tiptoed to his door, carefully opened it a crack, and peeped out. Disappearing away from him down the hall, obviously walking in an attempt not to be heard, he saw the back of Hugh Barribault.

Their host stopped in front of a closed door. Cobb saw him glance around. Quickly he shrank back, being careful not to draw

Barribault's eye. After a second or two, Barribault tapped lightly on the door.

Fortunately Melinda Franks was still dressed when the faint knock echoed in her room. She rarely went to sleep before midnight, and had just settled into the large floral-upholstered overstuffed chair to read. The sound was so light she thought it something outside the house. When it came again, there could be no mistake.

She rose and went to the door. Her eyes widened in astonishment to see Hugh Barribault standing in front of her.

"Forgive me for calling so late, Miss Franks," he said in scarcely more than a whisper. "If you are not too exhausted after the long day...would you perhaps join me for a drink?"

"I...uh...sure, I guess," replied Melinda.

"Meet me downstairs in the East Sitting Room—where we met with everyone this morning," said Barribault. "We will be less likely to be seen there."

He turned away and disappeared as stealthily as he had come, leaving a bewildered but adventurous Melinda Franks staring after him.

She followed three or four minutes later.

When she returned to her room half an hour later, her eyes were red. The instant she was alone and the door locked, she lay down on her bed and wept until sleep finally overtook her.

* * *

Meanwhile, alone in his room, having no idea what had transpired, Dugan Smythe had downed a third of a bottle of the best Scotch he had been able to find in the village. He would have the hangover of all hangovers in the morning.

The two men who were still awake in the great house at this late hour were finding themselves suddenly facing long past personal demons which they would deal with in very different ways.

FIVE

The Coterie

The fourth day's session began two mornings later at the earlier hour of 10:00 A.M.

Graham Whitaker walked in to see Father Smythe already seated in a green leather chair at one side of the room.

"It would seem you have commandeered that chair as your own," he said.

"It's the best of the lot," rejoined Smythe. "Here, why don't you try it?" he added, starting to stand.

"I was only joking!" laughed Whitaker. "I've already commandeered the wood Georgian desk chair over here. I must admit, however, to being a little envious of the pen stand and ink supply you have there on the table beside you."

"You had your chance, Whitaker!" chuckled Smythe.

After a continuation of the discussion of Dr. Cobb's Shakespearean theory involving not merely Sir Francis Bacon but also King James VI, followed by another of Graham Whitaker's short stories entitled *Mountaintop Melody*, and finally the introduction of Father Smythe's attempt to topple both religion and atheism in a single fell swoop, Barribault turned to a presentation of his vision for the Barribault Foundation and Barribault House.

The Eight had already been thoroughly briefed in the packets they had been sent before their arrival. Barribault now desired to expand his vision in more detail. The doubts he had begun to harbor about a few of the future partners he had chosen for his enterprise, he kept to himself. He still hoped to find a way through the mental quagmire of his concerns.

The fact was, these doubts were more than offset by his positive delight with young Melinda Franks. How could he possibly have anticipated discovering such a rejuvenating bond of love after so many years.

The morning's presentation had not taken the form of a discussion. After years of thought, planning, and consultation with experts, Barribault had the parameters well established by which his foundation and publishing company would function. There had, however, been a free flow of questions from seven of the eight as they sought to understand more accurately the sweeping vision in which they had been invited to share. Only one had been silent through the first ninety minutes. At last she could keep to herself no longer.

"But," finally interjected Jessica Stokes, "if you so strongly insist on the emphasis on traditional mores, how will we move into the modern mainstream? What of feminist and minority studies and publications? What of current philosophical and social and cultural trends?"

"*We*, Ms. Stokes?" queried Barribault.

"I merely assumed," Stokes began to reply, " —that is, you have repeatedly said that you desire all of us to participate in the future of your company, that you value our contribution and input. In that light I feel a responsibility to give it—I think your publishing vision is provincial and narrow, in the area of enlightened gender awareness most of all."

A few glances went round among the others as if silently to say, "What is she doing!"

"I wonder whether you have been listening to a word I have said, Ms. Stokes," replied Barribault. His tone was kindly, yet hinted unmistakably of rebuke. "Moving into the modern mainstream is the last thing I want to achieve. The whole point of Barribault House is to provide a traditional *alternative* to the modern mainstream. We are trying to *counter* modern trends, not embrace them."

"With such a business model, are you not dooming your efforts to be seen as old-fashioned, and thus a failure in the end, both financially and otherwise? Modernism does not merely mean that Kindles and ipads are replacing books, it also entails a range of issues that authors and publishers must address that would have been unthinkable a hundred years ago."

"I am a wealthy man, Ms. Stokes. Whether Barribault House succeeds financially is of little interest to me. I intend to publish books of a quality and with a perspective and outlook not seen for years. Whether the sales of those books will in every case recoup every dollar or pound invested in their publication will not be my chief concern. I intend to be ruled by no statistical equations of markup or profit margin. Of course it is an absurd business model, as you say. But it is *my* business model. This is how I have determined to invest my fortune. Certainly I hope that over the years others in the publishing industry, and readers of our books, will see the value in what we are doing and that, indeed, even financial success will follow. If not, I will go to my grave content in the knowledge that I contributed something of permanent value to the world of books and literature and publishing, and will have done my part to prevent modernity from poisoning our culture to the last man, and perhaps I should add, to the last woman. As for minority studies, they will have absolutely *no* part in Barribault House. Let a woman or a black or a Muslim or a Hispanic or Russian or a or a Hindu or a Korean or a white housewife from Iowa or Liverpool submit thoughtful, original, insightful, well-written books of traditional values and we will publish them because they are thoughtful, original, insightful, well-written books that promote traditional values. But we will publish them for no other reason. I hope I make myself clear, Ms. Stokes."

"I...*suppose* you do," said Jessica slowly, taken aback by the obvious scolding. "I merely...I assumed that the traditional values you spoke of were primarily concerned with quality and integrity in how you ran your business. I did not expect such a bias against much that modernity is contributing to culture and society to dictate the *content* of every book as well."

"You consider my outlook not only provincial, but biased?"

"It is obvious, isn't it," replied Jessica.

"Is it biased of me," said Barribault, "to acknowledge clear historic facts that I have gleaned from my study of nations and cultures that have come before us?"

Stokes did not reply.

"In any event, the traditional values I speak of concern not quality only, but content and worldview. Marriage, honesty, truth, responsibility, absolutes, accountability, sexual purity...the entire Greco-Roman and Judeo-Christian ethic will be woven throughout the fabric of our company, and in the content of the books we publish. Thoughtful books, but thoughtful as based on a traditional foundation."

"I don't understand then," said Jessica, "your selection of Father Smythe's book, which, as I understand it, attacks traditional Christianity in no uncertain terms."

"That, Ms. Stokes, is a perceptive observation. How does his book fit with my traditional outlook? In a way, perhaps, it is the exception that proves the rule. I found it original and thoughtful. It made me rethink some of my own spiritual ideas that I realized had become clichés. I do not agree with most of Father Smythe's conclusions. But I felt that he raised honest issues in a thought-provoking way that actually, in the end, helped to strengthen my own perspectives. So while such may not have been his intent, his book deepened my own traditional outlook."

"And if a lesbian or feminist or Islamic author presented his or her ideas with equal originality that caused you to rethink your own ideas, what then? Would they be afforded the same open-mindedness that you have given Father Smythe?"

The room was silent as it awaited Barribault's response.

"You handle yourself very well, Ms. Stokes," he said after a moment. "I honestly am not prepared to answer your question at this time. I will only say that you make a valid point. I shall have to think about what you say further. If my bias is indeed inconsistent, perhaps—well, as I say, I will think about it further."

* * *

As the meeting broke for lunch thirty minutes later, Graham Whitaker drew alongside Mike St. John in the corridor.

"What did you think of that nonsense of Smythe's?" he asked in a low voice out of the side of his mouth.

"I should probably offer no comment," smiled St. John. "Professional ethics, you know. The clergy must stick together in spite of our differences."

"I share the good Ms. Stokes confusion over Barribault's desire to publish Smythe's book. Original perhaps, but hardly traditional."

"In spite of what he said about his spiritual ideas, I do not take Barribault for a religious man. I don't know how much stock I would place in his evaluation of spiritual concepts."

"Perhaps not, but why would he endorse a lambasting of Christianity by a so-called clergyman?"

"It is the old shell game of trying to preserve the emotional comfort of spirituality absent the reality of its content."

"True enough. Smythe as good as admitted that he didn't *really* believe God existed at all, but recognized the good of religion to mankind whether there was anything to it or not. The whole premise is logically absurd. I found myself wondering if he really even is a priest. Do you recall how he seemed to fumble Barribault's question about Episcopalianism and Anglicanism, almost as if he was not aware that they are one in the same?"

"I don't know that I would read too much into that. Barribault was giving it to him pretty good. I think he was just flustered."

"I don't know. He seems more con man than priest to me."

Mike laughed. "You are a suspicious one."

"Not that I am a religious man," added Whitaker. "I just don't like hypocrisy. If he doesn't believe in God, get rid of the collar."

St. John laughed again. "Religious pretext is one of the oldest con games in the book. In my business you see it every day. As a renowned Scotsman of the nineteenth century once said, most of the unbelief in the world can be traced to the unbelief of the clergy, or words to that effect. If the truth were known, my profession is not one of the most admirable in the world."

"An interesting observation from a clergyman.—Got anything interesting planned for the afternoon?"

"I thought I might walk down to the beach and get my toes in the water," replied St. John. "Maybe the dolphins will be out. What about you?"

"No plans. I spent an hour in town yesterday. The shop called Abra Bits and Collectables is worth a visit if you are that way. I picked up a book by one of my favorite authors in an original 1952 first edition for only eight pounds."

"I shall definitely include it in my afternoon's agenda."

* * *

About three o'clock Jessica Stokes walked toward the rose garden. She paused and for the briefest moment her heart fluttered.

For a second or two she considered turning around. But then the next she found her steps moving slowly past the hedge and entering the expansive garden. Only one other individual was present, seated on a wood bench thirty or forty feet away reading a book and chuckling to himself. She walked forward.

"Hello, Mr. Whitaker," she said. "Lovely day, isn't it, especially in such glorious surroundings."

Whitaker glanced up.

"Ah, Ms. Stokes—yes, no place lovelier than a rose garden on a warm day."

"What are you reading?"

"Oh, just a little bit of nothing—a book I picked up in town yesterday. *Pigs Have Wings*, if you want to know."

"Oh…I've not heard of it."

"I'm not surprised. An obscure bit of fluff, nothing more.— Won't you join me?"

"Well, perhaps…if you don't mind the intrusion."

"Not at all.—So, what's the academic atmosphere like at Manchester?" asked Whitaker in the tone of one making conversation, "as liberal as everywhere else? What is it you teach?"

"Introductory philosophy."

"Ah, yes…Voltaire, Spinoza and their sidekicks. Only *liberal* philosophers, or do you also include the works of St. Paul?"

"Of course not. Why would we study a ranting supernaturalist?"

"Not a very open-minded view," chided Whitaker with a smile. "I thought you prided yourself on being a tolerant and open-minded modernist."

"I do."

"Paul of Tarsus is probably the most influential philosopher in the history of western civilization. But because he was a Christian, you deny him a seat at the table."

"I wouldn't have taken *you* for a Christian, Mr. Whitaker."

"I'm not. I was speaking of open-mindedness, not religious belief."

"You don't think I'm open-minded?"

"My, my but we do jump to conclusions, don't we," laughed Whitaker. "I did not say that, Ms. Stokes. I only pointed out that it does not strike me as open-minded to teach the philosophy of western civilization and ignore the influence of Paul of Tarsus.'

"You are entitled to your opinion, Mr. Whitaker."

"Thank you. But honestly I meant nothing critical, it was only an observation."

It fell quiet a moment.

"Do you mind if I make another observation?" asked Whitaker after a moment.

"Of course not," replied Jessica, "though perhaps I should be wary."

"I hope what I have to say will be helpful," rejoined Whitaker. "It's just this—I would be a little more careful, if I were you, Ms. Stokes."

"Please call me Jessica…that is if you don't think it a terribly familiar request of me."

"Not at all. You know us Americans—informality is our middle name. Return the favor, please."

"But you are *Dr.* Whitaker?"

"True, but we already have more Ph.D.s per square inch than is good for any group so small. *Dr.* Cobb. I assume Father Smythe is a *Doctor* of Divinity. I don't know about St. John. I think Congregationalists tend to be more relaxed about those kinds of things."

"And then there is Miss Franks," Whitaker went on, "who *will* have her Ph.D. in Literature when she completes her studies at Cambridge."

"Please—don't mention Miss Franks!"

"A sore point, I see."

"She grates on me."

"And then there is you," said Whitaker, "—the enigmatic Jessica Stokes. Perhaps you are a Ph.D. as well."

"Not yet—though I am working in that direction."

"In any event—we have one confirmed, two maybe, one soon-to-be...and with a line-up like that, I prefer to bow-out of the doctorial ranks. A simple *Graham* will suit me fine."

"Request granted, then," smiled Jessica. "So what were you saying I should be careful about?"

"Are you sure?"

"I cannot back down now."

"All right, then—I would simply think you might be a little more cautious in vocalizing your liberal views?"

"You consider me liberal?"

"Barribault obviously does."

"Do you?"

"I cannot imagine that you would deny it."

"I think of myself as representing the mainstream of modern enlightened thought."

"Coming from a university campus myself, I would not necessarily object to that characterization. Perhaps you do, though you must realize that what seems mainstream in academia is in reality much farther left than the general culture, whether enlightened or not. I think that you consider Barribault hopelessly behind the times. But he may be more representative of a greater cross section than you realize. I would only change one word in what you just said, and say that you indeed represent the mainstream of modern *liberal* thought."

"I know that argument," rejoined Stokes. "But I believe that enlightened liberalism is on the vanguard of progress in every age, leading society into new times in necessary ways. Truth, and the advancement of civilization is always on the side of liberalism, not conservatism."

Whitaker chuckled lightly. "Are you honestly not aware of the bias inherent in such a statement?"

"*Bias?*" rejoined Jessica a little heatedly. "You're accusing *me* of bias?"

"You called Barribault biased."

"But he is clearly a conservative, and prejudice is all on the side of conservatism."

Now Whitaker laughed openly. "You must know how ridiculous that is,' he said. "Your statement itself is *completely* prejudicial."

"How can you possibly say such a thing?"

"You have undone your own argument," rejoined Whitaker. "I say that not as a conservative arguing against liberalism, but as a simple matter of logic. Actually, I am probably more similar to you in my views than you may realize. I am simply aware that bias exists everywhere on the spectrum. Liberals are often *more* prejudiced than conservatives simply because they are blind to their own inconsistencies."

By now Jessica's face was red, whether from anger or embarrassment, it was difficult to say. She glanced away.

"My only point," said Whitaker at length, "as you yourself said, is that Barribault is *not* a liberal. He is a traditionalist. I have no idea what might be either his politics or his religion, nor do I care. That is his business. However, this plan for his publishing company is so far-reaching and creative in its approach, only an open-minded and forward-thinking man could dream it up. On the other hand, literarily his views are traditional. I can only assume him a cultural and social traditionalist as well. Yet you seem bent on trying to enlighten him to the necessity of embracing modernity."

"Everyone has to embrace it eventually."

"That's my point—no they don't."

"The momentum of modernity cannot be stopped."

"That is your opinion. You don't know that for a fact."

"History confirms that my opinion is right."

Again Whitaker broke out laughing. "There is your bias showing through again."

"How so?"

"Claiming that history proves you right. Barribault disagrees. Study the fall of Rome, Jessica. If you're going to make the arguments you do, you need to study your history more carefully. You liberals accuse conservatives of being closed-minded, but you are making as hidebound a series of statements as it is possible to make. If you keep it up, you are going to offend Barribault and there could be unpleasant consequences."

"Those who don't embrace the changes necessitated by the advances of feminism and gay and minority rights need to be offended, if that's what it takes for them to see the truth."

"Again, history doesn't confirm your view. Besides, Barribault is paying the bills. Our futures are in his hands. It is not our responsibility to enlighten him. In a sense, we work for him."

"I don't."

"If you cash his advance check, you do. The responsibility that comes with our selection is that we have become part of *his* literary vision. It strikes me that you may be working at cross purposes with that. You are so intent on voicing your views that you cannot see that this is not the right forum in which to further them. I would go so far as to say that here, in this setting, in these circumstances, you do not have the *right* to attempt to further them. By accepting his terms, we are agreeing to advance *his* vision, not our own."

"You expect me to be silent?"

"*I* expect nothing, Jessica. I am only trying to offer what I hope is good advice—to put your agenda and your viewpoints on the back burner. Publish all you want in that direction later in your writing career, and with another publisher than Barribault House. Honestly, I'm not arguing for or against any point of view or lifestyle, only about the wisdom of your outspokenness. It is your defensiveness that I believe is out of place, not your ideas themselves. In another setting, I would say the exact same thing to a conservative who was not giving *you* a fair hearing. I simply do not think it is wise of you to offend Barribault. I suggest you apologize to him for what you said this morning."

"Apologize...why? I did nothing wrong."

Whitaker shrugged. "It's up to you," he said.

* * *

Shelby Fitzpatrick walked leisurely along the railway viaduct between Cullen and Portknockie with an old cloth volume in one hand along with a brown leather journal. Everyone she met greeted her with the same words—*Fine day!*

Like Jessica Stokes, the thirty-four year old Californian was a modernist. But as a psychologist she had learned to cut people a little more slack for views and experiences that varied from her own. She was about 5'6" in height, of slender build but not abnormally thin like the model types that abounded where she came from, with straight brown hair cut short almost in Beatles fashion. Normally every inch the professional woman in appearance, on this day she had taken the enjoyable prerogative of donning a worn out pair of Levis, and, in place of an expensive blouse, a faded green sweat shirt whose arms had been cut off at the elbows.

The loose clothing felt great!

What a welcome tonic this week was to her spirits. After almost three years without a vacation, in the non-stop environment of her psychology practice, she felt as though she had stepped back into a Victorian novel—into this very novel she held in her hand that had been set right here in Cullen in the 1870s.

She drew in a deep breath of sea air, then walked to a bench along the path and sat down. She spent ten minutes noting some observations from earlier in the day, then opened the novel she had brought with her. She read for another forty minutes, until the sharp cry of a gull drew her attention to the sea. It was a gorgeous blue today. The sight drew her with the desire to feel the sand between her toes.

Shelby rose, continued along the path to a point at the third green of the golf course, where she turned off the high viaduct path, descended steeply into the middle of the golf links that sat between beach and highway, crossed the fairways until she reached the long expanse of dunes above the beach. There she stopped, took off her shoes and socks, clutched them and her books tightly, and ran down the final descent of rocky sand until she felt the foamy sea water on her feet. The chill sent an invigorating thrill through her body. It wasn't, however, as cold as she had expected. She bent down to fold up the bottoms of her jeans, then turned parallel to the line of the shore, and continued westward at ankle depth in the water as it ebbed and flowed over the sand.

She had walked perhaps two hundred yards, with the great red stone of the Bored Craig on her left, when she was surprised out of her dreamy reverie by the sound of her own name.

"If it isn't the soon to be renowned novelist Shelby Fitzpatrick," a man's voice said ahead of her.

She glanced up to see thirty-six year old Mike St. John jogging toward her, trouser legs rolled up to the knees and splashing as he came in the tide.

"Hello, Mr. St. John," she said, pausing as he lumbered toward her. "It appears we both had the same idea today."

"I would think for a Californian this water would freeze your toes off."

"It's not as bad as I expected," replied Shelby.

"Does everyone in California surf?"

Shelby laughed. "Hardly. I have never surfed in my life. We're not caricatures, Mr. St. John, anymore than all Scots wear kilts."

"It's just that California has such an image."

"Most of it fictitious, I assure you...or at least that image is limited to a very few."

"An illusion shattered. Nothing is sacred these days."

"An odd comment coming from a minister," observed Shelby as St. John fell into step beside her.

"A mere figure of speech. So, what does my fellow novelist think of the gathering thus far?" asked St. John.

"Your fellow novelist?" repeated Shelby. "You are making the two of us one of the little cliques within the eight?"

"How do you mean?"

"Surely you've noticed the natural cleavages within the group—by gender, by age, by outlook, by temperament. You've got the two crusty fifty-something men, Cobb and Smythe. You've got the two aloof observers, Mr. Whitaker and Dame Meyerson. You've got the two career women who keep to themselves—Melinda Franks and Jessica Stokes."

"You're more a career woman than young Miss Franks. I would think that group would include you and Ms. Stokes."

"I suppose you're right. But the two of us haven't had a single discussion. There's no chemistry. I might also lump you and Father Smythe as a subset of clergy, but you seem to have no more in common than I do with Miss Stokes."

St. John laughed. "I like your analysis," he said. "You are a true student of people."

"A psychologist has to be. So does a writer...or a novelist, I should say, to invent believable characters. But in your original observation about we two novelists, you omitted Ms. Stokes. The novelist sub-set would be three."

"You're right. I forgot—historical, whodunit, and thriller. Still, I don't see the three of us having too many palsy-walsy intimate discussions."

"But you and me?"

"We're having one now, aren't we?"

"I would hardly interpret passing the time of day as an intimate discussion. We just happened to meet on the beach, although I have to admit, this is more than I've ever spoken to a minister in my life."

"You don't go in for ministers?"

"Our paths don't usually cross. But honestly, no I don't particularly go in for them, as you say. I hope I'm not so cynical as Dr. Cobb. But I am certainly no fan of organized religion."

"Oh, it's not so bad. Nor are we men of the cloth."

"What you stand for is?"

"How do you mean?"

"Always asking for money, all the ritual, the wars of religion—how a man like you who seems halfway intelligent can throw in with a system with so much blood on its hands...it is beyond me. I may not consider myself an atheist, but I have nothing but contempt for Christendom as a whole."

"Strong words."

"The entire premise of Christianity I find loathsome—we are right and everyone who doesn't agree with us is wrong."

"I would hardly call that the foundation of Christianity."

"What is, then?"

"The account found in the gospels of the New Testament."

"Point well taken. But *a* premise of most Christians remains the conviction that 'we are right and everyone else is wrong.' I believe that all religions contain truth. I find the exclusivity of most Christians repulsive."

Mike did not reply. They walked slowly along in silence.

"Do *you* believe that Christianity is right," asked Shelby at length, "and all other religions wrong?"

"Not necessarily," Mike replied. "I agree that all religions contain truth."

He paused for a moment.

"Let me ask you a question," he went on. "If several children are set to solve the sum two plus two, and give answers of sixteen, nine, eighty-seven, one-hundred-fifty, and five…would you say that any of the answers are *nearer* the right answer than the others?"

"Of course."

"In the same way I would say that though all religions may point toward truth, some are nearer ultimate Truth than others."

"Namely, Christianity?"

"If I didn't believe that, I wouldn't be a Christian. I don't see how that makes me exclusivist. It strikes me as the ultimate realism. I am simply a man who is trying to find truth and who has arrived at the conclusion that in the Christian message I come closer to it than elsewhere."

"That sounds exclusivist to me."

"Then I am sorry. But I think if you observe me long enough you will not see me judging everyone who doesn't agree with me. I have my hands full trying to live my faith myself. I may poke fun at a man like Dr. Cobb occasionally, but not because I think I am better than him, but for the same reason you are questioning me now—because most of the world's judgmentalism actually comes from the point of view he represents, not from Christians at all. I'm just trying to knock a few of the barnacles off *his* knee-jerk judgmentalism toward Christianity."

"There is plenty of blame for intolerance to go around. Still, Christians have been most reluctant of all to face their hypocrisy."

"I would not argue that point. But are you not falling prey to the pitfall of throwing the baby out with the bathwater, of discarding the message because the messenger is a hypocrite?

What if the message, notwithstanding the messenger's hypocrisy, is true?"

"How else is it to be judged but by its messengers? If Christianity is a religion that purports to teach people how to live, and no one lives by its teaching, how reliable can that teaching be?"

"No one?"

"No one I have ever met."

"Maybe you haven't met the right Christians."

"Are you placing yourself in contention as a radiant example of Christian virtue?" said Shelby, making no attempt to hide her sarcasm.

Mike roared with laughter.

"Not in the least!" he said. "I am merely a humble minister. I make no pretext to virtue whatever."

"That's another thing I have never met."

"What's that?"

"A humble minister."

"Gently, Miss Fitzpatrick—you're coming close to stepping on toes. It is, *Miss*? Now that I think of it, I don't know whether you are married?"

"Yes...*Miss*. No, I've never been married. As for stepping on toes, I am of the view that a few more toes stepped on might be good for the Christian enterprise."

By now they had reached the end of the beach. They turned back in the direction from which they had come and parted about ten minutes later halfway along the sweeping shoreline.

* * *

As Shelby returned to Cullen House, she saw their host walking alongside a tall hedge in the garden with Melinda Franks, her hand through his arm and leaning against his shoulder.

Her eyes widened at the sight. The next moment they crossed the lawn and disappeared around the far end of the house.

"A little mischief going on if you ask me," she heard a voice say behind her.

She turned to see Briscoe Cobb approaching.

"I...don't know about that," she said. "But it does look...more than a little surprising."

"I'll let you in on a little secret," said Cobb, drawing close and speaking on a confidential tone, "the other night I saw Barribault creeping down the hallway. He stopped and knocked on Miss Franks' door. Whatever is up, it's been going on for a few days."

"You don't really think...?" began Shelby.

"All I know is what I saw, and now this. It's not that hard to put two and two together."

* * *

That evening's dinner was unusually subdued.

Both Jessica Stokes and Shelby Fitzpatrick had been left out of sorts by their respective conversations earlier in the day with Graham Whitaker and Mike St. John, though for markedly different reasons.

The two men, however, were in rare form.

"I say," said Whitaker as if talking to himself, "this meal is worthy of Anatole's steak and kidney pie."

A few eyebrows raised around the table.

"I don't follow you, Whitaker," said Father Smythe. "What do you mean?"

"Oh, nothing," replied Whitaker, vowing again to watch himself more closely about his closet literary passion. He hardly noticed the subtle grin that crept over Mike St. John's face.

The meal progressed. For several minutes St. John seemed to be nursing a private joke. Finally he could contain himself no longer and began to chuckle.

"By the way, Graham," he said, "it *wasn't* Anatole who dished up the steak and kidney pie."

Whitaker shot him a keen glance of disbelief. Had he heard him aright?

"Who then?" he asked, a grin forming on his lips.

"If you will recall," answered St. John, "they were at Totleigh Towers, home of the Bassett scourge, when Madeline imposed the diet that led Gussie Fink-Nottle to prowl the house at midnight in search of sustenance, not at Brinkley Court. The steak and kidney pie was produced on that occasion by substitute cook Emerald Stoker, who had taken the post at Totleigh because of unfortunate investments on the turf."

Whitaker laughed to find another devotee of like mind able to converse so fluently in the language of Wodehouse.

"You astound me, St. John! Yes, it all comes back. And let me see...the horse in question...right, Sunny Jim if I am not mistaken."

Now it was St. John's turn to laugh with delight.

"I want to know who Anatole and all these other people are...Sunny Jim of all things!" said Smythe a little peevishly. "I do not appreciate an inside joke unless you let everyone else in on it. Private conversations like that are grossly inconsiderate."

"You are entirely right," said Whitaker, taking the rebuke in stride. "Very thoughtless of me. I apologize. St. John and I were referring to a book we both know which I had misquoted. But as it may bore the others, why don't you come to the Library with me later and I will show you the book and you can read it for yourself."

"I am not so interested that I want to read a whole book," said Smythe, gradually settling his ruffled feathers back into place. "I shall see."

"The invitation is open anytime."

Slowly the conversation drifted into other channels.

* * *

While they were enjoying dessert later, Hugh Barribault walked in. He greeted everyone warmly and invited them to join him for after dinner drinks in the Library.

As he glanced around the room, reminded of what she had seen earlier, Shelby's gaze followed Barribault as his eyes came to rest momentarily on Melinda. She did not look away or seem embarrassed by his look. She returned his smile with one of her own.

Later that night after everyone had retired to their rooms, Shelby Fitzpatrick heard sounds in the corridor. She went to the door, opened it, and looked out. But she was too late. Whoever it was had disappeared toward the stairway.

Muffled voices in low tones still could be heard. Soft steps were climbing up to the third floor.

Whitaker and Smythe going up to the Library, she thought. Though on reflection as she closed her door, she was certain that one of the voices she had heard was that of a woman.

Six

Differences

The days progressed, gradually the Eight became more relaxed and spontaneous. If they could not yet be called *friendships*, a few relationships began to form among them that might become friendships in time. There were also several cleavages and undercurrents of animosity that, while not perhaps so visible, yet contributed a spicy intensity to the mix, which, for the perceptive among them, added multiple layers of interest to the gathering.

The Breakfast Room saw fewer private cloisters of ones and twos. Dinners became longer, the discussions around the table ranging further afield, the laughter less cautious. They no longer saw one another as threats. No gamesmanship was necessary. They sat at the apex, living the dream of all aspiring writers. With the exception of Mike St. John, the men enjoyed brandy and cigars together—though St. John enjoyed the company of the other three no less that he did not indulge with them. The women found it more difficult, though occasionally they could be heard giggling together. The barriers had truly come down when stately Dame Meyerson and flirtatious Melinda Franks had a little too much wine one evening and went outside in the rain together, stumbling about and giggling like tipsy teenagers. Even Hugh Barribault, observing the display from the privacy of his own apartments, could not prevent a smile. He had more reasons than it would be wise to divulge for being interested in the two women. For the present, to see them drunk in the rain was value for money in anyone's book.

But wide divergences of viewpoint and worldview were bound to surface too. Perspectives on political correctness and religion were not the only areas where strongly held differences existed.

Meanwhile, the increasing intimacy and frequent meetings between Barribault and Melinda Franks did not go unnoticed. Reactions were as varied as their personalities, though most kept their opinions to themselves. In a setting like this it did not do to be known as a purveyor of gossip. Briscoe Cobb had injudiciously let slip his observation of Barribault at Franks' door to Shelby Fitzpatrick. Beyond that little was said. But they had all seen enough to cause them to take notice.

Briscoe Cobb, the first to have suspected the affair, was returning from a short walk across the stone bridge about 7:30 in the evening, where he paused to enjoy the final remnants of his pre-dinner cigar. He had never been accused of being a man particularly sensitive toward others. But experience had taught him that cigar smoke was not the favorite fragrance of the rest of the world, and that in mixed company his thrice daily ritual was a pleasure best enjoyed in private.

Dusk was long past. Though the hour was not late, the sky, obscured by the small forest of beeches and Scots pines surrounding Cullen House, was dim. Only the lights from the great house behind him lit the pavement and bridge beneath his feet. The pleasurable gurgle of the burn passing through the small valley forty feet beneath him accented the peaceful evening with the pleasurable music of nature, along with doves in the distance in the canopy getting ready to call it a day.

As he leaned over the low stone wall of the bridge staring into the darkness, Cobb became aware of footsteps coming out of the night from the opposite side of the bridge. Slowly the shadowy outline of a figure came into view, lit but faintly by the house lights behind him. He waited.

"Dr. Cobb, I presume," said a woman's voice.

"You, ah...have me at a disadvantage," he said slowly, peering into the dark. Another second or two went by. "Is it...ah, Ms. Stokes!" he added as Jessica's form became recognizable. "I thought I was the only one out exploring the forest in the dark. You must have the eyes of a cat to have known me from such a distance."

"Not really," said Jessica as she walked to his side and stopped. "I had another clue than sight—my sense of smell."

"Right, of course. The cigar! Very good. I apologize if it bothers you. I had no idea anyone else was around. I'll just toss this stub in the brook and be done with it."

"I don't mind so much, actually," rejoined Jessica. "I know it doesn't fit my feminist persona, but cigars don't offend me so much. Cigarettes I find appalling. But my father smoked cigars and the smell always reminds me fondly of him. But you really ought to quit, you know. It's not good for you."

"We all need our little vices. Surely you have your own."

"I am afraid so…chocolate!" said Jessica.

"Not so much a vice," rejoined Cobb. "Now they say chocolate and wine and coffee are all beneficial to your heart. I am simply waiting for cigars to be added to the list."

"You may have a long wait! But heart or no heart, they are not beneficial to the waistline—at least not in the case of chocolate."

"It is my considered opinion, though I am admittedly a mere bachelor, and an aging one at that, that you have very little to be concerned about, Ms. Stokes. You have a figure that men would slay dragons for."

Jessica laughed. "How terribly suggestive of you, Dr. Cobb."

"Not a bit of it. Just the truth."

"Well, you are very kind. Still, I have to watch that I don't overdo it."

They were silent a few moments gazing into the night.

"Have you had the opportunity to, shall we say, observe our host and young Melinda Franks?" asked Cobb at length. In his voice could be detected a hint of fun.

"It's disgusting if you ask me," rejoined Jessica.

"You can't think there is anything to it?"

"Things may not always be what they appear. In this case, I think it is obvious that *something* is going on. I saw them just a while ago, disappearing into the rose garden in the dark. A man of his age should know better."

"Neither are you particularly fond of Ms. Franks?"

"Why do you say that?" asked Jessica.

"I've noticed."

"Well, you're right. She is a tart if you ask me. I've seen her flirting with you too."

Cobb laughed. "She's tried her wiles on all the men. Apparently Barribault is the only one to succumb."

"Well I don't like it. We are supposed to be equals in this project. I don't like the idea of her worming her way into his affections. It puts the rest of us in an awkward position."

"There is no element of female jealousy involved?" chided Cobb.

"Of course not. How can you suggest such a thing?"

Cobb laughed. "Just making sure."

"What would I have to be jealous of? Hugh Barribault is hardly my type."

"What is the joke?" asked another voice in the night, this time a man's. Slowly from the direction of the house, Graham Whitaker came into view. Dame Meyerson was at his side, her hand through his arm. Greetings went round the group of four.

"I heard laughing, did I not?" said Whitaker.

"We were just discussing the amorous activities of our host and our young poet and colleague," said Cobb.

"You have noticed?" said Whitaker with a humorous tone.

"Everyone has noticed," said Dame Meyerson at his side. "Hugh is—that is, Mr. Barribault is making a fool of himself. But he always did have an eye for the young starlets."

"Is that true?" asked Jessica.

"Believe me, it's true."

"Do you really consider her a starlet?" asked Whitaker. "A decent poet, perhaps, especially for one so young. But I doubt she will be the one to emerge from all this as a household name. Personally, I put my money on Fitzpatrick to eclipse us all in reputation. She could well become the next Michener."

"What are Barribault's motives, then?" asked Cobb.

"Do you really need to ask?" rejoined Jessica. "I would think it is obvious. She is a pretty young thing...he is a man."

It grew quiet as they pondered the implications.

"Do we all assume she is after his dough?" said Whitaker after a long pause.

"Graham!" exclaimed Dame Meyerson, unable to keep from laughing. "You really are the frozen limit! Do you make light of everything?"

"Who's making light of it," said Whitaker, laughing along with her. "I merely raise the obvious point that we are all thinking—he is rich and single, and she is an attractive and intelligent young woman."

"You really are awful, Graham," repeated Dame Meyerson.

"You are right, of course," rejoined Whitaker. "A gauche American without decorum or taste. And speaking of taste, I believe if we do not begin to move back toward the house, we may be late for the dinner bell. Dame Meyerson," he added, turning in her direction and leading her back across the bridge in the way they had come a few minutes earlier.

Cobb offered his arm in turn. Jessica took it, and they followed toward the house.

"Has anyone seen Father Smythe in the last few hours?" asked Cobb as they went.

A few shakes of the head and replies in the negative came from the other three.

* * *

A sharp wind came up during dinner, and rose steadily. They retired together to the Drawing Room after the meal. All eight still found themselves together an hour later, perhaps feeling an increased sense of camaraderie from the tumultuous conditions outside, none particularly sleepy or anxious to be the first to make a move toward their respective rooms. The conversation flowed congenially for some time, probably because it had touched on nothing controversial.

That was about to change.

Unable to keep his annoyance at religion from spilling over from time to time, after a lull in the conversation Briscoe Cobb turned toward Mike St. John.

"So tell me, St. John," he said. "I understand you are not presently active in the pulpit."

"That's right. I've been taking an extended leave of absence."

"Does your leave of absence indicate a change in your point of view?"

"You mean a change in my beliefs?"

Cobb nodded.

"In other words, have I lost my faith?"

"I didn't intend to be quite so crass about it," smiled Cobb, "but in a nutshell...yes."

"No, Dr. Cobb," said Mike, returning the other man's smile. "Sorry to disappoint you, but no loss of faith was involved then, or has resulted since."

"Do you think that disappoints me?" persisted Cobb, unable to let a potential bone of contention lie.

"I think you would take a certain delight in seeing a clergyman abandon his faith."

"Why do you think I would be pleased," rejoined Cobb, avoiding the nub of St. John's remark.

"Because you are a debunker, Dr. Cobb."

"What do you mean by that?"

"You relish tearing down rather than building up. Your interest is not so much discovering truth as debunking the beliefs of others. Therefore I think a minister losing his faith would be right up your street. On the other hand, were a man to stand up and say, *This I believe*, I have the feeling that your first response would be to argue against that belief—whatever it was—in an attempt to tear the man down and expose the holes in his beliefs."

The twinkle in Cobb's eyes from a moment earlier quickly disappeared. Even before St. John finished, he was squirming with irritation to have the tables turned on him in view of the others...and by one whom he dismissed as an intellectual lightweight.

"You call me a debunker?" he said heatedly.

"I would stand by that," replied St. John.

"On what basis?"

"Just what I said. Whenever anyone tries to make a positive point, especially about belief or matters of faith, your initial response is skepticism. It is almost as if while you are listening to what the rest of us might be saying, you are mentally constructing a list of countering arguments by which you can blow holes in whatever point we have been trying to make. I don't consider that to be the best nor most logically solvent method of dialogue and intellectual intercourse."

"Are you not doing precisely the same to me right now?"

"That point could certainly be made," nodded St. John. "I will readily admit that I have been your favorite target because for some reason you seem to have particular antipathy toward Christianity, as least as represented by the evangelical clergy. So I may be equally unqualified to render an objective opinion on the matter. But this is how your responses have struck me. You do not respond by saying, *Hmm, what truth might there be here?* but rather, *I reject your premise at the outset.*"

"What of it? If that's how see it, why shouldn't I speak my mind?"

"Oh, by all means. I appreciate your candor."

"Is there no place in your view for constructive and intellectual critique of shoddily held ideas?"

"Certainly. I love such honest dialogue. What I object to is critique as an *automatic* response. A man or a woman's belief is, if I may use the word, a sacred thing, to be treated with honor and respect. If there are inconsistencies present, they may be addressed. But not always immediately, and not necessarily by me. I can honor a man or a woman without necessarily endorsing every tenet of their belief system. What I object to is your *automatic* rejection of anything based on faith. Is there no room for the *possibility* that I may occasionally have something constructive to offer in the way of truth. From the moment you learned that I was a minister, you have treated me with a dismissiveness that ill-becomes a scholar such as yourself. I think the others would agree that you tend to react with knee-jerk anti-faith responses."

St. John glanced about the room. Most of the women were watching the discussion unfold with wide eyes and were not about to render an opinion. Dame Meyerson and Father Smythe had subtle smiles on their faces, obviously enjoying the exchange.

Graham Whitaker now surprised everyone by jumping into the fray.

"I think Mike has a legitimate point, Briscoe," he said. "You do usually weigh in on the negative side of things, no matter what the topic. I haven't heard you once all week say, *That is a good point. I shall have to think about that*, or *That is an excellent question*. I've heard Mike say almost those very words on numerous occasions. That first night when you two tangled on the existence of God and I commented on some point of Mike's that made sense to me, you shot me down in what I thought was a fairly rude exchange. Don't get me wrong. I'm not a religious man. I take no sides on the veracity of any spiritual issue. But from where I sit, if I was looking for a fair and objective response on some opinion of *mine* that I had offered, I think I would be more likely to get it from Mike than you. I agree with him that you are a debunker more than a seeker of truth."

"I suppose what it boils down to," added Mike, "is that you seem very close-minded to any hint of the idea that faith can actually point toward truth. I would think the more intellectually sound approach would be to say, I don't *know* whether faith points toward truth, but at least I am open to the possibility."

"You call me close minded?"

"Toward matters of faith and religion...yes, I would," replied St. John.

"And are you any better?"

"I don't know. Who am I to say? But when you make a point, I do try to listen objectively and give it a fair hearing. Some of your ideas on Shakespeare, for instance, I do not agree with. But I have said nothing. I listen and try to weigh them fairly, realizing that you have studied the bard more deeply than I have. I am therefore obligated to give you a fair hearing. In the same way, I would venture to guess that I have probably studied matters of faith more deeply than you have. I only make the point that that may likewise give me the right to an objective hearing."

'So the conclusion of all this," said Cobb sarcastically, "is that you are more qualified to know the truth than me?"

"Good heavens, Dr. Cobb," laughed St. John good-naturedly, "you have heard every word I said, and I said nothing like that. You are drawing an illogical conclusion. I have only said that debunking is not necessarily the best means to arrive at truth."

"That's the trouble with you Christians. You can dish it out but can't take it."

"It sounds to me, Dr. Cobb," said a voice none would have expected to weigh in on the discussion, "that you have taken hold of exactly the wrong end of the stick."

All heads turned in the direction of Melinda Franks.

"Mr. St. John is right," she went on. "You are constantly poking fun, making subtly critical remarks, as if you are the only one with any brains around here. You are especially critical of Mr. St. John. You treat him like a child just because he is outspoken about his Christian beliefs. Why shouldn't a Christian be able to defend himself? Now that he has spoken up, you don't like it. I would say that it is you who can dish it out but can't take it."

"All right, everyone," interjected Mike before Cobb could reply, "we don't need to beat this dead horse anymore. I didn't intend it to go this far. Argument accomplishes nothing. I apologize, Dr. Cobb, if I have been unkind or have spoken unfairly. I was only trying to make a point. So let me, if I may," he went on, glancing around the room, "throw out a general question that may shed light on what I maintain is an increasing bias against Christianity in our time. Let me pose the following. If Mr. Barribault chose us to sit on his publication committee, and two books came to us for consideration presenting a perspective on society and culture—one from a traditional and conservative Judeo-Christian perspective, and the other from a secular progressive and liberal perspective, and if we could only choose one...which book would we publish?"

"Wouldn't it depend, as Mr. Barribault has said, on originality of thought?" said Shelby Fitzpatrick.

"All right, then...both are equally well written, and equally original?"

"We all know where *your* loyalties would lie, don't we, Mr. St. John?" said Jessica.

"*Do* you?" rejoined Mike.

"I don't mind putting my cards on the table," said Dame Meyerson. "All things being equal...I would vote to publish the book that most accurately represents our time—which is a liberal and progressive era."

"Hear, here!" chimed in Cobb. "I vote with the good lady!"

"I too," assented Jessica.

"And we know where you stand, St. John," added Cobb. "So that makes it three to one."

"Not so fast," rejoined Mike. "Actually, I would abstain for the present, until I had read both books—with as much objectivity as I was capable of. I would not *automatically* vote in favor of the one that fell in with my own personal views. As a representative of the company, I would have a responsibility to try to see things objectively, beyond my own personal opinions— which is exactly the point I was trying to make about bias. The fact that you three arrived so quickly at a decision that agrees with your own personal viewpoints reveals a subjectivity that ill-becomes a publication committee."

Graham Whitaker was by now chuckling.

"Do you find this amusing, Mr. Whitaker?" asked Jessica.

"Actually, yes—I do," answered Whitaker. "Mike set us a trap to see whether we had been paying attention to his point about objectivity and avoiding knee-jerk reactions...and you three fell right into it. The correct answer to the conundrum is neither the Christian book nor the secular book. The correct answer is *abstain*. Since none of us have read them, either vote reveals bias unsupported by fact. I cast my vote with Mike— abstain."

"Abstain," now added Melinda. "That makes it three to three. What about you, Shelby? You've said nothing. And you, Father Smythe," she said turning toward the Anglican priest, "surely you would vote for the Christian book."

All eyes now followed hers to rest on Father Smythe.

"You forget the half title of my book, Miss Franks," he said, " —*The God Delusion*. I would certainly not classify myself as an evangelical."

"How can you talk about God being a delusion and wear the collar of a priest?" asked Melinda. "Like Mr. Whitaker, I don't consider myself a religious person, but at least I believe in God. Isn't it hypocritical to be a priest when you *don't* believe in God? I can't understand where you're coming from."

"I have wondered that myself," interjected Dame Meyerson. "I also find it curious."

"I do believe in God," rejoined Father Smythe. "I believe that God exists in the minds of men who need him to exist in order to explain the great unknowableness of the universe."

"But you don't believe that he *actually* exists, as a being, as a person, as an entity who is actually *there*?" asked Whitaker.

"What do you mean by *being*? What do you mean by *there*? Where is there? If God exists as a force in men's minds, is that the *there* you mean?"

"You're talking in circles, Father Smythe!" laughed St. John. "Do you believe that God, as a being separate from men, lives and exists?"

"As a force in the mind of mankind, yes. Separate from mankind, no."

"Therefore, a delusional force in the mind of man"

Smythe smiled significantly. "I will present you one of the first copies of my book when it comes off the press," he said, 'and you shall judge for yourself. I would only add that for one who read the likes of Karl Rahner and Hans Urs von Balthasar, not to mention Hans Kung, at seminary, such progressive accommodations to modernity are not scandalous in the least as a fundamentalist might view it. Perhaps slightly left of the mainstream, but accepted by many on the vanguard of current theology. But returning to the *res* as put to me by Miss Franks, absent more information than we have at present, notwithstanding your adroit parry, Mr. Whitaker, to divert attention from Mr. St. John's hypothesis, I would have to cast my vote with the tide of modernism rather than the antiquated Judeo-Christian framework which is on its way to the scrapheap of history."

"Four to three," said Dame Meyerson, clearly enjoying the exchange.

All eyes now turned toward Shelby Fitzpatrick, who still had not spoken. As she listened, she had been writing in the notebook she carried with her everywhere. At last her pen stilled and she appeared deep in thought.

"I find myself on the horns of an awkward dilemma," she said at length. "I am not exactly a tie breaker because technically we don't have a tie. I can either create a tie by siding with the abstainers, or vote with the progressives and put the thing out of reach. So who do I side with and whom do I offend among my colleagues. The complexities are perplexing."

"Come on, Shelby," said Melinda, "don't keep us in suspense!"

"Surely a Californian must be a modernist," urged Cobb.

"While it is true that personally I would tend to side with the progressive point of view, there are two other factors to be considered. Most importantly, the premise of Mr. St. John's hypothesis is that we eight, while sitting on the committee of Mr. Barribault's publishing company, found ourselves presented with a decision. Given that premise, I would have to ask myself in good faith how it was my responsibility to represent Mr. Barribault's publishing vision. The decision would not merely be mine to make in a vacuum according to *my* outlook. While I might personally be in sympathy with a progressive point of view, I would recognize my responsibility to publish along with more traditional lines according to the business model and vision established by the company's owner. I'm sure Mr. Whitaker during his tenure as an editor faced this exact situation, having to base his decisions on company policy and vision rather than his own personal taste."

Whitaker nodded.

"In other words, my own views would have to be subordinated to company policy. That is not to say I would necessarily vote in favor of the traditional manuscript and reject the other, only that I would want to withhold a decision until I knew how Mr. Barribault saw the thing. If he gave both his wholehearted support, all other factors being equal, I would probably vote in favor of the progressive manuscript."

"That's it, then—five to three," said Cobb enthusiastically. "Progressivity carries the day!"

"Not so fast, Mr. Cobb," said Shelby. "I did not vote yet. Not knowing Mr. Barribault's take on the two submissions, I said I would *withhold* a decision."

"You mentioned two factors that would influence your vote," said Vanessa. "What is the other?"

"As much as I disagree with him on most things, my other point is that from a strictly logical perspective, I think that Mr. St. John and the abstainers have had the best of the argument. Their reasoning holds more water. You other four, meaning no offense, have all voted emotionally and subjectively and on the basis of your own opinions. In that, Mr. St. John is absolutely right. Logic and reason and objectivity is all on the side of Melinda and Mr. St. John and Mr. Whitaker. In the end I might indeed vote with the progressives. But at this preliminary juncture, I would have to abstain."

A variety of reactions went round the room, nods of approval and shakes of the head in various degrees of annoyance.

"The perfect remedy to any dispute," said Whitaker. "Stalemate."

He rose and stretched with a long sigh. "And that, I believe, is my signal to retire to my room to my Erle Stanley Gardner. I left Perry Mason planting a knife in the shrubbery to coerce the murderer into a confession. Good night, all."

One by one the others rose as well and slowly drifted from the room. At length Mike St. John and Father Smythe were left alone.

"So here we are, the two clergymen, what, Father Smythe?" said Mike at length.

"I do not fancy us comrades of faith," said Smythe a little irritably. "You were pretty hard on Dr. Cobb. I am not sure I don't agree with him that your fundamentalist brand of Christianity is growing tiresome."

"You consider me a fundamentalist?" laughed St. John.

"You find that humorous?"

"I have to say I do."

"Are you telling me that you *don't* consider yourself a fundamentalist?"

"I don't define people—myself included—with labels. But I suppose it shows how little you understand a man like me who is *not* a fundamentalist, yet who takes his faith very seriously— more seriously it would appear than you do."

"Go to hell, St. John," said Smythe angrily, rising and walking toward the door. "You give us all a bad name with your unbelievable intolerance and judgmentalism."

In another few seconds Mike St. John was left alone in front of the dying fire in the hearth. At length he rose and followed Smythe from the room.

The great house was now quiet. A clock somewhere struck a single chime. Probably eleven-thirty, St. John thought. Though it might even be 12:30. He had been paying no attention to the time. He climbed the dimly lit central stairway and started down the corridor toward his room. Suddenly ahead he heard a door open then close softly, followed by footsteps retreating away from him. He paused. Then, driven by curiosity, he quickened his step and hurried ahead.

Rounding a corner he was just in time to see at the far end of the hall the vanishing color of yellow disappearing into a room on the right. A second later a door softly closed. The only woman who had been wearing yellow this evening was Dame Jennifer Meyerson.

Mike tiptoed on past his own room to the end of the hall. Just as he suspected...it was Graham Whitaker's room.

Graham Whitaker, you rascal! he whispered, though just as quickly he chastised himself for the thought. Perfectly innocent, of course. She was a married woman, not to mention fifteen years his senior.

Satisfied that he had witnessed nothing untoward, but nonetheless intrigued, Mike returned to his own room, and in ten minutes was sound asleep.

SEVEN

Reservations

The relaxed atmosphere of literary retreat being enjoyed by the Barribault Eight, as they were dubbed by the media belied the buzz of activity being carried out in the second floor offices of the newly christened Barribault House. Barribault's staff was moving full speed ahead into the early stages of production for the release of its first eight titles, coordinating everything from cover design concepts, to early editorial work on each manuscript, as well as promotional plans and arrangements for book tours and signings for the new literary stars.

In addition to their group discussions focusing on the literary vision of Barribault House, meetings had also been scheduled for each of the eight to meet with various arms of the production staff to discuss cover design, book layout, marketing ideas, as well as final contractual legalities. Most importantly, all were scheduled to begin working with the editor assigned to each project to strengthen the craft and clarity of overall presentation.

The previous day had seen Shelby Fitzpatrick and Father Dugan Smythe meeting alternately with six or eight different members of the staff in the office complex, and beginning the lengthy process of working with editors to turn their brain-children into the eventual reality of published books. Barribault had also met privately with both to discuss their respective projects in detail.

Barribault had not yet decided in which order to publish the eight books. To attract the most interest from the widest cross section of readership, he had tentatively decided to lead with a fiction title, probably Mike St. John's *Conundrum at Craigeivar Castle,* followed by Melinda Franks' collection of poems a month later, and continuing at successive monthly intervals. Not all the selections would create the same interest or produce the same sales potential. Therefore, the various genres represented had to be released randomly. Shelby Fitzpatrick's massive *Song of the Western Mountains* would probably be released last, with Jessica Stokes' *Ratchet* falling somewhere in the middle. He was also aware of the name recognition Jennifer Meyerson brought to the table that would insure high interest and sales. Her book of essays should no doubt precede Cobb's and Smythe's works in inaugurating Barribault House's non-fiction lineup. Graham Whitaker's short stories might fit anywhere in the sequence.

Mike St. John and Melinda Franks were scheduled to spend the afternoon today with editors and the publishing staff. As he was just finishing a private lunch in his study, Hugh Barribault's assistant Cynthia Gordon entered holding two sheets of paper.

"What is it, Cynthia?" said Barribault glancing up. "From that look on your face I assume you do not bring good tidings."

"I am afraid I have some unsettling news, Mr. Barribault," said Miss Gordon. "You remember the computer sleuth I have been in touch with in Australia?"

Barribault nodded.

"He has been slow getting his reports back to me. I had all but given up hearing anything. But now I have begun receiving emails from him almost daily about the eight men and women. He is somehow digging up facts that did not turn up in our investigations. I cannot imagine how they escaped us with the exhaustive research we did."

"The responsibility for that is mine," replied Barribault. "I was more anxious to study the writings that were sent in than the people themselves. It was only as an afterthought that I realized the need to look into their backgrounds. What we did was cursory at best. So what do you have there?"

"Some information that just came in concerning two of the men." She handed him the first of the papers.

Barribault took it. His face clouded as he read, slowly shaking his head. "Unbelievable...how *could* this get by us?"

"I am sorry, Mr. Barribault."

"I will talk to him and if there is no exculpatory explanation, I will have to cancel the contract and make a new selection. It will set us back months. But I don't see any other choice."

Barribault exhaled a long sigh.

"And the other?" he said

"It's about Mr. St. John," replied Miss Gordon.

Barribault looked over the brief report with concern.

"I am sorry, Mr. Barribault," said Miss Gordon. "I don't know what to say."

"It is not your fault, Miss Gordon," replied Barribault. "You did the best you could...we all did our best. As I say, if anything it is my fault for driving this train too quickly. We should have waited until we knew all there was to know. But we're in it now, so I will have to decide what to do.—This information concerning St. John may have a ready explanation. I will speak with him this afternoon."

* * *

Mike St. John and Melinda Franks arrived at the publishing offices at two o'clock. Miss Gordon introduced Melinda to the editor who would be overseeing her project, then turned to Mike.

"Mr. Barribault would like to see you in his study," she said. "If you will come with me I will take you there."

Mike followed. Two minutes later he found himself seated opposite Hugh Barribault.

"I have today learned," began Barribault, "about the trouble you apparently had in your church several years ago. Why did you not bring this to our attention on the biographical sketch you were asked to write after your selection?"

"I explained that my wife had died and that I subsequently took a leave of absence."

"But the rest...you indicated nothing of it."

"I did not consider it pertinent."

"What about the other woman?"

"There was no other woman, Mr Barribault."

"This report says there was. The allegations are serious and damning."

"I really have nothing to say," replied St. John calmly.

"I want to know what happened."

"I am sorry, but I really have nothing more to say."

Barribault stared back as if he had not heard correctly.

"Look, Mr. St. John," he said, in a tone registering a curious mix of sympathy and annoyance, "I like you. I *very* much like your book. Just between you and me, it was the first of the manuscripts to be selected. You were the first of the eight, though that must remain between the two of us. Your writing craft and technique are astonishing for one with no background in literature...for a minister, no less. You have a bright future. I am about to make you a star, as well as a wealthy man. But my authors must be men and women I can trust. I don't say they have to be squeaky clean. But they represent me. They represent my values. I can't have something like a sordid love affair come out, especially from a Christian minister. It would tarnish the whole image of Barribault House. You must understand."

"Yes, I do. I recognize what you are trying to do, and I respect it."

"Then just tell me the truth. I will believe you. If the reports are true, we will figure out the best way to deal with them. But I have to know. Just be honest with me."

"I truly wish I could, Mr. Barribault," said Mike. "But I can say no more. I am conscience bound to silence."

"Even if it costs you everything? I can still pull the plug on your book, you must understand that. No contracts have yet been signed."

"I hope it will not come to that."

"It will if you don't change your mind and make a clean breast of it. If you don't, I will have no choice but to investigate the matter further. The consequences may not be pleasant for you."

"I am sorry, sir—I wish I could."

Barribault looked away and shook his head as he exhaled deeply. He had never encountered quite such calm defiance.

"You are a frustrating man, St. John. What am I going to do with you? You put me in a very difficult position. I hope you change your mind. You may go. Tell Miss Gordon to start your session with the promotional people—on the assumption that you will still be a Barribault House author—then send her to me. Go on, St. John—I am angry with you and do not want to talk to you further. I might lose my temper."

Mike rose and left the room. Five minutes later Miss Gordon returned. Barribault had not fully cooled down. Having brooded on the exchange, however, he was calm enough to recount most of the specifics of the conversation for his assistant to embody in the form of a formal memo so that no misunderstanding would arise later as to what had transpired. He wanted no one suing him for breach of contract. Now that doubts had entered his mind about Mike St. John's ethics and morals, he intended to leave nothing to chance.

Unfortunately the other sheet she had brought him earlier contained information far more serious. If true, it would require yet more decisive action.

* * *

Two morning's later Hugh Barribault rose early as was his custom. He made himself tea in his room and sat down in his favorite chair with cup and manuscript. But he could not concentrate on his work. Over and over his mind replayed yesterday's tense exchange with the authors who now lay under a cloud of suspicion in his mind.

Perhaps this whole thing had been a mistake!

By 8:30, after two more cups of tea and a plate of oatcakes in his study, he set aside his manuscript. The Eight would be in the Breakfast Room by now, but he wanted to see none of them yet. He left his study by the narrow back stairway, continued by it down to the second, then the first, and to the ground floor, where he slipped out of the house and walked south, crossed the stone bridge, and several minutes later had circled around and down to the burn and was making his way along its side toward the Sea Gate. In fifteen minutes he stood on the shore just west of the Seatown.

The tide was midway out. The curving expanse of white sand enclosing Cullen Bay drew him. His mood was subdued. He needed to think.

By ten o'clock Barribault had circled back around into town under the old railway viaduct and was making his way through its gray streets. His steps unconsciously led him, as they often did, to John Thompson's shop.

The bell on the door sounded as he entered. He was relieved to see that his friend had no other customers.

"Morning, John," he said. "Hope you don't mind a non-paying browser come to get away from his troubles."

"No bother at all," replied the antique dealer. "But I thought this week was the culmination of everything you have been working for."

"The first few days were brilliant. It is an eclectic group and I find the discussions stimulating. But…"

His voice trailed away and he sighed deeply.

Thompson waited.

"It's just that you make assumptions about people," Barabault went on. "You assume, because of someone's writing style or content, that you share more of a common outlook than is actually the case. It may be a chance intersection of lines that are not actually parallel or going in the same direction at all."

"A colorful image—for people as well as lines."

"I had built up such hopes for this new publishing venture. However, I am coming to think that it may have been a mistake."

"Surely you don't mean your entire dream?"

"Perhaps not. But I was probably mistaken to think I could build it upon people I didn't know. Perhaps writers have to be like actors, playing roles that may be much different than who they are themselves."

"Fiction writers, you must mean?'

"Predominantly, I suppose. But what about poets—are they responsible only to capture sensations they feel themselves, or do they also take on personas in their poetry that may not reflect their own?"

"You are thinking perhaps of your own young poet Melinda Franks?" said Thompson.

"Actually I wasn't thinking specifically of her, though I do confess she has occupied my mind much of late. A delightful young lady. She is—"

Barribault paused.

Thompson eyed him with an expression of question.

"Let me just say that she has been the unexpected bright spot of the week," Barribault added. "In spite of that, I have begun to harbor doubts about some of the others. Not in their ability as writers, but doubts about whether they share my outlook sufficiently to help me launch this enterprise. I cannot entrust all I've worked for into the hands of people who will be at cross purposes with my vision, people who might even tarnish the image and reputation of Barribault House. I can't have feminists and extramarital affairs and someone who's gone through AA or a priest who's been accused of stealing from the collection plate…the thing would become a laughing stock after my years of speaking out in favor of tradition and—"

Barribault stopped suddenly. A sheepish look spread over his face. "Sorry, John," he said. "I got carried away."

"Surely you don't expect to find perfect people?" asked Thompson.

"No, not perfect…but integritious. "People with backbone, character, virtue, even nobility…as old-fashioned as that sounds—people who know right from wrong and who live by their principles."

"You are doubting that you have found such people?"

"In a word, yes. I wonder if I should just kibosh the whole thing. I would have to eat loads of crow, and it would cost me a million pounds—I would have to let them all keep their checks—but then I could start from scratch."

"Are you thinking of substitute manuscripts, perhaps?"

"I suppose that is a possibility."

"How would you like to see mine?" asked Thompson, glancing toward the drawer where his manuscript lay.

"Some other time, John," replied Barribault. "I'm too distracted to give it my attention just now. You haven't actually finished the thing, have you? I thought it was just something you were piddling with in your spare time."

"No, it's pretty much finished," said Thompson.

"Well, good for you. I will definitely have to take a look at it one of these days," rejoined Barribault as he walked to the door.

John Thompson sauntered to the window and watched the man disappear up the street. Usually he enjoyed Barribault's visits, but today his words grated on him. More than merely grated, they made him angry. The man had no idea. He had been working on his book for three years, had entered it in Barribault's contest, had suffered the humiliation in silence of having it rejected...and all the while Barribault came into his shop every few days without so much as a clue. The man had even helped himself to *his* ideas over the years, and included them in his own books without so much as a word of gratitude or acknowledgment...yet he had no time even to look at his manuscript.

With smoldering resentment, Thompson turned and walked back into his workroom. He sat down and took out his frustrations in attempting to improve the mechanism for the second fillable quill, whose various parts lay on his worktable. He worked steadily for an hour, revolving dark thoughts in his mind, until he was finally interrupted by the bell on his door signaling the entry of his first customer of the day.

* * *

Hugh Barribault returned to the mansion he called home by the lesser used country gate east of the house. The walk was longer, but in his present frame of mind he wanted to run into none of those men and women, perhaps out for a morning stroll, about whom he had begun to harbor doubts.

Approaching the great house thirty minutes later, he planned to dart in by one of the side entrances and make his way up to his own apartments unobserved.

Rounding the east corner of the north wing, however, he had not anticipated encountering Dame Jennifer Meyerson making a leisurely early tour of the rhododendron arbor with coffee cup in hand. By the time he saw her only twenty feet away, it was too late.

She walked toward him with an expression of inevitability and acknowledgment. But no smile of greeting came to her lips.

"So here we are, Hugh," she said, "alone again at last."

"So it would seem," rejoined Barribault.

"It must have been quite a shock for you to find *me* among your eight finalists."

"I was not surprised," replied Barribault. "You have made quite a name for yourself over the years. As I read your book, I felt your insight and the wisdom of your experiences and travels coming through on every page."

"You haven't changed!" laughed Dame Meyerson. "Still able to deflect attention away from unpleasant topics with your golden tongue."

"I mean every word."

"Where was all that praise a few days ago when I was giving my presentation. You went after me so hard I thought I was back in Hollywood. I was on the verge of leaving. I don't need your money, Hugh. And I certainly don't need any more humiliation at your hand."

"You're right. I am very sorry about that morning. I had not anticipated it—I suppose more emotions came back than I realized were there. I sincerely apologize. Please don't judge me by that exchange. Honestly, I am proud of you...and delighted beyond words to find you among my eight finalists."

"You are...*proud* of me?" said Dame Meyerson in a confused tone. "An odd expression to use considering what you did to me."

"That was many years ago. Ancient history, as they say. What's now is now. Here we are together again with a chance to make a new beginning and turn your book into a best-seller. I have no doubt that we will be able to make you into a highly respected spokeswoman for contemporary culture."

The words seemed to fall, if not on deaf, certainly on ambivalent ears.

"And just forget what happened? Pretend it never was?"

"I see no other course to pursue."

"I will never forget, Hugh. How can you expect me to forget? Publishing my book is hardly due compensation. No, Hugh, don't expect *me* to forget."

She turned and walked away, leaving Barribault watching her back in silence. When she had disappeared around the far end of the house, he continued on toward the side door and inside.

In the following days Miss Gordon came to Hugh Barribault several more times as new information arrived from her computer sleuth. Interesting revelations came to light about several more of the Eight that was not as disturbing as what she had initially brought him about the two men but nonetheless disquieting. Barribault's doubts now rose far beyond a few vague misgivings.

What was he to do?

More and more the conviction deepened within him that his only recourse was to cancel the entire result of his contest, apologize, eat the necessary crow, and start from scratch, perhaps with a reduced list of titles by those whose names managed to remain untainted after this latest round of investigations.

At length he summoned Cynthia Gordon to his office.

"Miss Gordon," he said. "I have decided to speak personally and in private with each of the individuals about whom questions have arisen. I will put before them the information that has come to light, and either receive a satisfactory explanation or take appropriate action. I will decide afterward what is to be done. In the meantime, I want you to type up a thorough dossier on each. I realize we have essentially compiled this already, but I need a revised file complete with the new information. Document everything meticulously. There could be legal consequences. I especially need you to ferret out any word or detail on the original applications and questionnaires that may, in light of this new information, now be seen as not entirely accurate. I will depend on you to make sure that we have a reliable record and proof of what has been my intent and what has been the information we have had at our disposal."

"I understand, sir. I will begin today.

"Then I will want to meet with you immediately after each interview to record in detail exactly what has been discussed. We must walk very carefully in this."

"Would you like me to set up the automatic recorder, Mr. Barribault?"

"I think not. If any of these people have not been entirely candid and truthful, I do not want to compound the problem by secretly tape recording them. They would be furious if they found out. I mustn't add duplicity to duplicity."

EIGHT

Shopkeeper and Authors

D ame Jennifer Meyerson walked away from Cullen House along the tree lined drive toward town with many mixed feelings she could not easily identify. After yesterday's exchange with Hugh, she had been unable to concentrate on anything. She had skipped breakfast, silently endured the morning's meeting, and was in no mood for small talk around the luncheon buffet. If the others wondered why she wasn't among them, let them eat cake. She had her own problems to think about.

Ever since she and Hugh had laid eyes on each other after all these years, she had progressed through a flurry of ups and downs. For so long she had dreamed of this moment…and what she would say. Especially for the last month since learning she had been chosen as one of the Eight and *would* see him soon. She had saved up so many venomous phrases, even practiced them. They had all evaporated in an instant.

She knew she didn't still love him. Whether she actually hated him, of that she wasn't quite sure.

Until yesterday's chance meeting, they had not spoken a word alone together. She wondered if anyone else *knew*.

John Thompson unlocked the door of his shop at two o'clock after lunch and went inside. He had scarcely put the few pages of manuscript he had been working on safely back in their drawer when he heard the door open again behind him. He turned to see a stately, gray-haired woman enter, whose presence carried a look of fading yet still stunning beauty. Suddenly his shop seemed drab and dingy alongside the luminescence of her elegant carriage.

"Dame Meyerson," he said greeting her. "Good afternoon."

"How do you know me?" she replied with a smile.

"Your reputation precedes you. And I keep close tabs on national news. I would have known you even without Hugh's little shindig."

"And you, I take it, would be the renowned Mr. Thompson," said Dame Meyerson.

"At your service," replied Thompson with a nod of the head and slight bow. "Now it is my turn to ask…how did *you* know?"

"Your little shop has become quite the talk of our gathering up at Cullen House."

Thompson laughed. "I hope you are not disappointed. As you can see, it is a small shop, but I try to make up for the diminutive size with a unique selection."

"I can see that at a glance," said Dame Meyerson as she walked slowly about. "You have many interests—vintage clothes, old cameras, glassware, photographs and prints, a great number of antique keys and locks, Persian rugs—what are these?" she asked, pointing to several colorful items of woven wool hanging on pegs above the rugs.

"Also Persian," replied Thompson. "Camel salt bags. The two sides…just here," he said, removing one from its hook to show her, "they fit over the camel's hump."

"How intriguing! I thought I'd been everywhere, but I've never seen the like in my life. And books everywhere, from floor to ceiling and filling every nook and cranny…but I understood your specialty to be old pens."

"Pens are indeed one of my passions, along with keys and locks, vintage cameras, and, as you note, Persian weavings."

"A man of many talents!"

"Perhaps better said, a man of many *interests*…step this way, my lady," said Thompson with a gesture of the hand. He led her toward a small room at the back of the shop, three of whose walls were filled with books, and the fourth of which contained shelves devoted to the writer's art.

A sharp intake of breath signaled her pleasure at the sight.

"Mr. Thompson—it's marvelous!" she exclaimed. "This could be a museum not a store. Just look at these ink wells! And the pens," she went on, drawing close and lifting several in succession to examine them closely. "You have Parker, Sheaffer, Cross, Waterman. I am partial to the old classic Duofold myself."

"I see that you are a lady who knows her pens! And I have to agree with you—the Duofold of the early 20th century, in my opinion, represents the classic writing instrument. I do like some of the Sheaffer nibs which are generally stiffer. But there is nothing like the slight flexibility of a classic Parker."

"And just look at this lovely traveling box. It is in perfect condition.—What is this—an actual feather quill!"

"It's just for fun. I attach nibs to the feather."

"But what is this one."

"Something I am tinkering with—an actual fillable quill."

"I can see that this must be a true passion."

"No more than every amateur. I try my hand at anything that comes to mind. I enjoy making things."

"Something tells me, Mr. Thompson, that there is more to it than that. Are you a man with secrets?" she asked, turning and casting upon him a coy and subtle smile."

"We all have secrets, Dame Meyerson," he rejoined with an expression of equal mystery.

"It sounds as though you are on intimate terms with our week's host. I doubt there are many who claim the privilege of calling *him* by his given name, as you did a moment ago."

"It is not the word I would use to describe our relationship," smiled Thompson.

"What word?"

"*Intimate.*"

Dame Meyerson's cheeks blushed slightly. "A slip of the tongue," she said. "But you *are* friends?"

"I would say so. Though one never knows who one's friends truly are, does one?"

Whatever Dame Meyerson might have said in reply was interrupted by the bell behind them.

* * *

Briscoe Cobb had not been much more interested in lunch than had Dame Meyerson. Some of the morning's discussion had probed uncomfortably close to topics he was not anxious to explore in depth. If what Thompson had said to Dame Meyerson was true about everyone having secrets, that harbored by Briscoe Cobb was one he was particularly anxious his host not discover. Had he only imagined it, or had Barribault cast him several inquisitive glances during the morning's proceedings? He was not eager to find out if his worry was well founded, nor relished the thought of Barribault pigeonholing him alone and questioning him further. As soon as he judged the coast to be clear, he executed a stealthy exist from the luncheon, crept downstairs and outside, and with a brisk walk made for the village.

When Dr. Cobb walked into Abra Bits & Collectables about half an hour later, after poking his nose into several other shops, the last person he expected to see was the elder stateswoman of their coterie.

"Ah, Dame Meyerson," he said as the door shut behind him and he saw the lady emerge from the back room with the shop's owner.

"Dr. Cobb," she nodded, then turned to the shopkeeper. "Thank you, Mr. Thompson," she said. "I am pleased to have met you. Your shop is delightful."

She extended her hand. Thompson took it and lifted it to his lips and lightly kissed the back of her hand. "The pleasure has been all mine, my lady."

Dame Meyerson smiled, nodded again to Cobb, and left the shop.

As Thompson and Dame Meyerson had been concluding their final exchange, Cobb had unconsciously begun scanning the spines on a nearby bookshelf. Suddenly his eyes nearly shot out of his head. What was *that* doing here! This was a piece of dynamite sitting in plain view for the whole world to see! He hesitated momentarily, then snatched the volume from the shelf and fished in his pocket for a ten pound note to buy the thing.

"Ten pounds, I believe," he said, turning toward Thompson, holding the cover open to the price while keeping the title obscured from the shopkeeper's vision and handing him the note in his hand. Hopefully, the man wouldn't recognize it and know what he had.

A look of hesitation crossed Thompson's face as he reluctantly reached for the note. He opened his mouth to say something, but the man interrupted his thoughts by speaking first.

"It would seem," began Cobb, attempting to make conversation and divert focus from his purchase, "that you and Dame Meyerson are..." He allowed his voice to trail away significantly.

"We only just met for the first time—a charming lady, don't you think?"

"I would agree," nodded Cobb, burying his purchase in the recesses of his overcoat. "If she is all she seems," he added, again significantly.

"None of us are *all* we seem," rejoined Thompson in a similar vein as he had to Dame Meyerson a few moments earlier. "We are all hiding something. Who was it—Mark Twain, I believe, who said that all authors are liars. That's not a quote, but it is something like it."

"Ah, but he was speaking of *fiction* writers, where make-believe is the author's stock in trade. It's different for non-fiction writers like myself."

"I wonder how different it really is."

"Why shouldn't Mark Twain say that novelists are liars— even his very name was a lie, a *non de plume* as we say in the trade."

"Are you saying that the use of a pseudonym like Twain is a deception reserved only for fiction writers? What about the Shakespeare-Bacon controversy? That is the subject of your own winning entry in the Barribault sweepstakes, is it not?"

"You keep up on things, I see! Actually that is but one small part of my work. In answer I would remind you that Shakespeare's plays, too, are works of fiction. So my premise still holds."

"And your own reputation untarnished with scandal. You win, Dr. Cobb," laughed Thompson. "I concede—no deception of identity allowed in the case of non-fiction authors such as yourself. Did I show you my refillable quill when you were in last?"

* * *

With sandwich in hand, Graham Whitaker left Cullen House and headed through the trees in the direction of town. He had last night finished the Blandings installment he had purchased several days before. Perhaps something new had come into to one of the town's shops in the meantime. He never went anywhere without a Wodehouse or two. In this case, however, he had assumed that the Barribault Library would contain, if not a complete set at least a modicum of offerings. He was surprised to find only three or four Jeeves and Woosters present. Enjoying at present one of his Blandings phases, he had instead sought his daily Wodehouse fix from the several shops in town that dealt in used books.

He had covered about a third of the distance along the tree-lined drive toward the town gate when he heard footsteps pattering up behind him. He turned just as Melinda Franks came alongside.

"Hi, Graham," she said with her usual exuberance.

"Hello, Melinda," he returned. "Walking into town?"

"It's a wonderful little village. Busy, friendly, always bustling. Have you enjoyed the ice cream yet?"

"Actually, I'm not a big ice cream man. Is it as good as they say?"

"I don't know. It's good, but the best in the world? I'm no expert so I can't say."

"Now the fish and chips at Linda's," added Whitaker. "About that I can weigh in with an opinion. I will say that they are the best I have ever had."

They reached the town gate and emerged onto the head of Grant Street, then continued two blocks along the gradual descent to the square. At Seafield Street they turned and made their way along the main street through town.

"What did you think of Father Smythe's essay on atheism this morning?" asked Whitaker as they went.

"Pretty heady stuff for a mere university student like me."

"You are as bright as anyone here," laughed Whitaker. "You play the game of being just a fun-loving coquet. But you don't fool me—there are depths you keep hidden. Your poems reveal more than you let on."

"What about you, Graham," said Melinda in a more subdued tone than usual. "Your stories do the same. You have suffered too, I can tell."

"You're right. Losing my wife was extremely difficult. It would not be far from the truth to say that my wife is an unseen presence between the lines of all my stories."

"That's wonderful. In a sad way, I mean. But it is wonderful that you are able to keep your love for her alive. How did she die?"

"ALS. She was in an experimental research program. But funding for the program ended. She died a year later."

"That is sad. I am sorry."

"Thank you."

"So do you think it true that it takes suffering to write well?"

"I don't know. Probably not in every case. All I can say is that in my own case I doubt very much that I would have been able to touch such deep themes and emotions otherwise. Not that I wouldn't give it all up and *never* see a book in print with my name on it to have my wife back. But things happen. You have to deal with life's griefs as best you can and try to keep alive your sense of humor and optimism."

"I know what you mean."

"Have *you* suffered, Melinda?"

She did not reply immediately. His question obviously struck a deep nerve.

Slowly she nodded. "I would say yes," she answered at length. "I know I am young and that people think me a flirt. But there are sorrows I bear too. I wear a mask like everyone. Those sorrows have been with me all my life. I suppose we are a lot alike, Graham. We put on a face of cheer and humor, while inside we carry our griefs in silence."

"And expose our deepest feelings through our writings."

Their serious conversation was brought to an abrupt end by the sight of Briscoe Cobb approaching along the walk.

"Well, well, my fellow colleagues in crime!" he said. Observing the serious expressions on their faces, he glanced back and forth between them.

"Why the dour expressions?" he said.

"We were just discussing the universal human predicament of suffering and whether it is a necessary ingredient to the writer's craft," replied Whitaker. "You caught us at a moment when we were both being sober and reflective."

"The last thing I would have anticipated from either of you!" rejoined Cobb. "My illusion of the poet and the short story writer have crashed against the rocks."

"Don't worry about me, Dr. Cobb," said Melinda, resuming her carefree demeanor. I promise not to be serious around you."

"I can take it, Miss Franks. I am, after all, a stuffy academic. It doesn't get more sober and less humorous than that."

"Where have you been, Dr. Cobb?"

"To the antique shop, just there," replied Cobb, his hand unconsciously probing his pocket where the book he had purchased remained securely hidden. He gestured widely behind him with his free hand. "Fascinating chap, the owner. Most wide range of interests and knowledge."

"I've heard about the shop but haven't been in yet," said Whitaker.

"It's worth a visit. Ask him to show you the fillable ink quill. Made it himself. I'm thinking about buying it, actually, though I suppose it's more a curiosity item than a practical working writing instrument."

Cobb continued on toward the square. A minute later the two authors walked into Abra Bits & Collectables.

"Hello," said Thompson, "—Miss Franks, isn't it?"

"Yes," replied Melinda. "You have a good memory. I've been in only once."

"I never forget a pretty face, to use a dreadful cliché. And would this be one of your authorial colleagues?" he asked, turning to Whitaker.

"This is Dr. Graham Whitaker," said Melinda.

"I am pleased to meet you. Dr. Whitaker," said Thompson, offering his hand. "I am John Thompson."

Whitaker nodded as they shook hands.

"You would be the American economist whose short stories were chosen in the contest," said Thompson.

"Right on all counts," replied Whitaker. "You are well informed."

"I followed the contest closely. The writer's craft is close to my heart."

"I am told you specialize in vintage pens and the like. There is a certain quill I've heard about I would love to see."

"My handicraft is acquiring a reputation, is it!" Thompson turned and led Whitaker further into the shop as Melinda went in the other direction to look at the dresses and hats. "It is back here, Dr. Whitaker," said Thompson.

He took the quill and handed it to Whitaker, who turned it over in his hand gently.

"I don't get it—how does it work?"

Thompson took it from him.

"You twist this part of the nib here," he said, "—like this. Out comes the snorkel...you dip the tip into ink, pump the plunger two or three times to fill...twist the snorkel again and it retreats and disappears back underneath the nib...and voila!—a quill with enough ink to write eight pages."

"Absolutely ingenious. An amazing device! It looks lethal—the end I mean, what you call the snorkel...it looks like a hypodermic needle."

Thompson laughed. "A sinister thought! It's not supposed to poke into anything but an inkwell."

"Still, it's a dangerous looking thing. Does it work?"

"Absolutely. It's fully loaded with the writer's poison, if you'll pardon the pun—actually, my own special ink which I make as well. Why don't you give it a try—here's a sheet of paper," he added, setting a blank sheet down on the shelf in front of them.

A minute later Whitaker handed the quill back to its owner.

"Well, Mr. Thompson, I must say I am very impressed," he said. "An extremely inventive device. I can see that someone definitely could write a book with that.—But what I really came in for was to see if you had any Wodehouse. I picked up one of the Blandings novels a few days ago from one of your colleagues down the street."

"I do believe I have two or three," replied Thompson. "They would be, let me see...back here on this wall—right, yes...here are a few."

"Great, terrific!" exclaimed Whitaker, looking over the spines and taking one off the shelf.

"Did you find what you were after, Graham?" asked Melinda, wandering in his direction as she continued absently to peruse the shop's shelves.

"Very possibly so. But look at this quill here, Melinda...it's remarkable. Just the thing for the creative poet."

"Do you write by hand, Miss Franks?" asked Thompson.

"Believe it or not—I know I'm young, Generation X and all that, or maybe I'm Y or Z by now, who knows, blackberries, ipads, and Kindles...but actually I do. I cannot even imagine composing a poem on a computer screen."

"Then perhaps my special handmade quill is indeed the perfect instrument to give you the inspiration you need."

"According to Dr. Whitaker, what a writer needs more than a good pen, is to suffer personal loss."

"That's not exactly what I said," laughed Whitaker. "I believe I said that it probably wasn't *necessary* in every case, but that it had played a prominent role in my writing. Actually you never revealed your own view on the matter."

Melinda did not reply. Instead she turned and hurried from the shop, leaving Whitaker and Thompson staring after her in bewilderment.

* * *

Shelby Fitzpatrick sat alone in the Lunch Room of Cullen House. Father Smythe had just left with Jessica Stokes, following closely on the heels of Mike St. John who had departed a minute earlier.

She withdrew a pen and a folio-sized leather notebook from her briefcase, opened it on the table in front of her, and began to jot down a few notes on the morning's proceedings.

It was no ordinary notebook but represented years of observations in her chosen field—observations of a wide cross section of people encountered in every conceivable situation of human contact, interaction, and relationship. She had been gathering data for years for a research project she hoped one day to publish. The moment the plans for this week at Cullen House had been sent to her, she knew that this week would provide a singular opportunity to observe a unique combination of gifted individuals, all strangers, in a controlled setting with a minimum of distractions and outside influences. It was a veritable hothouse of fascinating psychological character study and intriguing interchange. She had already filled several pages with handwritten observations, in which Jessica Stokes, Father Dugan Smythe, Mike St. John, and Hugh Barribault himself were thus far the primary participants.

A ray of sunlight glistened through the window and reflected brightly off the page in front of her. The sight reminded her that it was too nice a day to spend inside. She packed up her things, went upstairs to her room to drop off her briefcase and purse, then set out for the shore with notebook and pen in hand.

Walking down past Cullen's harbor, she made her way eastward at the shoreline, past Muckle Hythe, and around the point to the old Salmon Bothy cove. The return up around the climb to the outlook known as Nelson's Seat was steep, but the reward was well worth it. The point offered one of the most spectacular views of the Moray Firth anywhere. All of Cullen Bay spread out gloriously westward, the Bothy and its protected bay directly below and to the east. And on a clear day the mountains of Sutherland were easily visible almost to John o'Groats.

As Shelby climbed the last few yards of the path, she saw a familiar figure seated on the bench at the peak in front of her. She walked forward.

"Melinda?" she said tentatively as she approached, sensing something wrong.

Melinda Franks looked toward her in surprise. Her eyes were red. It was obvious she had been crying.

"Melinda…what is it?" said Shelby sitting down beside her.

"Oh, nothing," replied Melinda, sniffing and trying to smile as she brushed at her eyes. "Just feeling sorry for myself."

"Did something happen?"

"No, nothing like that. Mr. Whitaker and I came into town and went to that antique shop. We were having a nice talk but I lost it."

"Did he say something to offend you?"

"No. Graham is as nice a man as I could imagine. I just…I don't know…"

"That's all right," said Shelby, placing a hand on Melinda's arm. "I didn't mean to pry."

"That's okay…it would feel good to tell someone. I am adopted, you see. Sometimes the sadness of…you know…not knowing, of never knowing my mother…sometimes it just overwhelms me and I have to cry. I'll get over it. Sometimes it's painful, that's all."

"Melinda, I'm sorry."

"Please, don't tell any of the others. Everyone is so much older and more sophisticated than me. I don't want them to think I'm a baby."

"No one will think that, believe me. Your poems are incredible…and sophisticated. Besides, I'm only five years older than you, and Mr. St. John is thirty-six I believe. All three of us are the youngsters of the group."

"But everyone admires you for the scope of your novel. What you read this morning was amazing."

"Don't worry about your standing, Melinda, believe me. It takes a very special kind of talent to write moving poetry. Not everyone can do it, and those who can't have a secret admiration for someone with your gift. Even the two crusty old curmudgeons Cobb and Smythe, they know *they* can't do it. With Mr. Barribault backing you, you are going to become a very famous poet. The rest of us will be standing in line to get *your* autograph!"

Melinda laughed.

"What is that notebook you always have with you?" asked Melinda. "I see you writing in it all the time, sometimes when nothing is going on."

"Just my observations about life and how people handle situations."

"Is there anything in it about me?"

"Perhaps a word or two," smiled Shelby.

"And the others?"

Shelby hesitated before replying.

"Let me put it like this," she said after a moment, "I don't own a camera. Some people take photographs. I prefer to make *written* observations of what I see and hear. My notebook is my collection of written photographs of people I have known—hundreds of people. I want to remember things about them that a photograph would not reveal."

"I see...I think. Anyway, it's none of my business."

"Would you like to go into town and get an ice cream?" asked Shelby.

Melinda smiled, still a little sadly.

"Thank you. You've been very kind to me. But I think I would like to be alone a little longer. Sometimes it's good to let things go all the way into the depths. Cleansing, you know. There have been some major revelations this week...good things but emotional things. I will tell you about them when the time is right. Right now I just need to let it settle, I suppose."

Shelby nodded, took Melinda's hand, gave it a squeeze, then rose, and walked the rest of the way past the Caravan Park and cemetery toward Cullen.

* * *

Father Dugan Smythe and Jessica Stokes, as if drawn by the same invisible force acting upon the rest of their number on this particular afternoon, also found themselves in town after lunch. The conversation between them since setting out, agreeing to walk to town together, and through the entire half mile walk, had been more than a little superficial. For two individuals who shared so much on the political correctness side of the spectrum, the flow of soul and feast of reason was notably absent between them. Both were inwardly relieved when they parted at the square, Jessica turning down the street, and Father Smythe moving in the direction of the Paper Shoppe for his daily purchase, then to Abra Bits & Collectables.

"Hello, John," he said as he entered the antique shop, "how go the retail wars?"

"Afternoon, Father," rejoined Thompson. "I've had a good day of it," he went on. "The sale of a rug always makes a day."

"Sold that quill of yours yet?"

"No, but a number of lookers. Most of your lot, actually. I think you're the—what…the fifth from the House in today. Word of my quill seems to be spreading."

"Are you still at work on a second?"

"It's back on my work table as we speak. I think it may turn out better than the first, though the nib's a little sharp—I have to watch that I don't poke myself!—Do you mind if I ask you a question?"

"Not at all. I thought we were good enough friends by now that you wouldn't have to ask."

"Point well taken. All right then, and this is coming from an avowed agnostic so please don't take it wrong, but the idea of the confessional has always struck me as the supreme arrogance of the Christian religion. The idea that one human being can absolve the sin of another, and that a few rote prayers with a set of beads is capable of making it all go away…it is just inconceivable to me that intelligent people believe it. So I would like to know what it is like to sit in the confessional and hear confession."

"I am an Anglican, John. I thought you knew that. We don't have the confessional."

"Ah, right…I suppose that slipped my mind. So you've never had the experience?"

"Why don't you ask your friend Barribault about it? He's Catholic. Though he could only enlighten you from the lay side of the thing."

"Hugh Barribault is a Catholic?" asked Thompson with obvious surprise.

"So I understood."

"I've never heard such a thing and I *thought* I knew him as well as anyone in Morayshire. He's never uttered a religious word to me as long as I've known him, or been known to attend mass or church of any kind."

"Hmm, that is odd," rejoined Smythe. "Perhaps I am mistaken," he added with a light laugh. "I thought I'd read it somewhere."

* * *

Mike St. John had dozed off for half an hour in his room after lunch. When he woke and went downstairs, then outside, he found the place as good as deserted. Having no way of knowing that his seven colleagues were already in the village or thereabouts, he too struck off toward town.

Meanwhile, Shelby Fitzpatrick had come into the village and, had wandered through a few narrow lanes before finding herself emerging onto Seafield Street. As she passed The Willows, through the window she saw Jessica Stokes at a table with a cup of coffee. She entered and walked toward her.

"Hello, Jessica," she said, greeting her with a smile.

"Oh...Shelby—hello," said Jessica, glancing up. "Won't you join me"

Shelby sat down on the opposite side of the small table.

"Your presentation this morning about your book was very impressive," said Jessica. "You must have done a mountain of research."

"I suppose I did. At first I was just interested in my family's roots. It didn't feel like research. When I finally woke up to the fact that, *Hey, I'm writing a historical novel!* that's when I realized I had better get my Wales history accurate."

"I can't wait to read it."

"From what Mr. Barribault says, we are all going to read one another's work in manuscript form, as preliminary editors prior to the books going into production, complete with notes and recommendations. That will be an exciting process. He certainly seems to want us involved. I think that's unusual."

"I wouldn't know. I've never been published."

"Nor I. But I have several professional colleagues who have. They do nothing but complain about editors making changes without consulting them. It doesn't seem there's going to be any of that with Mr. Barribault. He seems to value our input. What about your book—what kind of research did you have to do?"

"Not so much really," answered Jessica. "It's a contemporary thriller, so mostly I had to read up on the pharmaceutical industry, which provided the setting for the plot. I like to think that my knowledge of people and modern society and the cultural climate of the times was the foundation rather than research per se."

"That makes sense. And you will unveil it on us tomorrow. You must be excited. The best saved for last."

"Hardly that!" laughed Jessica.

"I thought you were originally slated to present your novel and read to us from it yesterday."

"I don't know why Mr. Barribault changed the schedule. He said he wanted to see me later this evening. Perhaps he will explain it to me."

"A private interview—lucky you! Are you nervous?"

"I don't know. Should I be?"

"I don't know. He's probably going to rave about your book before your presentation."

Shelby glanced at her watch. "Oh, time's getting away from us. It's a few minutes after four. I wanted to pop in at that antique shop. And we meet again at five. I suppose I'd better be off."

"I'll join you...if you don't mind," said Jessica, rising with her.

They left the shop and walked across the square.

John Thompson was just returning from his workroom at the back of the shop as they entered.

"Ah, ladies, unless I am mistaken here are two more of the illustrious Barribault clan," he said, greeting them warmly. "This makes seven of you this afternoon to visit my humble shop. You would be, let me see...one of you would be the Californian, Miss Fitzpatrick, and the other Miss Stokes from Manchester, if memory serves."

"Very good!" laughed Shelby. "As you can no doubt tell from my grating accent, the Californian is me! I am Shelby Fitzpatrick. And this is Jessica Stokes."

"It is *Ms*. Stokes," added Jessica.

"Happy to make your acquaintance," nodded Thompson.

"We have come not only to browse around your shop," said Shelby, "but mostly to see this famous pen everyone is talking about."

"*Is* everyone talking about it?" laughed Thompson.

"It has come up in conversation several times. Word has it that you specialize in writing paraphernalia."

"Guilty as charged. What is on tap for this afternoon's session?" asked Thompson.

"I believe we are to be graced with more of Dr. Cobb's wisdom," replied Shelby.

"Ah yes, your resident Shakespearean expert. Is he as brilliant as the news reports have it?"

The two women glanced at one another with indeterminate expressions.

"I don't know, probably so," answered Shelby slowly. "I'm sure he thinks so. Just between you and me, however, I find it all rather tedious. But I'm no highbrow like Jessica here."

"It doesn't get more highbrow than psychology," said Jessica.

"Not really. You just have to know people, and be able to read what they're not saying more than what they are. It's not rocket science. It simply takes insight into motivations...why people respond as they do. But *your* field...philosophy! Now that's highbrow in my book."

"So does Dr. Cobb know his stuff, Ms. Stokes?" asked Thompson.

"I think so," replied Jessica. "His theories are interesting. I don't know Shakespeare that well, but Mr. Barribault seems to think them original. He has said that Dr. Cobb's book is the most original Shakespearean study since MacDonald's *The Tragedie of Hamlet,* which is over a century old. I thought every rock about Shakespeare had been turned over by now."

"Jessica will present her novel tomorrow," said Shelby. "She even has a private interview this evening with our host."

"Aren't you the lucky one," said Thompson with obvious interest. "What's the occasion?"

"I don't know," replied Jessica. "He said he wanted to talk to me."

"Well, brush up on your Victorian style! He's a stickler for the old-fashioned ways. Believe me, I know. This shop is the site of many a lengthy discussion—from book ideas to the plight of modernity. I sometimes think half Hugh's plots have been hatched here."

An expression it was difficult to identify crossed Jessica's features. She nodded but did not reply, then began wandering about the shop. Shelby, meanwhile, drifted toward the adjacent room. There, out of sight of the other two, she took out her pen and jotted down a few lines in her notebook. She was just putting the cap back on her pen when Thompson walked toward her.

"Ideas for your next book?" he said. "You've found my pen and paraphernalia section too, I see."

"Yes, most impressive. And the famous quill!"

"Let me show you how it works."

From the nearby room, Jessica Stokes was listening intently, but remained where she was. She therefore did not observe the demonstration.

* * *

Mike St. John rounded the corner and turned onto Seafield Street as the two women left Abra Bits and Collectables ahead of him. For a moment the idea flitted through his mind of running to catch them. Instead he continued along the pavement, then turned into the shop.

Thompson had just settled into his chair when he heard the bell and glanced up. He did not immediately recognize St. John. The newcomer's stumble over the step as he entered, nearly upsetting a vase on the nearest shelf, did nothing to endear the fellow to the shop owner at the end of a long day. He took him for a bumbling tourist—probably American—and glanced toward him with an impersonal nod of acknowledgment, then opened the book in his lap about the Picts.

As he read, however, Thompson kept a wary eye on his lone customer. Experience had taught him, in a shop as close as his, with glass shelves and delicate items everywhere, to keep a sharp eye out for galoots with two left feet.

The man wandered toward the back room without upsetting any fixtures. Thompson began to think that he had perhaps misjudged him. He glanced up from his reading about a minute later to see the man approaching him with his handmade snorkel quill in hand.

"How much do you want for your quill?" he asked in perfect Aberdonian Scots.

"Sixty quid," replied Thompson. "Do you know how that pen works?"

"Not exactly. The nib is vintage Sheaffer, which obviously accounts for the price. A nice Sheaffer gold nib is so exquisite as to be priceless. I take it you have removed it from one of their snorkel refill systems that, let me think…if memory serves they were produced in the 1950s."

"Right on all counts! It was 1952 to 1959, to be exact. You know your pens."

"Not really," replied St. John, "but I have heard about this one of yours. Does it actually work?"

"Just like the original Sheaffer. Heard about it…where? I know there's been some talk about it up at the muckle hoose—perhaps you've heard—Hugh Barribault's hosting a small gathering of writers."

"That's where I heard about it too."

"Oh, how's that?"

"I am staying up at the House. I'm one of those infamous writers you mentioned—Mike St. John's the name, from Aberdeen."

"Oh, well that explains it. I didn't recognize you. All of your colleagues have been in looking at it today, too."

"But no takers?"

"It's mostly a curiosity item, I suppose."

"I'm not so sure. I would like to think it practical as well. Matter of fact…I'll take it!"

"Just like that?"

"If it were done when 'tis done, then 'twere well it were done quickly, as the man said."

"Ah, very good—*Macbeth*, I believe. You know your Shakespeare as well as your fountain pens."

"Or Wodehouse…pick your bard," said St. John. He began fishing his wallet out of his trousers and pulled out two twenty pound notes, and a ten and a five.

"Oops, sorry…I've only got fifty-five. I'll come back tomorrow."

"Fifty-five quid and it's yours, Mr. St. John. Put it to good use. Write a book with it and make me proud…and maybe famous as well! I'm already at work on a second. You can let me know your suggestions. If you have any trouble with it, bring it in and I'll make whatever adjustments are needed to get it working properly."

"A deal. You'd better give me a full demonstration. Though I've known of them for years, I've never actually owned a Sheaffer snorkel system pen."

"It's quite simple really," said Thompson, taking the quill from him and removing a bottle of ink from a nearby shelf. Your biggest challenge will be keeping the feather looking nice. I'm not concerned about the nib and working parts themselves. You should probably keep it in a box of some kind to protect both quill and nib. It would look nice in an inkwell or stand, but it would then be unprotected. It's not the sort of thing you want to let lie around on a desk."

"Perhaps you can be looking for a suitable box," said St. John. "I will be around for a few more days and will check in with you."

"Will it be safe...taking it now, as it is?" asked Thompson, still a little concerned about the man's dexterity.

"I think so. I shall be very careful. If you have a bag that will get it safely back to my room. It will be undisturbed there—though I will try it out of course!—until we devise something in which to store and transport it."

"So what is your specialty among your literary colleagues?" asked Thompson. "I know it is not Shakespeare—that is reserved for Dr. Cobb."

"No, nothing so erudite as that I'm afraid," replied St. John. "I've written a novel—a murder mystery, actually. *Conundrum at Craigievar Castle* it's called."

"Oh right—now it comes to me...you're the minister!"

"*Was* a minister. There are two of us clergymen in attendance. Have you met Father Smythe?"

Thompson nodded. "He's become something of a regular to my shop. To be honest, I pegged him for the quill. He has been fascinated with it from the moment he first saw it. But you beat him to it. What do you mean you were a minister? Have you retired...or on sabbatical?"

"Just a spot of bother at my church. Rather than fight it out and try to vindicate myself, I resigned. That's when I began writing, so it all worked out for good as Paul says."

"Paul who?"

"The Apostle Paul, in his Letter to the Romans."

"Ah yes, right. And you haven't returned to the pulpit since?"

"Not yet."

"But you will?"

"No decision on that score yet. My future, you might say, is undetermined. I shall have to see how God leads. I've been given a once in a lifetime opportunity to support myself by writing, and I am enjoying it. I am in no hurry to rush a decision about the formal ministry. Pastoring a church is stressful work. You're always 'on,' so to speak. I cannot imagine finding time to write in such an environment. Though I miss aspects of church life, this has been a good break—rejuvenating to the soul, as it were."

"Right."

"I am just waiting to see how it all pans out.—But," St. John added, "I am going to be late for our next meeting if I stand here jabbering much longer!"

"Let me get you that bag for your quill."

A minute later, with St. John's purchase as safe for transport as they could make it, the minister turned toward the door.

"Won't I be the talk of the dinner table tonight with my new quill!" he said. "I feel a best-seller bubbling up inside me already. I will see you in a day or two, Mr. Thompson."

John Thompson watched Mike St. John leave with a pang of melancholy. He had made the quill to sell, yet it had attracted such interest that his shop now felt forlorn without it highlighting his writing display.

He would get to work finishing a second version of his line of writing quills tomorrow.

Thompson returned to his chair and his study of the ancient civilization of the Picts. However, he found himself unable to concentrate. His reflections turned to the fascinating string of visitors the afternoon had brought to his shop. All the Barribault Eight in a span of less than three hours.

And they all had stories to tell.

Why had they confided in him—a man unknown to them all a week ago? Did the atmosphere of his shop possess some strange ether that acted as a truth serum to all who entered? He had long noticed the same thing with Hugh Barribault. From the first time they met, Barribault had confided things Thompson doubted he told the postman, the butcher, or the clerk at the Co-op. Why did his shop bring out such a side to people, this openness to lay themselves bare seemingly without knowing they were doing so?

His mind replayed the visits of the last few hours.

Dame Jennifer Meyerson, the dignified public stateswoman...the very expression on her face spoke of mystery itself. She had asked him if he had secrets. Yet her tone revealed that she was deflecting attention away from her own...secrets that somehow, unless he was mistaken about that momentary tinge on her neck, had to do with Hugh Barribault.

Dr. Briscoe Cobb, snobbish Shakespearean expert...from the moment he made his insignificant purchase, he had become agitated, nervous, his manner oddly changed. If everyone had secrets, what were Cobb's? He knew the book, Thompson thought to himself—a cheap pulp historical mystery by an unknown called Brenda Carr. Who she was he hadn't the foggiest notion. He had been lucky to get more than *one* pound for such a book! It was an altogether worthless bit of trash—hardly the caliber of reading one would expect of an Oxford don. Why had the book affected him so strangely?

Melinda Franks, younger and more beautiful than any successful poet had the right to be...but had he not detected an expression of sadness in those bewitching blue eyes? What lay behind it? And had he noted a glisten of tears flood those eyes as she left the shop in such haste?

Dr. Graham Whitaker, to all appearances jovial and carefree, an instantly likeable man. If Cobb's interest in pulp novels was curious, what about this Ph.D.s fascination with the lightweight farce of P.G. Wodehouse? Still more curious was Miss Franks' comment about Whitaker's belief in suffering as the key to good writing. Perhaps it was true, Thompson thought. But how did suffering and humor interweave in the depths of this man who was obviously motivated by deeper complexities than met the eye?

Father Dugan Smythe, Anglican priest...he was the one among them all who seemed no more nor less than just what he was—a professional clergyman. That's why Thompson liked him—he put on no airs about his religion. Thompson had met more than his share of religious types over the years. His distaste for them was palpable. But Smythe could engage on any topic knowledgably without sounding like a preacher denouncing sin from the pulpit. His comment about Barribault being Catholic had been peculiar. A simple mistake, it seemed unaccountably to unnerve him.

Shelby Fitzpatrick, the young energetic Californian with the enegmatic notebook...what was she hiding in those pages she kept from public view?

Jessica Stokes, the self-styled and insistent *Ms.*...what insecurities made her so touchy about her womanhood, so determined that her persona be defined as feminist though it went against the grain of everything Hugh Barabault was about?

Mike St. John, innocent misunderstood pastor or perhaps defrocked minister...what was the real story behind his resignation?

Thompson smiled with irony and a hint of envious acrimony. He doubted any of them realized what they left behind, and how much he knew about them. He, on the other hand, had revealed nothing about himself. None of them, not even Barribault, knew *his* secret...that he yearned to be one of them. And *would* have been if Barribault's staff had had eyes to see the genius of his own work.

The fools, Thompson thought. They would see one day. Then Barribault would realize the talent that had been in front of his nose all this time.

* * *

It was some twenty minutes before five o'clock. Jessica Stokes and Shelby Fitzpatrick were walking leisurely along the lengthy paved entryway into Cullen House after brief visits to a couple more shops in town.

Gradually they heard footsteps running behind them, growing louder as they came. Curiosity overcame Jessica first. She glanced around to see Mike St. John lumbering after them.

"Oh, it's *him*," she said softly, sounding less than enthusiastic. "Do you suppose if we walk fast enough, we could get to the house before he catches us and bores us stiff?"

Shelby turned back, then chuckled at Jessica's comment.

"A good plan," she whispered. "But I'm afraid it's too late. He's nearly upon us. We shall just have to steel ourselves for the ordeal."

"Hello, ladies!" Mike called out behind them. "Slow down for a tired comrade."

Resigned to their fate, at last they stopped and waited for his panting approach. He swept toward them in a flurry of wheezing, sweating, dishabille, then stopped, bending over with hands on knees for a few moments to catch his breath.

"Whew! I haven't run so hard in years!"

"What was the hurry, Mr. St. John?" asked Jessica coolly.

"To catch the two of you...and keep you company the rest of the way."

"You needn't have put yourself out."

"Oh, no bother at all." Mike rose from his knees, inhaled again deeply, and again they set out alongside one another.

"So, here we are," he said, "—the three novelists of the group, what."

"You do like to classify people, don't you, Mr. St. John?" said Shelby. "I thought we were done with that. That is another of Christianity's fatal flaws—the obsession to divide and segregate humanity...sheep and goats, I believe you call them."

"You know your New Testament!" remarked St. John enthusiastically.

"Not at all. I have just read enough to know why I dislike Christianity. As a psychologist, well over half the problems I have to deal with in people stem in some way from religious teachings that have done nothing but confuse and conflict people at the deepest levels."

"I am sure that is true. Christianity's truths, misunderstood and mistaught, indeed have the power to do great harm. It grieves me as much as it angers you. But as to erecting artificial divisions within humanity, you are right...that has always been one of Christianity's many Achilles' heels. I certainly had no intention of doing the same with our little gathering of eight. If I caused offence, I apologize to you both."

"If you think that our being novelists creates some sort of unspoken bond or affinity between you and me," now said Jessica, "you are very much mistaken, Mr. St. John. Speaking for myself, I despise religion—in all forms. You and I are probably as different in outlook as any two individuals could possibly be."

"Ah...I see," rejoined St. John. "I shall in the future try to avoid any comment that hints at a connection between our respective crafts. Do you mind, however, if I make an observation?"

Jessica shrugged, as if to say she could not care one way or the other.

"Yours does not seem to be an incredibly tolerant position, given that in the lexicon of political correctness, tolerance is one of the foundation creeds of modernism. How is it that liberalism is allowed to stamp down hard on Christianity while demonstrating tolerance and open-mindedness to every other perspective, no matter how quirky or debased? It's a question for which I've never managed to get a satisfactory answer."

Neither did Mike St. John get one now. The faint sound of what might have resembled a *humph* was all that met him in reply. Fortunately they had by now arrived close enough to Cullen House that the three were able to gradually begin moving apart to go in their own directions. It was obvious that neither of the two ladies particularly appreciated the probing questions of the clumsy and unconventional clergyman.

NINE

The Ultimata

Hugh Barribault was not a man generally prone to self-recrimination. He had grown up surrounded by the privileges afforded by money, and had inherited the self-assurance that went with it. His father's death seven years before had thrust him into even more rarified echelons of wealth and power, adding all the more to his sense of poise and invulnerability. He had done his best to manage the fortune and affairs of the late Winston Barribault prudently and thoughtfully. Weighing among the myriad of causes to which his father had given so liberally, however, and a hundred others clamoring for new funding every year, remained a full time job for several of his staff. With so much responsibility, and the inevitable accompanying deference shown a man in his position by everyone with whom he came into contact, Hugh Barribault walked with head held high and the confident gait of a man who knew who he was and for whom things had mostly gone exactly as he wanted.

Only two episodes in his life could be said to have gone wrong. In truth, though there were two women involved, they comprised a single long episode in his memory—a memory scarred by heartbreak, guilt, and uncertainty about his conduct. He had tried to make up for it by recapturing the values of the far distant past if not the religious foundation out of which they had grown.

Suddenly those same sensations were coming back to haunt him. He was not sure how to deal with the self-doubts these last several days had hurled at him. The idea that he had *blundered*, perhaps badly, that he had made *mistakes*, that he had made *bad* decisions that may cost him dearly…these were sensations he had not faced in decades.

Unfortunately, in the days since the initial shadows of doubt had begun to gather over the integrity of "the Eight," Miss Gordon had brought to him additional revelations of potential incongruities that would be anything but pleasant to deal with. But if anything, Hugh Barribault was a man who could make decisions. That he had not had to make any difficult ones in the matter of the contest before this present hour of trial made doing so now all the more imperative.

Barribault hardly slept that night. Fits of wakefulness were interrupted by troubled nightmares of lawsuits and damning press releases, with visions of plummeting sales of his books and value of his holdings, culminating in the horrifying specter of having to sell Cullen House at auction to pay his taxes before venturing out into the cruel world as a penniless pensioner. And the presence in the house of the two individuals who had stirred up so much turmoil out of the past added yet more heavily to his mental and emotional perturbation.

He woke with considerable relief, but nevertheless in a cold sweat and breathing heavily. Within minutes he determined, come what may, today he would meet with the parties causing him such unrest concerning the publishing company. If Barribault House was destined to flounder on the rocks of his own foolishness in having hastily launched such an enterprise without sufficient due diligence, let the ship of his fortunes sink now and have done with it. As for his agitation from deeper personal causes…he would try to get hold of Forsythe in France to discuss that.

He drank his morning tea with a renewed sense of calm. By tonight he would decide what course to pursue—whether to fold the tent of Barribault House, whether to limp forward with a curtailed number of initial publications and try to explain it publicly as best he could, or whether to postpone the company's launch until alternate entries could be selected from among the dozen or so that had not quite made the final cut the first time around. Those seemed his only three options.

He went out for a walk about eight. A chill had set in during the night, along with an autumnal breeze that portended mischief to follow.

He would have preferred to cancel the morning's session. At the moment nothing could interest him less than a critique of the final chapter of Mike St. John's whodunit where the detective went round the room with insinuations pointing toward everyone present before finally unmasking the real murderer. It was such a contrived mystery-genre formula. But he had to admit, Mike St. John had pulled it off. He had won himself a place among the "Barribault Eight" as a result. For the present, at least. Rather than arouse suspicions, therefore, he would go through with it and get the day off to as normal a start as possible.

* * *

Hugh Barribault walked into the Drawing Room at 9:55. The company was all present save one. If anyone was missing, he would have anticipated it being the Stokes woman. After yesterday evening's unpleasant and heated exchange, he almost expected to find her packed and gone in a huff. But she was present, in her usual seat, eyes in her lap, appearing subdued and not anxious to pick a fight in front of the others.

"Good morning, gentle people," said Barribault, mustering as much enthusiasm as he was able. "We are on pins and needles to learn from Mr. St. John who *done* it, as the saying goes. It looks, however, as though we are one friar short of a quorum."

He took a seat and several minutes of desultory chit-chat and superfluous conversation followed.

"Did you hear on the radio," asked Dame Meyerson, glancing about the group, "about the terrorist incident in the middle of the night"

"No, what happened?" asked Barribault.

"I just chanced to turn on the radio while I was making tea. It took place in Glasgow sometime after midnight. I only heard it briefly…a bomb at one of the train stations, no one killed, but considerable damage."

"Do they know who was responsible?" asked Cobb.

"Not for certain," replied Dame Meyerson. "They think Muslim terrorists…the usual suspects."

More conversation about the incident followed. About 10:15 Father Smythe hastily entered the room. He had obviously been outside in the chilly morning. He wore an overcoat, with a folded newspaper protruding from one of the oversized pockets. His face was red from the cold.

"Sorry, I'm late," he said. "Out for a bit of a ramble and the time got away from me."

"Been into town so early, Father?" asked Barribault.

"Nothing so ambitious," replied Smythe rubbing his hands together. "Just strolling about your lovely grounds. But it is definitely cold this morning."

Mike St. John eyed him carefully, eyebrows drawing down in thought. Smythe took off his coat, folded it with care as if it contained something more delicate than a newspaper, then sat down and awaited Barribault's address prior to the morning's presentation.

The morning proceeded. After Barribault's presentation on the role of the mystery novel in the historical development of the fiction genre in general, he turned the floor over to Mike St. John.

"I have been looking forward very much to your presentation, Mr. St. John," he said, "about your perceptions of the mystery genre generally, and why you—especially as a religious man—think that its popularity remains undimmed, and how you came to develop such a cunning sleuth as Miles Madison. So…the podium is yours. Give us your thoughts, then we will enjoy hearing the final chapter from your book.—Oh, but I almost forgot…rumor has reached me that you purchased John Thompson's clever quill."

"I did indeed," answered Mike.

"We all admired it, but you came away with the prize. Does it work?"

"I wrote a letter to my sister with it yesterday."

"Perhaps you would give us a demonstration."

"If you would like. I'll just run up to my room and get it."

Mike hurried from the room, nearly tripping over an occasional table in front of the couch.

"Don't run too fast, Mr. St. John," murmured Shelby. "We would like you and the quill to get back in one piece."

A few snickers went round the room. By now Mike's clumsiness was well known to all.

"Ah, the sainted Stinker Pinker," smiled Whitaker. "Heart of gold and a terror as a prop forward for Plank's rugby squad, but otherwise nothing but three left feet."

No one offered comment. Not only was Mike's ungainliness well known among them, so too was Graham Whitaker's predisposition to mumble Wodehousian asides that no one understood.

Mike St. John returned two minutes later, both himself and quill intact. He set the quill and a small bottle of ink on the writing table that stood at one side of the room that also served as lectern. He had also brought several sheets of blank paper. He demonstrated how to fill the quill, which several of the number had already observed in Thompson's shop, then handed the quill around in turn to let everyone write a few lines with it on paper.

"It is remarkably fluid," said Shelby, handing the quill to Melinda. "I expected it to be...I don't know, more awkward."

"I could definitely write a poem with this!' said Melinda. She handed the quill to Graham Whitaker, who, after a few squiggles, merely nodded with an amused smile, and passed the quill to Father Smythe.

"To be honest," he said, "I'm afraid of the thing. My fingers are too fat and arthritic to wield something so delicate. I don't want to spoil your treasure, St. John—here, Cobb, you try it."

Briscoe Cobb took the quill from him gently, almost like he was handling a tiny baby, and with keen interest. He cradled the quill carefully between thumb and forefinger, resting the nib on the end of his middle finger, and bent down and proceeded to write out several flowing lines of glistening black ink. He clearly found it a pleasurable sensory experience. At length he nodded, then glanced up, stood back, and handed the quill to Dame Meyerson who was standing at his side.

The stately lady stooped over the table, made a few swooping ornate lines on a fresh sheet of paper, smiled faintly, then rose. "It reminds me of learning to write as a child," she said. "Not the feather, I mean, but there is nothing like the nib of a fine fountain pen." She handed the quill to Jessica Stokes.

Jessica looked at the ingenious thing in her hand, an odd look almost of puzzlement shadowing her face briefly, then set the quill back on the table and stepped away.

"Don't you want to try it, Jessica?" said Mike.

"No I don't," she answered. "I've seen enough."

Gradually everyone returned to where they had been sitting. Barribault sat down with the others as Mike took his place behind the table. After a presentation of ten minutes, he took out the last chapter of his manuscript and read aloud the first half of the chapter. The floor was then opened for a discussion not only of the writing, about which a few suggestions were made, but mostly concerning the unfolding of his clues pointing toward the potential suspects. One by one they made their predictions of the solution to the many conundrums Mike had posed, before listening to the author read the remainder of the chapter as it built toward a final climax.

But what should have been one of the most lively discussions of the week never quite managed to get off the ground. Except for Graham Whitaker, who carried on a spirited banter with Mike from the floor, humorously poking fun at his clues but also offering a number of shrewd insights, the rest of the group was listless, seemingly distracted. Jessica Stokes offered not a word and sat unexpressive, silent, and brooding. Father Smythe's mind was clearly elsewhere. Questioned a time or two, it was obvious that he had been paying little attention to the clues. Shelby Fitzpatrick seemed bored by it, yawning occasionally and glancing out the windows at the wind in the trees. Briscoe Cobb seemed more intent on make jabs about St. John's liberal use of religious clues in his book. Dame Meyerson did her best to contribute, but neither did her heart seem in it. More than a few of the number seemed more interested in the quill lying in front of Mike St. John than his reading of his text. What each was thinking as they stared absently at it, however, it would have been impossible to say.

As for Hugh Barribault, he made a gallant effort to keep the discussion animated. But he too was distracted by the press of concerns that recent days had brought to bear on him. Eventually the climax moved to an inevitable anti-climax of St. John's revelation. If this was any precursor to the enthusiasm with which his book would be read by the public, thought Mike morosely as he gathered his manuscript and placed it in his briefcase, he was in big trouble. His first novel was going to bomb!

After a morning that was bright, breezy, and warming considerably after Smythe's early ramble, the wind was now whipping into gusts. As everyone stood and moved in the direction of the Lunch Room, serious clouds were appearing in the sky to the west.

"Unless I miss my guess," said Barribault, "we are in for some heavy weather before evening. Anyone considering a walk or a stroll through the woods or town might be advised to get it in sooner rather than later."

Jessica Stokes left the room hurriedly under a cloud. The others filed out one by one.

Father Smythe draped his coat over his arm and disappeared quickly up to his room.

Shelby left thinking about a walk to the shore.

Graham Whitaker and Dame Meyerson joined forces as they made their way to investigate the Lunch Room.

Briscoe Cobb wandered outside, shivered and thought better of it, and sought the Smoking Room where he lit a cigar and sat down to enjoy it in solitude.

"A good effort, this morning, St. John," said Barribault as the two men left together.

"The group was unusually lethargic," said Mike. "Or so it seemed to me."

"The change in weather, no doubt. It does strange things to the mood. If you don't mind," Barribault added, "I would like to speak with you privately for a moment or two."

"No bother...right now?"

"Meet me in my study...say in ten minutes."

* * *

Mike St. John knocked on the door of Hugh Barribault's study and entered.

"Sit down, St. John," said Barribault. The smiling cordiality from minutes earlier had disappeared from his face.

Mike took a seat across from Barribault's desk.

"I told you when we spoke before," Barribault began, "that you compelled me to look more deeply into the allegations that surfaced in connection with your church in Aberdeen."

Mike sat listening without expression, only nodding in acknowledgment.

"I have done so. One of my associates in the city sent me a report gained from interviewing a number of church leaders and from access he was given to church records. It is not a pretty sight, Mr. St. John. Financial impropriety is perhaps the worst of it, but my God, man—having an affair with another woman in your church, right in your own home while your wife lay dying in the next bedroom. No wonder they asked for your resignation."

Barribault paused and drew in a long sigh.

"What do you have to say for yourself?" he asked.

"I am sincerely sorry, sir," said Mike, "but nothing more than last time."

"You refuse to answer the charges?"

"I do."

Barribault shook his head in obvious frustration.

"I don't understand you, St. John. Don't you know that I can make or break you?"

"I do."

"Still you refuse to answer my questions?"

"I will answer your questions, but I will not refute the charges."

"Are they true, then?"

St. John remained silent.

Barribault's frustration finally gave way to anger. His fist slammed down on his desk. "What does it take to wake you up to the seriousness of this!" he cried.

"I am fully cognizant of the seriousness of it, Mr. Barribault. But as you were compelled to investigate, I am compelled to remain silent."

"Have it your way, then, and to blazes with you! I told you before—I like you. I love your writing. All things being equal I am inclined to trust whatever you tell me. But you have to help me out. As things stand, you leave me little choice."

He sighed again in exasperation.

"I will give you another day to come to your senses. By noon tomorrow I want an explanation. I want you to give me good reason to keep you on. Otherwise I will have no choice but to remove you for moral reasons from the Eight. You have twenty-four hours. Now get out, St. John, before I become seriously angry and pull the plug on you right now."

From where she had stopped when walking along the corridor after hearing Barabaut's outburst, and had strained to listen to the ending fragments of what sounded like an argument, Jessica Stokes now quickly resumed her way, breaking into as much a run as she was capable of. She just managed to round the corner and duck out of sight as Mike St. John opened the door and stepped into the hall behind her.

* * *

Meanwhile, downstairs in the Lunch Room, most of the others were sipping tea or coffee or nibbling at oatcakes, cheese, or fruit as Jessica walked in.

"I was hoping to put my toes in the ocean this afternoon," said Shelby. "I think I will go change and drive to the beach before the predicted storm hits. Anyone care to join me—Melinda, Jessica…?"

"I would!" replied Melinda. "A walk on the sand with dark clouds blowing in…that sounds fun."

"Are men invited?" asked Cobb, entering the room shortly after Jessica after completing his cigar. "I don't know about toes in the water, but the sea air always clears the brain."

"As many as my car will hold!" answered Shelby. "Whoever wants to go, meet me out by the garages. By the way, has anyone seen my notebook?" asked Shelby. "I'm sure you've noticed me with it...leather, dark brown. I haven't been able to find it."

"When did you have it last?" asked Graham.

"Last night, for certain...I took some notes. By this morning's session and Mr. St. John's unmasking of his killer, it was gone."

Twenty minutes later Shelby and Melinda, and Professors Cobb and Whitaker were motoring out of the grounds by the main entry.

Mike St. John left his interview with Barribault preferring to be alone. He made his way to the observation deck on the roof to see what the sky portended. He had a book from the Library under his arm and sat down to read in one of the roof-chairs until it turned cold or started to rain.

Dame Meyerson and Jessica Stokes, who had not yet formed a meaningful camaraderie, nor seemed likely to, found themselves alone in the Lunch Room. Dame Meyerson mumbled a few words excusing herself and went to her room. Feeling deserted, and a little annoyed at the world in general, Jessica left the house to see if Nature might accomplish more for her perpetually peevish spirits than lunch with her fellow authors had been able to.

The storm came on. By three o'clock the skies over Elgin were black. Though the rain had not yet unleashed itself in the environs of Cullen, most of the guests at Cullen House were by then cozily back inside and awaiting the inevitable. A fire blazed in the East Sitting Room on the first floor where most of the entourage gradually wandered and a few were now scattered about reading.

Coombes came through the door about 3:30 with a tray containing the first of the afternoon tea things and began setting them on the sideboard. Melinda did not return from the shore with Shelby and the two men. No one had seen her in several hours.

Several rose to pour themselves tea. They heard the door behind them open and Hugh Barribault walked in.

"Did you enjoy yourself at the shore, Miss Fitzpatrick?" he asked.

"Very much, although we seem to have lost Melinda. We waited, but I'm afraid eventually we came back without her."

"Actually, it was her I was looking for. If anyone should chance to see her—"

"She is just walking across the bridge in the back," said Father Smythe, entering the room and picking up the lingering fragments of the conversation.

"Ah, good," said Barribault. "Please tell her that I've just run up to my study for a moment, but that I will meet her in the garden…at the stone bench."

As he turned away a few looks were exchanged, though no one offered comment.

Barribault reached the door, then paused and turned back into the Sitting Room. "Oh, and by the way, for reasons into which I need not go I have decided to cancel our session later this afternoon. There are matters I am trying to attend to. Please spread the word to those who are not here. In consequence, we will dine at seven this evening instead of eight, at which time I will join you."

* * *

Dr. Briscoe Cobb returned from the excursion to the beach and went to his room where he found an envelope on the floor that had been slipped under his door.

Dr. Cobb, he read on a single sheet.

I would like to speak with you in my office at four o'clock, if such would be convenient for you.

I am,

Sincerely,

Hugh Barribault.

Cobb set the brief note down on his writing table. His eyes unconsciously flitted to the adjacent bureau where he was keeping his few personal belongings.

He glanced at his watch. 3:20. Perhaps time for a cup of tea first.

At four o'clock sharp, Briscoe Cobb knocked on the door of Hugh Barribault's office as Mike St. John had before him.

"Come in, Dr. Cobb," he heard Barribault's voice from inside. He opened the door and entered.

"Sit down, please, Dr. Cobb," began Barribault. Cobb did so. "As you are no doubt aware," Barribault continued, "after our selection of you eight finalists, guided by the detailed questionnaires we asked each of you to fill out, we conducted as thorough an investigation into each of your backgrounds as was practical. The purpose was to have complete biographical information to use to publicize your books, and simply so that I would know you all well. We certainly did not anticipate finding anything untoward. Unfortunately, in a few cases, that has been the result of our ongoing inquiries. I should have delayed the announcement until this process was complete. Nevertheless, with new information now coming to light, it is not such as I can ignore. Some of these things I have only learned in the last few days, creating more than a little awkwardness."

Barribault paused and drew in a breath.

"As you also know," he resumed, "from the outset there were very strict rules and guidelines for the contest in which you participated.—You *were* aware of these guidelines, were you not, Dr. Cobb?" he added, probing intently into Cobb's face with searching eyes.

"Yes...yes, of course," replied Cobb, unnerved by Barribault's manner.

"And you understand that I must have people engaged with me in this enterprise whom I can trust implicitly, and who can bear up to the most rigid scrutiny in all matters of ethics, integrity, and propriety—people who will represent me in everything I stand for?"

"Of course."

"Then I am puzzled, Dr. Cobb."

"Puzzled...by what?"

"Dr. Cobb...I know about Brenda Carr."

If Cobb had been thrown a curve by Barribault's statement, he did his best not to show it.

"I am afraid you have me at a disadvantage, Mr. Barribault...I don't know what you mean."

"You've never heard of Brenda Carr?"

"Not that I am aware of."

"Come, come, Cobb," smiled Barribault. "You can take off the mask. I *know*."

Ten minutes later, Briscoe Cobb emerged from the Barribault study, his face flustered, and stormed away in silent fury.

Only one other of the eight knew of Cobb's meeting with their host. Graham Whitaker had been trying to find a chance to speak with Hugh Barribault alone ever since arriving in Cullen. He had decided to make his own opportunity on this particular afternoon, whether Barribault was receptive to what he had to say or not.

He arrived on the third floor. Even from some distance away he heard the angry voices of the two men from behind the closed door of Hugh Barribault's study. Realizing that his own timing could not have been worse, he immediately turned and began to descend the way he had come.

The moment Cobb left him, as he had after Mike St. John's departure, Hugh Barribault sent for Miss Gordon. When she arrived he recounted in exacting detail the conversation just as it had taken place. There must be no mistaking later what was said and by whom.

* * *

When the brief dictation and note-taking were done, Miss Gordon rose to go.

"See if you can locate Miss Stokes," said Barribault. "—Excuse me...*Ms.* Stokes. If she is about, please send her up to see me."

Ten minutes later, Jessica Stokes in her turn sat down in Hugh Barribault's office.

"Have you considered my offer, Ms. Stokes?" Barribault asked.

"It was hardly an offer," said Jessica, doing nothing to disguise her annoyance. "Not even a request...more like an ultimatum."

"Please, Ms. Stokes, I had hoped we could settle this amiably. My request was made in good faith. You will be published and will have your advance check. Surely you realize as well as I that we will never be compatible as business partners. We view everything about the world from opposite perspectives. Our goals and objectives would be constantly warring with one another. You must see that I can not allow such strife to exist at the heart of my company. I am simply asking you to be happy with your success, and then to graciously step away and not pursue a longterm publishing relationship with the company. But rest assured, I will do all that is in my power to make this first book a success for you."

Stokes sat listening in silent irritation.

"Before making any decision," she said at length, "I would like to know where I stand legally."

"No contracts have been signed," rejoined Barribault, "if that's what you mean. If you are thinking of suing me for breach, I would not recommend it. I have said that you may keep the hundred thousand, and that your book will be published. Any aspiring author in the world would kill to find themselves in such a position. Besides that is the very practical fact that solicitor fees could easily drain you of that entire amount overnight...and that I maintain relationships with some of the best solicitors and barristers in Scotland. You would find yourself, I believe, in very deep waters."

"I could sue for discrimination."

Barribault could not prevent himself breaking out in laughter.

"You liberals love to see discrimination under every rock. On what grounds would you sue? How have I discriminated against you—by offering you one hundred thousand pounds as an advance for a book by an unpublished author?"

"You are discriminating against me as a woman, for my progressive views."

"As far as gender discrimination, that would be hard to prove in light of the fact that I selected four women and four men."

"It will be *three* women if you cast me adrift."

"I may select another woman as your replacement."

"You may not."

"True. All publications by Barribault House, and all future contest winners, will be selected on the basis of merit not gender. As for my not wanting progressivity to influence the public image and direction of my company...it is my company. I am free to operate it as I wish."

"As long as you stay within the law. The law forbids discrimination."

"Come, come, Ms. Stokes, don't persist in being ridiculous about this. I *could* stop payment on your check and refuse to publish your book. You might sue for breach of a *verbal* contract. But it would be very difficult to prove. Instead, I am offering what for most people would be a small fortune."

"It would seem you hold all the cards, would it not?" rejoined Jessica sourly.

"So do you agree to my terms?"

"That I just step aside and quietly disappear...no, Mr. Barribault, I do not agree."

"You really want to push this?"

"I intend to consult my solicitor, that is all I will say. Good day, Mr. Barribault," she added, then rose and left the office.

* * *

Graham Whitaker emerged onto the third floor of Cullen House a second time, deciding to try again to find Barribault alone. He was just in time to encounter Jessica Stokes turning onto the stairway with considerable heat in her manner.

"Jessica..." he said as they met.

"Hello, Graham," she nodded, not slowing and hurrying down the steps.

Whitaker gazed after her a moment, then made his way down the corridor where he stopped in front of Barribault's study and knocked on the door. Behind her, still close enough to hear the knock, Jessica Stokes paused. Curious, she tiptoed back up the way she had come.

Expecting Miss Gordon, Barribault bid his visitor enter. He looked up in surprise to see Graham Whitaker walking through the door. Jessica reached the landing just in time to see her fellow author disappear inside.

"Oh...Mr. Whitaker, it's you," said Barribault.

"I hope you don't mind the intrusion," said Whitaker, "but I have been hoping for a chance to speak with you."

"Not at all...sit down. What can I do for you?"

"Actually, it's about your father, Mr. Barribault—your father and my wife."

"Your wife? Surely you are not suggesting a connection between my father and your wife."

"I'm afraid I am, Mr. Barribault."

"They are both dead."

Just then a knock sounded and Miss Gordon entered to consult with her employer about the Stokes interview. She stopped abruptly as she saw the back of Graham Whitaker's head.

"Oh—I didn't know you were with someone," she said. "I am sorry—excuse me."

She turned to go. "I will ring you presently, Miss Gordon," said Barribault behind her.

Melinda Franks paused at the far end of the corridor as she saw the door open and Mr. Barribault's assistant exit his study. After remaining alone in the garden after their brief meeting earlier, she had come up the back stairway Barribault had shown her, emerging at the distant end of the hall away from the main staircase. She waited until Miss Gordon disappeared in the opposite direction, then crept slowly forward. Gradually she heard voices and realized Barribault was not alone. She retreated again to the end of the hall. Once more she waited in the shadows.

When an emotional Graham Whitaker left the study ten minutes later, Melinda hesitated another minute or two, then again walked toward the study. Unlike the others who had entered these private precincts on this day, she did not pause to knock on the door. Confident of her reception, she turned the latch and walked straight inside.

* * *

Melinda Franks walked out of Hugh Barribault's private study. She wiped at her eyes but could not stop the flow of tears. She began to walk away when Barribault came out into the hallway after her. Hearing his footstep, Melinda turned. Barribault took her in his arms for a moment, then stepped away and bent down and kissed her on the cheek.

From behind a column at the head of the stairs, Dame Jennifer Meyerson watched with combined compassion and cynicism. She knew more intimately than any of the others how persuasively Hugh Barribault's charm was capable of undoing a young woman of delicate sensitivities.

When the sounds of Melinda's sniffling and footfall had receded into the corridor in the distance, Dame Meyerson stepped out from her hiding place and walked with almost equally confident step to the same door from which Melinda had just come. With an air almost of bravado, she turned the handle and entered. Hugh Barribault stood across the room, his back to the door, obviously in deep thought.

"So, Hugh," said Dame Meyerson coolly, "another young conquest. It has always been your particular—what should I call it...your special knack—"

At the sound of her voice, Barribault spun around. His face was red and his eyes aglow. "How dare you walk in here and assume such a thing!" he cried angrily.

"Do you deny it?"

"Categorically.

"You really are too much, Hugh. And at your age! You just don't have the goods anymore."

"Leave me, Jennifer...please, not now. Just go!"

Dame Meyerson laughed a sardonic and bitter laugh. "So, you would cast me adrift...again?"

"Not now, Jennifer. I'm not in the mood for your mind games."

"A game is it? What happened to all your soothing words of before—so happy I was one of your finalists...so proud of me. Was that too a game, Hugh?"

Barribault did not reply. His anger had vented itself. He resigned himself to the pointlessness of further engagement. He walked to his chair and sunk into it, thoroughly spent.

"What did you come here for, Jennifer?" he said softly. "To gloat, to threaten, to blackmail me...what is your game? What do you want, Jennifer."

"Only to see you suffer, Hugh. Nothing more."

She turned and walked out of the room, leaving Barribault, at long last, alone for the rest of the afternoon.

TEN

The Storm

_____

The afternoon waned.

Coombes kept the fire in the East Sitting Room well stoked with fresh logs. Even the crackling flames, however, could not prevent a heaviness descending with the gloom outside, portending a storm that could last days. Darkness fell earlier than usual on account of the thick covering that blanketed northern Scotland.

Pre-dinner cocktails were served.

The rain began to pour down about the very moment Coombes opened the Dining Room doors to announce dinner. To all appearances having put the trying afternoon behind him, Hugh Barribault was back to his customary personable self. If major changes were in the wind as to the make-up of "the Eight," whether the *Eight* would soon be the *Six* or the *Four*, or whether he would take his plans in completely different directions than originally thought, he gave no indication of it. Most of those who had endured painfully private interviews that day likewise gave no indication of their thoughts. Jessica Stokes, however, sat silently nursing an attitude. And Dame Meyerson, who always enjoyed her wine, drank even more liberally than usual of the expensive light Beaujolais.

By the time the main course was over, rain was slashing against the windowpanes with so much force it might have been hail.

"This *is* getting exciting!" commented Dame Meyerson, her animation showing the effects of the Beaujolais.

Two more of the party, in addition to Stokes, remained subdued. Neither Melinda Franks nor Father Smythe seemed to enjoy the onslaught against the Moray coast. The others of the group, however, were invigorated by the display. Even resident curmudgeon Briscoe Cobb found himself throwing out an occasional parry in response to Graham Whitaker's wry humor. Whitaker's responses, however, as he eyed Cobb carefully two or three times during the evening might have indicated that after what he had overheard that afternoon, he thought Cobb trying just a little *too* hard to be jovial. Protesting too much in the Shakespearean jargon that was supposedly Cobb's specialty. What was he trying to hide, thought Whitaker, that he must work so hard to cover up the anger that had boiled over a few hours before.

Halfway through coffee and dessert, a specially delivered batch of fresh ice cream arrived from the Cullen Ice Cream Shop, Barribault rose. His face looked pale.

"I am terribly sorry," he said. "I am not feeling well. I think I am going to find it necessary to bid you all good evening."

A few words of protest arose. Barribault attempted a smile as he waved them off with his hand.

"I apologize for being a poor host," he said. "I hope to find myself in better fettle tomorrow. Until then, however, I think it best that I get some rest. Enjoy the rest of your evening. Good night."

The men rose in their chairs with nods and comments of regret. Good wishes and expressions of sympathy and appreciation for his hospitality continued around the table from the women as Hugh Barribault made his way, a little slowly—with a barely perceptible limp that had dogged him since his military days slightly more noticeable than usual—toward the door.

"If Coombes should happen by to check on your needs before I talk to him, would you please ask him to come up to my apartment?"

A few more nods followed Barribault at last from the room.

"That is a shame," said Shelby. "He didn't even finish his ice cream."

"I agree, it is unfortunate," said Mike St. John. "However that brings me to a question I would like to pose. Everyone says Cullen ice cream is the best...but is it really? What's your consensus? Is it actually any different than what anyone can buy out of the freezer from any market?"

"What a thing to ask at such a time," said Shelby Fitzpatrick irritably. "Good heavens, Mr. St. John, our host is feeling ill and you are asking us to evaluate the merits of ice cream? You really are too much sometimes."

"Do you really think so?" rejoined St. John with an innocent smile. "I thought the lighter touch might be the perfect antidote to keep things from bogging down."

"Always a crack or rejoinder!" muttered Shelby, shaking her head in disgust.

"It's only eight-forty-five," persisted St. John. "I don't want to give up on the evening so soon."

"Nobody's giving up on the evening. It's just that a little decorum is occasionally called for."

"I think you are being too hard on poor Mike," interrupted Graham Whitaker. "I understand what he was trying to do. Speaking for myself, Mike," he added, turning toward St. John, "—yes, I think this ice cream *is* superior."

"That's more like it!" laughed St. John. "What about the rest of you?"

"Perhaps you and I can finally agree on something," replied Briscoe Cobb. "Maybe not on anything else, but about the ice cream, I endorse yours and Whitaker's view."

"But you don't know my view," said St. John. "I was only canvassing the rest of you. I did not divulge my *own* opinion in the matter."

"There you go again, parsing words," sighed Cobb, shaking his head. "I extend an olive branch and you make light of it."

"Just trying to be accurate, Mr. Cobb."

"Don't you two ever get tired of arguing with poor Mr. St. John?" said Melinda Franks, glancing back and forth between Fitzpatrick and Cobb. It was the first time she had spoken in probably fifteen minutes. "This whole thing would be a bore without him," she added. "I'm tired of you always criticizing him. I think I will go up to my room."

She rose and left without another word. The others stared after her in bewilderment.

"She has been acting strange most of the week," said Briscoe Cobb, glancing around the table. "Distracted, you know. It is obvious there is something going on between her and Barribault."

"Going on, what do you mean going on?" asked Shelby.

"We all know what I mean," rejoined Cobb. "I mean *going on*. We've all seen them together."

"Good God, man, get a grip on yourself," said Father Smythe. "Listen to what you're saying. It's preposterous."

"I think Father Smythe is right," said Shelby.

"I saw him kiss her," said Dame Meyerson.

Several gasps of astonishment went round the room. "Granted it was a mere peck on the cheek. But what would Shakespeare say, Dr. Cobb—a kiss is a kiss is a kiss."

"Perhaps he would be more likely to phrase it, a kiss by any other name is still a kiss," corrected Cobb.

"It's all damn nonsense!" muttered Smythe. He now rose and walked from the room.

"He's in a snooty tiff!" said Dame Meyerson. "What did we do to deserve that?"

"My attempt to lighten things up with the ice cream motif has certainly backfired," said St. John, a little subdued. "Honestly, I meant nothing by it. But if I have offended anyone else, I sincerely apologize."

"It's not your fault, St. John," said Dame Meyerson. "The storm has frayed a few nerves. Along with this delicious Beaujolais, of course. The electrical impulses outside get under people's skin…at least that's what I've heard."

"So here we are…down to six of us," said Whitaker. "To follow up on Mike's theme about the evening yet being young…let me see, we are too many for bridge, but…right, six is perfect for poker!"

"Poker!" exclaimed Dame Meyerson in a shocked tone. "Mr. Whitaker, please. There are ladies present."

"The merest suggestion."

"I am afraid you will have to find something suitable for five," said Jessica Stokes, now also rising from her chair. "I am going to bed too. I have a headache."

The others watched her depart, as they had the previous two, and continued to spoon out the last of the ice cream.

"I think she *always* has a headache," muttered Cobb. "The way she walks around with her nose in the air."

Slowly Whitaker cracked a smile. Gradually more smiles followed, until outright chuckles spread around the table. Only Mike St. John did not join into the merriment.

"I have to admit, that woman is a cold fish," nodded Shelby.

"Snobbish, I would call it," put in Meyerson.

"I have tried everything," added Shelby. "She does not let her guard down for anyone."

"All right, then," said Mike, "we agree that Ms. Stokes may not be everyone's cup of tea. I am sure she has her reasons, so I suggest we let her be. As for the rest of us—let's make a pact. No one else leaves this room."

"What are you getting at?" asked Shelby skeptically.

"We must salvage this evening," replied Mike. "If this is my last evening with you all, I intend to enjoy it."

"What are you talking about?" said Dame Meyerson. "You're not leaving us?"

"Oh, sorry…a slip of the tongue," answered Mike. "I meant nothing. By the way, Miss Fitzpatrick, have you found your notebook?"

"No, but…" she said in an uncertain tone. She did not finish the sentence. She too had been thrown by Mike's statement.

"So…" Mike continued, anxious to prevent the discussion returning to his inadvertent comment, "I propose a plan to insure that we remain and enjoy the next few hours together. When one of us leaves, we all leave."

"Hear, hear!" said Whitaker. "Well done, St. John—a masterful stroke!"

"And since I know nothing about bridge, that sounds like a perfect activity for you four. Why don't the rest of you explain it to me as you play. I've always wanted to learn."

"I am up for it," said Dame Meyerson. "I would fancy a lively game of bridge, as long as we have some vintage port to go with it. I never play bridge without port on hand."

"Then I suggest an addendum to Mike's pact," said Whitaker. "Rather than *this* room, let us repair upstairs to the Parlor where, unless I am mistaken, Coombes will have a nice fire burning for us. As I recall there is a game table that should suit our purposes admirably."

They nodded and all rose and left the Dining Room together. A few minutes later they entered the Parlor where they had spent several evenings.

"Ah yes, this is more like it!" said Dame Meyerson, at sight of the fire and cozy room.

"I shall check our host's supply as per your request," said Whitaker walking across the room toward the well-stocked wet bar. He opened an oak cabinet and scanned the bottles on the shelves inside. "It appears that you have a choice, Mrs. Meyerson," he said across the room after a quick inspection of the contents. "It seems we have Paul Masson, Ficklin, or Cockburn's. No orange juice, however, St. John."

"I don't think that will be a problem," smiled St. John. "Gussie is not among us."

"There is also a bottle of eighteen year Napoleon cognac."

"That's good enough for me!" exclaimed Cobb. "You pour, Whitaker, I'll find the cards!"

"Dame Meyerson?" said Whitaker.

"I cannot imagine Hugh Barribault even allowing Paul Masson in his house. But Ficklin Madera is my label—perfect for bridge."

"I don't want to spoil a good party," said Shelby as Whitaker gathered bottles and glasses on a tray, "but I'm afraid I don't know how to play either."

"That throws a bit of a spanner into it," said Cobb. "Bridge is no good with three."

"We'll teach you both as we go," said Whitaker as he approached. "Nothing to it. If you can handle Gin Rummy, you can learn Bridge. You two sit over there beside each other. You won't be partners exactly—you'll have to partner with...Dame Meyerson, would you like to take on the assignment?"

"Absolutely."

"Good. Then Dr. Cobb and I will sit adjacent, and the three of us will explain it to both of you."

Fitzpatrick looked none too pleased with the prospect of learning Bridge beside the annoying Mike St. John. But by this time in the evening she was reluctant to throw a wet blanket over the plans. She walked around the table and sat down next to the minister.

The port and cognac flowed and the game got underway. Gradually the two neophytes managed to pick up enough of the rudiments that everyone, including Shelby, was able to enjoy themselves.

* * *

Meanwhile, the intensity of the storm increased. The wind howled around the towers and turrets of the great House, occasionally sending an eerie whistle down the chimney followed by a tiny puff of smoke or brightening of embers. The trees throughout the grounds, some of them three hundred years old, were swaying dangerously in a wild tumult of leaves and branches. Down at the shore, by this time the ocean was a positive cauldron of black waves battering the harbor wall and sending giant plumes of spray high over it into the streets of the Sea Town.

"This is wonderful!" exclaimed Whitaker as a blast of rain hit with such force it threatened to blow the windows into the room. "Here we are hidden away in an old castle during a terrific storm! I did not expect to step into a gothic romance when I signed up for this gig! I must say I am enjoying this immensely!"

"We Scots strive to give satisfaction," rejoined Mike St. John, with the hint of a grin.

Whitaker returned his look with an amused and knowing expression. "Very good, St. John," he said with a nod. "You continue to remind me that I have met my equal."

Another blast shook the windowpanes. Almost the same moment the door of the room opened. Juxtaposed as the two events were, the unexpected sound behind them startled the table of card players. Two or three hearts leapt into their corresponding throats. All five heads turned to see Father Smythe returning. He looked a little agitated, but forced a smile as he approached.

"Father Smythe," said Whitaker amiably, "come...join us. We are enjoying a game of bridge."

They made room for the priest as he pulled a sixth chair toward the table.

"I, uh...I apologize for leaving in a bit of a huff," said Smythe. "Had a few things on my mind."

"Don't mention it," said Dame Meyerson. "Have a glass of port. It always settles my nerves.—Mr. Whitaker, bring Father Smythe a glass."

Whitaker rose, went to the wet bar, and returned.

"Actually..." Dame Meyerson said, "I am afraid I may have been steadying my nerves just a teeny weeny bit *too* much. But then, what the hell!"

"Oops," she said as a few eyebrows went up at the unexpected expletive. "I fear I have committed a lapse of decorum! But you only live once," she added, pouring herself yet another glass. She lifted it to her lips, then paused and glanced at Mike St. John.

"I am sorry," she said, "but I really have no alternative—I find that I am going to have to break our pact. I simply must return to my room briefly. Whether it is decorous or not to say it...the powder room, as it were, has become a rather urgent necessity."

St. John laughed. "I think we may make an exception in such a case," he said. "I propose, then, a modification to the pact— personal breaks allowed when accompanied by another consenting adult, presumably of the same sex, to insure that anyone who leaves returns."

"Agreed," nodded Dame Meyerson, rising, slowly enough to make sure her knees didn't wobble. "Thank you. So who will take me to the little girls' room?"

"It would appear, as the only woman left, that I am nominated for the honor," said Shelby, rising to join her.

"I would like to claim a similar exemption," said Briscoe Cobb.

"Duly noted," nodded Mike. "Perhaps a break in the festivities would be in order. Why don't we agree to suspend the pact for ten minutes, while all who feel the need go about their business."

"I will accompany you, Dr. Cobb," said Graham Whitaker.

Nods and agreements went around the table. Cobb, Meyerson, Fitzpatrick, and Whitaker rose, leaving newcomer Father Smythe at the table. The two clerics were left alone together.

"What is this pact they were talking about?" asked Smythe.

"After you and Mr. Barribault and Melinda and Ms. Stokes left us earlier, we made a pact that no one else would leave, that we would spend the remainder of the evening together until we were all ready to retire."

"Ah, I see. Any particular reason?"

"Only that I thought the evening was too young and the storm too wild and exciting not to share it with one another."

Slowly the others returned, first Dame Meyerson and Shelby walked in together. About five minutes later Graham Whitaker returned alone.

"Where is your charge?" asked Mike.

"I'm afraid I must have lost him. I thought perhaps he had come out while I was still in my room and returned here alone. I see I was wrong."

It was probably fifteen minutes before Briscoe Cobb sauntered back into the room. His face was slightly flushed, as if he had been under some exertion, but he did his best to reenter the room casually. With Father Smythe now on hand, and the beginners progressing nicely, a new round of the game was begun with the two novices venturing to play on their own. Mike sat with Graham Whitaker beside him as coach, opposite Briscoe Cobb. Dame Meyerson took the part of Shelby's assistant, partnering opposite Father Smythe.

The rain pounded and the wind blew. The game continued to occupy their attention.

An hour or more passed.

"This is brilliant!" said Mike St. John after the completion of a hand. "We have all the ingredients for a first class murder mystery. I think I feel a new book coming on!"

At the word *murder*, it fell silent. The darkness outside seemed to invade the room like an invisible spectre. A few involuntary shivers crept up several spines.

Suddenly a blinding light and a crash of thunder exploded almost together, rattling the windows and shaking the great house to its foundations. The two women jumped out of their seats.

"That was too close for comfort!" said Smythe, running a finger around his neck and collar.

Seconds later a great pounding thud rumbled the foundations again.

"What was that!" cried Shelby.

"I think Mr. Barribault just lost a large beech!" said Whitaker, jumping up and running to the window. "I am from timber country, and you can take it from me, that was the sound of a giant tree hitting the ground."

He pressed his face to the window between his hands. "I see nothing," he said.

"What did you expect to see out there?" asked Cobb.

"Fire, perhaps," answered Whitaker. "A lightning strike like that can set a tree ablaze in seconds. With this rain I doubt there is any danger, but—"

He stepped away from the window, obviously thinking.

"Still," he said, "with Barribault sound asleep—"

"No one could have slept through *that*!" said Shelby.

"I would feel better if we checked to make sure there's no start of a fire. I am going to run up to the roof and have a look."

"You will get soaked...not to mention blown right off!" exclaimed Dame Meyerson. "Especially if you've had as much of this port as I have! We mustn't have any drunks falling off roofs!"

"I'll go with you," said Mike St. John. He rose and followed Whitaker toward the door.

"Be careful!" called Shelby after them.

The two men left the room and hurried along the corridor together. "To be honest, Mike," said Whitaker as they went, "you tend to be...don't get me wrong, I'm only concerned for your safety—but I know I don't have to remind *you* about Stinker Pinker. If I didn't know better I would assume your two left feet act a Wodehousian ploy."

"I wish it was, old man," laughed St. John. "But any similarity between myself and the lovable curate is purely coincidental."

"Just the same, I would feel more comfortable if you *weren't* on the roof with all this wind."

"Are you saying I'm clumsy?" chided St. John.

"Let me put it this way...I was thinking that we ought to check the front of the house too. I'm fairly certain that crash came from the east. Why don't you go downstairs and see what you can see out the main door while I check the roof?"

"Right."

The men parted at the central staircase. Whitaker ran up two steps at a time while St. John hurried down toward the ground floor.

* * *

Back in the Parlor, the storm seemed to abate the moment Cobb, Fitzpatrick, Meyerson, and Smythe were left alone. It grew preternaturally quiet.

"Suddenly it's very spooky around here!" said Dame Meyerson.

The two older men made an attempt at small talk but without much success.

"I need to stretch my legs," said Father Smythe at length, rising and walking toward the door.

"Wait," called Dame Meyerson after him. "What about the pact?"

"It's not my pact," he rejoined. "I'm bound by none of St. John's tomfoolery."

He disappeared, leaving the others staring after him.

"The good father remains in a grumpy mood!" said Dame Meyerson. "He's a stuffed shirt if you ask me. He's given me a sour taste in my mouth all week. Let him go, I say."

Five minutes later Graham Whitaker returned, hair and shoulders wet but not quite soaked to the skin as Dame Meyerson had predicted.

"Anything amiss?" asked Shelby.

"Nope—nothing but darkness in every direction," replied Whitaker, walking over to stand in front of the fireplace. "We'll have to wait until morning to see where the tree is down and if there is damage. I did hear voices from the direction of Barribault's apartments, however, as I came down from above. The crash must have awakened him too."

"Who was he talking to?"

"I assume he was probably on the phone—maybe to one of his groundsmen. I really didn't stop to think about it."

Whitaker glanced about the room.

"Where is Father Smythe?"

"He broke the pact," said Shelby.

"And why are you alone," said Dame Meyerson. "Where is Mr. St. John?"

"He went downstairs to check out front. I thought he'd be back by now."

"We assumed he was with you."

Another five or six minutes went by. At length they heard footsteps, though not from the direction they had anticipated. Instead of coming from the main corridor, they heard the faint echo of descent from the floor above them. A minute later Mike St. John reentered the room through the door on the opposite side from that where he and Whitaker had departed. His hair and clothes were dry.

"Did you see anything out front?" asked Whitaker.

"Not a thing," replied St. John.

"Where did you come from just now?" asked Cobb.

"The back stairway. Then I got myself lost and wound up a floor too high."

"What back stairway?" asked Shelby.

"There are two ways to get into all these rooms," replied Mike. "Haven't you explored the place? I love an old castle. There are a dozen stairways all around us besides the central grand staircase.—In any event, I am glad to see everyone still here."

"We wouldn't think of breaking your pact, Mr. St. John," rejoined Dame Meyerson.

"Not quite everyone," said Shelby. "Father Smythe was not fond of the idea. He snarled at Jennifer when she reminded him of it."

Before anyone spoke further, the door opened and Father Smythe returned and found the chair he had left.

"So, shall we pick up the game?" said Mike. "I think I am just beginning to get the hang of it. The night is young and no murders have been committed yet."

"No more cards for me, I think. And please, let us have no more talk of murders!" said Smythe. "I am, after all, a peaceable man of the cloth. However, I am well enough lubricated now that nothing anyone says can possibly upset me. And with that—" he added, rising and pausing to steady himself with one hand on the arm of his chair, "—I say, that cognac goes to the head! As I was saying, with that I propose to bid you all a good evening. As I made clear, since I was not included in your original pact, I do not intend to be bound by it. Good night, one and all."

He moved slowly toward the door, not exactly unsteady on his feet but carefully and deliberately.

"That is a little curious," said Dame Meyerson.

'What's that?" asked Whitaker.

"Why did he come back at all if he was just going to sit down and then get up a minute later and leave?"

"What time is it, anyway?" asked Shelby.

Cobb glanced at his watch. "Quarter till midnight," he answered.

"Then I think the pact has served us well enough for one evening," said Dame Meyerson. "What do you say, Mr. St. John?"

"I would agree to our breaking it for the night—if consent is unanimous...excluding my clerical colleague."

Nods and comments of assent went round the table.

"Then shall we follow the remains of the good Father Smythe upstairs?" said Whitaker.

"He may need a hand getting up them!" said Dame Meyerson as she stood. "Actually...I may too. I definitely had too much of that port!"

"I shall be happy to assist you," said Whitaker, rising offering his arm. She took it and they walked toward the door.

Shelby also stood. Following Whitaker's example, Briscoe Cobb offered his arm and they fell into step behind the other two.

"Good night, everyone," said Mike St. John, wandering toward the hearth. "I will follow you presently."

When they were gone and he was left alone the minister sat down in an overstuffed chair, his eyes drawn to the red-orange coals of the dying fire. It had been well over two hours since Coombes last fed it and the flames were gasping their last. Mesmerized, however, Mike sat staring into it longer than he planned, pondering many things.

The clocks throughout the house had just begun to chime the midnight hour when at last he rose, turned the lights of the room out behind him, and made his way upstairs, assuming himself by now the only one in the historic house still awake.

ELEVEN

The Quill

Briscoe Cobb woke from a deep sleep, such as Macbeth's wife could only long for, to a loud crash above him. As his room sat somewhere directly below Hugh Barribault's study and the adjacent Library, his first thought was that a bookcase had fallen over.

Instinctively he sat up and turned on the bedside light. He was not particularly anxious to investigate. What if there *were* ghosts in this mouldy old place? But whatever had fallen was too heavy for a ghost to have knocked over if they had mistaken being able to walk through it. And somebody might have been hurt. Reluctantly he rose and looked about for where he had tossed his robe.

Dame Jennifer Meyerson, in the intervening hours since the breakup of the bridge party, had developed a monstrous headache. What the devil was she thinking, all that talk about port... then guzzling three-quarters of a bottle! And that after a stiff portion of dinner wine to boot. How could she have forgotten the way the stuff affected her? She had fallen asleep almost before her head hit the pillow, soused to the gills, and awakened an hour or two later, the effects of some of the alcohol gradually wearing off, but with her temples beating two bass drums with her head between them.

When the crash came from above, muted though it was by walls and floor and ceiling and carpet, it shot a piercing gong through her skull and sent her flying off her bed like a rocketing pheasant. Had Whitaker been present to diagnose a solution to the problem, he would surely have offered some crack about her needing one of Jeeves's specials, to which she might have likely have sent back an unkind rejoinder about what he could do with Jeeves and his blasted specials. She had, of course, heard of P. G. Wodehouse—though wouldn't have known whether it was pronounced *Wode* or *Wood*—but had never actually read any of his books. It wouldn't have mattered. It was certain that Coombes—who had never heard of Jeeves or his creator—had not, and thus no hangover-curing specials would be forthcoming.

Dame Meyerson eased her way to the door, not so much out of curiosity like the others, but to put a stop to the infernal ruckus already brewing outside. The moment she opened the door, however, while not exactly forgetting her headache, she could not help being drawn into the unfolding mystery of what had caused the sound.

Leaving the dinner party early, Jessica Stokes went straight to bed, read for perhaps half an hour, and then fell asleep. As was not unusual, she only slept three or four hours. When the commotion suddenly erupted from somewhere in the house, Jessica was seated at the writing table in her room jotting down her impressions of the day and what she intended to do about what had taken place. She jumped at the sound, and for reasons she could not have explained quickly pulled the chain on the desk lamp and found herself sitting in pitch blackness. With careful step she rose and felt her way to the door.

Dugan Smythe, for reasons of his own, was also less than anxious to get involved. That people were stirring, however, meant that he could not reasonably avoid it. He would have to shrewdly execute his moves to join them so as not to call attention to himself.

Advanced as the night was, Melinda Franks had not yet fallen asleep. The events of the last few days had culminated after her return from the sea and her private late afternoon interview with Barribault. How could she possibly sleep?

Shelby Fitzpatrick had been dreaming of her favorite beach just north of San Diego when the noise from above awakened her. She sat up quickly in bed, trying to collect her wits and remember where she was. Footsteps in the hall acted on her simultaneously like a magnet and a caution. She stood, eased on her slippers, and crept to the door.

Remarkably Mike St. John did not wake up. He slept right through the racket that had startled the others and was now bringing them one by one out of their rooms. It might have been that his room sat some distance down the corridor from Cobb's, and that therefore the crash from above had not been as loud. Or perhaps, having gone to sleep with an occasional thunderclap still sounding from the storm as it proceeded east, his brain had grown accustomed to the noise. Yet as footsteps and soft voices began to disturb the still air of the west wing of Cullen House where the guest rooms were located, the sounds invaded his dreamless sleep. Slowly he came to himself.

The night was still black, but there could be no mistaking it— there were whisperings in the corridor. Mike St. John may have been a minister, but the mystery writer in him also lay near the surface. He rose, grabbed his robe, crept to the door, opened it a crack, and peeped out. One or two figures whom he could not immediately identify walked by, followed by a third. When they were past, he rubbed his eyes another time or two and slipped noiselessly from his room.

The door across the hall opened the same moment. Shelby Fitzpatrick emerged, blinking back the remnants of sleep. She and Mike saw one another. Their eyes met. Neither spoke. Then Shelby followed Mike after the others.

Graham Whitaker had drifted to sleep with his recently acquired Blandings novel. The crash above him awakened him instantly. This was too good to pass up! Reminded of the safe-cracking episode involving Wooster and Spode, he leapt out of bed, threw on his trousers, and rushed into the hall to investigate as if he had been Sir Watkyn Bassett suspecting the theft of his silver cow creamer.

Several of his authorial colleagues advanced toward him in the dimly lit corridor.

"You all, uh…I presume you all heard that too?" asked Whitaker.

"What was it?" asked Melinda at the head of the troop of investigators, walking toward him.

"Don't ask me," replied Whitaker. "It was obviously loud enough to bring us all out of our rooms."

"What is going on?" came the voice of Father Smythe. Whitaker looked past the others to see the priest approaching from behind Mike St. John and Shelby Fitzpatrick.

"We heard a crash?" replied Whitaker, glancing behind him.

"If you ask me," said Cobb as the others came toward him where he stood waiting at his door, "I think a bookcase fell in the Library. I believe it came from straight above me."

"How could a bookcase fall in the middle of the night?" asked Dame Meyerson irritably. "It must have been more thunder."

"The storm is long past," said Smythe. "There's been no thunder for hours."

"Shouldn't someone go see what it was?" said Jessica Stokes.

"Yes, you go investigate…the rest of us will go back to bed," said Dame Meyerson. "Does anyone have any Excedrin? I've run out since the last time I was in the States."

"It's hardly up to us," said Smythe. "Oughtn't Barribault or his people see what's going on? We don't want to snoop around. We *are* guests."

"Barribault's rooms are on the next floor," said Mike St. John. "He must have been awakened too."

"Has anyone seen him since he left us after dinner?" asked Dame Meyerson, placing a hand, gently, to her forehead.

"Not me," said Smythe.

"Nor me," added Cobb.

"I certainly haven't," said Jessica in a defensive voice. "I've been in my room the whole time."

"No one's accusing you, Ms. Stokes," said Dame Meyerson. "We just need to know."

"What do you mean *accuse*? What are you suggesting?"

"Nothing…I meant nothing at all. Good heavens, we're just trying to find out what happened."

"How would *any* of us have seen him?" said Shelby. "We left together and have been in our rooms ever since...well, *most* of us left at the same time," she added.

"I wonder if any of his staff are about," said Mike, walking past his reluctant colleagues. "What do you think, Cobb...Whitaker?" he went on. "Should we go upstairs and have a look?"

"Fine with me," nodded Cobbs.

In truth, Hugh Barribault's eight literary guests were not the only ones stirring within the walls of Cullen House.

Housekeeper Merideth Walton and her husband heard nothing as their apartment in the old kitchen wing was separated by a great distance. Nothing in the main house ever disturbed them. And cook Constance Fotheringay could sleep next to a train track.

Butler Reginald Coombes, however, sprang out of his bed — in his case, a floor above the Library — as if the green ghost of jilted Lady Sylvia, or of his own predecessor butler Steven murdered by the mad laird, had personally roused him. He knew the sound that had awakened him instantly. Having heard it once in his life — though that was many years ago — he would never forget it. It was the unmistakably horrifying sound of a grandfather clock — with bells and chimes and weights and pendulums and chains and glass and intricate brass mechanisms — crashing face down on the floor.

It took him a minute or two, fumbling frantically with buttons and laces, to dress. Even in an emergency, he could not permit himself to be seen without trousers, shoes, white shirt, and coat. The tie in a case like this was optional. Managing to reduce his dishabille to the minimum his conscience would allow, he trundled from his room and made for the stairs.

In dignified haste, the descending Coombes saw the assembled party of awakened literary guests, all eight of whom appeared present, climbing up from below. He paused as he reached the third floor landing from above.

"Ah, Coombes," said St. John at the head of the entourage as they navigated the last few stairs, "we were just talking about you. Not knowing what was going on, we felt you would be the one to investigate. Mr. Barribault himself is apparently still asleep in his room."

"Where is his bedroom, by the way?" asked Whitaker, as he and Cobb came up behind St. John.

"On this floor, above your rooms," replied Coombes, pointing down the hallway, "at the end of the corridor there."

"Could the noise have come from there?" asked Whitaker.

"I do not believe so, sir," replied Coombes. "I distinctly heard the clock in Mr. Barribault's study fall."

"The clock? We thought it must be a bookcase."

"No, sir. It was a clock. I fear very much that it was Mr. Barribault's antique seventeenth century French library clock. He prized it highly, sir."

"Then I suggest we have a look, Coombes," said St. John. "If anything is amiss, either from the storm or some other cause, you should rouse Mr. Barribault and notify him immediately."

"Yes, sir."

Maintaining his aplomb even in such trying circumstances, the butler led the way to the study. The eight followed silently. He expected to find the room locked, but as they approached, in the dim light of the corridor, they saw that the door stood slightly ajar. No light came from within. Coombes opened the door, stepped inside, and flipped on the nearest light switch. An immediate gasp of horror escaped his lips.

The three men followed him inside. On the floor, strewn about for ten feet in every direction, was broken glass and pieces of brass and lengths of chain. Exactly as Coombes had foretold, the great clock lay face down in front of them. The back and sides of the heavy oak case obscured sight of the full extent of the catastrophe. Merely from what was visible scattered about the floor, however, it seemed probable that death had visited this place, and that the huge clock would never chime again. Coombes, trembling, merely stood staring down from above it with a pale face.

"That clock was priceless," he said after a moment. His voice was close to tears.

Mike St. John, however, was not looking at the dismembered clock. His eyes had strayed to the far side of the room where he saw two shoeless feet protruding from behind Hugh Barribault's desk. He stepped past the rubble of the clock and walked across the study floor.

"We won't find Mr. Barribault in his room," he said. "I'm afraid he is over here."

Slowly the others followed. There lay Hugh Barribault motionless on the floor next to a gray leather couch. His face was pale but looked calm, with eyes closed, as if he were asleep. On the low coffee table beside him sat an open wine bottle, one empty glass, and an open clothbound book, to all appearances a novel. Barribault was half covered by a wool tartan blanket, strewn over him as if he had grabbed it while falling and pulled it down with him. There was no other sign of a fall. Instead, it almost looked as if he had simply fallen from the couch and gone to sleep on the floor. A wet black stain oozed from beneath the blanket on his left side. At sight of it, more gasps of shock sounded. All four of the women reached for whatever happened to be nearest them—whether a bookcase or one of the men's arms—to steady themselves.

"Is he...?" said Jessica Stokes.

"Does anyone know CPR?" asked Cobb.

No one replied. They were all thinking the same thing, that it did not look like CPR would help.

Mike St. John knelt down and placed several fingers to Barribault's neck. As he did he glanced up at Graham Whitaker. "I'm no expert," he said tentatively. "I don't feel anything...Whitaker—try his wrist."

Whitaker knelt down beside their fallen host, lifted his right arm with one hand and probed the veins of Barribault's wrist with the other.

"No pulse," he said.

Coombes and the other six stood silent and pale in a semi-circle around them. St. John stood and walked to Barribault's feet. The others stepped back to make room.

"I don't really know about this," he said, kneeling again. "I used it in my book...but I suppose it's worth a try."

He grasped the sock of Barribault's right foot and pulled it off. Jessica Stokes and Dame Meyerson glanced away, as if the mere removal of a sock portended what they all feared.

St. John took hold of Barribault's big toe.

"That's disgusting!" said Shelby, swallowing hard.

Mike glanced at Graham Whitaker. "Feel his foot, Whitaker," he said. "I don't want to make this call by myself."

Mike leaned back. Whitaker came round and clasped his fingers over Barribault's five toes. He nodded.

"Definitely cooler than the wrist," he said.

"That was my conclusion," sighed Mike. "Rigor mortis always begins in the extremities—"

Dame Meyerson gagged, grabbed at her mouth, and hurried from the room.

"—There is no rigor yet," St. John went on. "But the body is beginning to cool."

"The top of his big toe is stone cold," nodded Whitaker. "There's no doubt about it—he's dead."

Swallowing hard, her face white as a sheet, Jessica Stokes turned away and followed Dame Meyerson. The two remaining women stared down at the floor in disbelief. They were thinking very different things.

"He must have been dead for some time," said Father Smythe after a silence of several seconds. "The blood's dry and black. What do you think, suicide?"

"It's *not* dry," said Mike St. John. He reached down and touched the stain on the blanket. "Look, still wet and fresh."

"Then why is it so dark?" asked Smythe.

St. John rubbed the dark glistening liquid around on his fingers. "Because," he said, "it's not blood. This is ink—black ink, though it seems peculiarly thick and gunky."

"Has no one noticed that bit of white under the edge of the blanket?" said Shelby. "Unless I am mistaken, it's the tip of a feather."

She knelt beside Graham Whitaker, and pulled the blanket away revealing Barribault's left arm and chest.

Protruding from Barribault's bare arm was a quill to all appearances identical to the one Mike St. John had bought from John Thompson's antique shop. Its snorkel tip was extended to its full length. The feather was bent and slightly scruffed, as if gripped by a fist not fingers, and the tip driven into Barribault's vein inside the elbow. Mingled ink and blood stained the arm, some still oozing from the wound, and had dripped down into the carpet below.

Shelby glanced up. "Mr. St. John," she said slowly, " — it's...*your* quill."

All eyes turned and came to rest on Mike St. John.

Melinda Franks burst into sobs and fell to her knees beside Shelby. She bent down and kissed the dead face several times, mumbling incoherently. Just as suddenly, she climbed back to her feet and ran hysterical from the room.

TWELVE

The Inspector

"**O**bviously, we need to notify the authorities," said Mike St. John when the echo of Melinda's emotional departure had subsided.

Without a word, Coombes walked across the Library floor to the telephone.

"The authorities are well and good, St. John," said Father Smythe. "But until they get here, what we really need to do is lock you up."

Notwithstanding the sobriety of the occasion, Mike could not help laughing.

"Lock me up...why?"

"So you can't make an escape in the night."

"What are you talking about?" laughed Mike again.

"Clearly the police have to question you. They will want to know why you did it."

"A minute ago you were suggesting suicide," said Mike.

"That was before I knew your quill was sticking out of his arm."

"Don't be ridiculous, Smythe—"

Mike stopped as Coombes returned to the small group. "I fear that we will not be able to notify anyone," he said. "The phone is dead."

"That big tree that went down," nodded Whitaker. "It would not surprise me if there were others too. It was a terrific storm."

"A mobile phone would come in very handy about now," said Mike. "Coombes, are you certain? I mean, there's not a mobile phone anywhere in the house, not even for emergencies?"

"Not that I am aware of, sir. Even Miss Gorden is not allowed to bring one with her to work."

"Somebody has to drive into town," said Shelby.

"I'll go," said Whitaker.

"I'll join you," said Mike.

"You're going nowhere, St. John," said Smythe. "If you won't stay voluntarily, then I don't know what we will do. But there are seven of us."

"I will make no attempt to escape, then," replied Mike.

"All right, then I'll drive into town alone, if that satisfies you, Father Smythe," said Whitaker.

Smythe made no reply to the comment that sounded more like a jab than a joke.

"The nearest station will be Buckie, sir," said Coombes. "Whether the station will be manned, I cannot say."

"At least I will be able to find a telephone," rejoined Whitaker. "Hopefully one that works." He turned and left the house for the second time that night.

No one expected to see Graham Whitaker for at least half an hour. He returned in less than ten minutes. The others were still in the study trying to decide what they should do. They had been rejoined in the meantime by Dame Meyerson and Jessica Stokes, who considered company at a time like this almost worth having even if she had to find it in a room shared with a dead body.

"I'm afraid I'm going nowhere. Downed trees are blocking all the entry drives. It's pitch black. I couldn't see five feet in front of me. We'll have to wait until morning and walk out."

"That means we have to stay the rest of the night in this place...with him...like that," said Jessica.

"Not to mention with a murderer on the loose."

"Don't talk nonsense, Smythe," said Whitaker. "It has to be suicide. Who would have a motive to kill him?"

No one uttered a word, though expressions of question and uncertainty registered on several faces.

"Well," said Father Smythe after a moment, "I suggest that you women go back to your rooms and get what sleep you can while we men keep vigil here."

"Surely you don't intend to spend the rest of the night here…with Mr. Barribault lying there?" said Shelby.

"What choice do we have? Nothing must be disturbed until the police get here. I for one don't intend to let Mr. St. John out of my sight."

"You can't be serious," said Dame Meyerson, "thinking that a minister had something to do with this?"

"I agree. It had to be suicide," said Jessica.

"You may be right," said Smythe. "But it also may be that somebody killed him. That's why we have to stay together—keeping a pact like your bridge pact. You too, Coombes."

"All that's pointless if someone snuck into the house and snuck out again," interjected Mike St. John. "Whoever it was—though I'm not discounting suicide either—is long gone by now…that is if someone killed him."

"*Your* theories are hardly credible, St. John," said Smythe. "It's your hypodermic quill sticking out of his arm."

"Well I am too shocked and tired to stand here arguing," said Shelby. "The idea of someone killing him is too unbelievable. I don't know about the quill. But I am going back to Melinda's room to see if she is okay. You men can decide what to do."

"Not so fast," said Briscoe Cobb. "If Smythe is right and this is murder, it could just as well have been one of you women."

"Don't be absurd, Dr. Cobb," retorted Dame Meyerson. "What motive could any of *us* have to kill him?"

"Just as much as any of us men. Why do you assume foul play must originate from the hand of a man not a woman? As to motive, I happen to know that you knew Barribault years ago."

"What are you talking about! That's ridiculous."

"Not so ridiculous. I overheard you talking to him."

"You're daft!" said Dame Meyerson angrily. She turned and walked to the door. Jessica and Shelby followed.

The five men were left alone.

Whether any of them *really* believed one of their number had killed Hugh Barribault, especially Mike St. John, it would be difficult to say. They were also still reeling from the grisly discovery. Though they showed their shock differently than the four women, their thoughts and emotions at the sight were no less volatile. More than one present, however, had reasons for perpetuating the St. John theory.

"There is no reason why all five of us have to stay together the rest of the night," said Graham Whitaker. "I am going back to my room. If you would like, Mike, you can join me. If the rest of you want to keep vigil, as you put it, that is up to you. I will return at five to put in my stint guarding the body, as it were."

"Sounds good to me," said Mike. The two men left the room.

Cobb, Smythe, and Coombes were left alone.

"I suppose he's right," said Cobb. "We might as well split this up. Coombes, if you want to go back to your quarters, we will be fine here. You could perhaps relieve one of us at three or four."

"Very good, sir."

As soon as he was gone, Smythe spoke up.

"You don't actually think it was one of the women, do you, Cobb?"

"I have no idea. It's as plausible as that one of us or St. John or Whitaker did. I'll admit I don't care much for St. John, but you aren't serious in thinking he did it?"

"Why not? There's his quill."

"I suppose you're right. The man is lying dead over there. *Something* happened. Except for that beastly clock which looks heavy as sin, any of the women could have done it just as well as anyone else. Though how they overpowered him long enough to stick that quill in his arm is a mystery. What do you think, that the quill was laced with poison?"

"An interesting twist. So you're saying that the quill may be more than just a prop, but the actual murder weapon?"

"I was just thinking out loud," replied Cobb.

"We might as well make ourselves as comfortable as we can. It is going to be a long night."

* * *

Morning did not come quickly for the inmates of Cullen House.

First light found Graham Whitaker and Reginald Coombes dozing intermittently in the Barribault study. For all his talk about watching Mike St. John like a hawk to make sure he didn't make a run for it, Father Smythe had returned to his own room after being relieved by Whitaker, as had Dr. Cobb. Within half an hour the others were preparing themselves for what would likely be a long day and gradually wandered down to the Breakfast Room. Nor did Father Smythe seem altogether surprised to find Mike St. John along with the rest. By then Constance Fotheringay had awakened with news of the tragedy. She was too beside herself to put out much beyond coffee, tea, oatcakes, and hard-boiled eggs.

In spite of Father Smythe's suggestion that the study must be guarded, seven of the eight found themselves together again in the Breakfast Room, looking haggard, most of the women with red eyes.

"I would say it is time for a walk to the village to try to get through to the police," said Whitaker, walking in bundled up in his overcoat and hat. "Does anyone want to join me?"

"Anyone except St. John," said Father Smythe, renewing his theme from earlier.

"If someone's going to try to escape, it could just as well be me," rejoined Whitaker.

"Then we should all go together—we four men."

"You're not going to leave us women alone?" said Dame Meyerson who had been gulping aspirin like candy for the headache of all headaches. The sound of her own voice beat like a hammer against the inside of her head.

"Coombes is on his way down," said Whitaker. "You will be safe enough with him."

What Dame Meyerson thought of the stuffy butler as a guardian of their welfare was apparent by the expression on her face. She made no reply.

Ten minutes later the four men walked out into the wet cold drizzly morning to make their way, over two fallen trees and through much evidence of the night's storm, to the village.

* * *

Even before they had completed their walk back to the house thirty minutes later, sirens approached from the direction of Buckie.

"We should wait for them here," said Whitaker when they reached the first of the great fallen beeches blocking the drive.

"Who put you in charge?" asked Cobb, who was by now straining from the early walk. Nor had the scratches and mud on his arms and legs from climbing over the downed trees done much to improve his mood.

"Simply a suggestion," replied Whitaker. "Go on ahead if you like."

"So you can make a getaway?" said Father Smythe.

Whitaker burst out laughing. "So now *I'm* your prime suspect! I thought you had Mike pegged for the honors."

"I'm keeping an open mind," rejoined Smythe.

"Well then, wait with me...or go on to the house. I don't really care. I'm sure Coombes is a bundle of nerves. He would no doubt welcome the company. I am staying here till the police come. Say—" he said, then stopped and chuckled to himself, "— you don't suppose...naw, it's too corny."

"What?" asked Mike.

"I was just wondering if it was possible, you know, that the butler did it."

"You are too much, Whitaker," said Smythe. "Making jokes at a time like this. Do you never stop?"

"Well *somebody* did it. I am just throwing out possibilities...though my vote is still suicide. I don't see what else it *could* be. I have to say, however, that quill stuck in his arm is a complete mystery."

* * *

Meanwhile, Coombes retired to his quarters. There, with shaking fingers, he proceeded to don the outer crust of proper British butler in anticipation of a visit from the local constabulary. The four women remained together in the Breakfast Room.

Melinda was disconsolate and said little, breaking every few minutes into renewed weeping. Gradually the other three began to voice opinions on what might have happened.

"I cannot believe a man like Hugh Barribault capable of suicide," said Shelby. "He was so animated, so full of life...so optimistic and excited about everything."

Neither Jessica nor Dame Meyerson offered an immediate response. Both had good reasons at this point for keeping their own counsel. Eventually Dame Meyerson spoke.

"If you're right," she said softly, still conscious of ringing inside her skull, "it means that somebody actually *killed* him. Do you think...I mean is it possible that one of the men...who else could it be?"

"Why not one of the staff?" said Shelby.

"Why would they choose right now to kill him? Some of his people have been with him for years."

"To throw suspicion on us. But most of his staff don't live in the House. I think there's only Coombes and Miss Fotheringay and Mr. and Mrs. Walton."

"I can hardly imagine any of *them* as a killer," said Dame Meyerson.

"Nor Coombes," said Shelby. "The man's afraid of his own shadow."

"There aren't many other possibilities. I don't think Miss Gordon stays here. All the publishing staff have homes elsewhere."

"How can you all make so light of it!" Melinda suddenly burst out.

"We're not making light of it, Melinda," said Shelby. "We're just confused about what could have happened."

"He's dead!" Melinda sobbed. "Isn't that enough? Why can't you just let it be?"

She jumped up and ran from the room, leaving the other three women staring after her.

"She is certainly strung tight this morning," commented Dame Meyerson after a few seconds of silence.

"I wonder what the police will think when they find out what was going on between those two," said Jessica, finally coming out of her silence.

"Why do they have to find out?" said Shelby.

"You're not suggesting covering it up?"

"Maybe not that exactly, but why bring it up? This is hard enough on Melinda as it is."

"They are bound to find out," said Dame Meyerson. "Even if we say nothing, Dr. Cobb's sure to start blabbing. He's been beating that drum since the beginning." She did not again mention the kiss she had seen only yesterday, which confirmed beyond a doubt that the relationship between Hugh Barribault and Melinda Franks had indeed progressed far beyond that of publisher and author.

* * *

The police cars finally came into sight, screaming through Cullen with lights flashing and sirens at full volume when most of the town's inhabitants were still trying to decide whether to get out of their beds. The lead car screeched to a stop before a great fallen tree in front of which stood the four authors. A lanky man of some 6'4" stepped out. He was dressed in baggy trousers, a hastily knotted tie, and a grey wool coat that had been ready for replacement at least five years before.

"Ah, I believe this would be our Inspector Witherspoon, eh, St. John," whispered Whitaker, glancing toward Mike.

"On the trail of Alpine Joe and the black amber statuette," rejoined Mike in a low voice.

"I am Detective Chief Inspector Riggs," the man said as he walked toward them. "I take it you are the men who called?"

The four nodded.

"Which one of you's Whitaker?"

Graham Whitaker stepped forward. "I am Graham Whitaker," he said, offering his hand. "We spoke on the phone."

"Right. So you are one of the famous Eight, I take it?"

"As are all four of us."

"Who found the body?"

"All of us together. We heard a crash above our bedrooms. We came out of our rooms and gathered in the hall. Then we went upstairs together to Hugh Barribault's study."

"Why did you go up?"

"Because it was a tremendous crash, enough to wake us all up. We thought we should see what happened, or if someone was hurt."

"That's when you found Barribault?"

Whitaker nodded.

"Nothing's been disturbed since?"

"I don't think so. We took turns in the room for the rest of the night to guard against that happening."

"Why didn't you call immediately?"

"We tried. The phone was out."

"No one had a cell?"

"Barribault's instructions on that were clear—we were to bring no phones."

"Why didn't you walk to town to call?"

Whitaker paused and glanced at the others. "I went outside intending to drive in, but after seeing the damage from the storm, to be honest I didn't think of walking through the rubble. It didn't occur to me that I could make it in the dark. I suppose with a flashlight I might have made it."

Riggs stared back, not altogether satisfied with such a lame answer.

"Right, then, you had better show me. Let's go."

With the four writers leading the way through the foliage and struggling up over the trunk of the great tree, Riggs and a column of his men walked the rest of the way to Cullen House.

Within an hour crews were at work on the fallen trees. Soon the police and medical examiner's vehicles drove through and parked in front of the house. By then every village along the coast of northern Scotland was buzzing with the news that High Barribault was dead. By mid morning camera teams from every news organization in England and Scotland were speeding toward the scene.

*　*　*

Meanwhile, Detective Chief Inspector Riggs succeeded in gathering everyone from inside Cullen House in the large first floor drawing room for questioning. As other members either of the household or publishing staff gradually arrived, once their personal details were taken down by the policeman at the front door, they too were shown into the drawing room. Most had heard the news and had come immediately. A few simply arrived for work as usual to see the place swarming with police and to be told that their employer was dead.

"So as I understand it," Riggs was saying, "the eight of you who were Barribault's guests—you were all together in the corridor after being awakened by the crash. Then you went upstairs together?"

Nods went around among the eight.

"Who was actually the first to see the body?"

Glances went around. "I think it was you, wasn't it, Mike?" said Whitaker.

Mike St. John nodded.

"Did you touch anything, Mr....uh, Mr. St. John?" Riggs added after a quick glance at his notebook.

"I felt for a pulse," replied Mike, "then examined his extremities."

"He took off his sock," said Dame Meyerson. "I thought it was disgusting."

"Did anyone else touch anything?"

"I felt for a pulse too, on the wrist...then Mike asked me to feel the foot," replied Whitaker.

"Why?"

"Because it was cold. Mike and I were the ones who came to the conclusion that he was dead."

"What time was that?"

"Around one-thirty, I believe," replied Whitaker.

"Closer to two," added Mike.

"And you attempted to telephone immediately?"

"Mr. Coombes tried," said Shelby. "The phone was dead."

"Is that right, Mr. Coombes?"

"Yes, sir."

"Were you with the others when they discovered the body?"

"Yes, sir. I also heard the crash and arrived as the others were coming out of their rooms."

"And then?"

"We walked upstairs to the study, sir."

Just then the door opened and a uniformed officer led a young woman into the room.

"Ah, Miss Westbrook," said Riggs with obvious sarcasm. "How nice of you to join us."

"I'm sorry to be so long, sir," said the young woman. "I only got the call twenty minutes ago. I was sound asleep."

"This, ladies and gentlemen," said Riggs, turning back to those assembled in the room, "is Detective Sergeant Margaret Westbrook. She will be assisting in the investigation."

Miss Westbrook smiled a little nervously, then took a seat while the uniformed officer again left the room. She looked no more than twenty-five, though in reality was approaching her thirty-first birthday. She stood exactly one foot shorter than her boss. To say that he looked down on her would have been true from several perspectives.

"Who else was in the house, Mr. Coombes, besides Mr. Barribault's guests?" asked Riggs, turning toward the butler.

Coombes glanced at the cook and housekeeper. "Just those of us on the staff who work for Mr. Barribault, sir," he said. "There's me, Miss Fotheringay, Mr. Barribault's cook, and Mr. and Mrs. Walton. Mr. Walton is retired, sir, and Mrs. Walton is Mr. Barabault's housekeeper."

"I don't see anyone else," said Riggs, looking around the room. "Where is this Mr. Walton, then?"

"In our apartment, sir," answered the housekeeper. "We heard nothing. We weren't with the others."

"No matter. I want him here. I need to question everyone who was in the house last night. Go get him, Mrs. Walton."

"Yes, sir," said the housekeeper nervously. She got up and left the room.

"And what about this—"

Again Riggs consulted his notebook.

"—the secretary, Cynthia Gordon?"

"She is Mr. Barribault's assistant," replied Coombes.

"Where is she?"

"As soon as the drive was cleared, I walked into town to telephone her, sir. She lives in Keith. She will be here presently."

"Right, so what about this quill? I understand you have all seen it before?"

"It is a specially made writing pen," answered Dr. Cobb.

"Made...where?"

"By a fellow in the village," answered Cobb. "An antique dealer. I had seen it in his shop. I think most of the others had as well."

"How do you think it came to be here?"

"It belongs to Mr. St. John," said Father Smythe. "It's his quill."

"Is that true, Mr. St. John," asked Riggs, turning again to the minister.

"Actually...no," replied Mike. "My quill is still in my room where it has been since I bought it from Mr. Thompson's shop."

Expressions and exclamations of surprise went round the room.

"When was that...when you bought it, I mean?"

"Two days ago."

"There were two quills for sale?" said Riggs.

"I only saw the one in his case, Inspector," replied Mike. "I bought it. It is still in my room."

"That will be established in our search."

He turned and motioned to a uniformed officer standing by, and whispered a few words to him. The man left the room.

"You are going to search our rooms?" said Jessica as Riggs turned back to face them.

"Yes we are, Miss—"

Riggs paused again for a look at his notebook.

"Miss...uh, Stokes," he added.

"Why would you search our rooms?" she asked.

"It seems it would have dawned on you by now, Miss Stokes—you are all suspects in a murder investigation."

"Surely not *all* of us?"

"Of course all of you. So do not disturb anything in your rooms until my men are through. They have probably begun by now. I also want to make sure you are aware also that none of you may leave the house or grounds until we find out what this is all about. We will be questioning you individually."

He paused and glanced about the room one last time."

"All right, then, I think we are through here for now. You may go back to your rooms after they have been searched. Miss

Westbrook and I will take each of your statements. Until then you may remain in this room.—Mr. Coombes, and Miss....uh, Miss Fotheringay, please remain until the housekeeper and her husband return. I want to ask the four of you a few questions."

"I don't understand," said Jessica as her colleagues rose and began walking toward the door. "Why are *we* suspects...surely you don't think—"

"Look, Miss Stokes," said Riggs with annoyance, "a man is dead. According to Mr. Coombes the house was locked up tighter than a drum. There was a storm before midnight that cut the house off from the outside world making it unlikely that anyone from the town could get through in the middle of the night. Inside there were twelve of you—you eight and four members of the household staff. It seems obvious, doesn't it? One of you killed him."

Jessica Stokes left the room and Riggs turned again to the butler.

"Mr. Coombes," he said, "when did you last see Mr. Barribault last night?"

"Probably between nine and nine-thirty, sir."

"After he had retired from the dinner party?"

"Yes, sir. Mr. Barribault summoned me to his quarters that evening requesting something to help him sleep."

"And did you take him something?"

"Yes, sir. I brought him his usual tonic of a capsule of valerian root powder and warm milk."

"He was in his study?"

"Yes, sir."

"Was this a regular thing with him?"

"Yes, sir. He often had trouble sleeping."

"Did you see anyone else when you were attending to Mr. Barribault?"

"Actually, yes, sir. I encountered Father Smythe on the third floor. I asked if I could help him. He seemed to have lost his way and I directed him back to his room."

THIRTEEN

The Arrest

Cynthia Gordon, forty-seven, had never been married nor traveled farther from her native Scotland than Manchester, and that only once. Her interests were wide and varied and she was a great reader of every conceivable type of book. Coupled with a dogged efficiency toward detail, this made her perfect as a secretary and assistant for a writer like Hugh Barribault. That she was not particularly interested in seeing more of the world did not concern him. He was not widely traveled himself, though he had written convincingly about every continent on the globe. Meticulous research had always been Hugh Barribault's signature tune, with which, in the nineteen years she had been in his employ, Miss Gordon had proved invaluable. With the advent of the computer and internet age she had become all the more indispensable. He had no inclination to learn the intricacies of either, and she was fluent and skilled in both.

After taking a joint journalism and business degree from Aberdeen University, Miss Gordon worked several years out of her home in Keith as a freelance copy editor, mostly kept busy by two or three Aberdeen publishers. It was there she came to the well known author's attention. When Hugh Barribault had gone to one of these smaller publishers for a certain book of particular Scottish interest rather than his usual London house, she had been assigned to the project. Barribault had been so impressed, not merely with her editorial expertise but by her entire method, work ethic, and attention to detail, that he offered her a sizeable increase in pay to come work for him. In the years since she had become far more than a mere editorial and research assistant, but a full executive associate who virtually managed the bulk of Hugh Barribault's affairs.

Though not at present an actively religious woman, her childhood training in one of Scotland's fundamental Brethren sects had left one notable conviction of conscience indelibly imprinted upon her character. Boiled to its essence, it might have been summarized as: *Never speak against one's neighbor.*

The elder Mrs. Gordon had grown out of the rootstalk of the best of the old Scots school of child rearing. She taught her children the practicalities of *James* more than the theology of *Romans*. Chiefly she taught them to listen first, speak second, and never convey by speech or expression so much as a word against one's fellow man. If any stood condemned, let no word of it pass the lips of *her* sons or daughters. Accusation, like vengeance, belonged to the Lord. They were free to speak only of what their own eyes had seen or ears heard. All else was hearsay and thus the currency of loose tongues and gossipmongers.

The passing of her mother two years before brought much from that cherished past into Cynthia's consciousness with both renewed fondness and fresh import. More often these days she heard the beloved voice as clearly as if she were still a child. With the memory came heightened conviction to heed the wisdom of her mother's words: Say nothing to injure or do harm. Pass on no gossip. Impugn no motive. Neither blame nor curse, ridicule nor accuse. Remember that the tongue is a great fire. Therefore, tame your speech and seek comfort in silence.

After the initial shock of Mr. Barribault's death and the flow of tears following Coombes' telephone call, as she had driven in from Keith, Cynthia became aware of the precarious position in which she was likely to find herself. At first her primary emotion beyond despondency and grief, was utter confusion. Who would possibly want to harm Mr. Barribault? She did not initially consider that any of the eight might have had anything more to do with his death than one of the staff. Even as she drove into

Cullen she was still trying to convince herself that it must have been a horrible accident.

The moment the great house came into view a few minutes before eight, however, with half a dozen police cars and numerous officers swarming about the place, it dawned on her that the death of her employer was being considered a *crime*. She was thus likely to be questioned in minute detail. As Hugh Barribault's primary confidante during the recent days when doubts had arisen concerning certain members of the illustrious Eight, suddenly the question took on huge personal import:

How much should she divulge of what she knew?

Where would she draw the delicate line between her mother's injunctions and her own convictions, and the legalities involved?

The revelations and private interviews of recent days could be construed as providing motives against Mr. Barribault. Could she, with information she possessed, at best second hand and in some instances third hand, pass on what was no more than hearsay...when that information had the potential power to provide a motive for murder?

Her anxiety was confirmed the moment she arrived. Scarcely out of her car, she was descended upon by Detective Chief Inspector Riggs. In a brusque and peremptory manner, he grilled her with a barrage of questions. She immediately disliked the man. He was sniffing about for any word, any hint dropped from her lips upon which he might hang an accusation.

It was his job. She realized that. A detective dealt with crime every day. Of necessity he had to seek hidden motives. But Riggs's manner of treating everyone as a suspect grated on her sensibilities. She could tell as they spoke that he was even eyeing *her* as a suspect. He interpreted her every word through the filter of doubt and suspicion.

"All right, then, Miss Gordon," said Riggs in closing, "keep yourself available for further questioning. I presume you will be on the premises."

"I...I imagine so," replied Cynthia. "I don't exactly know what to do."

"I will be able to find you in your office, then?"

"Yes, sir."

"Where is that?"

"On the second floor, with the rest of the publishing offices."

Riggs turned to leave her. "Oh, and Miss Gordon," he added, "I will need to speak with Mr. Barribault's solicitor as soon as possible. Get in touch with him for me, will you?"

"I will try, sir. It may be difficult. I believe he is on the continent. But I will telephone his office immediately."

"I believe the phone lines are down. I'll have one of my people get you a mobile."

Riggs left her. Cynthia hurried up the stairs, breaking into renewed tears as she went. Arriving at last in the privacy of her office, she sat down and began to cry.

* * *

John Thompson knew the minute he looked up that the tall man entering his shop just after 10:00 A.M. was no customer. He rose from his chair and greeted him.

"I am D.C.I. Riggs from the Buckie police," said the man. "And your name?"

"John Thompson."

"You are the owner of the shop?"

"Aye."

"I take it that you have heard about the death of Hugh Barribault?"

"I have…a terrible tragedy. A great man and a good friend."

"You and he were friends?"

"Oh, aye."

"I understand you make handmade quills, Mr. Thompson?" said Riggs.

"I dabble in many things," replied Thompson. "I did make one I was particularly proud of. I just sold it to one of Hugh's author guests."

"Right…Rev. St. John. He told me. There was just the one?"

"Aye. But I have been at work on another."

"May I see it?"

"Come this way, Inspector," said Thompson, leading Riggs through the shop to his back workroom.

"It's right here on my—" began Thompson, then stopped. "What—I can't...it's gone!"

"What do you mean, gone?"

"I mean it's *gone*. I was working on it...let me see, day before yesterday."

"Are you saying someone pinched it?"

"I can't imagine it, right under my nose...but it's not here."

"You definitely made two quills? Were they identical?"

"More or less."

"This one you say is missing from your workroom—it looked just like the other?"

"Aye. The nibs were from two different original years, but to the uninitiated eye they would appear identical."

"You could tell the difference?"

"Oh aye."

"And the second was also able to hold and deliver ink?"

"Aye—it was ready to sell. But why such interest in my quills, Inspector?"

"Because one of them was stuck an inch into Barribault's arm, clear into the vein from the look of it. His skin near the wound was stained black. What I need to know from you is if it is possible that the ink could have been lethal."

Thompson returned to his chair and sat down, his face pale. He sat for a moment or two breathing heavily in obvious shock. When he spoke again, his voice was quivering.

"I can hardly imagine it, Inspector," he said. "But if what you say is true, if the entire ink supply was released directly into his arm, who knows but that it could have killed him."

"In other words, the ink may be far from harmless?"

"I cannot say. The ink I use is my own formula. I combine a mixture of herbs and plant dyes in a base of regular commercial ink. But it would take a chemist to determine the effect if ingested. Obviously that has never been the intended use of my ink so I cannot speak with certainty."

"And the mechanism itself—how does it work?" asked Riggs.

"I have a Sheaffer snorkel tip right here," said Thompson, rising again and walking to his shelf of pens. "It is from a pen exactly like this that I made the two quills."

Riggs watched with keen interest as Thompson demonstrated the action of the mechanism.

"The tip itself looks deadly," he said. "It's a tiny hypodermic needle—exactly like the one in Barribault's arm."

"Once stuck into his vein," nodded Thompson, "a few actions of the plunger would release the ink straight into his bloodstream. But to do so would require a victim already unconscious, would it not, Inspector?"

"It would take some effort to penetrate the vein with the tip of the quill," said Riggs. "It would not slip in quite so effortlessly as a medical needle. It is one of the puzzles of this case. Even with a sharp nib such as that, breaking the skin would require a relatively strong force. I am also surprised that the quill itself wasn't more damaged. The point is that no one would sit patiently and allow such a thing to be done. We are still working on that part of it. Not to mention that it would hurt like the devil. The ink and quill obviously do not tell the whole story. Something else had to have been used as well."

"You mean to render him unconscious *before* the tip of the quill was inserted into his arm?"

"Right."

A brief silence followed. Both men were reflecting on the puzzling details and apparent manner of Hugh Barribault's death.

"That is…*if* someone killed him," added Thompson as if the thought had just occurred to him.

"What are you getting at?" asked Riggs.

"I know it sounds grisly…far too bizarre for a man like Hugh, who was as sane as any man I know. But is it possible—I mean…have you considered suicide?"

"We consider all possibilities," answered Riggs. "Of course suicide is on the table. The automatic assumption in a case like this is either murder by a family member or suicide. In this case, with an unmarried man, naturally suicide jumps to the top of the list. But it hardly seems likely that he sat there and calmly stuck that pen in his own arm. There would be much easier ways of killing himself."

"What was he like when you found him?" asked Thompson. "Were there signs of a struggle...anything that would indicate another's involvement?"

"Nothing. At least not yet. Other than a large pendulum clock across the room tipped over onto the floor and smashed to bits—another curious fact that seems to have no bearing on the man's death. Barribault was just lying on the floor with the quill in his arm. If we are unable to find evidence of someone being with him at the time—a bump on the head, another poison administered, shall we say, in a less obvious manner than by your quill, then of course the conclusion may indicate suicide. All I am certain of at this point, whether homicide or suicide, is that someone was trying to make a statement with that quill. I've never seen anything like it in my life."

"How do you mean, make a statement?"

"I mean that whoever it was wanted to make a point about writing or writers or the writer's life... *something* about Hugh Barribault's profession. When we find the motive, we will find the killer, whether Barribault himself or one of the other twelve who was in the house at the time. I will know more when I get the pathology report. In the meantime, do you have a sample of this ink of yours? I want to have it analyzed along with what we found at the scene."

"Of course. You may take this along with you," he said, picking up a partially used bottle from a nearby shelf.

An expression crossed Thompson's face, as if something had just occurred to him.

"What is it, Mr. Thompson?" asked Riggs.

"A curious fact has come back to me. It is probably mere coincidence, but I do find it intriguing."

"In my business we do not believe in coincidences. Continue, Mr. Thompson."

"It is just this...on the day before yesterday—the day before Hugh's death—to a man and women, every one of Barribault's authors, all eight of them, came into the shop in succession. Everyone looked at the quill—the one I had out on display. They all showed a keen interest in it. Most of them handled it and I demonstrated its operation. I suppose any one of them might have taken a fancy to it."

"What are you suggesting, that they were all in on it together?"

"Nothing like that. Just a curious coincidence, I suppose."

Riggs took in the new information with obvious interest. "Well, we overlook nothing," he said. "As of right now they are all suspects. And was that when Rev. St. John bought it?"

"He was my last customer of the day. He paid for it and walked out with the quill."

"How much was it?"

"Fifty-five quid."

"I see. Well, I will also want you to come up to the house to examine the quill we removed from Barribault's arm."

"Of course, Inspector," replied Thompson. "Whatever I can do to help."

*　*　*

When Inspector Riggs returned to Cullen House, the medical examiner was loading Hugh Barribault's body into his van outside the main entrance.

"You're all done up there?" asked Riggs.

"I've got what I need," replied the man. "Your boys photographed everything. They found an open bottle of wine and two glasses on the desk. They're dusting them for prints now, and the whole room. My own work's ahead of me at the morgue."

"Let me know as soon as you can pinpoint the time and cause of death. You have a good sample of the ink?"

"I do."

"Check it with this," said Riggs, handing him the bottle from Thompson's shop.

The examiner climbed into his van. As he pulled away Riggs walked toward two uniformed officers standing at the door of the house.

"We need to station a car and a man at all the entrances to the grounds, Sergeant," he said. "Call in whatever help you need. A crowd is starting to gather at the gate in town. When the news people descend on us, I don't want them in here."

Riggs continued inside the house and went in search of Margaret Westbrook. He found her in the study where half a dozen men and women were examining every inch of the place for fingerprints.

"No one can figure out why the clock fell, sir," she said. "It makes no sense."

"How many times have I told you, Westbrook—nothing makes sense at first. Neither does it make sense that there is no sign of a struggle. We put the clues together one at a time. Gradually things fit together. Have you interviewed the women?"

"Yes, sir."

"And?"

"Same story as with everyone else—they were awakened from a sound sleep by a crash. They came out into the hall and went up to the study with the men."

"The boys find anything here?"

"Not yet. But the quill—the one Mr. St. John bought and said was in his room…"

"What about it?"

"It wasn't, sir. They turned his room upside down. There's no sign of it."

"What does the fellow say?"

"I haven't spoken to him. I thought you would want to question him yourself."

"Right. Anything else?"

"Only that the priest—the older one…Mr. Smythe—he said he wanted to talk to you."

"What about?"

"He didn't say. He made it sound secretive. But he didn't want to confide in me. I think he considers me too young to be a detective."

Riggs did not reply as he turned to go. He thought to himself that perhaps the priest was onto something.

He found Father Smythe in his room.

"Miss Westbrook said you wanted to see me," he said.

"Yes, Inspector," said Smythe, closing the door behind him. "I hate to speak against a fellow cleric," he went on in a confidential tone. "—I mean, I like the man. But from the moment I met Mr. St. John, I had the feeling he was hiding something."

"Like what?" asked Riggs.

"I don't know...something in connection with his last church."

"Such as?"

"I do not know the specifics—he has not chosen to confide in me, though I have made numerous efforts to draw him out. But knowing something about our profession and how churches function, something strikes me as amiss in his story."

"How do you mean?"

"Only that he is not presently in possession of a pastorate, yet neither is he on an official sabbatical. He calls it a leave of absence, but it has apparently been going on for some time. Something about it is odd. He is not telling the whole story, of that I am certain. I would be very curious about his present standing in his denomination."

"What possible bearing could any of this have on Barribault's death?" asked Riggs a little cynically.

"Probably nothing. It is simply something I thought you should be aware of. It has been my experience when people have secrets, especially if they lie about them, that they often point to deeper motives than meet the eye."

"Very true, Rev. Smythe," nodded Riggs. "Your profession and mine are perhaps not dissimilar. So is that all?"

"Yes. It is only that I wonder if things are on the up and up, if you know what I mean. I'm not saying the man's a murderer, only that there may be more to him than meets the eye. I hope you don't think I am trying to meddle in your business, Inspector. I simply thought you ought to know."

"We are well able to conduct our investigations thoroughly, and believe it or not, we usually get our man. But I will look into it," said Riggs, then left the room and again went in search of his assistant.

He recounted the brief conversation with Smythe.

"If there is one thing I've learned in this business, Westbrook," he said, "it is always look a gift horse in the mouth. When someone is trying too hard to be helpful, he is either the killer or a busybody. So I want you to find out all you can about our good Father Smythe. I want to know every detail of his past."

"I'll get right on it, sir."

"That goes double for St. John. Start with his denominational headquarters. Find out his current status. Then look into his last church and the circumstances of his leaving. You may have to run into Aberdeen and talk to those who were involved, especially whoever is pastor now. I have no reason to doubt Father Smythe except that I don't like civilians butting into our work. But we *do* have reasons to be skeptical about St. John, if none other than that it appears his quill was involved. The long and short of it, Westbrook, is that I want to know everything about *both* our two holy men."

* * *

By early afternoon the eight authors and Coombes were dragging from the sleepless night and long day of interrogations.

All Cullen House lay oppressed under a cloud of gloom. Both domestic and publishing staffs were overwhelmed with a sense of desolation. Uncertainty reigned over the household and publishing offices. What would happen to them now, no one knew. Would the new company go forward? None present possessed hard information concerning the specific provisions of Hugh Barribault's will, not even the efficient Miss Gordon. Nor had his assistant yet been successful in reaching the solicitor who held the Barribault will, Drummond Forsythe. The lawyer employed a year earlier for Barribault House, one Alexander Macmillan, had been hired to attend merely to the legalities of setting up the company and newly created foundation, to help administer those entities. He knew nothing about the provisions of the Barribault will or whatever trusts might have been established.

All work in the second floor offices was temporarily suspended. The future was suddenly very much in doubt, not only for Barribault's employees but also for the eight authors. Would Barribault House even continue?

No one yet had answers to these and a dozen other pressing questions.

Constance Fotheringay put out a buffet about noon for the guests and police, and another late in the day. She had no intention of preparing a formal dinner. None expected it.

Well before the day wound down, after two more interviews with Inspector Riggs and one with Detective Sergeant Westbrook, Cynthia Gordon reached a decision about the course of action she intended to follow. She would answer all questions as directly and simply as circumstances allowed. Where she possessed first hand knowledge from what she had personally seen or heard, she would try to give *yes* and *no* answers—attesting to facts only while avoiding the enticing drift toward speculation. She would volunteer no information and offer no opinion. What information had come to her, they would have to discover for themselves. What she kept to herself that fell into the category of informed possibility she would divulge only as a last resort to prevent any from being *wrongly* accused.

She did not have long to wait to test her resolve. Between 3:30 and 4:00 that afternoon, Chief Inspector Riggs walked into her office and sat down.

"We have uncovered information on both Mr. Barribault's men of the cloth," he said. "It appears that the questionnaires and biographical information on each of the eight which you gave me this morning were not entirely complete in the case of Rev. St. John. Were you aware of this, Miss Gordon?"

"Mr. Barribault had asked me to continue inquiries into all the authors," Cynthia replied.

"You did not answer my question," said Riggs.

"I am sorry, sir."

"So *were* you aware that the information provided was incomplete?"

"Not personally, sir. I had no reason to doubt what any of them said about themselves."

"But investigations were ongoing?"

"Yes, sir."

"By you?"

"Not directly."

"He had others working on it?"

"That's right."

"Did you know them? Were you privy to their findings?"

"I did not know any of the individuals involved. In some cases the information came to us by email. When it came, I passed it along to him."

"Did you learn more about Rev. St. John and his last pastorate that caused Mr. Barribault concern?"

"I know only that Mr. Barribault had further discussions with Mr. St. John, as he did with several of the authors."

"What I am asking you, Miss Gordon, is whether you know the substance of these discussions. Were you present, or were the meetings recorded?"

"No, sir, they were not."

Riggs sighed in frustration, but kept what he might have said in response to the woman's reticence to himself. He recognized that she was central to his investigation. He did not want to alienate her by demanding additional information. For all he knew she was a little dense, or else simply not yet thinking clearly after the shocking day.

"Very well, Miss Gordon," he said, "I take it you kept a record of Mr. Barribault's appointments?"

She nodded.

"I would like a list of all Mr. Barribault's interviews yesterday. Make it for the last two days—all his activities…where he went, whom he spoke with—everything. Leave out no detail. I would like it immediately, if you don't mind. I will be up in the study."

Riggs turned and left the office. He did not, however, return immediately to the study. Passing by a large window looking out toward the front of the house, he saw Margaret Westbrook's car approaching along the drive. He descended the staircase and walked outside. There he waited as she drove up and stopped.

"Did you turn up anything on St. John?" asked Riggs as Miss Westbrook got out of her car and came toward him.

"Actually, yes," she answered. "We uncovered quite a substantial dossier on the former minister."

"*Former?*"

"According to the people I spoke with, it seems that his leave of absence was less than voluntary. According to United Reformed headquarters, he is about to lose his license to preach altogether."

Westbrook handed Riggs the file. He perused it briefly.

"So, the man of God was embroiled in a messy and sordid scandal—good work, Westbrook. What more might the good Reverend be concealing? What about the older fellow, Smythe? Any dirt on him?"

"Clean as far as I can tell, sir," replied Miss Westbrook. She handed him a separate file. "Anglican priest, several parishes, no outstanding accomplishments, no evidence of anything untoward. Only sketchy information about his early life."

"We can get all that later. Anything else?"

"Not much before he turns up doing graduate work at the University of London. After that his life reads like the boring account of a clerical existence. He is apparently no more nor less than he appears."

"Right, a priest who is not sure if he believes in God, if I read him correctly—at least from the bits of his manuscript I looked at. I suppose it takes all kinds to make a world, what? No former connections with Barribault or any of the others?"

"Not that appear in his bio."

"Well, perhaps he is on the level after all. Right now, however, I want to have a few words with Mr. St. John."

Riggs walked back into the house with Miss Westbrook at his side.

Passing the second floor landing, they were met by Miss Gordon approaching along the corridor from her office.

"I have that list you asked for, Inspector," she said, "—of Mr. Barribault's activities over the last two days. For a few of the discussions I was present, otherwise I pieced together what I could from his desk diary." She handed him a single typed sheet.

"I see. Thank you very much." Riggs perused the paper quickly, mumbling to himself as he read:

Wednesday, noon	*Information comes through internet on Dr. Cobb and Rev. St. John.*
2:00	*Private meeting between Mr. Barribault and Rev. St. John.*
4:30	*Afternoon session with the Eight.*
Thursday	*No private meetings*
10:00	*Morning session with the Eight.*

4:30	*Afternoon session with the Eight.*
Friday morning	*Mr. Barribault went out early for walk, visited*
	John Thompson's shop, later tells me of
	nagging doubts about some of the Eight.
10:00	*Morning session with the Eight.*
4:30	*Afternoon session with the Eight.*
Saturday-Sunday	*Regularly scheduled sessions with the Eight. No*
	private meetings.
Monday, 10:30	*Morning session with the Eight.*
noon	*Another meeting with Rev. St John. Left Mr.*
	Barribault unsettled. I was not present.
4:00	*Meeting between Mr. Barribault and Dr. Cobb.*
4:30	*Meeting between Mr. Barribault and Jessica Stokes.*
Afternoon session with Eight cancelled.	
5:00	*Meeting between Mr. Barribault and Mr. Whitaker.*
7:00	*Early dinner with Mr. Barribault and guests. Mr.*
	Barribault retired early to apartment not feeling well.

"All right, this will be a start," said Riggs, looking up. "I may want to know more later. It is just as I thought, whatever was going on, he was clearly concerned about St. John. Tell me, Miss Gordon, do you have any idea why he wasn't feeling well that evening?"

"No, sir."

"Had he complained of being sick earlier?"

"No."

"Then it could be that he was unconscious simply because he was sick...or had been slipped something at dinner. Were you present at any of these private meetings?"

"No, sir."

"Do you know the substance of Mr. Barribault's private talks, say, with the young reverend?"

Cynthia's eyes dropped to the floor.

"Miss Gordon," said Riggs, "don't make me use the threat of withholding evidence in a police investigation."

"He...he, uh confronted Mr. St. John with certain allegations from his former church," answered Cynthia hesitantly.

"Just as I thought! And was this the substance of it?" he said, handing Miss Gordon the file put together by Miss Westbrook. It took Cynthia only a moment to see that it contained substantially the same information they had received earlier.

"Yes, sir," she replied at length.

"Unless I miss my guess, old-fashioned values and all, Hugh Barribault was not happy about it. For a year everyone in Britain has been reading of his plans to publish with high standards of integrity, which standards I can only assume, he intended to be reflected in his staff and authors. Am I right?"

"Yes, sir."

"Now he finds this…and not just from any of his authors, but a sordid skeleton in the closet of a *minister* no less. I would put money on the fact that he intended to drop Rev. St. John from the Illustrious Eight."

He looked at Miss Gordon with an expression of interrogation. It was clear he expected an answer.

"That was merely a possibility, sir," she said after a moment. "I know that he was trying to work it out with Mr. St. John so that such a drastic measure would not be necessary."

"They obviously did not get it worked out."

"I don't know, sir."

"And there we have discovered our motive for murder!"

Cynthia Gordon's eyes widened in alarm. Before she could speak further, Riggs spun around and strode along the second floor corridor that led to the guest rooms. He walked straight into Mike St. John's room, where he found the suspect reading.

"St. John," nodded Riggs.

"Hello, Inspector," said Mike cheerily. "Any progress?"

"I believe so. You have noticed, I am certain, that when you returned to your room this morning the quill you had purchased, which you claimed was still in your possession, was gone."

"I assumed your men took it when making their search."

"They did indeed conduct a thorough examination of your room, and all the rooms," said Riggs. "But the quill was *not* here as you claimed. Nor have we found a second quill anywhere."

"That is odd."

"Perhaps," rejoined Riggs. "Perhaps, however, there never was a second quill. Information has also come into my possession concerning the circumstances of your leaving your pulpit— circumstances you lied about in the information you provided to

Barribault. When he learned of your duplicity, he was furious. Am I correct?"

"He was concerned, yes."

"He was more than merely concerned. Did he give you a chance to explain, to defend yourself?"

"He did."

"Did you explain matters to his satisfaction?"

"Not to his satisfaction, no."

"And thus he planned to remove you from the Eight and cancel publication of your book."

"He did not say it in so many words. I assumed that was the direction in which things were moving."

"But you were not about to let that happen. You snuck to his room either during or after last night's bridge game. That is when you killed him. That is motive and opportunity, along with the murder weapon which was yours."

Mike sat listening with incredulity, though he remained calm. Riggs paused briefly, then added:

"Mike St. John, I am arresting you for the murder of Hugh Barribault."

Fourteen

Questions

Though the reality of Hugh Barribault's death gradually sunk in over the course of the day among the Eight, that one of their number might actually be a *murderer* still seemed too remote a possibility to be believed. Seeing the genial Mike St. John led out of the house in handcuffs and whisked away to a jail cell in Buckie, sobered the collected ensemble of staff and guests at Cullen House into renewed disbelief.

Several of the police cars left the scene to accompany the prisoner. As word of the stunning arrest circulated through the house, rooms gradually emptied. A general drift downstairs resulted toward the lunch room, where tea and edibles were set out.

"Is it really true," said Melinda Franks as she eased into a chair next to Shelby Fitzpatrick, "—they haven't actually arrested Mike?"

"It's true," replied Shelby. "I saw them from my window taking him away…in handcuffs, no less."

"Handcuffs!"

"It's always whom you least expect," said Dame Meyerson, sitting down next to Melinda. "I would have suspected myself ahead of Mr. St. John."

"The man had a hidden life," added Briscoe Cobb, joining the gathering with a cup of tea in hand. "That's what I overheard.

Barribault was apparently going to kick him off the author's list and send him packing."

"I don't believe a word of it," said Dame Meyerson.

"How can they arrest him when they don't even know how he did it?" said Melinda sadly. Her eyes were puffy and her face still red.

"It was his quill," rejoined Cobb. "Filled with poison ink, they say."

"Something more must be involved," insisted Dame Meyerson

Through the door now walked Inspector Riggs with Graham Whitaker. They were obviously in the midst of a heated discussion. Conversation around the table stopped instantly. They had not seen Graham Whitaker so worked up all week.

"—most ridiculous thing I've ever heard," Whitaker was saying.

"You don't deny it was his quill," said Riggs.

"I don't know about that. Even if it was, anyone could have taken it from his room. As far as his movements last night during the storm, I was away from the bridge game too. Several of us were. Mike wasn't the only one who could have snuck up to the Library. You might as well arrest *me*, Inspector."

"Are you confessing, Mr. Whitaker?"

"Of course not. I doubt Mike confessed either?"

"No, but neither did he deny it. What about his private interview with Barribault, when Barribault told him he was going to cancel the contract for his book."

"Are you positive that is what he said?"

"As positive as I need to be. I've got convictions on less."

"Then your justice system must be sadly lacking," rejoined Whitaker. "In the States you would be laughed out of court on such flimsy charges."

"Careful, Whitaker. We don't need you Yanks telling us how to do our business. We happen to have invented the criminal justice system."

"What about the fact that there were others who met with Barribault privately yesterday as well as Mike. I happen to be one of them. I saw others coming and going too. Why don't you arrest us?"

"Who might you be speaking of?"

"I'm not about to give you more fuel for your absurd theories so that you can arrest someone else when Mike turns out to be innocent. Suffice it to say that Hugh Barribault probably had issues to be resolved with all of us. I'm sure that's part of the publisher-author relationship. You can't just arrest people on a whim."

"Look, Whitaker," said Riggs, growing perturbed, "I know my business. I don't arrest people on whims. Now I want to know who else you saw alone with Barribault yesterday."

"You'll have to find that out on your own, Inspector," said Whitaker and turned and angrily left the room. Already he regretted saying as much as he had.

The appearance at that moment of Father Smythe saved Riggs from the discomposure of several sets of eyes staring at him.

"Ah, Father Smythe," he said, "just the man I wanted to see, along with the rest of you," he added, turning toward the table where the four were seated. "We have, as I am sure you are by now aware," he went on, "arrested Rev. St. John for the murder of Hugh Barribault. He has been taken into custody and is on his way into Buckie at this moment.

"What about the rest of us, Inspector?" asked Father Smythe. "I mean, do you have any idea what is to become of...well, this whole thing...the publishing company and our books?"

"I have no way of knowing. You will have to consult with the Barribault staff and legal team. I suggest you talk to Miss Gordon."

"With the case solved so quickly," Smythe went on, "obviously our meetings with Barribault are over. Are we free to leave?"

"No one is going anywhere today anyway," replied Riggs. "I want you all here through tomorrow at the very least. I know we have taken preliminary informal statements, but we will need more thorough statements from each of you for the trial. I am afraid I am going to have to ask you to remain here for the time being. Spread the word to the others if I don't see them all."

"Damned inconvenient, I'd say," said Father Smythe after Riggs had left the room. He sat down at the table with the others. "Having to stay here with all this business going on."

"More shocking than inconvenient," said Shelby, miffed by Smythe's tone. "I for one think it's awful."

"Not if St. John did it," said Cobb.

"You can't believe that," said Shelby.

"He could have just as well as any of the rest of us. Any of the rest of *you*, I mean…anyone except me. I certainly didn't do it. Anyway, why not St. John? As I recall last night, when we all left, he remained behind in the Sitting Room. How do we *know* he went straight to his room?—So, what do you think…will we be able to keep our checks?"

"What a thing to bring up at a time like this," huffed Dame Meyerson. "Goodness, Dr. Cobb!"

Meanwhile Riggs was in conference with Margaret Westbrook.

"We've about wrapped it up here for the day, Westbrook," he said, "you can go any time. Be here early tomorrow. We have to complete the statements from everyone, as well as figure out exactly what happened. On your way out, while I'm finishing up here and setting the schedule for guards at the gates and here at the house for the night, would you stop by that antique shop in town—Abra Bits and Collectibles, it's on the high street. Tell the fellow there to make himself available tomorrow morning. I'd like him to come up and identify the quill so we can link it definitively to St. John. Say around ten o'clock."

* * *

Margaret Westbrook, known to her friends as Maggie, drove out of Cullen after her brief visit to John Thompson's antique shop with many thoughts swirling through her brain, not the least of which was the conviction that her blundering boss had arrested the wrong man.

When she first envisioned a career as a police detective she had had visions of training under various incarnations of Sherlock Holmes and Hercule Poiroit, and then rising herself to become a future female Scots legend of investigative prowess.

She had not been prepared for being assigned to someone so obtuse as Inspector Dick Riggs. How did such men rise to become *Detective Chief Inspector*s at all? She had heard of the Peter Principle. But even that fell short of satisfactorily accounting for such a man being where he was. She could hardly imagine him solving a case at all without the help of the supporting cast of police men and women who regularly filled in the gaps. Subtleties entirely escaped him. It was a sore trial to follow him lurching randomly from clue to clue without logically connecting the dots. The worst of it was being treated as a hapless neophyte. Every possibility she suggested, if reasonable, became his *own* discovery. Her only consolation was that this present assignment wouldn't last forever. For now she was able to work in that part of Scotland she loved best, with the convenience of being able to remain at home. But when the chance for advancement came, whether to Aberdeen, Dundee, Edinburgh, or Glasgow, she intended to jump at it.

The drive home from Cullen to Fordyce was only three miles. As she approached the Fordyce Road opposite Sandend on the A98, a sudden thought struck her. If Riggs was still wrapping things up at Cullen House, it might be her only opportunity to interview the arrested man alone.

She braked, turned around at the Sandend intersection, and seconds later was speeding back the way she had come. She continued through Cullen and westward toward Buckie. Ten minutes later she pulled up in front of the police station where Mike St. John was being kept in a holding cell pending transfer to Elgin.

She walked inside.

"Hello, Sergeant," she said to the office on duty. "I would like to question the prisoner Inspector Riggs brought in earlier."

"Sure, Maggie," said the man, rising and leading the way toward the rear of the station. "It didn't take you and Riggs long to crack this one!"

"Well, you know the Detective Chief Inspector," she said. "He's a bulldog."

Sergeant Murray led her to a row of three cells and unlocked the door to the first. Inside Mike St. John sat on a plain bed staring at the opposite wall. He glanced up as she entered, then stood.

"You can leave us, Sergeant," said Miss Westbrook.

"You sure, Maggie? According to Riggs the man's a killer."

"I'll be fine," she replied.

Thirty seconds later Margaret Westbrook and Mike St. John were alone.

"I don't think I need be worried, do I, Mr. St. John?" said Miss Westbrook.

"Why do you say that?" asked Mike.

"Because I'm not in the presence of a killer, am I?"

Mike smiled knowingly but said nothing.

"I didn't think so. There are probably few more dangerous things for a detective to think, as the old adage goes, than that she is a good judge of character. *Everyone* believes that. Probably ministers and detectives are the worst of the lot. In this present case, however, though I still have no idea what actually happened to Hugh Barribault during the middle of last night, I do think I have a pretty good idea who *didn't* kill him. So if you are willing, I want to ask you a few questions."

"Of course. Would you like to sit down? I'm afraid all I have to offer you is an edge of this bed."

Maggie nodded. They both sat down.

"I know I am young," Maggie began, "but I think I can say with confidence that you can trust me. I also think I understand at least some of your reasons for keeping your own counsel. I hope you will be candid with me as far as your conscience and convictions will allow."

"Fair enough, Miss Westbrook," nodded Mike. "You are plain spoken. I will return the level of trust you show me by speaking candidly myself...as far as my conscience and convictions will allow."

"Good. Then as a further measure of that trust, I want you to call me Maggie."

Mike nodded.

"Now then," she said, staring straight into Mike's eyes, "we both acknowledge that a man is dead and we want the same thing—the truth. So I am going to ask you directly—did you kill Hugh Barribault?"

"No," replied Mike.

"Was it your quill that was found?"

"That I don't know. I could have sworn absolutely that it was in my room the morning after Mr. Barribault's death. Apparently I am mistaken. Your people did not find it. I have been puzzling over that ever since. I have no answer to give you."

"All right, we'll leave that for the present. Now according to Miss Gordon, you were not the only one to have had a private interview yesterday with Mr. Barribault. There were apparently problems cropping up with several of your colleagues."

"That I know nothing about?"

"But if you did, you wouldn't tell me, would you?"

Mike smiled. "I see we understand one another. No, I would not."

"But there were problems with you?"

"Yes."

"Would you care to tell me about them?"

"Not in detail. But I will tell you that Mr. Barribault was seriously considering canceling the contract for my book unless I gave him information that I was not at liberty to divulge."

"That did not concern you?"

"Of course it concerned me. But I was unable to tell him certain details of my situation. Without that information, he intended to remove my book from his list."

"That was a price you were willing to pay to keep silent?"

"It was."

Now it was Maggie's turn to smile. "I see I have not misjudged you," she said.

She drew in a breath, then removed a single sheet of paper from her briefcase. "This," she said, "is a list of apparent interviews with Mr. Barribault in the days leading up to his death."

She handed the sheet to Mike.

"You are obviously featured," she said. "But you are not the only one. Do you know anything about any of the other private interviews, or whether they were similar in nature to yours?"

"Nothing," replied Mike. "I am speaking without constraint of conscience—I honestly know absolutely nothing. As far as I know I was the only one whom Mr. Barribault had doubts about. I have no idea whether others were being similarly questioned."

"What do you know of Jessica Stokes and her background?"

"Nothing. She teaches at Manchester, I believe. Other than that, her life is a sealed book to me."

"Did you and she have any personal exchanges this past week?"

"Let me think...no, not that I recall—only small talk...you know, the sort of thing. Come to think of it, several days ago, walking back from town I ran into her and Miss Fitzpatrick. I walked to the house with them. The conversation was light and only lasted a few minutes. I don't know if that counts as a personal exchange."

"I see," nodded Maggie. "What is your impression of Ms. Stokes?"

"I would not care to comment."

Maggie smiled. "I didn't think I would get away with that, but I thought it worth a try. Would you say that you and she hit it off?"

"Not particularly. We didn't gravitate toward one another and strike up conversation. But I would not say that I hit it off with too many others of the group either. Ministers don't always make the best first impression. We rarely go into new encounters with the benefit of neutrality if you know what I mean. It has been my experience that it usually takes ministers longer to form meaningful relationships."

"Were your views and hers, your outlook on life and the world, shall we say, compatible?"

"I would not care to speculate."

It fell quiet a moment.

"All right, Mr. St. John—"

"Please, Maggie, return the favor—it is Mike."

"All right, then...*Mike*," she smiled. "I think that is all for now. I just needed to hear some of these things for myself. I hope you won't be too uncomfortable here for one night. I am reasonably certain it will be no longer than that. But on behalf of...well, on behalf of *me*—I apologize for this inconvenience."

Thirty minutes later the young Scots detective was back home and on the telephone to several contacts in Manchester she had managed to come up with earlier in the day.

* * *

Maggie Westbrook slept well that night. Her peace of mind was not due to the knowledge that she had solved the case. Too many uncertainties still loomed for that. But she was reasonably confident she possessed sufficient information to free an innocent man having to put up with *durance vile* one night more than he should have to.

She was back on the scene at Cullen House by 7:30 the following morning. She did not, however, confront her boss with what she had learned until after the visit from John Thompson from Abra Bits and Collectibles two hours later, the outcome of which she had half expected. It took the Inspector, however, by complete surprise.

Riggs led the antique dealer into the study. Maggie followed.

"This is the room where we found Mr. Barribault's body," he said. "It was right over here."

"What is this clock doing strewn about in such shambles?" asked Thompson.

"We don't know," replied Riggs. "It is apparently what awoke the household and led to the discovery of Barribault. But we are a bit stumped how it is connected. From the condition of the blood and body, Barribault had already been dead for some time."

"From the look of it I would say it is...that is, this *used* to be a very valuable clock—eighteenth century by the look of it. I doubt it will ever keep time again."

"We're leaving it as it is for now until we figure out why it fell."

"You're positive it is murder?"

"We're keeping our options open, but that's what it looks like. The quill is here on this table," said Riggs, leading Thompson across the room past the body-outline taped to the floor. Thompson made his way slowly, seemingly much disturbed by the scene where his friend of fifteen years had met his end.

Riggs stopped in front of the table. Thompson slowly walked to his side and looked down at the quill.

"May I handle it, Inspector?" he asked.

"Yes, anything you like. We've taken what we need for fingerprints. And of course we are testing the ink."

Tentatively Thompson reached out, picked up the quill, and drew it near for closer inspection.

"Yes," he said, "this is definitely my quill—the one that was stolen from my workroom."

"What?" said Riggs in confusion. "This is the *second* quill?"

"Right."

"Not the one you sold to St. John?"

"Oh, no. This is the other one I was working on, as I told you. It was definitely still in my shop after I made the sale to the minister. I presume I will be able to have it back? I can get fifty quid for it. Maybe more if it was used to kill Hugh—a collector's item, you know."

"Uh...yes, of course—after our investigation is complete," said Riggs, obviously perplexed by Thompson's revelation.

"And...wait a minute," said Thompson, scrutinizing the tip of the retractable nib which was still in the extended position, "—yes, it has been modified since I saw it last."

"Modified, how?" asked Riggs.

"Look here—the point of the nib has been filed slightly on three sides, creating a very sharp point. Now it begins to make sense that it could have penetrated the skin so easily."

"How so?"

"Someone has turned this more than figuratively but *literally* into a hypodermic needle. With a point like this, it would take very little pressure to poke through the skin into the artery. If we had the other you would easily see the difference...or the pen in my shop I showed you yesterday. Though this nib will never write very well again."

"Right—we will want to do a comparison for our investigation. This certainly throws a different light on it."

"In what way, Inspector?"

"This makes whatever happened premeditated. It was no crime of momentary anger or passion. If someone modified the quill, they *planned* this."

"So where is the other quill, Inspector?" asked Thompson, " — the one the minister bought?"

"Actually, I don't know. This is the only quill we've found. We had assumed it the one you sold."

"Not a chance of that."

When they were through, Riggs led the antique dealer downstairs and outside. The two spoke again briefly, then parted. When Thompson was on his way back to town, Maggie approached.

"May I have a word, Detective Chief Inspector?" she asked.

"Of course, Miss Westbrook," said Riggs, still baffled by the turn of events. "What is it?"

"It is just a theory," she said, "but it has occurred to me that we may have the right motive but the wrong author."

"What are you talking about, Miss Westbrook?"

"I made some calls yesterday and last evening, following up on the list we received from Miss Gordon."

"And?"

"I think there may be reason to suppose that Mr. St. John was not the only one of the Eight Mr. Barribault may have been considering removing."

"Who else then?"

"Ms. Stokes for one."

"What is the basis for this conjecture?"

"From certain individuals I spoke with, classes she has taught, a thesis she worked on as an undergraduate, and a reputation that has followed her for some time...I think there is reason to suppose that Jessica Stokes may be a lesbian."

The word hit Riggs with the unexpected force of a bucket of ice water in the face. But nothing in his expression revealed it. He was clearly intrigued, but did not want to show it and thus give credibility to Miss Westbrook's theory.

"If you're right, what of it?" said Riggs after a moment. "This is the modern age. Don't tell me you're not a liberated young woman, Miss Westbrook?"

"I don't know whether I would be considered liberated or not, Inspector. Nor am I passing judgment. I simply find myself intrigued to imagine what might have been Mr. Barribault's reaction had he made the same discovery."

"Is this theory of yours based on your woman's intuition, Westbrook?" said Riggs in a chiding tone. "You should know by now that in our job we rely on facts not feelings."

"Maybe there is a little intuition involved," rejoined Maggie. "I'm sure you don't deny that part of detective work is learning to read people, and sometimes reading more into their expression and carriage than they tell you. All I am saying is that if he happened to discover a sexual orientation in such stark conflict with traditional values as homosexuality, I cannot imagine that Hugh Barribault would have been happy about it."

"You don't propose we arrest her on this hunch of yours?"

"Not at all. But with the quill now established as *not* Mr. St. John's, and at least one more of the Eight found potentially to possess the same motive, my only point is that in their standing with Mr. Barribault there exists no difference between Mr. St. John and Ms. Stokes. No one saw her the entire evening while the others were playing bridge. As far as opportunity, she had *more* than St. John. He has an irrefutable alibi for a good part of the evening when he was with the others. Stokes has none at all. If we find that Barribault was killed relatively early in the evening, I would say that puts *her* in the lead position."

"Or one of the others who did not participate in the bridge game."

"Yes—Franks and Smythe, I haven't forgotten them. The crusty old cleric and the young beauty."

"No doubt you have motives lined up for them as well?"

"No. But like you said regarding suicide, I am keeping all options open. Either the young Franks or the aging Smythe may have motives we haven't found yet."

"What do you suggest then?" asked Riggs, unable to prevent a hint of condescension in his tone.

"Either arrest all three on suspicion, or else release Mr. St. John. They all could have the same motive—that Barribault was going to dump them. As I see it, they stand or fall together."

"We don't know that in the case of the Stokes woman. We have no idea what she and Barribault talked about."

"Only because she hasn't admitted it. Are you going to punish Mr. St. John for owning up to the fact that Barribault was thinking of canceling his contract?"

"I'll think about what you say, Westbrook," said Riggs. "In the meantime, I'm working on some leads of my own."

* * *

In actual fact, D.C.I. Richard Riggs had no leads at all.

He was still reeling from Thompson's revelation about the quill. Most of his annoyance toward Maggie Westbrook stemmed from the conviction that she was right—that they had no solid evidence on which to hold the minister. Of the three essentials— motive, opportunity, and evidence—the evidence was almost non-existent, and the motive too was thin. But he had to play the thing carefully so as to avoid the unthinkable—the appearance of having made a rash arrest, and then being upstaged by a woman…one half his age at that.

It did not take him long to determine the best way to deal with the inevitable. As soon as Westbrook was out of sight, he went to find the uniformed officer in charge of the guard detail.

"Simmons," he said, 'we have just learned that the murder weapon—that is, the quill in question—was in fact not Rev. St. John's at all. This does not remove him from suspicion. We still know he was in Barribault's doghouse. However, without a clear link to the quill, I've decided it might be best not to hold him…until we find that link. I want you to go into Buckie and see to his release on my authority. Have Sergeant Murray call my mobile if he has questions. Then bring St. John back here where we will keep close watch on him. Make clear that he remains a suspect and under no circumstances is to leave the premises."

"Yes, Inspector," replied Sergeant Simmons.

"Before you go, however, have all your men—except those at the gates…have them report to me. We need to initiate a new search of the rooms, of the entire house if need be."

"For what, Inspector?"

"For a second quill…which is actually the first quill—the St. John quill."

"I will see to it."

Forty minutes later a knock came on Jessica Stokes' door. She answered it. There stood D.C.I. Riggs.

"Miss Stokes…" he said, "if I might have a word with you?"

"Yes, come in. Actually, it is Ms. Stokes."

"Ah, right…sorry, uh…*Ms.* Stokes."

Riggs stepped into the room, closed the door, and took out his notebook and pen.

"As I understand it," he began, "you were alone the entire evening of Mr. Barribault's death…after dinner, that is. You did not participate in the bridge game?"

"That's right. I went to bed early."

"Yes, right. I understand you had a private interview with Mr. Barribault earlier that same day."

"I did, but how…that is, I understood that to be confidential."

"Nothing is confidential in a murder investigation, Ms. Stokes. It is my business to know everything. Was the meeting with Barribault the cause of your headache? You were upset by it…angry perhaps."

"Of course not. What are you suggesting?"

"Just trying to be clear on what happened and why."

"I want to know how you knew about the meeting. Who is talking about me behind my back?"

"Nobody. We are simply trying to piece together a picture of events leading up to what took place that night. In actual fact, the information was provided by Mr. Barribault's secretary, Miss Gordon."

"The bitch!" exploded from Jessica's mouth. "What gives her the right—"

"Please, Ms. Stokes. She was only answering our questions."

"Of course…sorry. I meant nothing by it."

"It may interest you to know that yours was not the only name on the list. We asked her for an account of Mr. Barribault's schedule. Several names were mentioned. So, would you care to tell me the substance of your conversation on that occasion with Mr. Barribault?"

"No, I would not."

"I can force you, Ms. Stokes."

"How?"

"There are always the courts."

"You can't bully me, Inspector."

"If I put you in the witness box, you will have to tell the truth or go to jail? Before it comes to that, however, I can arrest you for withholding evidence."

"I am withholding nothing. What Mr. Barribault and I discussed has nothing to do with his death."

"I'll be the judge of that."

"It has no bearing on anything, I tell you. It was personal. What does it matter anyway? I thought you had your killer."

"Mr. St. John is being released."

"You've cleared him?"

"No. But he is being released pending additional evidence. It may be that that evidence could involve you as well."

"Don't be absurd, Inspector. What evidence? I have nothing to do with Rev. St. John."

"Look, Ms. Stokes, I have reason to believe that Mr. Barribault had become aware of certain facts about you...facts that if true would have led to his cancellation of your book contract."

"That's a lie!" Jessica shot back, eyes flaming. "Who told you such a thing?"

"No one. That's what detectives do, they ferret out the truth."

Jessica took a deep breath and forced herself a second time to calm down.

"I am sorry, Inspector. I forgot myself. Of course...you have the right to ask me anything you like. I apologize."

"No need," replied Riggs. "All right, then, let me ask again— what did you and Mr. Barribault discuss?"

"I still fail to see why I should have to answer that."

"I am afraid I must insist."

"All right, all right! It was nothing, really. Just...uh, a few specifics pertaining to my book contract."

"I see. And after your meeting with him, Barribault cancelled the scheduled afternoon session. Do you know why?"

"No I don't know why. He had already done so. It had nothing to do with me. That was the first thing he said when I went to his office. He asked if I'd heard there was to be no session later and that dinner had been moved up to seven."

"Ah...right. Then later, you did not participate in the bridge game?"

"No, I had a headache and went to my room."

"You spent the whole evening alone?"

"I took something for my head and tried to read. But I went to bed shortly after that."

Riggs thought a moment, pretending to look over his notes. In fact he was trying to figure out a way to ease into the big question gracefully. But tact had never been Dick Riggs's middle name. Thus he lurched forward in his usual bumbling manner.

"You said your meeting with Barribault was personal?" he said.

"That's right," answered Jessica. "The substance of it was between the two of us, no one else."

"Were you having an affair with him?"

"What!"

"You heard the question, Ms. Stokes."

"I resent the implication."

"Please answer it."

"No I was not."

"You weren't attracted to him?"

"The man was twenty-five years older than me!"

"Wealth is a powerful incentive, Ms. Stokes."

"Not to me."

"Then I will ask it another way...are you or are you not gay?"

If Mike St. John withdrew into silence rather than defend himself, Jessica Stokes was bound by no such chosen constraint of character. When confronted by accusation she more resembled a cornered alley cat.

"Go to hell, Inspector!" she spat. "That's none of your business!"

"I am making it my business, Ms. Stokes. It may especially be my business before this investigation reaches its conclusion...if it proves to be a motive for murder."

"Then go talk to Melinda Franks, the little hussy!" she hissed. "She's the one who was cozying up to Barribault. Ask any of the others. They all knew the two were messing around. She wasn't with them that night either. She probably went straight up to Barribault's apartment and spent the evening with him!"

Again Riggs checked his notebook. The handwritten scrawlings on the paper swam before his eyes. He desperately needed to collect his thoughts. This was a juicy one! He hadn't once suspected the Franks girl. Yet what was a more perfect motive for murder than a hasty affair gone suddenly wrong!

"Ask Cobb. Ask Dame Meyerson—they saw them!" Jessica ranted on angrily. "And since when is being gay a motive for murder. Believe me, if you arrest me on that basis, I will have you up on discrimination charges the next day. As for the private meetings...I heard Mr. Barribault yelling at Mr. St. John in his office. They obviously were arguing about something. And Graham Whitaker went into Barribault's office after I did—*alone*. Have you questioned him about *his* business with Barribault? Have you asked him if *he's* gay!"

They were coming off the bat a little fast for Dick Riggs. If there was one thing he could do with the best of them, however, it was keep his cool.

"No, uh...but I intend to," he mumbled, still trying to focus, "—about his business with Barribault, that is. Yes, I am of course aware of the Whitaker interview. Don't imagine I am singling you out, Miss...uh, Ms. Stokes. It would be a mistake to assume that. All leads will be followed with equal vigor."

* * *

While Riggs was attempting to wrap up his heated exchange with Jessica Stokes, Sergeant Simmons drove up to Cullen House with Mike St. John. It was twenty or thirty minutes before noon. Detective Westbrook was waiting for them. She took charge of the freed prisoner and accompanied him upstairs.

"You don't look too much the worse for wear," she said.

"Not an experience I would want to make a regular habit of," rejoined Mike. "But once for the Memoirs is tolerable. I do feel dreadfully dingy. The first thing I want to do is take a shower and get into some clean clothes."

As they left the second floor landing and walked down the corridor toward Mike's room, a latch sounded on their left. Shelby Fitzpatrick stepped into the hall. She saw them and paused. For a brief instant her eyes met Mike's. A peculiar expression flitted across her features.

"Mr. St. John," she said, clearly surprised. "You're, uh...welcome back."

"Hello, Shelby."

"So you've been released?"

"For now at least, thanks to Miss Westbrook. But according to Mr. Riggs, I remain the prime suspect. I don't know if I am technically under house arrest, but that is the impression conveyed to me."

"You are not under house arrest, Mike," said Maggie. "But to make things easier on you—actually, to make it easier on me too!" she added laughing, "what do you say to keeping that a secret between we three."

"Agreed," consented Mike.

Shelby glanced back and forth at the minister and detective, surprised at the level of friendliness between them.

"Well, I am glad you are back," she said. "I was shocked when I heard that Inspector Riggs had arrested you."

As if on cue at the mention of his name, Riggs walked out of Jessica Stokes' room further down the corridor, obviously agitated. He saw the three gathered in the hall and walked toward them with the best imitation he could muster of nonchalance.

"So you're back, are you, St. John?" he said.

"Yes, thank you very much, Inspector," replied Mike with a smile. "I don't think I would want to spend too many nights in your facility."

"Don't read too much into it, St. John. They did tell you, didn't they, that you are still being watched very carefully?"

"They did, yes. But just as a point of clarification, am I still a suspect?"

"Absolutely."

"Perhaps I should rephrase that—am I under house arrest and confined to my room?"

"Not technically, no…but—"

"Ah, good," interrupted Mike before Riggs could qualify his words. "Then, ladies," he said, turning briefly toward Maggie and Shelby, "I bid you good day.—Thank you again, Inspector," he added to Riggs, then opened the door to his room which stood nearly opposite Shelby's, and disappeared inside.

Riggs was left staring at the closed door in silence, the two women inwardly amused at Mike's adroit handling of the exchange.

"I was just on my way downstairs for a cup of tea and perhaps a bite of something," said Shelby.

"I'll join you," said Maggie.

The two walked off leaving Detective Chief Inspector Riggs standing in the corridor alone, still more than a little overwhelmed by the revelations of the last ten minutes.

Slowly at length he followed Shelby and Detective Westbrook downstairs. He was not close enough, however, to see them detour outside for a few words alone.

* * *

Jessica Stokes had been listening to the faint sounds of the conversation in the hall with her ear pressed against the door of her room. When she was satisfied the coast was clear, she opened the door a crack and peeped out. The corridor was empty.

She went to her bathroom, doused a washcloth with cold water then wiped her face and the back of her neck. After a few deep breaths, she left her room and walked downstairs after the others. What she wanted right now was people, a crowd…anyone! She would endure no more private sessions with Riggs if she could help it. If further conversations took place, she wanted witnesses to see the man's buffoonery for what it was.

Jessica entered the Lunch Room to see Riggs, his back to her, standing beside a table where Graham Whitaker, Briscoe Cobb, and Dugan Smythe were all seated. Neither Shelby nor Miss Westbrook were present.

Hesitating momentarily, she turned to leave. A moment later, however, she was arrested by Riggs's voice behind her.

"...that you both met privately with Barribault on the afternoon of his death."

Jessica paused in the corridor outside the door and listened.

"I did...yes," answered Cobb.

"What about?" asked Riggs.

"I, uh...just routine matters."

"There were private meetings going on with all of us, Inspector," said Father Smythe. "Not just with Mr. Barribault but also including talks with his staff."

"What kind of talks?"

"Editorial and legal matters."

"He told us...when was it—" said Graham Whitaker, glancing toward the other two, "two or three days earlier...that he was setting up meetings for all of us."

"For what purpose?" asked Riggs.

"To begin the process of finalizing contracts for our books, and moving toward the editorial and production stage I assume."

"Ah...right. And you, Mr. Whitaker, did Mr. Barribault ask to see *you* privately that afternoon—the day of his death?"

"No," answered Whitaker.

"Ms. Stokes says otherwise."

"Then she is mistaken."

Suddenly Jessica Stokes was striding back into the lunch room. This time she did not slow down. If Inspector Riggs might have benefited from Shelby Fitzpatrick's workshop on the subtleties of human psychology, even more so might Jessica Stokes. When perceiving a threat, whether real or imaginary, she lashed out without forethought of consequence. Nor was she attuned to the danger implicit in protesting too much.

Forgetting her initial thoughts toward Graham Whitaker, she marched toward the table.

"Graham, what are you talking about?" she said. "I saw you as plain as day."

Knowing the voice, Riggs unconsciously rolled his eyes and turned to meet the inbound Stokes Express.

"I recall meeting you on the landing as *you* came out of Mr. Barribault's study," said Whitaker. "Your face was red and you were angrier than a wet hen."

"I was no such thing!"

Whitaker laughed. "Have it your way, then," he said.

"I was just...Mr. Barribault and I had had a spirited discussion, that's all," Jessica said, speaking to Riggs. "Be that as it may, I waited on the stairs, Graham," she said again toward Whitaker. "I know what I saw, and it was *you* going into Mr. Barribault's study. And you, Dr. Cobb," she went on. "You and he had words too. I saw you when you came outside earlier—your face was flushed—"

Riggs had finally had enough. "*Miss* Stokes!" he shouted. "This is none of your affair. Please leave the room! I am trying to conduct an investigation. If you don't leave us alone, I have a good mind to arrest *you*. I am still not satisfied with some of the answers you gave me."

"You can't be serious, you big lout! You don't seriously think I had anything to do with it!"

"That does it!" exclaimed Riggs. "I am not charging you with murder but with interfering with a police investigation."

He took her by the arm. "Come with me!"

Riggs forceably led Jessica from the room in a huff and took her in search of Sgt. Simmons.

"Simmons, this lady is under house arrest for obstruction," he said. "Take her to her room and have one of your men stand guard."

When the sergeant and his fuming new charge were out of sight, Riggs returned to the three men in the lunch room.

"She won't pester us any more for a while," he said. "Now, Whitaker," he said, "what's this all about between you and Barribault? I don't much care for the Stokes woman. But she was definite about seeing you. I don't like being lied to. Did you or did you not have a private meeting with Hugh Barribault?"

"You asked if he had asked to see me," replied Graham. "He did not. But I did talk with him. I had been trying to find him alone most of the day actually, concerning a private matter having nothing to do with our books. Ms. Stokes is right—we passed one another on the landing, then I went in to see Mr. Barribault."

"Did you and he argue?"

"No."

"What did you need to see him about?"

"Actually, it was concerning my wife."

"I thought you were a widower."

"I am. My *late* wife, I should say."

"Would you care to elaborate?"

"I would prefer not to. Honestly, it has nothing whatever to do with all this."

"If I insist?"

"Then I would tell you. But under protest."

"Duly noted."

"*Do* you insist?"

"I'm afraid I must."

"All right," said Whitaker. "But this is personal and private, Inspector," he added with a glance toward the other two men. "I hope you can appreciate my feelings, and understand why I protest being forced to divulge it."

Riggs nodded. "You two won't mind if I speak with Whitaker alone," he said to Cobb and Smythe. Their mealls completed, the two rose and left the room together. The Inspector took a chair at the table and waited.

Graham Whitaker sat staring down at the floor for a minute or two, marshaling both thoughts and emotions.

"It was about eight years ago," he began softly, "that my wife was diagnosed with a rare form of ALS—what we in the States call Lou Gehrig's Disease. Much positive research was being done by the Harvard Medical Center and my wife was admitted into their trial program. She seemed to be responding well and we were hopeful. Among the chief donors for the research program was aging Winston Barribault, Hugh Barribault's father. As you may know, he died seven years ago. According to the terms of his will, all philanthropic donations were suspended and the senior Barribault's assets placed in trust for Hugh. His reasons were understandable. He wanted his son free to administer the Barribault fortune on his own, and to be in a position to determine for himself which directions he wanted his *own* philanthropic efforts to go. His motives were understandable, but for some of the Catholic schools and other medical facilities that depended on his funding, it made things very difficult. Harvard was in the same boat. The suspension of funding was a major blow to its program. As it did not rank in importance alongside cancer and AIDS and Parkinson's research, the ALS program was the one to be cut from the Harvard Medical Center's budget. My wife died a year later."

Whitaker's voice had grown low and hoarse. He sniffed and wiped briefly at his eyes with the back of his hand.

"It was simply an unfortunate circumstance of timing," he went on. "At the time that we received notification from Harvard about the Barribault will and the discontinuation of the ALS program, the name Barribault meant nothing to us. After my wife's death, I began to write but I still knew nothing about Hugh Barribault. It was only after the writing contest was announced and I was well into the process that I put two and two together and learned that Winston and Hugh Barribault were father and son. I determined if I happened to be lucky enough to be one of the contest winners, that I would do everything in my power to talk to Mr. Barribault about the importance of the ALS research. I hoped to convince him to resume funding for the program as his father had done. Obviously it would do me no good. My wife was already gone. But his money could save other lives. I did not see myself as a crusader for the cause, I was simply a man who lost a wife he loved and wanted to tell Hugh Barribault about it."

"Were you bitter, Mr. Whitaker?" asked Riggs.

"I hope not...I don't think so. How could I blame Barribault? It wasn't his fault. Neither he nor Harvard were doing anything but following the terms of the will. But if I happened to find myself in a position to influence the Barribault Foundation, I wanted to use the opportunity to push for new funding to find a cure for the disease that took my wife's life. What therefore began as a coincidence, my future linked with Hugh Barribault, by the time I arrived here had become something of a mission I suppose you might say. That is what I wanted to talk to Mr. Barribault about."

"How did he take it?"

"He listened with the utmost respect and compassion," replied Whitaker. "I think he was moved by my story, and saddened that such unintended consequences resulted from his father's attempt to show *him* the respect of a father. It was simply a sad set of ironies converging, with my wife's life in the middle. In the end, Mr. Barribault said he would think very seriously about what I had told him, and weigh it heavily in his future plans."

Long before he had completed his story, Shelby Fitzpatrick and Maggie Westbrook had approached the lunch room after a brief stroll together outside. As they drew closer they heard the sounds inside of what was clearly an emotional outpouring from one of their number. By unspoken consent they paused and stood listening in the corridor unseen through the open door. By the time Whitaker fell silent, both sets of eyes were wet.

Riggs took it all in thoughtfully, however, with dry eyes. It was silent for several moments.

"A powerful motive for revenge, some might consider your story, Mr. Whitaker," he said at length.

"No doubt," rejoined Whitaker. "But I happen to be a man who doesn't believe in revenge."

* * *

Dick Riggs left Cullen House about 12:30 and drove into town. Passing through the Town Gate at the head of Grant Street, a crowd of some fifty locals and half that many journalists, recognizing the car, swarmed toward him. Cameramen were on their heels. Within seconds the narrow roadway was so clogged it was impossible for him to move further.

He had left the house to get away from the clamor and try to collect his thoughts, not to be besieged by cameras and reporters and curious onlookers. Realizing his plight was hopeless, however, he succumbed to the inevitable and opened his window.

"Detective Chief Inspector!" shouted a dozen voices at once.

"Inspector...Inspector...what can you tell us?"

"Nothing to report at this time," said Riggs.

"Has there been another arrest?"

"Not at this time."

"What about the minister?"

"He has been released."

"Do you have any suspects?"

"We have several persons of interest."

"Which ones?"

"I'm afraid I cannot divulge that at this time."

"When do you expect to release details?"

"When we have them."

Riggs slowly tried to inch his car forward. By degrees the crowd slowly moved back. Gradually he was allowed to pass.

He drove past the high street, onto a quiet side street where he parked. He removed his coat, then walked through a narrow lane back down toward the town square hoping he would not be recognized. From there he found his way to one of three or four eateries and sandwich shops available. He sat down at a corner table as far from the door as possible. After ordering, he took out his notebook and pen and tried to put his progress thus far into perspective.

Suspects: he wrote.

> *St. John.*
> *Stokes.*
> *Whitaker.*

The potential motives were obvious.

The first two had been exposed by Barribault as something less than the sterling characters he had hoped for from his authors...at least in his, Barribault's, opinion. And his was the only opinion that mattered. In a moment of rage, when he confronted them with the decision to bounce them...why might one of them not have killed him?

With Whitaker, the motive was clearly revenge for his wife's death.

Right, he said to himself. The Whitaker motive was the strongest. Half the cases he encountered had revenge somewhere in the mix. Yet he couldn't help liking the fellow. What jury would convict such a sincere man? He would have the women in tears and feeling sorry for him. Before he could hope to successfully press a charge against Whitaker, he would literally have to find the smoking gun in his hand—or the smoking quill.

As for St. John and Stokes—he *didn't* particularly like either of them, but the evidence against them was thin. Actually there was no evidence, except for the circumstantially speculative which was based on their private meetings and the gaps in their alibis during the night of the murder. Either of them *could* have done it.

The sequence of events during the bridge game...everything hinged on that. He had to get that timeline nailed down. Who could he most reliably depend on for information? St. John and Whitaker were both there, but not only had they left at the same time to investigate the storm, they were both suspects. He could hardly ask *them*.

That left—

He looked back over his notes.

Omitting St. John and Whitaker...the bridge game was left with Fitzpatrick, Meyerson, Cobb...and Smythe for part of the evening.

Meyerson—the stately diplomat's wife...if he couldn't trust a woman like her, who could he trust?

Smythe—the staid old priest, uninteresting but probably reliable despite his initial doubts.

Fitzpatrick—the American psychologist...he hadn't made up his mind what he thought of the lady. He couldn't quite get a read on her.

Cobb—the scholar and academician...he was wary of Cobb. Could the Stokes' menace be right about him hiding something?

Nor had he yet had a probing interview with young Melissa Franks. He needed to find out whether she really was fooling around with Barribault. Like Stokes, she had no alibi.

Not that he could base anything on the rantings of the Stokes woman. But the affair scenario was ripe with intrigue.

What about the household and other staff? Nothing had turned up on any of them resembling a potential motive. But he could omit no one from consideration.

He would put Westbrook on that. It would get her out of his hair while he went on with his investigation with the Eight.

* * *

D.C.I. Riggs returned through the Town Gate at 2:00 o'clock. This time he did not stop for questions. Arrived back at the house, he immediately sought an interview with Dame Jennifer Meyerson, Shelby Fitzpatrick, and Dr. Briscoe Cobb. He met with them in the second floor Sitting Room.

"I am trying to piece together a detailed timeline of the events of the night in question," he began. "From my earlier notes I gather that the three of you were the only ones who were never alone the whole evening. I hope you can help me."

"I don't know how much help I will be, Inspector," said Dame Meyerson with attempted humor. "I was drinking rather heavily. My memory of events is fuzzy at best."

"I'm sure we shall manage," said Cobb. "What would you like to know?"

Riggs took out his notebook. "Right, then," he said. "Dinner was at seven. All of you along with Mr. Barribault dined together. Mr. Barribault complained of not feeling well and left early. Did he have anything to drink?"

"I don't remember if he had any cocktails. He was drinking wine along with the rest of us, wasn't he?" said Shelby, glancing around at the others.

"Could he...I am just thinking out loud," ventured Cobb, "—might he have already taken something?"

"You're wondering if he was poisoned?" rejoined Riggs.

"I don't mean to be macabre, but yes, that is what I was thinking?"

"In other words...taken it, or been given it. That is a possibility, Dr. Cobb. As yet, however, there is no indication of poison administered through the mouth or stomach. Only the ink. Of course we are investigating that angle thoroughly. But as far as you can all remember, he drank nothing different than any of you? How many bottles were there?"

"I remember that clearly enough," said Dame Meyerson. "I was enjoying the wine selection that evening, so I noticed. Coombes had opened three bottles—we all shared them freely, as I recall...Hugh along—er, Mr., Barribault along with the rest of us."

"So after Barribault's departure," said Riggs, "what happened next?"

"Melinda left as well," said Shelby.

"Not until you two had given Mr. St. John the third degree," said Dame Meyerson.

"I would hardly call it that," rejoined Shelby.

"What else would you call it? You and Dr. Cobb have been belittling Mr. St. John all week. That's why Melinda said she left—that she was sick of it."

"All right, so we gave the man a hard time," said Cobb. "I didn't like him from the start. I couldn't help giving him a bit of his own back."

"Why did he bother you?"

"He wore his religion on his sleeve. I don't like people who pretend to be saints."

"That's not my read of the man," said Dame Meyerson. "I find him pleasant and courteous enough. But he speaks up when someone makes an illogical statement. For my money, Dr. Cobb, *you* are the one who started the rift with Mr. St. John."

"How me?"

"You jumped on him from the very beginning. You poked and jabbed at Christianity from the very first time we were together. I saw it in your eyes. You have an attitude against people of belief. You were asking for it. When Mr. St. John mildly stood his ground, you now accuse him of pretending to be a saint. That's rubbish."

"So Franks left?" said Riggs.

"Then these two started talking about *her*, that she and Mr. Barribault were fooling around together," said Shelby.

Riggs glanced back and forth between Dame Meyerson and Dr. Cobb.

"That's right, we did," nodded Cobb.

"I didn't believe it then," said Shelby, "and I still don't."

"And you, Mrs. Meyerson?" asked Riggs.

"From everything I saw...yes, I definitely think there was something going on."

"Who left next?"

"Father Smythe," said Shelby. "At least...didn't he leave before Jessica?" she said, glancing at the other two.

"I can't remember," said Dame Meyerson.

"It was Smythe," said Cobb. "He became irritated at the talk about Miss Franks. Ms Stokes was still there at that point. Then Mr. Whitaker suggested a game of poker. That's when she left the room."

"I'm afraid we all ganged up on her a little after her departure," said Shelby. "In any event, that's when we adjourned from the Dining Room and went upstairs to the Parlor, and the brandy and scotch and port began to flow."

"So you were then down to five—you three plus the other two men, St. John and Whitaker."

"I believe that's it," nodded Cobb.

"Then what?"

"We played bridge instead of poker," said Dame Meyerson, "and I became, I believe, a little tipsy. Father Smythe came back an hour or two later."

"Don't forget the storm," said Shelby. "It began to rage terrifically outside. That's when Father Smythe returned. What was it, maybe around ten by then? We used the pause in the game to take a powder room break."

"Did you leave alone?"

"Not exactly," said Shelby. "Mr. St. John had come up with the notion that we remain together for the rest of the evening so that we would all quit together. So we took our powder room break in pairs—Dame Meyerson and I went up to our rooms together, and back down. And you, Dr. Cobb, you and Mr. Whitaker went together."

"What about the other two men?" asked Riggs, glancing at his notes, "—that would be, at that point...the two ministers?"

"They remained in the Parlor together," answered Shelby.

"So none of you were alone, except briefly when you went to your own rooms?"

There was a brief silence. Shelby glanced toward Dr. Cobb, as if waiting for him to speak. When he said nothing, she looked toward Dame Meyerson.

"What are you waiting for, Dr. Cobb?" said Dame Meyerson. "Tell him."

"Tell me what?" said Riggs.

"That he *didn't* rejoin the rest of us for ten or fifteen minutes, long after Mr. Whitaker had returned."

"Is that true, Dr. Cobb?" asked Riggs.

"Well, yes, but what of it?"

"Where did you go during those fifteen minutes?"

"Nowhere. Just to my room."

"Fifteen minutes is more than ample time to kill someone."

"How dare you?" retorted Cobb. "I was indisposed, that's all. Stokes and the Franks girl were alone the whole time…for hours. Smythe was alone half the evening. Why are you making such a fuss over ten minutes?"

"Minutes make the difference in a murder investigation, Dr. Cobb."

"St. John and Whitaker were gone longer than that later—after the lightning and downed tree."

"When was that?"

"Not much later," said Shelby. "We heard a great crash. Mr. Whitaker said a tree had been struck by lightning. He and Mr. St. John went to investigate."

"How long were they gone?"

"Whitaker returned first, maybe five or six minutes later," said Cobb. "And remember," he added, glancing toward the two women, "—he said that he heard voices in Barribault's apartment."

"I thought he just said he heard him talking on the phone."

"I remember distinctly—he said *voices*."

"In any event," said Riggs, noting it in his book, "that establishes the fact that Barribault was still alive then."

"*If* you take Whitaker's word for it," rejoined Cobb. "He and St. John had parted by then, so no one else heard the alleged voices or phone call."

"If he had been on the phone to one of his staff or groundskeeper about the storm," said Dame Meyerson, "they would be able to corroborate it."

"No one has mentioned a call from Barribault that night," said Riggs. "We'll have to keep open the possibility that there was someone else in his room. We will check the phone records as well. At the time this took place, St. John was still missing from your group?"

"No, now I remember," said Shelby. "Father Smythe also left when they were checking about the tree. Mr. St. John returned five or so minutes after Mr. Whitaker."

"It was odd, too," said Dame Meyerson. "He said he'd been out of the house, but his clothes were dry. I admit that by then my head was a little light, but as I recall it was raining quite hard. Not even his hair was wet…and he came back from upstairs not downstairs, though he seemed perfectly composed. Then of all things, Father Smythe came back and joined us yet again — acting very strange I thought, his mood completely changed."

"Yes, but only long enough to pop in and depart again for a third time," said Shelby.

"It sounds like he was behaving strangely all evening?"

"He was, but he complained of having too much to drink just like me," said Dame Meyerson.

"Eventually we had all pretty much had enough," said Cobb. "It was eleven-thirty. I looked at my watch and told everyone what time it was, and we finally broke up. Dame Meyerson left on Whitaker's arm, and Miss Fitzpatrick and I followed."

"And Mr. St. John?" said Riggs.

"He remained behind. He said he was coming momentarily."

"But none of you actually saw him leave?"

The three shook their heads.

* * *

When the three were gone, Riggs leaned back in his chair and closed his eyes. Everyone, it seemed, had opportunity. At some point in the evening *every* one of the eight had been alone — in the case of Fitzpatrick and Meyerson, but briefly, yet nevertheless alone. And where in this baffling case was the *motive*?

After what he had just heard, his delay in returning to the game, staying after the others left…his money was still on St. John. But Whitaker…Stokes…young Franks — there remained questions surrounding their movements too. And the priest Smythe had by all accounts acted oddly that night too. What had *he* been up to during the time no one saw him?

Riggs drew in a deep breath and opened his eyes. *All right, Father Smythe,* he thought to himself, *what secrets have you been keeping from me?*

He rose and left the room. After receiving no reply to the knock on Smythe's door, he found Sgt. Simmons downstairs at the front entrance.

"Any idea where the good Father Smythe has got to, Sergeant?" he asked.

"Yes, sir. He came out about an hour ago. He's in the rose garden. I'm keeping an eye on him."

"Good man."

Riggs found Smythe, as advertised, in the rose garden. He was seated on a stone bench, head slightly bowed, to all appearances deep in thought.

Riggs approached slowly. Smythe made no move or gesture to indicate that he was aware of his presence in the least. Finally Riggs cleared his throat.

Smythe started slightly, sat up straight, and turned toward the sound.

"Oh...Mr. Riggs, I am sorry—I didn't hear you."

"It is I who should apologize," rejoined Riggs. "I am afraid I startled you."

"Think nothing of it," smiled Smythe. "Just absorbed in my own thoughts. Actually, I was praying—occupational pastime, you know. But please—were you looking for me? What can I do for you?"

"Yes, I was. I wondered if you would mind a few questions?"

"Not at all. The sooner you are able to solve this case the better for all concerned. Actually, that is one of the things I was praying about."

"What specifically, Father?"

"I was praying for you, Inspector."

"For me?"

"I was praying that God would give you wisdom and discernment to sift and sort through all the confusing aspects of this case, and solve it speedily."

"I don't know that I like the idea of being prayed for. Police work is based on fact not superstition."

"I would object to your use of the word superstition. Nevertheless, as I say to my doubting friends…what can it hurt?"

"I don't even believe in God. The here and now, that's all there is in my book. We've got to make the best of it we can."

"Ah, Chief Inspector, everyone believes in God, in his or her own way."

"I know a trap when I see one, Father Smythe. You would lure me into a pointless discussion of theology and belief. But I'm a practical man, so I will resist the bait."

Smythe laughed good-naturedly. "At least you are able to see the humor in our differences."

"I hadn't taken you for such a religious man…in that way, I mean—praying and that sort of thing."

"We all have our complexities."

"No doubt. Well, I still need to ask you a few questions," said Riggs.

"Of course, of course. I am happy to help. We need to get this terrible business behind us."

Riggs sat down on a wet and weathered wood chair across the path from Smythe and pulled out his notebook. "I've been speaking with some of the others," he began, "trying to nail down precisely where everyone was on the night of Mr. Barribault's death."

"And you wonder why I did not participate in the bridge game?" said Smythe.

"That isn't exactly how I planned to phrase it, but something along those lines. I need to account for everyone's whereabouts at all times."

"Originally I left after dinner, a few minutes after Melinda, and went to my room."

"Where you stayed…?"

"I remained there alone for, it must have been a couple of hours. There was a great storm raging outside and I couldn't sleep. So I went to find the others and joined their bridge game for a while."

"And after the tree came down, a few of the men went to investigate and you were still there."

Smythe nodded.

"Then you left again. Did you go to your room a second time?"

"That's correct. Needed a break, you know."

"But you returned to join the others a third time, but only briefly."

"By then it was breaking up. I said my good-nights and went to my room for the last time where finally I was able to get to sleep."

"At no time during the evening did you pay a visit to Hugh Barribault?"

"I wouldn't forget to omit a detail like that, Inspector," laughed Smythe.

"Did you and he have any private discussions during the week as he had had with some of the others?"

"No, I never saw him alone. I presume my time would have come along with the rest. He was, as you remember, setting up meetings with all of us."

"Right." Riggs glanced over his notes, and slowly rose. "I think that will be all for now," he said. "Thank you for your time, and continue to remain available."

"Of course. And if you do not object, Inspector, I will continue to pray."

"Whatever suits you, Father," rejoined Riggs as he walked away. As he made his way toward the house, it occurred to him that such a statement from Mike St. John would grate on him and smack of the overt religiosity he hated. Why did it not irk him in the same way coming from the older Father Smythe? Maybe the man's gray hairs earned him a little respect, or at least the benefit of the doubt.

But prayer wasn't going to solve this case. God wasn't going to help him. At the end of the day, St. John and Smythe were cut from the same clerical cloth. But he couldn't very well arrest Smythe for praying.

* * *

Midway through the afternoon, Riggs received the call he had been waiting for. The medical examiner was ready with his report. After a brief conference with Miss Westbrook, he left the house and walked to his car. He opened the door and saw a book laying on the driver's seat. A folded sheet of paper was sticking out the top of it like a bookmark.

He picked it up, then got in and sat down and opened the leatherbound volume. It was obviously a notebook of some kind, about half of which was filled with handwritten notes, the latter portion blank. The folded sheet had been inserted to indicate the last two pages of entries.

Riggs unfolded the paper.

Detective Chief Inspector, he read in a hand clearly distinct from that of the journal, *I found this notebook beneath one of the davenports of the sitting room on the second floor. I thought you should see it.*

The paper was unsigned.

Whatever it was, Riggs thought, it would have to wait until after his drive to police headquarters in Elgin. He would peruse the thing tonight.

* * *

Meanwhile, during his absence, Detective Sergeant Margaret Westbrook was busy with a few interrogations of her own. She spent a good part of it questioning the domestic staff, from Coombes down to part time gardeners. If a motive or additional information existed from that quarter, however, she had been unable to get a whiff of it.

She left early and stopped in the village on her way home. Having grown up only three miles away in Fordyce, she knew every inch of the town, and had some passing acquaintance with most of its inhabitants as well. Perhaps she could pick up something in passing that they would not share with a stranger.

Maggie had an ice cream, then visited several of the town's shops, walking about casually, making small talk as if she were merely passing the time of day, greeting those she met not as a detective but rather as a friend. They were all more than willing, indeed eager, to talk about the case—nothing this big had happened around here since the queen's visit in 1961.

She went into the Paper Shoppe. There was the familiar face of Keara Long behind the counter.

"Good afternoon, Keara," she said.

"Hello, Maggie," rejoined the shop owner, greeting her with a warm smile. "Hoo's yer mum?"

"Weel, Keara."

"Gie her my best. Tell her tae come an' tak tea w' me one day."

"I'll aye du that, Keara."

"So, ye're on the big case, are ye? We'll one day be seein' yer ain name in the headlines o' all the papers there on the rack aboot oor ain lassie solvin' the mysterious murder o' Cullen Hoose."

"I dinna ken aboot that," laughed Maggie. "I'm aye tryin', ye ken, but maist o' the headlines'll be for the Glasgow terrorists fit was that same day. No one's payin' much attention tae Cullen Hoose, I'm thinkin'."

"Oh, I dinna ken aboot that. Tis a parcel o' 'em stayin' o'er at the Seafield Arms—reporters an' the like."

"Aye, ye're richt there. They're up at the gate at all hours. A body canna gae in or oot wi'oot 'em shoutin' a' at once. But fin there's headlines tae be got my chief likes tae keep them for himsel', ken?"

"Aye, tis a man for ye!"

"Nae yer Alan."

"Ye're in the richt—he's no a man fit seeks the spotlight like the maist o' 'em. So what div ye think—was it one o' the authors, div ye think?"

"I dinna ken, Keara. Had tae be one o' them, or one o' the household, or some one fit snuck in til the hoose an' back oot again. I canna think it o' Coomes or Constance or the twa Waltons, or any o' the Barribault folk like Miss Gordon. Tis a' a puzzle."

"Could a body hae snuck in fae toon div ye think?"

"Ye mind hoo wild it was that nicht. Gien someone drove til the hoose, they might no hae been heard. But then there's the fallen trees, an' they couldna hae won oot wi'oot leavin' their car tae be found trapped inside o' the gates by the trees. An' there wasna a car there the naist mornin'. They might hae walked in, but by nightfall the hoose was locked up, so how'd they get in? Coombes checked ilka door afore he went up til his room for the nicht. He's a stickler, they a' say, for lockin' up at nicht."

"Must hae been one o' the eight, then. But I've aye spoken wi' them a' an' none o' 'em luiks like a killer."

"Tis one o' the first lessons they teach ye," said Maggie. "Criminals luik jist like the rest o' folk. Ye maun luik past the smilin' faces til what's inside. Are ye sayin' they a' came intil the shop?"

"Oh, aye. Some o' 'em but ance or twice, though one o' 'em was in ilka day for his *Daily Telegraph*."

"Wha was that?"

"The priest, an older gentlemen. Alan spoke wi' him maist days. Said he couldna get on wi'oot his news o' the day, an' he was followin' the terrorist story fae the first day o' it."

"Ah, weel...I best be getting' on. Mum'll be waitin' tea for me," said Maggie.

"Dinna forget tae tell her tae come see me."

"I winna, Keara."

FIFTEEN

The Notebook

D.C.I. Richard Riggs drove to the entrance of Cullen House the following morning a few minutes before eleven o'clock hot on the trail of what he hoped would be an arrest. He had read much that interested him in the notebook left in his car, especially the last few pages of entries. He had the coroner's report with the time and cause of death. All taken together, he now had a pretty good idea of what had taken place.

This time he stopped at the gate and got out of his car. Again he was besieged by news people and the ever present crowd from the village anxious for news.

"I have a brief statement," he announced. "I am hopeful that there will be an arrest in the case of Hugh Barribault's murder later today, certainly within forty-eight hours. The coroner has placed the time of death between 10:00 P.M. and midnight on the night of the 26th. The cause of death was poisoning by the joint effects of valerian root and nicotine, probably homemade and introduced into the body intravenously, not by food or drink. The lethal dose of nicotene was injected into his arm through the tip of the quill found attached to his arm when the body was discovered. The valerian root, however, may have been taken previously as a sleep aid."

The group of listening reporters exploded with questions. Riggs waved them off.

"I will answer everything when we know more," he said loudly over the din. He got back into his car and continued through the gates toward the house.

He found all eight authors in the Sitting Room where he had instructed D.S. Westbrook to assemble them at 11:00 A.M. He walked in with a confident flourish, leather notebook in hand.

All heads turned in Riggs's direction.

"Ladies and gentlemen," he said, "I asked Miss Westbrook to gather you together because there have been some developments in the case that I think will be of interest to you all."

Before he could continue, Shelby saw the book he was holding.

"Is that...that *is* my journal!" she said excitedly, rising and coming toward him as if expecting Riggs to hand it to her. "Where did you find it?"

"Never mind where I found it, Miss Fitzpatrick," rejoined Riggs. "If you don't mind, please take your seat."

"But that's my notebook. I've been looking for it for days."

"I know very well what it is, Miss Fitzpatrick. It is in my possession now. Fascinating reading it makes too, I must say."

"You read it!" exclaimed Shelby. "You had no right to do that, Inspector. That journal contains my own private observations. Please, I must insist you give it back to me."

"I shall give it back when I am jolly well ready and not before," retorted Riggs. "I'll thank you not to talk to me in such a voice. Now sit down, Miss Fitzpatrick, before I bring in one of my officers and use force."

"Use force! What...on me?"

"If I have to."

Shelby stood staring, stunned into silence.

"I'm sorry, Inspector," she said after a few seconds. "I didn't mean to sound demanding. All I want is my notebook back. What on earth could you be interested in it for? It's got nothing to do with you or anything."

"On the contrary, Miss Fitzpatrick, it has a great deal to do with our business here."

"In what possible way?"

"I believe it provides us with the identity of Hugh Barribault's murderer."

"You've got to be joking!" laughed Shelby. "The contents of that book have nothing to do with anyone but me. I am conducting research for a book, Inspector. There are hundreds of personality profiles included that go back many years. Besides, it has been missing since before Mr. Barribault's death."

"Yes, well...we shall see about that."

"It certainly gives you no right to talk to *me* like this," rejoined Shelby, getting heated again and unable to comprehend Riggs's tone, "—especially to threaten me?"

"I have every right."

"*What* right?"

"You are a suspect in a murder investigation, Miss Fitzpatrick."

Shelby's mouth dropped.

"A *suspect*?" she said in disbelief.

"More than that, you have become *the* suspect."

"I don't believe what I'm hearing," said Shelby. "On what grounds...what possible motive could I have?"

"There is motive aplenty in what you wrote in here," said Riggs, raising the book toward her.

"I wrote nothing incriminating in the least, toward me...toward anyone."

"Hugh Barribault might disagree, Miss Fitzpatrick. Especially after you tried to blackmail him and he refused."

Shelby's face went white where she stood in the middle of the room. At last she realized how serious the Inspector was. Slowly she wobbled back and crumbled into her chair. There she sat motionless and silent.

"Now then..." said Riggs, lifting the journal, "I will read a few selections so that we all might see your treachery for what it is—"

From where she was seated, D.S. Westbrook sent a glance in Shelby Fitzpatrick's direction. A look of horrified chagrin was apparent on Shelby's pale face.

"—Let me see," Riggs went on, opening the journal and turning to the middle of the book, "ah, yes—here we are, after you arrived here with your colleagues. *It is a most intriguing gathering,*" he began to read. "*All present are obviously talented and skilled, intelligent, good writers, students of people. And yet everyone is on guard as well, sizing up the situation, as well as one another, some trying to impress, others cautious...one sees such a variety of expressions in the eyes, the glances, the subtleties — it is a greenhouse of forced relationship, all of us thrust together in a controlled setting, never having seen one another before and suddenly required by circumstances to relate to one another, competitors in a way as well as colleagues...*

"Curiously, some do not seem afraid of offending our host. JS, for instance, seems determined to offend him at every turn. Others do not care what anyone thinks, whether HB or their fellow authors, as is obvious in the case of young MF and the unceremonious MSJ. Others mask their thoughts and feelings behind various facades, of dry wit (GW), of superior detachment (FDS), or of scholarly hauteur (BC)...

As Riggs read, a few heads turned in Shelby's direction, obviously not appreciative of having been the object of her observations.

"But let us move along," said Riggs, turning another few pages. "Some of the more recent entries are more to my liking. Yes...here we are. *I have been watching the many interactions with great interest,*" he read. "*Supposedly we all arrived here as strangers to ourselves and to HB. But having spent many years observing people and trying to understand what makes them tick, my instinct tells me that we are not all the strangers we appear. Though I have no proof, I am reasonably certain that among our number are some who have crossed paths before. Not with one another (at least I see no indication of such). But in at least two cases, I am convinced that my fellow authors knew HB prior to this week.*

"*If true, More important, however, than the subtle personal machinations, what does this fact make of the contest itself. Did HB know when selecting them? Did they enter the contest thinking they would receive favorable treatment because of prior association with HB? These questions puzzle me. Does this make the contest a sham — supposedly objective but potentially exposed as treating certain individuals different than the rest? There exists the possibility that HB did not know their identities ahead of time. The judging of entries was supposedly conducted blind, without names divulged until after selections were complete. When did HB become aware of these identities — that is the intriguing question. What did he know and when? And were this revelation to be made public, how would that effect*

HB's plans and the future of Barribault House? A cloud of suspicion at the outset could doom everything.

"HB himself is a fascinating psychological study. On our very first night together, his identification and greeting of aka JS was carried off as if meeting for the first time. But the countenance had drawn my attention before. I saw a look in the eyes of knowing. Those eyes told a story of intrigue—and unless I miss my guess, from many years earlier. I am convinced this is not their first meeting. A similar chemistry is at work in the other case, though it seems curiously one-sided. As improbable as it seems, I cannot tell if HB is even aware of it. Yet how could a prior relationship be known to one and not the other?

"In any event, the relational mix in these two cases is fascinating and compelling, and obviously impacts not merely the contest itself, but subsequent interactions between us all. If HB was not aware of these identities, but is aware of them now, how will that effect his decisions regarding their books and further involvement in his company?

"Then there is the fascinating MF. Is she somehow involved? If so...the connection escapes me entirely.

"Nor is it merely a prior meeting...there is more to it. It is how JS has watched him all week. I am convinced something more is involved—something powerful, a secret of import that HB would not want to come out. In short, the situation seems rife with possibilities for the potential of blackmail—"

Sounds of astonishment went round the room. Riggs glanced up from the journal. All eyes were riveted on him as if he were reading from Mike St. John's mystery.

"And what would HB do if blackmail were attempted?" Riggs continued. "Would he cancel the contract? Would the gamble be worth it for mere revenge? It hardly seems likely. Yet whatever secret binds them together from the past, revenge might indeed be a more powerful incentive than financial reward and fame and book sales. Money, sex, power, greed, revenge...these are among the strongest psychological motivations of humankind. And if I am right in my observations...where does that place me? I might blackmail them both!

But I think I will satisfy myself with HB. He is so filthy rich he will not miss a few hundred thousand for my silence, to keep his reputation intact and whatever secrets he has from coming to light. I will look for an opportunity to approach him. It may be in the end that *my fiction book will not be that for which this gathering proves of the greatest benefit for me. HB has secrets that I alone now know...how much will he pay for me to keep them quiet?"*

Riggs paused and again glanced about the room. His eyes came to rest on Shelby where she sat with an expression of total disbelief.

"I think that is enough for our purposes," he said after a moment. "It is my contention, Miss Fitzpatrick, that Hugh Barribault not only refused your attempt to shake him down...he was furious, not only by your attempt to blackmail him, but also at your use of his forum to carry out your own private research project. He accused you of accepting his kindness and hospitality on false pretences. After your little game did not succeed, he demanded that you depart at once, leaving your check for £100,000 behind, and voluntarily withdraw your book from consideration from publication and yourself from any further connection to himself. The two of you argued. He gave you time to think about it before he took matters into his own hands, turned you over to the police, and made your dismissal public. That's when you began to formulate your plan."

Shelby was too flabbergasted as she listened to utter a sound, other than a faint gasping for breath.

"After the bridge game broke up that night," Riggs went on, "you snuck up to his room with a bottle of expensive wine pretending to make amends with feigned apologies. You offered him a drink as a peace offering, with wine you had spiked with valerian root, which, added to what he had already taken had the effect of a Mickey Finn. When he fell over unconscious, as a symbolic gesture of your rage at being ousted from the literary world of your dreams, you took the quill you had stolen from Mr. St. John's room and whose nib you had filed to a razor-sharp point, then you drove it into Barribault's arm, and squeezed out the poison ink into his bloodstream."

Riggs paused as if for maximum dramatic impact.

"Shelby Fitzpatrick," he said after a moment, "I am arresting you for the murder of Hugh Barribault."

He took a step toward her, when an unexpected voice broke the heavy silence.

"If I might be permitted a question, Inspector—" interrupted Mike St. John.

Riggs turned toward him, obviously perturbed.

"—how did Miss Fitzpatrick happen to have the quill at the time...and merely as a point of correction, you recall that it wasn't *my* quill that was found with Mr. Barribault."

"Right. I meant to say the quill she had stolen from Mr. Thompson's shop," rejoined Riggs, recovering himself. "As for how the quill happened to be there, she obviously brought it to show him, probably as a distraction to throw him off guard. Perhaps she told him she had bought the second quill. She might have claimed to have brought it to him as a gift. She had it with her, that's all that matters.—Now, Miss Fitzpatrick," he said, walking toward her, "I'm afraid I will have to ask you to come with me."

Six of her fellow authors and one young Detective Sergeant watched in silent disbelief as Shelby stood and glanced around helplessly as Riggs took hold of her arm and led her across the room. Mike St. John, however, rose to his feet and hurried after them.

"Inspector," he said as Riggs approached the door, "I wonder if I might have a moment with Miss Fitzpatrick...in private?"

Riggs stopped and eyed him questioningly.

"Why?"

"I *am* a minister, Inspector."

"You want to offer spiritual solace?" Riggs asked, cracking a sarcastic smile.

Mike did not reply, allowing his silence to be taken for a reply in the affirmative.

Riggs let out a sigh of resignation. "All right, you can have five minutes," he said. "But remember that I am keeping my eyes on you too, St. John. Don't think I've forgotten."

He led them through the door and to a small adjacent parlor.

"You can talk in there," he said. "I'll be waiting here. Five minutes, St. John."

* * *

Mike closed the door behind them as he and Shelby entered the small private lounge. At last Shelby's annoyance and disbelief gave way.

"If you intend to offer me spiritual solace," she began, taking her anger out on the nearest and most accessible target, "believe me, I'm in no mood—"

Mike raised a hand and shook his head gently.

"Have no fear, Miss Fitzpatrick," he said. "I never offer spiritual counsel unless it is asked for."

"What then? Why do you want to talk to me?"

"Merely to say that I know you are innocent, and to encourage you, if you can, to say nothing. Go along with what must seem like a great outrage for now."

"It doesn't appear I have much choice, does it?" she retorted, shaking her head in frustration. "That Riggs is really a piece of work!"

"He does tend to be a little impulsive," smiled Mike, lowering his voice and glancing toward the closed door. "Why don't we sit down over here?" he said, indicating two chairs a little further away.

When they were seated, he continued.

"I spent a night in Inspector Riggs's jail. I won't say it was pleasant, but the time will pass. I hope you will not even have to be there an entire day. Put up with it without arguing. Don't give the inspector additional ammunition against you. I will do all I can to make sure you are out as soon as possible."

"What can you do?"

"You would be surprised what a minister can get away with."

"But he suspects you too."

"Temporarily, but this too, I believe, shall pass. Unless I badly misread her, I am convinced that we have an ally in Miss Westbrook."

"How so?"

"I was watching her as Riggs laid out his imaginary case against you. Her face registered as much disbelief as yours. The moment he said, *Miss Fitzpatrick, I am arresting you*, her eyes flashed with fire for the briefest of seconds. I saw genuine anger. She knows her boss has made a huge blunder. His theory has too many holes to be believed. There are no witnesses to your supposed argument with Barribault. You were never seen going to him in private. Nothing connects you to the quill. I would have heard if you had left your room after we had all retired that night. No, you have nothing to worry about—Miss Westbrook will not let this charge stick."

Shelby began to calm. She looked down at the floor for a moment, more than a little taken aback by Mike's gracious manner and his obvious kindness toward her.

"I hope you don't mind my asking," she said, "but why are you so sure I am innocent? And why would you risk your own standing with Inspector Riggs...for me. I mean, I haven't exactly been very nice to you."

Mike smiled. "I'm not bothered by that," he said. "People have to get to know one another. Sometimes it's a slow and bumpy process. Trust isn't something that comes all at once. I know I have rough edges. I know I haven't been your favorite person here. Sometimes it takes people a while with me. But my motives are mostly good. Usually people figure that out in time. As to why I know you are innocent, there are two reasons. One, do you remember that evening we were discussing which of two books we would vote to publish?"

"Shelby nodded.

"I knew then that you were one who could allow logic and reason to outweigh personal opinion. Your esteem for Barribault's vision above your own ideas tells me that you would not murder to gain your own ends."

"And the second reason?"

"I saw your innocence on your face that night Mr. Barribault was killed...when we all wandered out of our rooms into the corridor wondering what had woken us up."

A strange light came over Shelby's face. It was followed by the hint of a smile.

"What did you see on my face?" she asked.

"I saw genuine surprise...question...uncertainty," replied Mike. "That may seem a small thing, but I believe it is very significant. Like you, Shelby—you don't mind if I call you Shelby? At this point the formality of *Miss* and *Mister* seems a little strained."

"I agree," nodded Shelby.

"What I was going to say is, like you, my profession requires that I study people. You keep a journal of your impressions, and—"

"Oh…I *am* sorry about what I wrote about you! I was just—"

"It's nothing, forget it," said Mike, brushing it away with another wave of his hand. "I thought it was funny, and I *am* a klutz. My point was that both a psychologist and a minister have to be able to see beneath of the surface of what makes people tick. Because our rooms sit nearly opposite one another, and because we both came out of our doors at almost the same instant, pulling on robes and rubbing eyes and trying to shake ourselves awake, I realized I was observing your very *first* reaction. When I saw that look on your face, it was like a window into your soul, to use a shopworn phrase. I *knew* that you genuinely had no idea what was going on. It was not a look you could have faked. As the night progressed, and we all went upstairs…then we found Mr. Barribault…of course there were many comments and exclamations and we were all shocked…or pretending to be…through all that I never saw the same look on anyone else's face that I had seen on yours. At this point I have no idea who killed Hugh Barribault. It could have been Coombes for all I know—the disgruntled butler. I am only *absolutely* sure of two individuals in this entire *ménage* that has been thrown together…*you* did not kill Hugh Barribault, nor did I."

"There is another possibility," said Shelby. "What if *you* are the murderer, Mr. St. John?

"And this is all a ruse?"

She nodded.

"Then we would be pitting my skill at deceiving you against your skill as a psychologist to see through my charade. It would indeed be a delightful game of wits—an interesting dilemma for us both. But I trust you will weigh in on the side of character in the end."

"Even your saying that might be part of a ploy to win my confidence."

Mike shrugged and smiled. He had said enough. She would have to decide if she could trust him on her own.

"Well, Mr. St. John," said Shelby, forcing an embarrassed smile, "all I can say is that I'm grateful you are willing to try to help me."

Anything else either might have planned to say was cut short by a peremptory knock on the door, followed by the brusque entry of Detective Chief Inspector Riggs to take charge of his prisoner.

* * *

With Shelby Fitzpatrick securely in the back seat of his car under the watchful eye of Sgt. Simmons, Inspector Riggs walked back into the house and up the stairs to the Sitting Room where the six remaining authors, now rejoined by Mike St. John, were talking feverishly amongst themselves. Sighs of relief were mingled with many shakings of the head and numerous variants of, "I would never have expected it of *her*!"

"If I might just have your attention for a minute more," said Riggs as he walked into the commotion of discussionary astonishment.

All heads turned in his direction.

"All that remains for the case to be solved to my satisfaction," he said, "is a confession, which I am confident will be forthcoming this afternoon. While I am seeing to that, I will want final statements from each of you. There are a few loose ends to tie up. Assuming Miss Westbrook is able to get that business concluded today, by tomorrow you will all be free to resume your lives. I assume there will be aspects of this nasty business you will have to attend to with the Barribault people. That is of course between you and them. But as far as our investigation goes, you will be free to go. You will be notified if and when a trial date is set, presuming we are not successful in obtaining a confession. As you discovered the body as a group together, you will all no doubt be called as witnesses. That is all...and I thank you for your cooperation."

Riggs turned and strode from the room.

Sixteen

The Detective Sergeant

Margaret Westbrook hardly slept all night.

She turned over for what must have been the thirtieth time and once more looked at the clock on her nightstand:

4:07.

It was no use. More sleep was impossible. She might as well get up, shower, dress, fix herself a strong pot of tea, and plan out her moves for the day ahead, which could make or break her career as a police detective. If things went badly, *she* might be the one in jail by day's end!

She couldn't think about that now. She knew what she had to do. She had known most of the night.

From the moment she had walked into Cullen House and met the cast of characters in this extraordinary case, the American psychologist had occupied the very bottom of her list of potential suspects. Even Riggs, she thought, obtuse as the man could be, would never turn and look seriously in Fitzpatrick's direction. Her sudden arrest yesterday had taken Maggie so by surprise she had hardly been able to utter a peep for five minutes. The rest of the day, finalizing the interrogations of the other seven as well as a few on the household and publishing staff, passed like a tedious blur of futility. By then the statements were becoming a little too scripted, too carefully thought about, too conveniently self-protective.

244

It was not the first time Maggie Westbrook had seen her boss distracted by a wild goose chase. He usually managed to wander back toward the truth. But this situation was different. He had given all the other principle players in the drama leave to go home and return to their lives. It wasn't that they would be unable to contact them later. But once everyone was gone, the dynamic changed. Stories and alibis became more difficult to check. Evidence could be destroyed.

This was the time, when they were still all together at the setting of the murder, to get to the bottom of it. By tomorrow, with the Eight scattered to the four winds, it might be too late.

Maggie slipped on her robe and stole quietly into the kitchen. Trying not to disturb her sleeping parents, she put on the kettle for tea.

Even before she got out of bed, she knew she had to keep the authors here for another day at least. She would have to be sneaky about it, and do whatever she did behind Riggs' back. If she blew it, her ploy might cost her her job.

By five o'clock she was dressed and ready, drinking a third cup of tea and waiting for the newspaper. At five-thirty she telephoned Sgt. Simmons at home.

"I'm sorry to wake you so early, Sergeant," she said. "It's Maggie Westbrook. Is any of your detail coming to the house today...Cullen House."

"No, Maggie," replied Simmons sleepily. "Riggs sent us all home yesterday."

"That's what I thought. I'm sorry, Robbie, but I need a man or two today...early."

"How early, Maggie?"

"By seven."

"Ow—" Simmons groaned. "How about one for seven, another at eight?"

"We'll manage that. I'll be there at 6:30 myself, just in case."

"What's it all about, Maggie."

"The case isn't quite as solved as the Detective Chief Inspector thinks. I want to make sure no one has an early getaway planned. I'm reasonably certain none of them would take off in the middle of the night—it wouldn't look good. But I have the feeling there might be some activity around daybreak. I want to intercept it."

"All right, I'll be in at seven."

"Thanks, Robbie. But not a word to Detective Chief Inspector Riggs until I have something solid to take to him. By the way, do you know what he is planning for today?"

"Not really, only that he's got a meeting in Elgin with some of the brass from the Council office.

"Do you know what time it is scheduled?"

"Ten, I think."

"That should give us time, then."

"You'll be for it if he finds out, and me too for going along."

"Just say you were following orders. As for me, I'm willing to risk it—as long as I'm able to find something solid before Riggs asks for my badge."

* * *

It was still dark at 6:17, under a thick covering of clouds, as Detective Sergeant Margaret Westbrook proceeded quietly through the iron gates of Cullen House and slowly drove along the half mile entry to the imposing and historic building. As she approached, the entire north wing was black. A few lights burned in the domestic quarters and kitchen area, as well as in two or three of the second floor guestrooms. By degrees the great house was already coming awake for the day.

She drove past the kitchen wing and around to the row of garages at the back of the house. As she had half suspected, one garage door stood open. In front of it stood an expensive dark blue Mercedes, boot open with one suitcase already inside. Somebody was obviously planning an early departure. She hadn't come a moment too soon.

Maggie pulled up behind the Mercedes, stopped, got out, and waited.

A minute or two later she heard voices from inside. A door opened on the landing above. Two figures in overcoats, talking as they came, descended the outside flight of stairs to the paved terrace surrounding the garages.

"...such a relief to get back to the real world..." a woman's voice was saying.

"...an interesting interlude, I must say," rejoined the man with her. "Unpleasant of course, but grist for the mill of our memoirs, what?"

"Actually, my husband has been talking about writing his memoirs about the diplomatic—" the woman began, then stopped as she reached the bottom of the flight of steps. She stood gaping, a small suitcase in her hand.

There stood Detective Sergeant Westbrook..

"Good morning, Dame Meyerson," she said cheerily. "Hello, Father Smythe," she added, glancing part way up the staircase to Father Smythe where he stood holding a large suitcase. "The two of you are planning to get an early start, I see."

"Yes," replied Dame Meyerson, "Father Smythe graciously offered to drive me into Aberdeen. There I will get a flight to London later this afternoon. I decided to take him up on it."

"And you, Father Smythe?" asked Maggie.

"Back to Edinburgh for a few days, then I'll push on south."

"You're both up early."

"Four hour drive," said Smythe. "I like to get on the road before the school traffic, you know. If you don't mind, this bag is heavy—I'd like to get it the rest of the way down."

"Of course," said Maggie. She and Dame Meyerson stepped aside and Smythe descended the rest of the stairs. "You didn't want to get Coombes to help you?"

"Didn't want to bother the poor man. Probably not even up yet."

Smythe lugged the case to the open boot at the back of his car and hoisted it in with the other. "I think that's me," he said, turning to Dame Meyerson. "Do you have anything else upstairs?"

"No, this is it. I believe I am ready."

"Then Miss Westbrook," said Smythe with a nod and a smile, "it seems it is time for us to say our farewells. It was very good of you to take the trouble to come and see us off."

"Actually, Father Smythe," said Maggie, glancing back and forth between the two, "I had no idea you would be trying to leave so soon."

"Then, why—"

"I came early in the event that any of you *might* be planning an early departure. I'm afraid I come as the bearer of unfortunate news…that is that you are not going to be able to leave just yet."

"What…why not?" exclaimed Smythe. "This is an outrage!"

"You are joking, Miss Westbrook," said Dame Meyerson, forcing a nervous laugh. "Please tell me this is just some quirky bit of Scots humor."

"I am afraid not, Dame Meyerson. I apologize for the inconvenience. I am sure we can get Coombes to help return your bags to your room. But the fact is, there may be new developments in the case very soon. I am afraid I am going to have to insist that you remain on the premises."

"What kind of new developments?"

"I am afraid I cannot say at this time."

"Where is Inspector Riggs?" said Smythe in a tone that sounded hostile.

"He will not be here until later," answered Maggie calmly.

"I demand to speak with Inspector Riggs…now. I will not be ordered about by a damned underling. If he is not here, then get him on the telephone for me, or there will be hell to pay. I warn you!"

"I'm afraid that will not be possible, Father Smythe," said Maggie. "Again, I sincerely apologize for this inconvenience. Now if you will please both go back to your rooms, or perhaps breakfast has been set out by now. And, Father Smythe," she added, approaching him, "if you would be so good as to turn over your car keys to me…merely as a precaution, you understand."

"You impudent little—" began Smythe, his eyes glowing with unspoken wrath that it was well did not find verbal expression. "You will hear about this!" he said, slapping the keys into her outstretched hand. "You will all hear about it!"

He stormed away toward the house, and was followed in a slightly more dignified fashion by Dame Meyerson.

"Be in the Sitting Room at 10:30," Maggie called after them. "More will be explained at that time."

* * *

Left alone in the darkness outside the Cullen House garages, Maggie Westbrook let out a long sigh.

Well that went about as badly as possible, she thought to herself. She hoped the others would express their thoughts with a little less ire.

She walked to the front of the house in the darkness of the morning to await the arrival of Sgt. Simmons. He arrived fifteen minutes later. When she had apprised him of what to do, Maggie went inside. There she found the beginnings of activity in the Breakfast Room. She fixed herself another cup of tea and sat down to await the arrival of what were sure to be more disgruntled authors. What she really needed was to find a way to have a conversation with Mike St. John alone, without attracting attention to it.

The first to make an appearance after the staff had finished setting out the breakfast trays was Jessica Stokes.

"I thought we were all done with you people," she said, glancing without a smile toward Maggie.

"I am afraid not," said Maggie, trying to sound cheerful. "It turns out that there are some additional ends to tie up. We will be meeting in the Sitting Room at 10:30."

Jessica did not reply, and went dabbling about at the sideboards to all appearance as if she were alone in the room.

About 7:30 Maggie heard voices coming down the stairs. A minute later Graham Whitaker and Melinda Franks walked in. Maggie rose from the table where she had been sitting and walked toward them.

"Good morning, Mr. Whitaker…Miss Franks," she said.

"Detective Westbrook," said Whitaker, returning her smile. "You are here early. I didn't expect to see you today at all."

"I am afraid I have found it necessary to convene another meeting," rejoined Maggie. "I know it is inconvenient for everyone, but I would appreciate your being in the Sitting Room at 10:30."

"I had no plans," said Whitaker.

"I'm not going anywhere," sighed Melinda. "At least not today."

"Good, thank you," nodded Maggie, and wandered toward the door.

So far so good, she thought. If she could just get lucky and nab Mike St. John alone. She waited a few minutes in the corridor until the sounds of irate conversation drifted down from above. Quickly she ducked behind an adjacent column as Father Smythe and Dame Meyerson descended the stairway, Smythe still expressing his supreme annoyance at this interruption to their plans. They entered the Breakfast Room. There a wider audience gave yet further expression to his reaction to the ill treatment to which he was being subjected.

Alone in the corridor again, Maggie realized her chances of encountering Mike St. John next had increased to fifty percent. On stealthy step she dashed silently up the first flight of stairs, paused, then hurried up to the second floor just in time to hear a door opening down the hall in the direction of the guest quarters. She peeked around the edge of the corner.

It was Mike!

She ran toward him. "Quick, back into your room!" she whispered.

Taken by surprise, Mike hesitated. A moment later he found himself being dragged by the sleeve back into the room he had just left. A quick finger to her lips told him Maggie wanted silence.

They waited, perhaps two minutes. At length a door opened elsewhere along the corridor. Heavy steps came toward them, then slowly retreated. Maggie opened Mike's door a crack, in time to see Briscoe Cobb's back disappearing down the stairs. She waited another minute, then turned toward Mike.

"I needed to talk to you alone," she said.

"Is it about Shelby?" Mike asked.

"It is about everyone, including Miss Fitzpatrick."

"She is innocent, Miss Westbrook."

"Maggie, remember?"

"Sorry," smiled Mike.

"Yes, I know she is innocent. Our only problem is how to prove it."

"Is Inspector Riggs—"

"He has no idea I am here. I am running a great risk, but I hope the three of us—you and I and Miss Fitzpatrick—may be able to uncover enough to convince even him. Why do you believe so strongly that she is innocent?"

Mike recounted what he had told Shelby about the gathering in the corridor the night of the murder.

"Do you have any such strong convictions about who *may* be responsible?"

"No," replied Mike. "Honestly, having become so well acquainted with my fellow authors this week, I cannot believe it of any of them. Neither can I believe Hugh Barribault capable of suicide. I am probably too much an optimist to make a very good detective. I confess myself completely stumped. It seems to me that someone must have come in from the outside."

"I haven't forgotten that possibility," nodded Maggie. "Well," she added, "that is about it for now. I just needed to have an ally on the inside. I will be off shortly to Buckie to talk to Miss Fitzpatrick. One more thing. I need you to go down to the Breakfast Room now. Don't let on that you have seen me. We have to play out one more little charade."

Mike nodded, then left his room a second time where Maggie waited.

She walked into the Breakfast Room three or four minutes later, where conversation among the seven about recent developments was spirited. "Ah, good morning...Dr. Cobb, Mr. St. John—you are the only two I have not yet seen."

"If it is about this morning's meeting," said Cobb, "believe me, we know all about it."

"And you, Mr. St. John?" she added, turning toward Mike.

"Yes," smiled Mike. "We have all been vigorously discussing this change in the agenda. I will be there."

"Good. Then, I shall see you all at 10:30."

* * *

With a ten o'clock meeting in Elgin, Maggie assumed Detective Chief Inspector Riggs would be on his way out of Buckie no later than 9:15. She was positioned in her car down the street from the station at 8:45. A few minutes before nine, she saw

Riggs leave the station for his car, then drive away. She waited another five minutes, then completed the short remaining distance and went inside.

"Good morning, Alec," she said.

"Hi ya, Maggie," returned Sgt. Murray. "You just missed the Detective Chief Inspector. Are you in on that meeting with him in Elgin?"

"Not a peon like me!" laughed Maggie. "It's for the brass. I'm only here to do some follow up questioning of Miss Fitzpatrick."

"You know where she is," said Murray rising with key in hand to lead her back to the cell.

Maggie waited as he unlocked the door, then walked inside. She nodded to an obviously tired Shelby Fitzpatrick lying on the bed. Maggie waited until Sgt. Murray had returned to his post and they were alone.

Shelby rose and swung her feet over to the floor as Maggie sat down on the far end of the bed.

"I am sorry for this fiasco," she said shaking her head. "I know it's not pleasant here, but you will be out soon. I want to ask you some questions about your journal. Then I may need your help to prove your innocence."

"Obviously anything," sighed Shelby. "I hardly see what I can do from in here."

"I didn't mean in here. But we'll get to that in a minute. First tell me about your journal."

"There isn't much to tell, really," said Shelby. "It is simply a collection of my observations of people. I have been working for years on a psychological research project which I hope to publish one day. I take notes all the time. I admit I was using this opportunity to profile the others at the House, including Mr. Barribault. The uniqueness of the situation, a small group of strangers being brought together as we were, was a unique setting. I was hopeful that it would give me some unusual personal profiles I had not seen before."

"Did Mr. Barribault read it, as Inspector Riggs suggested?"

"I don't know," sighed Shelby. "It went missing days ago."

"Did you and he have a private meeting where it was discussed?"

"No. Everything Inspector Riggs said about that was pure fiction?"

"You did not see Mr. Barribault the night of the bridge game?"

"Not after he left right after dinner."

"And when the game broke up?"

"I went straight to bed."

"You neither saw nor heard anyone else?"

"Nothing...until I was awakened by the crash that brought us all out of our rooms."

Maggie drew in a deep breath. "All right," she said, "now we come to the question I have been waiting to ask you for almost twenty-four hours."

She paused again and looked into Shelby's face with a serious expression.

"I know I am young," she said. "I know you are an experienced psychologist who has made a lifetime's study of people. But I like to think of detective work as a sort of psychological chess game too. You have to be able to see people, see *inside* them...see what they are telling you in subtle ways...and what they are *not* telling you. Perhaps our two professions are not so very unlike each other."

"Funny," smiled Shelby. "Mr. St. John said something very much like that to me yesterday, about *his* profession and mine."

"I have been speaking to Mr. St. John this morning too. About you, in fact—trying to figure out how we can get you out of here."

"Thank you—I appreciate that very much!" added Shelby with an ironic laugh. "He told me after his stint in this place that he would not want to make a habit of it. Neither would I!"

"You won't have to."

"So what question did you want to ask me?"

"I am almost embarrassed to say," said Maggie. "You are an experienced psychologist, I am a novice detective whose boss thinks I am a dunce, but...I thought, when I was listening to Inspector Riggs read from your journal yesterday, I saw in your face something I think that you were *not* saying. And I think I was reading you correctly."

"A psychologist psychoanalyzed by a detective," smiled Shelby. "That is turning the tables!"

"All right then—my question is this: Did *you* write everything in your book that Detective Chief Inspector Riggs read?"

Shelby smiled. "You are a shrewd one. You saw that in my face?"

"I think so."

"Well, you were reading my reaction correctly. No, I did not write it all. All of a sudden I was shocked to hear him reading out of *my* journal, supposedly in *my* handwriting, what were indeed very incriminating words that were completely new to me."

"Why did you say nothing, and allow him to arrest you without a word of defense?"

"You may have seen me unconsciously glance around the room. Suddenly I felt very isolated and alone. I didn't know whom to trust. I wasn't afraid, exactly...but I realized I needed to let the thing play out and think very seriously about what I said and did from that point on. We call it keeping your powder dry. I didn't want to say too much too soon. Inspector Riggs was obviously misreading the whole thing. I didn't know at that point where you stood. As far as my fellow authors were concerned, it had to have been one of them who took my journal and then added to it. They had all seen me with it. I made no secret of it. So I felt vulnerable and isolated. I realized I'd better shut up until I figured out what to do. Better *not* to divulge that the words weren't mine just yet, I thought."

"I think you were wise. In any event, it is just as I suspected. I knew from the look on your face that something fishy was going on. You have no idea who it might have been?"

"None."

"When did you first miss the notebook?"

"A couple days before the murder. I don't know the exact moment. It simply dawned on me one afternoon that I couldn't remember where I laid it. I never saw it again until Inspector Riggs walked in yesterday carrying it in his hand. And there's something else too. I can't exactly be sure, I would have to see it...but something seemed missing in what I had written, or at least in what he read.—Where is my notebook...could you get it?"

"I'm not sure. Inspector Riggs may have kept it, but—wait just a minute."

She rose and went to the door. "Sgt. Murray!" she called. A moment later the sergeant came down the hall. They spoke in low tones, then he let her out and they disappeared together.

When Maggie returned ten minutes later, she was holding Shelby's journal.

She said nothing until she was inside the cell, and Sgt. Murray had returned to the front office and they were again alone.

"Where was it!" asked Shelby excitedly.

"In the evidence box," replied Maggie. "We need to go over this thoroughly and see if we can get to the bottom of what's going on."

She sat down beside Shelby. "This note was folded inside," she said, showing Shelby the paper addressed to Inspector Riggs. "Do you recognize the writing?"

"Not in the least," said Shelby shaking her head.

"Would you know the writing of all the Eight?"

"I think I would. Actually, I am a bit of a handwriting buff as well—an occupational sideline, you might say. But this is not a hand I have seen before."

Maggie handed her the journal. "All right," she said, "what do you see here?"

Shelby flipped open the pages to the final entries and glanced over them quickly. Slowly she began shaking her head.

"This is really remarkable," she said. "If I didn't know better I would think I *had* written these last two pages."

"But you didn't?"

"No. Whoever forged my hand knew what they were doing. This is the work of an expert. It would take an actual handwriting professional to know the difference. No wonder it fooled Inspector Riggs. It would fool me if I didn't know better! But wait...what's this?" she said, turning through the pages and examining some of the writing yet more carefully."

"What is it?" asked Maggie.

"A page is missing," said Shelby. "Look...right here—you can see the edge where it was torn out. That's the last page *I* wrote. It's gone, and that's where the forgery begins."

"All right—we need to go over this with a fine tooth comb, starting with your arrival in Cullen. We have to assume that whoever absconded with your journal read it all, and somehow saw in it the opportunity to frame you."

"I can't imagine that anything I wrote about anyone could have—"

"Somewhere in this book, Shelby—whether in what you wrote or what someone else wrote—are the clues that may help us solve this thing. We have to find them. Then I am going to get you out of here and we are going back to Cullen House together. I have an assignment for you. I need you to carry out a little sleuthing on my behalf."

"Can you do that—can you just release me?" said Shelby.

"Just watch me! True, if Inspector Riggs finds out before we come up with something, I'll be toast. But I intend to risk it. Now let's see what this journal of yours can tell us."

SEVENTEEN

The Search

At fifteen minutes past ten, Detective Sergeant Westbrook was speeding back in the direction of Cullen with Shelby Fitzpatrick at her side. Sergeant Murray had been more than a little reluctant to release the prisoner into Maggie's custody. But the paperwork was in order. She had signed all the necessary forms in triplicate. Most importantly, she outranked him.

Riggs was certain to hit the roof. That reality concerned them both, though for different reasons. Murray was praying that Riggs would not return to the Buckie office before his shift was over at noon. Maggie hoped she would have something to placate her boss by the time she saw him again. Otherwise, she might be looking for a new job by this time tomorrow.

On the way Maggie explained her plan.

"I don't know how much of Cullen House you have explored," she said, "but we were given detailed floor plans when the investigation began. There is a back set of stairs leading from the ground floor near the kitchen up to the third floor. It has direct access into some of the rooms adjoining the stairwell. It was once a servant's stairway, I believe. I will drive in by the farm road entrance and let you off at the back of the house. I hope you will be able to get through the kitchen and to this stairway without being seen."

"If one of the staff sees me, they are sure to cause trouble," said Shelby. "They all loved Hugh Barribault. They have likely heard by now that I killed him."

"We'll have to risk it. If they question you, simply say that I released you and they can ask me about it. Don't give them the chance to oppose you. Just keep going. Go to the second floor to your rooms. Listen at the end of the corridor to make sure all your colleagues have gone. They are to meet me in the Sitting Room at 10:30. I want you to search their rooms. If any are locked, I have a skeleton key that should open them."

"What am I looking for?"

"I don't know. Anything. Mike's quill, for one thing. Who stole it and why? Chemicals, pills, medicine…journals, letters, diaries…I honestly don't know."

"Anybody's room in particular that I should start with?"

"Not really. I know Mike didn't do it, but the other six are all still suspects in my book."

"If I find something?"

"Bring it down and try to signal me. I will try to see what I can learn about the notebook. Once you are through in the rooms, I may have to bring you in to face your accusers."

"If I accuse anyone, it's bound to hit the fan."

"Maybe that's what we need. We have to force someone to make a mistake. A heated argument might be just the thing.— Here we are."

Maggie pulled up at the kitchen entrance to the great house and stopped. "Here is the key. Good luck. Be as quick about it as you can. I'll stall for time."

* * *

Detective Sergeant Westbrook walked into the Sitting Room at 10:29. To her relief, a quick glance about the room revealed all seven authors.

"Good, I see you are all here," she began, trying to sound upbeat. It was obvious, however, that not all her listeners were delighted with the prospect.

"Under protest," said Father Smythe from his chair.

"Duly noted, Father Smythe," rejoined Maggie. "I apologize again for the inconvenience."

"Then would you be so good as to tell us when we will be free to go, and then get on with whatever it is that is so damned important. I have business to attend to in both Edinburgh and London. I need to be in Edinburgh tonight."

"It may be necessary for you to postpone your plans, Father Smythe."

"What the devil for? Surely you don't mean to detain us more than an hour or two."

"I am afraid it may be longer than that."

"What I want to know is why! What more is there to be done that involves us? You have your killer."

"It may not be quite so simple. I have already initiated proceedings for the dropping of charges and release of Miss Fitzpatrick."

"What!" exclaimed Smythe, amid a flurry of murmured astonishment from the others.

Meanwhile upstairs, Shelby Fitzpatrick had not anticipated the difficulty of her assignment. Ninety percent certain that Melinda was innocent, she decided to conduct a hurried search of her room first. The moment she walked in, however, a feeling of duplicity and deceit overwhelmed her. What right did she have to snoop among another person's private things? What if she discovered something truly personal that had nothing to do with the case? She would feel deceptive and dirty for betraying the fledgling trust Melinda had given her.

She stood in the middle of the room and glanced about for a few seconds, then realized she couldn't do it. As a detective, Maggie was probably so used to it she could look through someone's personal things without qualms of conscience. But she couldn't...not to one like Melinda.

She turned and left the room. In the deserted hallway once more she stopped, drew in a breath and took stock. She *had* to do this. Solving the case could well depend on it. Her own freedom might depend on it! She couldn't waste all day pondering the ethics of the thing. She had to move quickly.

That decision made, she hurried down the corridor and tried the handle of Father Smythe's room. It was locked. She took out the key Maggie had given her. Seconds later she was inside.

Downstairs, Maggie Westbrook was drawing out explanations with increasing difficulty as Father Smythe's questions became more pointed and irritable. More than once her eyes unconsciously drifted in Mike St. John's direction, as if silently pleading for help, though knowing he could do nothing that would betray their private confidences.

At last he spoke.

"Would you be able to tell us, Detective Westbrook," he asked, "on what grounds Miss Fitzpatrick is being released?"

"For much the same reason Detective Chief Inspector Riggs released you, Mr. St. John," Maggie replied. "Upon further scrutiny, the evidence is simply not strong enough to hold her."

"You are saying blackmail is not a strong enough motive?" said Dr. Cobb.

"We have no compelling reason to believe Miss Fitzpatrick was trying to blackmail Mr. Barribault."

"What about her journal? She explicitly spoke of blackmail."

"It is difficult to get a conviction based on someone's fanciful speculations, Dr. Cobb."

"She certainly had more reason to kill him than any of the rest of us," now said Jessica Stokes, who was still more than a little concerned about the prominence of *her* initials in the journal. She had wondered why the charge of blackmail hadn't come calling at her door too, as preposterous as the idea was—what could she possibly have to blackmail him about!—after what Riggs had read. Though she had been up at the crack of dawn with Meyerson and Smythe, her bags were mostly packed as well. She was anxious to get out of this place on the first convenient bus. She didn't even care what direction it went…just away from here!

Meanwhile Shelby left Father Smythe's room exactly as she found it. A closed suitcase sat in the middle of the floor where Coombes had left it. Otherwise the place gave all the appearance of a vacated hotel room. Nothing personal was anywhere. She certainly wasn't about to open the man's suitcase and rummage through his dirty underwear! If clues existed connecting Father Smythe to the thing, someone else would have to find them.

She moved next door to Dame Meyerson's suite. Her packed case sat on the floor next to the dressing table, also unopened since being brought back upstairs. On the bed lay an open cosmetic case. In this instance Shelby felt fewer qualms about poking through Dame Meyerson's things than she had Father Smythe's. It was not only that she was a woman, but because she had reason to think she might find something important.

Shelby knew what the initials *JS* in her notebook signified because she had written them herself.

It did not take long to find it. No attempt had been made to hide it. Though the years had been many, it was clearly more than an heirloom or keepsake from a bygone era of life. It was something the grand lady still used every day. Shelby wondered if her husband knew of it, and what the simple engraving signified.

With but a moment's hesitation, Shelby pocketed the silver compact and hurried on.

Across the hall she entered the room of the other "JS" without need of a key. The fleeting question passed quickly through her brain whether innocence or guilt could in some measure be detected by whether the need was felt by one individual or another to lock his or her door. Did it signify something to hide…or mere force of habit? Not that she wouldn't rather find something here, thought Shelby, than in several of the other rooms. In spite of the fact that they probably shared more in common with one another than anyone else here, she did not like Jessica Stokes. Other than an open bus schedule on the writing table, however, and a partially filled suitcase on the bed, she found nothing of much interest.

Two minutes later she was inserting the key into the lock of the room occupied by Dr. Briscoe Cobb.

* * *

Meanwhile Maggie continued to stall in front of several disgruntled authors.

"...and I regret to have to tell you," she finally said openly, "that you are not yet free to leave. We will certainly keep you informed of developments, and apprise you the moment there is—"

The sound of heavy footsteps intruded into her hearing, followed by the door being brusquely opened. She paused and glanced up at the interruption.

"Detective Westbrook," demanded the angry voice of D.C.I. Riggs, "what is the meaning of this!"

Riggs strode across the floor straight toward her until his face was less than a foot from hers. "I understand you have released the prisoner—"

"Only pending further evidence, sir," said Maggie, trying to remain calm, "which I hope will be forthcoming any minute."

"I don't even see her here!" exclaimed Riggs, glancing about the room in disbelief. "Who is guarding her?"

"She is upstairs, sir"

"Assuming for a moment that I believe you, Miss Westbrook," said Riggs, "the most important question is why all this behind my back? Are you trying to make points with the higher ups?"

"Not at all, sir. I understood that you had gone to Elgin and I did not feel this could wait. I assumed you would be notified and would come as soon as you were free. I am glad you are here now and that—"

Behind Inspector Riggs, through the open door, Maggie saw Shelby Fitzpatrick, out of sight from the others, trying to get her attention.

"Excuse me...just a moment, Inspector," she said. She hurried past him out of the room, leaving Riggs staring after her in angry bewilderment.

Shelby stepped further out of sight into a corner of the corridor. Maggie hurried to her.

"What did you find?" she asked.

"Not very much. I'm not very good at this I'm afraid.—This was in Dame Meyerson's cosmetic case," she went on, handing Maggie the round silver mirror-compact. The initials—"

"Yes, I see."

"It confirms what I told you about what I had written in my journal."

"This is dynamite!"

"Then this curious book I found in Dr. Cobb's room. I wouldn't have thought anything of it, except for where it was."

"I don't follow you."

"I don't know, but it...I had the feeling he was not intending to read it, but to *hide* it."

"Why?"

"I found it in a bureau drawer folded up inside a pair of trousers."

"Odd, but hardly incriminating."

"Still, I thought it worth showing to you."

Maggie nodded and opened the cover of the book. On the inside flyleaf she saw price and logo in the unmistakable hand of her father's antique dealing friend. She looked up again at Shelby.

"Anything else?"

"No...sorry."

"No sign of Mike's missing quill?"

Shelby shook her head.

"All right...good. You did well." She thought a moment. ""Go back to your room and wait there. If Riggs comes looking for you before I get back, tell him I told you to wait there."

Shelby nodded and was disappearing quietly back up the stairs just as Riggs, his patience at an end, emerged from the Sitting Room to see what had become of his assistant.

"What is going on?" he said.

"Certain evidence possibly pertinent to the case has come into my hands, Chief Inspector," said Maggie. "I don't want to say more until I follow up one additional lead in the village. If you could just bear with me and give me fifteen minutes."

Without awaiting a reply, she turned and hurried for the stairway.

"This better be good, Westbrook!" shouted Riggs after her. "Or there will be disciplinary action, I can promise you that. You have twenty minutes. After that, you will be dismissed from the case."

Already Maggie had flown to the ground floor and was outside running to her car.

* * *

The tires of Maggie's Vauxhall screeched to a stop in front of Abra Bits and Collectables just as John Thompson was walking up the street with his daily *Telegraph* under his arm. Maggie jumped out and followed him inside as he flipped around the "Back in Five Minutes" sign on his door to read "Open."

"Hello, Maggie," he said.

"My father told me to ask again about that key you are making for him if I saw you."

"Tell him I've nearly got it—a couple more days at most."

"Mr. Thompson," said Maggie, "I need to ask you about two items."

"You look in a rush!" laughed Thompson.

"The investigation of Mr. Barribault's murder is heating up," she said.

"I thought you had a suspect in custody."

"It's thin. Actually, there's no evidence at all. That's why we're checking other angles."

She dug into her coat and pulled out the book and the compact. She handed him the mirror case.

"It's not mine," said Thompson, turning it over in his hand.

"I know that. But could you give me an estimate of its age?"

"Hard to tell," said Thompson, examining the silverwork more carefully. "It's not nineteenth century, I can tell you that. I wouldn't technically call this an antique at all. It could possibly be pre-war, though I doubt it. The style is fairly definitely 1950s in my opinion, and probably American made. It's nice, a very expensive piece, but modern. Wherever you got this, someone bought it from a high-end jewelry store not an antique dealer. Who is JS?"

"That may come to light soon enough," replied Maggie cryptically. She stuffed the compact back in her pocket. "What about this book?" she said, handing Thompson the faded clothbound volume.

He took it without apparent recognition. As soon as he opened it, however, and saw his scribbled price inside, he nodded.

"Ah yes, right," he said. "I remember now—bought by the older chap, the Shakespearean fellow from Oxford. Odd, too, as I remember it."

"Odd...in what way?"

"For one thing, what interest could he possibly have in *this*?" he said, holding the book up in question. "Pure rubbish. The only reason I had it in the shop at all is that it came in with a load of other books. I never dreamed I'd get anything for it. I stuck it on the shelf to fill up space. I figured it was destined for the bin eventually."

"But Dr. Cobb bought it?"

"Yes, with no quibbling over the price—which was the most surprising thing of all. Only two people would buy a worthless title like that—someone who knew *nothing* about it, or someone who did. The first would pay maybe a quid or two, but no more, in the off chance they could get an afternoon's entertainment out of the thing. But someone who *did* know the book, wouldn't even pay that much. They wouldn't give a brass farthing for it."

"Then why did you have it priced at ten pounds?"

"An accident, really. I bought a crate of books from the widow of a man who used to have a shop in Fochabers. I didn't scrutinize them carefully, I just penciled in my little AB but left his prices. This was one of those he had wildly mispriced and I didn't catch it."

"How much did you sell it to Cobb for?"

"That's just the thing—he paid the whole ten pounds without batting an eye. Acted a little peculiar...but in the other direction, if you know what I mean—as if *he* had made the discovery of a great find and was anxious to hurry along the transaction before I changed my mind and charged him a hundred pounds. That's why I called it odd. I started to tell him he could have the thing for two pounds, but he just stuffed a tenner in my hand, jammed the book in his pocket, and that was that. A very peculiar exchange. He acted agitated the rest of the time in the shop."

"All right—that's what I wanted to know," said Maggie, taking the book from him. "Do you know anything about the author?"

"Nothing. A pseudonym is my guess. But after a piece of rubbish like that, it's no wonder she didn't want her identity known."

Maggie turned to go, then paused.

"One more thing, Mr. Thompson," she said. "Where were you in the evening of the 26th?"

"What do you mean? What kind of a question is that?"

"Just an innocent question. Routine."

"A little more than routine, Maggie, for a family friend."

"I am sorry, Mr. Thompson, but it was the quill from your shop that was involved in some way. There remains a mystery how it got from here to there."

"What are you insinuating, Maggie?"

"Nothing. It's just that thus far we have been unable to establish that it was ever in anyone else's hands than yours."

"It was pinched. I've made that clear enough."

"But when and by whom?"

"If I knew that, I'd tell you."

"But because you can't, I have to ask where you were that night."

"To answer you, then, I was home."

"All evening."

"That's right."

Maggie nodded and left the shop. Thompson watched her through his window, thinking to himself that he may have misjudged young Maggie Westbrook.

Eighteen

The Exposé

M aggie glanced hastily at her watch as she ground her car to a stop in front of Cullen House. She had been gone, by her reckoning, nineteen minutes. She hoped she was still on the case.

She ran inside. A fuming D.C.I. Riggs, glancing every few seconds at his watch, and an impatient Father Smythe stood closeted in intense discussion to one side of the room. Graham Whitaker, chuckling lightly about something, was seated beside Dame Meyerson, with Briscoe Cobb listening in a chair opposite them. Melinda Franks looked agitated, almost distraught, beside Mike St. John who was speaking softly at her side. Jessica Stokes sat alone, her face registering a perennially sour expression warning all possible intruders against making a closer approach.

"So, you made it under the wire, Westbrook," said Riggs scornfully. He turned and approached her. "Father Smythe has just been telling me of your little game early this morning as he and Dame Meyerson were attempting to leave. He is considering harassment charges. All I can think, Westbrook, is that you concocted this scheme of yours long before my meeting and deliberately kept me in the dark. That does not look good for you."

"I came early simply to tell them to delay their leaving," said Maggie a little hesitantly. "I didn't want to bother you so early.

By the time I went in to fetch Miss Fitzpatrick, you were on your way to Elgin."

"That's as it may be, but don't think I will forget your shenanigans."

"If you will hear me out, Chief Inspector," said Maggie, "I hope I will be able to make you understand. I will just go and bring Miss Fitzpatrick down," she added and hurried again from the room.

Sighing impatiently, Riggs walked again toward Father Smythe and tried to conciliate his ire. The man of God was resuming his seat when Maggie reentered the room with Shelby at her side. All eyes went instantly to their fellow author, who, now as a murder suspect, looked very different in the eyes of all except Mike St. John. Their stares were cold, hard, suspicious.

Ever vigilant, Riggs' eyes went straight to the leather notebook in his impertinent young colleague's hand.

"What are you doing with that, Westbrook?" he said in an importune tone. "I put that in the evidence lock-up."

"I thought we might need it, sir," replied Maggie calmly as Shelby took a chair apart from the others. "If you will just bear with me, I think you will be very intrigued, as I was, with what Miss Fitzpatrick has to say about the final entries in her journal which you read yesterday."

Without awaiting a reply, Maggie immediately turned to Shelby.

"Miss Fitzpatrick," she said, "will you please tell the D.C.I. Riggs exactly what you told me when I came to question you in your jail cell."

"I told Miss Westbrook," said Shelby, addressing Inspector Riggs, "that I did not write all of what you read from my journal."

"What...who did, then?" asked Riggs.

"I have no idea, sir. I assume whoever took my journal?"

"Are you now saying that the notebook wasn't merely misplaced...but that someone stole it?"

"I honestly don't know, sir. All I know is that it was missing for several days. I couldn't find it anywhere. The next thing I knew you were pulling it out yesterday and reading from it."

"And you say what I read was not written by you?"

"Only part of it, sir. When you began, yes, those were my words. Then came a point when suddenly I realized I was listening to words I had never heard — or written — before."

"Let me guess...when it turned incriminating against you," said Riggs sarcastically, "that's when the words were no longer yours?"

"Actually, that is true."

"Very convenient too, wouldn't you say?"

"I don't say anything, Inspector. I am simply telling you the way it was."

"Yes...well, we shall see about that. I saw no change in the handwriting."

"Neither did I. Whoever forged my hand was more than unusually clever about it."

"You've seen the book since I confiscated it?"

"Miss Westbrook had it when she was interrogating me. She showed me the journal and I was able to point our where my entries ended and the added portions began. The last page in my hand had also been torn out."

"Ah, I see. Well, as I say, this makes it rather convenient for you."

"Please, Chief Inspector," now said Maggie, "if you will allow me, I think you will see that it is very possible that the added portions may very well have been intended to accomplish exactly what they did."

"Which is?"

"Falsely incriminate Miss Fitzpatrick."

"Perhaps you would like to explain in more detail."

"Of course, Inspector," replied Maggie, "with Miss Fitzpatrick's help.—Now, Miss Fitzpatrick," she said, turning toward Shelby, "if you would please tell Inspector Riggs what you told me."

She walked across the floor and handed the journal to Shelby. Shelby opened it to the final few pages of writing.

"As I explained to Miss Westbrook," Shelby began, "I have been keeping this journal of observations in conjunction with my professional practice for many years. Perhaps it was unwise of me to continue doing so here. I regret it now. I apologize to any of you," she said glancing about the room, "whom I have offended by what I wrote. Honestly, I meant no harm. I have come to care about you all during this week we have shared together. In retrospect I truly am sorry. I should have left the journal in my suitcase and never opened it. It has always been intended only for my private use, and no one's eyes but my own. It is unfortunate that you read it, Chief Inspector, without asking me about it first. All of this could easily have been cleared up if you had exercised a modicum of sound judgment rather than being so hasty to condemn me."

"What exactly are you accusing me of, Miss Fitzpatrick?" retorted Riggs.

"Of handling this whole thing badly, Chief Inspector. I think you have blundered almost in the extreme. You owe several of us apologies. So far you have put two of us in jail and a third under house arrest, all without a shred of evidence."

"If you don't watch yourself, you may find yourself—"

"Please, Miss Fitzpatrick," interrupted Maggie, "it would be more helpful if you concentrated on the journal. Tell the Chief Inspector where your writing leaves off."

"Yes, sorry." Shelby again looked down at her notebook and scanned the pages a moment. "Here it is. I think you began reading about here, Chief Inspector," she said, "where I was talking about this being a relational greenhouse of diverse personality types. That is where I made a few unfortunate comments about the others."

Again she glanced about the room and smiled sheepishly.

"I have used initials instead of names for years," she went on, "mostly to save time and space, but also to protect confidentiality in case anyone should ever read what I had written. In some cases, as in this instance, some initials may have double meanings or seem to refer to more than one person. Then…let me see, it goes on…yes, I was talking about some of the people having met HB prior to this week. Obviously that is a reference to Hugh Barribault, and the passage is in my own hand. I did believe that in more than one case…and I still do—as I wrote here."

"Who are they, then?" asked Riggs. Gradually Shelby had succeeded in getting his attention.

"I would rather not divulge that just yet, Inspector," said Shelby. "After all, I may be wrong. I would not want to say anything that casts suspicion on anyone."

"But you believe it?"

"From what I observed, yes. However, my observations are not infallible."

"All right, then—go on."

"My writing continued through the remainder of this page," said Shelby as her eyes slowly scanned the familiar writing from her pen. "I was speaking about my fascination with Mr. Barribault and the effect on the future of his writing contest and publishing company if it were discovered that he had known one or more of us prior to this week. I was just thinking aloud, you understand—that's the nature of my notes. They are not scientific."

"Understood, Miss Fitzpatrick. Get on with it, please."

"I wondered aloud if Mr. Barribault was aware of the identities of these individuals who had caught my attention. I was also speaking specifically of my interest in his relationship with someone I called JS, and that in spite of the little game they were each playing this week of pretending to meet for the first time, my firm conviction they had actually met before. I spoke of this being a fascinating psychological study for one in my profession. And there were also two other initials I mentioned where some involvement seemed indicated beyond what was true for most of us. But you will note that I said clearly, *if* my observations were correct—"

D.C.I. Riggs was tired of beating around the bush.

"All right, I've heard enough," he said, then turned away from Shelby. "So why don't you tell us about your previous meeting with Barribault, Miss Stokes," he said. "Did you and he have an affair, and then you killed him when it went wrong?"

Jessica stared back at him with a blank expression. "I have not the remotest idea what you are talking about," she said.

"Come, come, Miss Stokes," persisted Riggs. "I already have one motive pinned to you. Who else could be this JS Miss Fitzpatrick is talking about? If you knew Hugh Barribault before arriving here, that's enough to build a solid case. It will go easier for you if you come clean."

"Detective Chief Inspector," interjected Maggie Westbrook, "perhaps if would be most helpful if Miss Fitzpatrick could explain why she is certain that the final portions in her notebook were written by another hand." She turned to Shelby. "Please continue, Miss Fitzpatrick."

"I admit," said Shelby, "that the handwriting is amazingly similar. I remarked to you earlier, Miss Westbrook, that this forgery was carried out by an expert."

"But you can tell the difference?"

"Actually, it is easy to see once you know what to look for."

"Which is?"

"Besides the fact that I remember writing these words at the bottom of this page here, there is also the change in ink and pen type."

"Pen type, Miss Fitzpatrick?" repeated Riggs, cynicism again creeping into his voice.

"Yes, sir. I use a roller ball. The ink flows fluidly from the point in a way similar to that of a fountain pen. There is no need to apply pressure to the page. You can see in all the previous pages of my journal, there are no indentations from pressing into the paper with my pen. I write with a very light hand, and a roller ball works perfectly for me. However, as I reached the end of this page…right here," she said, pointing as she held the journal up to him, "the ink began to fade. My roller ball cartridge was running out of ink. You can see it easily. The last words on this page, as you read earlier, are, *I am convinced something more is involved—something powerful, a secret of import that HB would not want to come out. In short, the situation*—and there the page ends, Chief Inspector. My roller ball was running out of ink. You can see the words fading. I distinctly recall moving up to the top of the next page to finish the sentence. Then I stopped and put in a new cartridge before continuing on."

"And do you remember what those words were?"

"I do. I wrote, *In short the situation*…a new page…*is full of personal and relational intrigue*. That last word *intrigue*, I recall, was nearly non-existent on the page. But you know how it is, you want to finish your train of thought."

"How do you remember the exact words so clearly?"

"I just do. The term *relational intrigue* is one I use fairly often. It seems to me to sum up much of what goes on beneath the surface between people. Maybe that's why I remember it. Also that my pen was running out of ink."

"What did you do then?"

"I put in a new cartridge, I copied over the words *personal and relational intrigue* to make them more legible, then I went on."

"And do you recall your next words exactly?"

"No. I was talking, I think, more along the same lines about the mystery of Mr. Barribault's associations. But then I remember getting off on a tangent and writing some thoughts about the antique shop and Mr. St. John having bought the quill he showed us...I don't recall exactly what I said."

"And you cannot read it to us?" said Maggie.

"No. That last page of mine was torn out. You can see it clearly, Chief Inspector," she added, again turning the open journal in Riggs' direction. "Where the writing goes on, what you read to us yesterday...someone else wrote it. And you can see that it was written by a ball point pen—the slight indentation from the pressure on the paper is easily visible on the reverse. The ink, too, flows in a different pattern. Here, Chief Inspector, I'm sure you will see what I mean."

Shelby stood and walked a few steps and handed her journal to D.C.I. Riggs. He squinted at the bottom of the one page and top of the other.

"Yes, I see what you mean."

"And the ink at the top of the new page, is dark," added Shelby. "The fading of the words from the previous page, with the torn out page between them, has completely disappeared."

Riggs continued to scrutinize the journal carefully.

"All right, you have made your point, Miss Fitzpatrick. So your contention is that the journal should be read in this way. Let me see, I'll begin here...*there is more to it. It is how JS has watched him all week.* This is in your hand, you say."

Shelby nodded.

"Then you continue, *I am convinced something more is involved—something powerful, a secret of import that HB would not want to come out. In short, the situation*—here the page ends, and the rest of what you wrote was torn out?"

"That's right."

"And someone *else*, pretending to write in your hand, picked up where you left off and with a different pen wrote... *seems rife with possibilities for the potential of blackmail. And what would HB do if blackmail were attempted?"* Riggs continued. *"Would he cancel the contract? Would the gamble be worth it for mere revenge? It hardly seems likely. Yet whatever secret binds them together from the past, revenge might indeed be a more powerful incentive than financial reward and fame and book sales. Money, sex, power, greed, revenge...these are among the strongest psychological motivations of humankind. And if I am right in my observations...where does that place me? I might blackmail them both! But I think I will satisfy myself with HB. He is so filthy rich he will not miss a few hundred thousand for my silence, to keep his reputation intact and whatever secrets he has from coming to light. I will look for an opportunity to approach him. It may be in the end that my fiction book will not be that for which this gathering proves of the greatest benefit for me. HB has secrets that I alone now know...how much will he pay for me to keep them quiet?"*

Riggs lowered the journal. The room was silent.

"A very interesting theory, Miss Fitzpatrick. You believe someone went to such elaborate lengths to incriminate you for the murder? Why would they do that? Why single you out?"

"I honestly don't know, Chief Inspector. I assume to cover his or her own tracks."

"But why you?"

"I don't know. Maybe they simply found my journal and thought it up later. I don't know. I'm no detective. But it strikes me that if you could find who took my notebook, you may find your murderer."

"Things are not always that simple. Nevertheless, we will dust it for prints. There is also the possibility that you did all this yourself—tore out the page, changed pens—to *pretend* to implicate yourself in a way that would throw suspicion toward an imaginary journal thief."

"That is completely ridiculous, Chief Inspector," said Shelby. "You don't really believe that."

"I believe what the facts tell me. In the meantime, Miss Stokes," he added, turning again toward Jessica, "I haven't forgotten about you."

"Look, Chief Inspector," replied Jessica, "I have already admitted that Mr. Barribault found some of my modern views difficult. Yes, we had a private meeting about it. He did not know if he could be comfortable with a liberal and a progressive in his company. He went so far as to request that I have no involvement other than having my book published and then step away entirely. I admit that we argued. Yes, I was angry and I told him what I thought. But in the end I went back to my room more heartbroken and humiliated than anything. How would you feel, Chief Inspector, to have everything you believe ridiculed in such fashion, and to be in a setting where you know no one likes you and then be told by your host that he wants nothing to do with you? I went to my room thinking how soon I could get out of this place, and eventually cried myself to sleep, Chief Inspector," said Jessica, glancing down and choking momentarily. "I certainly did not dream up a plan to kill Mr. Barribault. I just wanted to get away."

The room again went silent.

"That's all well and good, Miss Stokes," said Riggs, unmoved. "But Miss Fitzpatrick seems convinced that you and Hugh Barribault had a prior relationship. I want to know if that is true."

"Excuse me, Chief Inspector," said Shelby. "You misunderstand. I never said such a thing. You cannot accuse Jessica on the basis of anything in my journal."

"You wrote about JS and HB."

"I was not referring to her."

"There are the initials JS in black and white."

"They are not hers, Inspector. She is not JS."

Now it was Riggs' turn to stand gaping.

"Who is, then?" he asked after a second or two.

Shelby hesitated, Slowly she turned to face Dame Meyerson.

"Do you want to tell him?" She said. "Or should I?"

A few murmurs accompanied the turning of heads toward Dame Meyerson.

"Why is everyone looking at me?" she said.

"Who is JS?" demanded Riggs, looking back and forth between the two women.

"I have no idea what you're talking about," said Dame Meyerson.

Riggs looked back toward Shelby.

"Look here, Miss Fitzpatrick," he said, "you are trying my patience. You claim innocence, yet refuse to reveal what you know. I might understand…you don't want to point fingers. You don't want to be the snitch, as we say in my profession. You can have your relational intrigue, but I prefer to speak more plainly. If you know something, tell me or I will take you back to the jail myself and book you for withholding evidence. Maybe you are innocent, maybe you aren't. But for now, I want to know why you wrote what you did. You may not want to be a snitch, but do you want to cover for a killer? If you are innocent, I'm sure you want the truth to come out. Otherwise, I will have no choice but to consider this a conspiracy."

Shelby thought seriously a moment more, staring down at her lap. Slowly she began to nod and looked up at Riggs.

"You're right, Chief Inspector," she said. "Of course I want to help you find the truth. Neither do I want to seem as if I am accusing anyone of anything. I've told you, my observations *may* be wrong."

"All duly noted, Fitzpatrick," said Riggs impatiently. "Just get on with it."

Again Shelby nodded, then drew in a deep breath.

"Growing up in southern California," she began, "I was a great film buff. I subscribed to all the magazines and followed the lives of the stars—the old stars, I mean…the classic actors and actresses—Garbo, Davis, Stewart, Kelly, Garland, Hepburn, Astaire…all of them. Later I worked my way through U.C.L.A. as an undergraduate doing those film star tours in Hollywood. The pay wasn't good, but I loved it. I already knew a lot, but I boned up even more on film history and trivia. I had to be able to talk non-stop for two hours and keep people interested and convince them I was an expert. I got tired of the same material so I constantly tried to learn new things—tidbits and factoids and gossip. Actually I think that's where I started using the phrase 'relational intrigue.' That's what people wanted to hear about— the inside stories of the stars…*intrigue*."

She paused. Her eyes flitted briefly again in the direction of Dame Meyerson, seemingly as if expecting her to say something. But the older woman sat staring straight ahead like a statue. Shelby continued.

"That's how I knew about Jenny Swain."

"Who's Jenny Swain?" asked Riggs, not noticing the sudden burst flushing Dame Meyerson's cheeks.

Again Shelby's eyes flitted away momentarily. She saw the color, and the accompanying daggers from the eyes. She knew the latter were meant for her. But by no silent imploring could she induce Dame Meyerson to take up the story on her own. Thus Shelby continued.

"She was a Hollywood starlet."

"Never heard of her."

"Most people haven't. She only made four movies—meteoric rise, then sudden fall and she disappeared from the Hollywood scene. She was discovered rather late in life for the sex symbol image—her first movie was made when she was in her mid twenties. But she received rave reviews for the steamy role. She was immediately touted as the new Marilyn Monroe and Grace Kelly rolled into one, Rita Hayworth, Ingrid Bergman, Audrey Hepburn—sexiness and dignity, beauty and brains...and considerable talent as well. There was talk of an Oscar nomination for her third screen role, but it didn't materialize."

"This is all well and good, Miss Fitzpatrick," said Inspector Riggs in mounting impatience, "but what does any of that have to do with us?"

"I am getting to that, Inspector," replied Shelby. "This Jenny Swain knew Hugh Barribault."

A few raised eyebrows and expressions of sudden interest spread about the room.

"Right, now we're getting somewhere!" said Riggs enthusiastically.

"Barribault's first breakout novel about the Northern Ireland conflict," Shelby continued, "a book called *Love's Dry Tears*, was made into a highly publicized movie with Jenny Swain as the female lead. She was twenty-seven at the time, I believe. Most in the movie industry considered her poised to take her place among Hollywood's greats, and this was the movie they thought might launch her up to that level."

"So what happened? It obviously didn't."

"During filming she became involved on the set with a consultant for the producer. There was an alleged affair, which in Hollywood usually increases star power. But not in this case. This consultant with whom she was involved inexplicably turned on her. He saw to it that she was offered no more major roles for several years. This consultant, incidentally, happened to be the author of the book—a young upcoming new author by the name of Hugh Barribault. By the time the actress tried to make a comeback, it was too late—the luster of the bloom had faded. She drifted into obscurity. Eventually Jenny Swain reinvented herself by marrying up, as they say, into the British aristocrisy, where she became—"

"All right, all right!" suddenly exclaimed Dame Meyerson. "At least let me retain the dignity of telling it myself."

Every eye in the room turned toward her. Dame Meyerson drew in several deep breaths.

"Yes...I am Jenny Swain," she said. "I *was* Jenny Swain would be more accurate. It was another lifetime ago. And yes...Hugh and I were involved.—How dare you, Miss Fitzpatrick," she went on, turning toward Shelby, "drag me into it to save your own skin."

"I am sorry," said Shelby. "I recognized you when we first gathered and referred to you as JS just for myself, just for fun. But once all the questioning began...I didn't know what else to do."

"Don't worry Miss Fitzpatrick about it, Dame Meyerson," said Riggs. "It was bound to come out in our investigation."

"I don't know how, Inspector. You had no clue who I was."

"Be that as it may, I know now—so why don't you tell us about it."

"She's told what there is to tell," sighed Dame Meyerson, her anger subsiding. A sad nostalgic expression filled her eyes. "Hugh and I had an affair during the filming of *Love's Dry Tears*. It was actually quite wonderful for a time. It wasn't even really what you would call an affair. We were single consenting adults. No one was hurt. We were both unmarried. We shared some wonderful times together. Actually I was naïve enough to think he might ask me to marry him, and I would have accepted him. I was in love with him. But then...suddenly he changed. Something came over him. The change was dramatic, and suddenly it was over. His love turned to hatred. He became furious at me, saying horrible things I didn't understand, blaming me for the relationship as if he hadn't even been part of it. It was dreadful. I still have no idea why he turned on me as he did. I thought we cared for one another. But something happened that I never knew and that he never divulged. Eventually his hatred turned vengeful. It was as though he wanted to punish me for the affair. And he did. He ruined my career."

She let out a long sigh and looked away, blinking hard.

"Were you bitter?" asked Riggs.

"You bet I was bitter," rejoined Dame Meyerson, snapping out of her reverie. "My love eventually turned to hatred too. Funny how love and hatred can be two sides of the same coin. But I am a survivor, Inspector. I had no intention of letting it destroy me. I managed to make the best of it. I returned to England, which was my home. Eventually I married Sir George Lord Meyerson and was made a dame of the British Empire and have had a full and satisfying life. For me, Jenny Swain was dead and buried long ago."

"Until you came here and met Hugh Barribault again."

"I won't deny it. I had been speaking publicly for some time, and had begun to write some of my reflections and observations. When I learned of Hugh's contest, I thought what a delicious irony if I could sneak back into his life without his knowing it—not with any motive other than to turn the tables on him and prove—maybe to myself," she added with a reflective smile, "that I had made something of my life without him. I was shocked to be among the contest finalists. I must admit it stirred up many things when I suddenly realized I was one of the winners and was going to see Hugh again."

"*Your* opportunity for revenge, you might say."

"It was no such thing, Inspector."

"You can hardly deny that it looks bad, Dame Meyerson. These others may have had motives of money and greed. But you were driven by love and revenge, the oldest motive in the book—

a lifetime's silent desire to get even with the man who cast you adrift."

"Yes, I admit to the affair. Yes, it's true that I talked to Hugh a few times since arriving here. Yes, we argued. I was furious. He ruined my career. I had intended to come here and play the suave and dignified grand dame, but it was useless."

"Did you still love him?"

"No, nothing like that. I haven't carried a torch all these years. I love my husband. I have had a happy life. But the past still has power to hurt. The old feelings came back...yes, all the anger and resentment for what he had done. But I didn't kill him. When I left him he was still alive."

"I think there might be a different story to tell," persisted Riggs. "You admit to being drunk that night."

"I admitted to no such thing," retorted Dame Meyerson, her anger returning. "I was tipsy, that's all. I had had a little too much to drink. Is that a crime?"

"It depends on where it leads."

"It led me to bed."

"I contend that it led you back up to Hugh Barribault's rooms. Maybe you didn't plan to kill him. You were more than half drunk. You found him still awake. You argued again, more violently this time. He told you to get out. By now you were trying his patience. He may have threatened to remove you from the Eight. The alcohol went to your head. In the heat of the moment you lashed out. He fell and hit his head on the floor, not hard enough to kill him, but sufficient to knock him out briefly. By now you were wild with rage, not knowing what you were doing. A crime of passion followed. By the time you had come to yourself you were standing over the body of your former lover, looking at disbelief where you had stabbed him in the arm with the feather quill, leaving him there on the floor to die as the poison ink seeped into his blood. — All right then, Dame Meyerson," said Riggs, approaching her with a triumphant flourish, "I am arresting you—"

"Don't be absurd, chief Inspector," shouted Dame Meyerson, jumping to her feet. She strode across the floor and confronted him eyeball to eyeball. "You can't arrest me on the basis of such a fairy tale. You could *never* make it stick. You've made up the whole thing. You want a motive of revenge? Mr. Whitaker had far more need of revenge than I did. The man is responsible for his wife's death."

"We've been over all that, Dame Meyerson."

"And Ms. Stokes...he was about to send her away with a flea in her ear. So don't come dredging up something out of my past from thirty years ago and talk to *me* about revenge. He was also suspicious of the good Rev. St. John—don't forget that, Inspector. You've got motives for murder all through this room!"

"Hey," laughed Father Smythe, as if attempting to bring some levity into a room grown suddenly heavy with accusation. "What about me? Am I to be left out of all the fun?"

His lighthearted humor grated with dissonance against the echo of *murder* which still hung in the air.

Several glanced in Smythe's direction, hardly knowing what to think.

"Am I alone to be omitted from this barrage of accusation?" said Smythe, trying to laugh again. "After all, Dame Meyerson, fair is fair. Don't you have a theory about me?"

"How could I suspect you, Father?" replied Dame Meyerson, "with that collar around your neck?"

At least Smythe's ploy had succeeded in calming her down.

"But as you say, there is a member of the cloth under suspicion. If you point the finger at Rev. St. John, then you mustn't discount me on account of my collar. I too may have some sinister motive."

"All right, then, Father Smythe," said Riggs, "I'll play along—what motive might you have?"

"None that I can think of," laughed Smythe. "I am simply pointing out that we must keep open minds. Perhaps, Chief Inspector, we are all in it together."

"I am going to have to ask you to keep your theories to yourself, Father. Smythe," said Riggs. "You are helping nothing. We are not playing parlor games, this is a murder investigation. Now then," he said, turning again to face Dame Meyerson who had resumed her seat, "—I am not satisfied with your answers, Dame Meyerson. I may not have every point necessary yet for a conviction, but I am going to have to ask you to come along with me for now. I am charging you with suspicion of the murder of Hugh Barribault."

Again Dame Meyerson leapt to her feet.

"Then take me away, Chief Inspector," she said. "Put me in your silly jail. With my one allowable phone call I will ring up Number Ten Downing Street. Or Buckingham Palace. Pick your poison, Riggs. They will take my call at either place, Chief Inspector. The first thing I will tell them is your name, and what a bumbler you are. You want revenge...you want arguments...you want motive...why don't you ask our friend Dr. Cobb along with the others. I heard him arguing with Hugh too, and he sounded like a man angry enough to do something violent. Ask him who Brenda Carr is. I heard them arguing about her. You want a love triangle, ask *him*! Jenny Swain is past...gone...dead. Maybe your motive instead is this mysterious Brenda Carr!"

Shelby and Maggie looked at each other with expressions that silently shouted, *Did you hear that!*

Shaken by the Number Ten threat, D.C.I. Riggs was only too glad of a diversion that would allow him to back gracefully away from his previous statement. "All right, Dr. Cobb," he said, perfectly willing to take an accusation however foundationless and run with it, "suppose for a moment I decide to take Dame Meyerson's little tirade seriously—why don't you tell me about this argument you had with Mr. Barribault."

"I already explained that, Inspector," replied Cobb. "It was simply a meeting to discuss my book contract."

"Did you and he argue?"

"Not at all."

"That's not true, Dr. Cobb," interjected Dame Meyerson heatedly. "I heard you clearly."

"Then perhaps you can tell me who is this mysterious Brenda Carr?" asked Riggs.

"I have no idea."

"You have never heard the name?"

Cobb shook his head.

"Detective Chief Inspector," said Maggie from where she was sitting, "might you permit me to ask a question?"

"Of course, Miss Westbrook."

Maggie rose, pulling from her pocket the volume Shelby had given her in the hall.

"Perhaps, Dr. Cobb," she said walking toward him, "you could explain this." She handed him the book. He took it, turned it over in his hands, then glanced up at her with an expression of puzzled confusion.

"I don't know what you mean. I am not familiar with this book."

"You've never seen it before?"

"Not that I am aware of."

"Nor have you heard of it?"

"No."

Maggie opened the cover to the title page. "*Love on the Dunes by Brenda Carr,*" she read aloud, then glanced again toward Dr. Cobb. "I might believe you, Dr. Cobb," she said. "It doesn't really sound like your kind of reading—pulp fiction, tawdry romance...I might believe you, that is if you hadn't bought the book three days ago, paying at least five times its value, from the antique shop in town."

"That's a bloody lie! Who said I did?"

"The shop's owner, Mr. Thompson."

"Then he's lying!"

"I doubt that. I have known the man half my life. If you will just look here inside on the flyleaf you will see the *AB* in his hand. It is his personal logo. Every book is priced with it. He also keeps track of every sale. This book was sold three days ago for the marked price of ten pounds."

"All right, then, what of it?" said Cobb. "I bought it. So what?"

"Why did it make you so angry that I knew you had purchased it?"

"I don't know. You caught me off guard. What I would like to know is how you happen to have that book now, if, as you say, it is my property."

"I arranged for your room to be searched. It was found there."

"How dare you! You had no right!"

"This is a murder investigation, Dr. Cobb," interceded D.C.I. Riggs. Catching someone in a lie was blood in the water to his shark's nose. Maggie had caught Cobb in a lie and he was now ready to arrest *him* on the spot. "We have the right to search this whole house. So why don't you just tell me what is your relationship to this Brenda Carr, and why you and Barribault were arguing about her."

Cobb sighed. Contracts were legal documents. Once they were on the scent of his secret they were sure to uncover it eventually. You might hide an identity from the public, but you couldn't hide one from the police. He realized the jig was up.

"All right," he said in a resigned tone. "She's nobody."

"She's *somebody*, Dr. Cobb. Otherwise why were you and Barribault arguing about her?"

"Just because she is nobody," rejoined Cobb. "It's a pseudonym...a pen name. I am Brenda Carr. I wrote this trashy bit of fluff years ago when I aspired to be a fiction writer. I was a mere twenty-nine. I thought a woman's name would add to the cache. Who's going to read a romance by someone named *Briscoe?* Or *Cobb* either for that matter. Not much romance to the sound, you know. So I invented a new name—rather clever I thought myself at the time. I don't know why the thing was ever published. It died a quick death after selling probably no more than three thousand copies...though," he added almost wistfully, "it curiously went through three printings in the Scandinavian translation. In any event, Brenda Carr was never heard from again. Subsequently I was fortunate and rose in the ranks of academia, becoming what they loosely call a 'Shakespearen expert,' and eventually almost forgot the incident altogether. When I filled out the Barribault Contest questionnaire and answered in the negative about having been previously published, I honestly did not think of it as lying. By then, to my mind, Brenda Carr and her fleeting brush with the publishing world did not even exist."

"But Barribault found out?"

Cobb nodded.

"You argued?"

"I'm afraid that his accusations were rather pointed. I suppose I handled it badly precisely because he was right. He had me cold and I knew it."

"He threatened to remove you from the list of his published authors?"

"He didn't merely threaten. I was as good as gone. He told me to pack my bags and get out and leave the hundred thousand behind."

"So you killed him? You stole the quill from the shop and you killed him with it."

"Don't be ridiculous, Chief Inspector. I heard someone say that we were all in that antique shop the day before the murder. Any one of us could have stolen the quill. Besides that, I had no reason to kill the man. I have a good career. I am respected. I have as much money as I need. I'm not about to throw all that away. This contest is not a life changer for me. Besides, what's that they say about all publicity being good publicity. I have no doubt that major houses will line up to publish my manuscript when it is known that Barribault kicked me out. His murder only increases its publicity value."

"Adding to *your* motive for killing him."

"Nonsense, Inspector. You're grasping at straws. I admit that we argued…and yes, he was going to throw me out. But I didn't kill him."

"So you say, Cobb. We shall let a jury decide?—Miss Westbrook, go ask Sgt. Simmons to come in here please."

Maggie left the room and returned a minute later with the sergeant.

"Sgt. Simmons," said Riggs. "Put Dame Meyerson and Dr. Cobb into immediate custody. Take them to the station and hold them until I am able to sort the rest of this out. And, Sergeant," he added, "keep Dame Meyerson away from a telephone."

NINETEEN

The Witness

The sounds of a furious tumult of allegations directed by the accused against Detective Chief Inspector Riggs, Sgt. Simmons led away the two most recent of the Eight to be held. Gradually the the electrified atmosphere began to subside. Those remaining in the Sitting Room slowly stood to stretch their legs and draw in a few deep breaths.

"That was interesting to say the least," commented Graham Whitaker wryly, always ready to find the humor in any situation.

"Chief Inspector, I don't know if I speak for anyone else," said Mike St. John, "but I need a break. Would you mind if I ran up to my room?"

"Right, not a bad idea. Everyone be back in fifteen minutes. Somebody go find that cook lady and see about getting some tea brought in.—Miss Westbrook," he added, glancing around and seeing Maggie and Shelby Fitpatrick speaking softly together.

"Yes, sir," said Maggie, walking toward him.

"Run down to that shop in town for me, will you. Pick up a package of Paracetamol. My head is killing me."

He handed her a five pound note.

Maggie nodded, then turned away. She noticed Melinda Franks leaving the room with more than the expression of sadness that she had been wearing constantly since the death of

Hugh Barribault. Something more serious was reflected on her face. She returned briefly to Shelby Fitzpatrick.

"Take this back and replace it where you found it," she said in a confidential tone, handing her the silver compact from Dame Meyerson's room. "It looks like we won't need it after all. I'm glad she admitted it on her own. It would be best if you weren't seen. It would raise too many questions. I'm off on an errand for Inspector Riggs."

A few minutes later Maggie walked into the Co-op on the corner of Grant and Castle streets

"Hi, Maggie," said the girl behind the counter. "Solved yer muckle case, hae ye?"

"Na yet, Jennie. Tis a swither I maun say. But I'm jist come for a puckle o' Paracetamol the noo."

"Speikin' o' the muckle hoose, did Mr. Thompson git the key for the hoose sorted?"

"I dinna ken what ye're meanin', Jennie," said Maggie. "What key?"

"Mr. Thompson, ye ken, fae the shop—I saw him twa nichts syne...he was on's way up the street tae the muckle hoose. I thoucht ye might hae seen him."

"What nicht, Jennie."

"Oh, the nicht o' the cankert win', it was."

"What time was that, Jennie?"

"I got aff at nine, it maun hae been close efter that. I was jist leavin' the store an' he was walkin' up til the gate an' fiddlin' wi' somethin' in's hand. I saw it was a big key—one o' those rale big auld keys, ye ken."

"An' ye speiked til'm?"

"Aye, I spiered aboot the big key in's hand an' whaur he was boun'. I think I gae him a wee fricht speikin' til him fae ahind in the gloamin' that gait. He didna ken I was there, ken. He started fan he heard me, an' he tell'd me he had made the key for Mr. Barribault at the muckle hoose."

Maggie nodded with interest, then quickly purchased the headache tablets and hurried back to Cullen House. There she found her boss alone in the Sitting Room with a cup of tea.

"I have your Paracetamol, Inspector," she said handing him the package and change. "I have also just learned something interesting. Mr. Thompson, who told me he was at home that evening, was seen entering the grounds of Cullen House shortly after nine o'clock the night of the windstorm."

"The antique store man, the fellow with the quills?"

"Yes, sir."

"On the night of the murder? He was *here* that night?"

"My friend at the Co-op said so. I suppose she could be mistaken, but I thought you should know."

"That explains the quill!"

"She said nothing about seeing a quill, only a key."

"He could have had it hidden. Very good, Miss Westbrook."

"What do you want me to do?"

"You can start by telling me about this man. He's a family friend of yours, if I remember."

"For many years...of my mum's and dad's. All I know is what my dad says—he calls him a renaissance man...you know, someone who is interested in everything, can do anything. He was in the RAF as a young man—flew fighter jets I think. Then he worked for a time in the defense industry—some high-tech thing. He's an electrician as well—he helped my dad put in a new service in our house and wired my dad's workshop. But for most of his professional life he taught history at the University of Edinburgh."

"It would have taken him two lives to do all that."

"Maybe I exaggerated it, I don't know the details. I do know that he retired early to pursue a dream of dealing in the things of antiquity."

"Antiques, you mean? That's why he opened this shop of his?"

Maggie nodded. "He writes too," she said. "That's one of the reasons he's got so many writing things."

"Writes, how do you mean?"

"You know, writes books."

"Anything published?"

"I don't think so."

As they were talking, the others drifted gradually back into the Sitting Room and listened in. As the two police detectives paused in their discussion, they realized they were surrounded by Mike St. John, Father Smythe, and Shelby Fitzpatrick.

"I don't mean to eavesdrop, Chief Inspector," said Father Smythe, "but I can verify what Miss Westbrook just told you."

"In what way, Mr. Smythe?" asked Riggs.

"About Thompson's writing. He told me about some of his books."

"What did he tell you? What kind of stuff did he write?"

"Oh, history, fiction—I never actually read anything. He did tell me that he had entered a book in Barribault's contest."

"And?"

"Nothing came of it. It didn't even make the first round of cuts."

"What was it called, do you know?"

"No, sorry. But if you ask me, reading between the lines, he was upset about it. It grated on him. Barribault repeatedly encouraged him to write, yet did nothing to help him, and was mostly oblivious to the writing he had done."

"Enough to commit murder?" asked Riggs.

"I really could not say, Inspector," replied Smythe. "That is your area of expertise, not mine."

By now Graham Whitaker had joined the little group. Jessica Stokes, who came back into the room with Whitaker, returned to her chair.

"There is one other interesting fact about the good Mr. Thompson that you may not know," now said Father Smythe.

"And that is?" said Riggs.

"He also confided to me that the original idea for Barribault's blockbuster *Templar Timebomb* was actually his."

"Whose...Thompson's?"

"That's right."

"Why would he confide that to you?" asked Whitaker.

"We struck up a friendship, I guess you might say," replied Smythe. "I went into his shop whenever I was in town and we spoke of this and that. He told me that Barribault came in and chatted with him in the same way, that they spent hours talking about book ideas. When Barribault used his idea, Thompson anticipated some kind of credit, even remuneration. The book and movie must have made millions."

"What became of it in the end?"

"Nothing. Thompson never received so much as a brass farthing or a word of thanks from Barribault."

"Another motive for murder?" suggested Riggs. "I suddenly find myself very interested in this man. Miss Westbrook...go into town and bring him here for questioning.—Why don't the rest of you have tea while we wait."

* * *

Maggie Westbrook returned with John Thompson ten minutes later. The antique dealer was not pleased to have his business interrupted and having to lock his door in the middle of the day. He walked into the room at Maggie's side intending to give D.C.I. Riggs a piece of his mind. Seeing a half dozen other sets of eyes resting on him, however, momentarily deflated the sails of his annoyance.

"Sit down, Mr. Thompson," said Riggs without formality. He rose and began pacing the room thoughtfully.

Thompson sat down. Maggie found a chair beside him.

"It has come to my attention," Riggs began, "that you paid a visit to Hugh Barribault on the night of his death."

Thompson glanced around uncomfortably.

"I had business at the house, yes."

"What business?"

"Hugh had asked me to rekey a certain old lock. I had been working on fabricating a new key and needed to try it out."

"So you picked a stormy night, after dark, to sneak onto the grounds—"

"I did not sneak in, Inspector," said Thompson.

"What would you call it?"

"I walked straight in. I had a standing invitation. Hugh Barribault and I were friends."

"Such good friends that he stole book ideas from you?"

"What are you talking about?"

"Templar, what was it called, Father Smythe?"

"*Templar Timebomb.*"

"That's it—so what about it, Mr. Thompson?"

"I told you that in the strictest of confidence, Smythe," said Thompson angrily.

"Sorry, John," said Father Smythe. "The man is a policeman. I couldn't refuse to answer."

"So what about it, Mr. Thompson," repeated Riggs. "Did High Barribault steal an idea from you for one of his books?"

"I suppose that is one way of looking at it."

"Is that how *you* looked at it?"

"I did at first, yes. I was perturbed at him. I got over it."

"So tell me about this key."

"He asked me to make him a new key. I was working on it and needed to try it."

"In the middle of the night? Why didn't you go up when it was light?"

"I have a shop to run, Chief Inspector. It is open during the day. I can't just walk out."

"So you waited until dark?"

"I didn't *wait* until dark. That's when I happened to be free."

"Did the key work?" asked Riggs.

"Actually, yes. I was rather chuffed in fact."

"It was a stormy night to be out."

"It was. I remember thinking that some of the trees were swaying dangerously."

"Where did you have the quill when you went into the grounds that night?"

"What do you mean...what quill?"

"The pen quill you made that you were so proud of?"

"I *didn't* have it. I told you, it had been stolen from my shop."

"So you went in to the house, tried the key, and then left?"

"That's right."

"If I may, Chief Inspector," said Maggie, "—Mr. Thompson, you told me you were home all evening."

"I was, after I returned from the house and went home."

"You didn't consider your visit to Cullen House pertinent when I asked you where you were that evening?"

"Actually, it slipped my mind."

"And you did not see Hugh Barribault?" asked Riggs.

"No," replied Thompson.

"I am sorry to interrupt, and I do not mean to interfere, Inspector," said Graham Whitaker, "but I heard you, Mr. Thompson, up on the third floor. It has just come to me as I listen to you—it was your voice I heard from the direction of Hugh Barribault's study when I was going up to the roof to check on the fallen tree."

"That's a bloody lie—who are you to say it was me!"

"I am sorry, but I heard you," rejoined Whitaker calmly.

"That's right," said Mike. "When I was outside I thought I saw someone in Barribault's window."

"All right, Mr. Thompson, you had better give me the whole truth," said Riggs.

"The man's just saying that to cover his own tracks! He was probably on his way to Hugh's study right then."

"So you were in the house."

"Yes, I went up to tell Hugh the lock worked fine."

"Why did you lie about it?"

"I didn't think it was any of your concern."

"Everything is my concern, Mr. Thompson. I contend that you did more than just show him the new key. I maintain that you came here with your quill containing the poison ink you had yourself made, and that the presence of these other authors had filled you with a silent fury at the rejection in the contest of your own book, and your seething bitterness at being slighted by Hugh Barribault for so many years. You finally decided to get your revenge. You knew that it would be blamed on someone inside the house. So you killed him. Then you snuck back out through the same entry by which you had gained access to the locked house. John Thompson, I am arresting you for the murder of Hugh Barribault."

Thompson was so shocked by the charges, and so dumbfounded by Inspector Riggs' illogic that he sat shaking his head in disbelief. For the first time since the flurry of charges had begun, Maggie Westbrook found herself thinking that perhaps at last her chief had unwittingly stumbled onto the truth. Too many questions about the case suddenly made sense if her father's friend was indeed guilty—the missing quill, the poison ink, the motive of revenge, the handmade key allowing access to the locked house…and now an earwitness placing him on the scene.

The force of all the facts together was compelling. She had no word of objection, therefore, when Riggs approached her.

"Do you want me to take him into town, sir?" she asked.

"I'll take him into Buckie and book him myself," said Riggs. "You hang tight here, Westbrook, until I get back."

"So, Chief Inspector," said Smythe as Riggs, with Thompson in tow, moved toward the door, "it would appear that you have just about got it wrapped up here. You've got your killer at last. Presuming Miss Westbrook has no objections, are we at last free to go?"

"Probably so," nodded Riggs. "I'll be back in less than an hour. We will talk about it then."

TWENTY

The Flight

While they were gone, Mike St. John was thinking hard.

There were things involved here that were escaping everyone. He had the feeling Hugh Barribault himself might hold the key to it all. He went up to the Library. Barribault's office was still locked and off limits. But in the Library he soon enough located copies of all Barribault's books. He took a copy of *Love's Dry Tears* off the shelf and perused it briefly.

When he left the Library a few minutes later to rejoin the others, the volume was under his arm.

* * *

Rather than suffer the awkwardness of a car ride from Buckie back to Cullen House with Dame Meyerson and Briscoe Cobb badgering him about false arrest, D.C.I. Riggs instructed Sgt. Simmons to release the two authors and return them to the house while he saw personally to Thompson's arrest.

When he arrived back in Cullen some forty minutes later, Dame Meyerson was in her room attempting to get through to her solicitor on the phone. Cobb was cooling his heels waiting to take out his dudgeon on Riggs.

"My solicitor will be contacting you, Chief Inspector," he said heatedly the moment Riggs reentered the Sitting Room where most of the group except Dame Meyerson and Melinda Franks was still gathered, along with Detective Sergeant Westbrook. Trays of tea, coffee, and lunch things had recently been delivered. All but Cobb were clustered about the sideboards.

"You are free to pursue any means of recourse that may appeal to you, Dr. Cobb," returned Riggs with a slight condescending air. "But the law is on my side. It's been tried before. Believe me it won't get you far. As long as I have a strong motive, I am within my rights to arrest anyone—and you had plenty of motive."

"That is preposterous, Chief Inspector. You have been falsely arresting people for two days."

"I would be careful, Dr. Cobb. You don't want to threaten me. You are still on my A-list of suspects. You had probably the strongest motive I have uncovered thus far."

"You are always talking about motive. I don't think you would know a real motive if it bit you in the face. You want motive—what about the young strumpet who was playing around with Barribault. Why haven't you arrested her, Inspector? Got your eye on her for yourself?"

"Watch yourself, Cobb. You're not in the clear yet. I don't even know who you're talking about."

"The Franks girl, you boob—who do you think I mean. They've been having an affair since almost the first day. We all knew it. We saw it clearly enough. Yet this patently obvious fact seems to have completely escaped your notice. She is the one you should be talking to."

Riggs was inwardly furious to be spoken to in this manner. But Cobb's words shook him. He *had* been unaware of any hanky-panky going on between Barribault and the Franks girl. In the textbook of motives for murder, sex gone wrong topped the list. What if he had indeed overlooked the big one in all this?

"We are investigating all leads, Dr. Cobb," he said, doing his best to keep his cool, "including that one."

He turned away from Cobb and scanned the room.

"By the way, where is Miss Franks?"

No one replied.

"I haven't seen her for a while," said Shelby at length. "She left with the rest of us when we broke up an hour ago and went to our rooms. I don't think she came back after that."

"Go up and see if she is in her room, Miss Fitzpatrick," said Riggs. "This is as good a time as any to get to the bottom of her involvement with Barribault. Then we can put this behind us."

Shelby left the room. When she returned three minutes later, her words were the last D.C.I. wanted to hear.

"She's not in her room, Inspector," said Shelby. "I looked, but I can't find her anywhere."

D.C.I. Riggs's face paled. The news clearly stunned him like a sock in the jaw.

"Westbrook," he said, "alert the staff. Search the house. Find that secretary—what's her name...Gordon. See if she's seen her.—Anyone here know what kind of car she drives?"

"A yellow Mini convertible," answered Whitaker.

Riggs ran for the door shouting for Sgt. Simmons. He found him outside. They made for the row of garages at the back of the house. They were not locked. One stood open and empty. Quickly the two men hoisted open the doors of all ten. None contained a yellow Mini.

"She's gone!" exclaimed Riggs. "Blast it—I slipped up, Sergeant. I didn't have my eye on her!"

"I'm sure she'll turn up, sir. It may not be what it looks."

"No, my gut tells me this is bad. She must have slipped out when we were away to Buckie! Sergeant, call it in—put out an all points on Melinda Franks. It may have been almost an hour—she could be nearly to Aberdeen or Inverness."

He paused and rubbed his chin in thought. "What do you think—the A96, A98...maybe the 947 through Turriff?"

"Or the 95 to Grantown, even the 97 through Huntly down into the Grampians."

"Those are definitely the most likely routes. Move, Sergeant. There's not a moment to lose!"

* * *

D.C.I. Riggs walked slowly back toward the house. He hated to admit it, but he had blown it big time. He would give anything to avoid the questions that would be awaiting him inside. But he had to face it like a man.

He drew in a deep breath, then walked through the front door and back up to the Sitting Room.

"Well, unless Detective Westbrook turns up something which I don't expect," he said, "it would appear that young Franks has given us the slip. Perhaps you were right about her after all, Dr. Cobb. But we'll track her down. When we do, I'll nail her with a charge that will stick."

Not more than a few seconds later Detective Sergeant Westbrook returned with Cynthia Gordon at her side.

Riggs looked toward them with question.

"Anything, Westbrook?"

"No one's seen her, sir, if that's what you mean," replied Maggie. "But Miss Gordon has some news I think you will want to know."

"What is it, Miss Gordon," asked Riggs.

"I finally heard from Mr. Barribault's solicitor, Mr. Forsythe," replied Miss Gordon. "I just got off the telephone with him a short time ago."

"Where is he?"

"He is still in France, sir. But he is on his way. He told me that Mr. Barribault had dictated a new will to him by telephone just five days ago."

"Did he tell you the contents of that new will?" asked Riggs.

"He said he couldn't do that. But he said if you contacted him, if it bore on the case and you formally requested it of him, that he could divulge the basic gist to you."

"Then give me the number where I can reach him, Miss Gordon. I will go up to Barribault's study and telephone him from there. Perhaps he can tell me where I can find a copy of this new will."

* * *

The moment she heard that Melinda was missing, a knot seized Shelby in the pit of her stomach. She knew that Hugh Barribault's death had hit her much harder emotionally than it had any of the others.

In one thing Briscoe Cobb and the other gossipers were right. Something very personal and intimate had taken place between Melinda Franks and Hugh Barribault. But she was sufficiently experienced in reading people to know that it wasn't what they thought.

She, too, had observed the looks of tenderness, the smiles, the snatched moments alone, the hugs, the light in the eyes. That she was observing the blossoming of a wonderful love, Shelby had no doubt.

But it was a far different love than a crusty old coot like Briscoe Cobb could even imagine.

That's why she was so worried right now.

She had been listening intently from across the room to the exchange between Riggs, Westbrook, and Gordon. A minute after Riggs' departure, she casually left the Sitting Room and hurried upstairs as if going to her own room. Once she was certain she was not seen, she continued on up to the third floor and crept down the corridor toward the Barribault study.

The door was closed. From behind it she faintly heard Rigg's muffled voice on the telephone.

A quick glance up and down the hall confirmed that she was still alone. Gently she pressed her ear against the door, and listened.

For some moments all she could hear was an occasional incoherent comment or question, as if Riggs was mostly listening. All at once an exclamation burst out that was so loud Shelby heard it distinctly.

"Melinda Franks!" he cried. "Everything?"

Another silence.

"So, that's our motive tied up in a bow. We've got her!"

Shelby Fiztpatrick heard no more. She was already halfway down the corridor sprinting for the main stairway. She took a detour on the second floor only long enough to hurry into her room and grab her car keys.

She slowed so as not to be heard from the Sitting Room as she reached the first floor landing, then hurried down to the ground floor. She trusted Detective Westbrook completely. But right now, as Riggs had just told his sergeant, there wasn't a moment to lose.

She reached the garages at the back of the house. All the doors were still open.

Thirty seconds later her rented Volvo rounded the front of the house and was racing along the narrow entry road at thirty m.p.h.

* * *

Shelby was more than reasonably certain where she would find Melinda, and not where any police dragnet, on its wild goose chase, would ever think to look for her—on one of the highest and most treacherous overlooks near Cullen. She and Melinda had been there several times together.

All the way she prayed to the God she wasn't sure she believed in that she wasn't too late.

The distance wasn't far—about two miles from the house on the far side of the village. She and Melinda had walked here twice together. She drove through the streets, up Seafield as fast as the traffic would allow, then left and to the Caravan Park.

There, ahead…it was Melinda's Mini!

Shelby jammed her foot onto the accelerator and tore straight through the private lane of the Caravan Park as far as she could go, then stopped, jumped out with her car still idling, and sprinted for the footpath to the overlook known as Nelson's seat.

She reached it in less than two minutes.

Breathing hard, she slowed. There was Melinda at the edge of the precipice, staring down at the sloping bit of muddy grass that led to the high cliff above treacherous rocky shoals fifty feet below.

Shelby approached slowly. She walked past the bench where she and Melinda had sat looking out on the sea. An open book lay on it.

Melinda heard her step and turned.

"Hello, Melinda," smiled Shelby. "I had a feeling I might find you here."

"Go away, Shelby!" shouted Melinda. "Leave me alone."

"Why don't we sit down on the bench and talk."

"There's nothing to talk about Shelby. Please go. This is something I have to do…I have to do it alone."

"It doesn't have to be this way, Melinda. There are people who care about you."

"Don't lie to me, Shelby! No one cares. I have no one left. I never had anyone! This is the only way. It is my destiny, don't you see. It always has been. It had to end this way."

"Melinda, dear," said Shelby, taking another step or two toward her and reaching out her hand.

"Get back, Shelby. I warn you, if you come closer I'll run to the edge and jump right now. I don't want you to have to watch. You've been nice to me. But I have nothing to live for now. I promise, I will jump if you take another step. Just make it easier on us both and go away."

"Okay, Melinda, I'm sorry," said Shelby, backing away. "But you are wrong, Melinda."

"About what?"

"When you say you have nothing to live for."

"What do I have to live for? He's gone. The man I wanted all my life to love...and he's gone!"

"Melinda...he left everything to you."

"What do you mean?"

"Mr. Barribault's will. He left his fortune to you, and I think I know why, Melinda. It's true, isn't it?"

Melinda's eyes, already red, flooded with tears as she stared back at Shelby.

"He made a new will. His legacy is yours now. You have to carry on his work."

"Is it really...did he—"

"Yes, Melinda," smiled Shelby. "He did. You have to come back. He wanted *you* to carry on after him."

Suddenly Melinda burst into sobs. Shelby approached, without fear now, and took her in her arms. The two women stood together, both weeping in release and relief on the edge of the cliff for two or three minutes.

"I'm sorry, Shelby!" Melinda sobbed. "I'm so sorry...I didn't know what to do! I couldn't imagine going on."

"It's all right, Melinda," soothed Shelby stroking her hair. "You will get through it now. You will be strong. I know you will."

At last Shelby led Melinda back from the precipice to the bench. They both sat down. Several more minutes passed. Gradually the tumult of emotions passed. Melinda's jerky breathing slowly relaxed.

"What were you reading?" asked Shelby.

"The story of my life," answered Melinda softly.

They sat for some time. Melinda continued to calm, then by degrees told her the story Shelby had partially suspected.

In the distance slowly the sound of police sirens intruded into their hearing. As they came closer, Shelby realized they were meant for them. Melinda's car must have been seen.

She stood and looked down at Melinda.

"Why don't we go back," she said. "I think you are ready to tell your story now. I will help you."

Melinda smiled and stood with her.

"Don't forget your book," said Shelby.

"Believe me, I will never forget it."

Arm in arm they left the point and descended the path together. A minute later they met a relieved Detective Sergeant Margaret Westbrook hurrying toward them.

TWENTY-ONE

The Story

The mood in the Sitting Room of Cullen House two hours later that afternoon was more subdued than any gathering since the arrival of the Eight. Maggie Westbrook managed to convince Chief Inspector Riggs not to arrest Melinda Franks until he heard what she had to say, which Shelby had filled her in on as they made their way back to the house in Miss Westbrook's car. But Melinda needed an hour or two to rest and calm down, Shelby said. Reluctantly Riggs agreed, with the provision that Westbrook not let her out of her sight.

Riggs spent the time scouring Barribault's office for the missing will.

Sgt. Simmons retrieved the two women's automobiles, the Volvo and the Mini, from the caravan park and called off the all points bulletin.

The same intervening two hours Mike St. John spent in his room reading. *Love's Dry Tears* had long since ceased to be a mere novel to his inquisitive brain. He was a fast reader. Long before the two hours was over he was probing the story's depths on several levels. Without realizing it, he and Shelby Fitzpatrick were approaching the truth from opposite sides. Fate seemed determined for them to meet in the middle with a pooling of their collective insights.

As Mike walked into the Sitting Room a few minutes before 3:30, he sought Shelby with a quick glance, then walked toward her.

"We have to talk," he said in a low tone.

"About what?" she asked.

"About Hugh Barribault...and about Ireland."

Shelby's eyes bored straight into his with a penetrating stare. Had Mike divined that portion of the truth that *she* now knew? She would have to wait to find out. The room was filling again. The mere presence of Detective Chief Inspector Riggs was enough in itself to squelch any attempt at meaningful conversation. Shelby saw him enter the room and rolled her eyes.

"That Riggs is a fool," said Shelby under her breath.

Mike smiled. "Do you think so?" he whispered.

"I would call it obvious to the most casual observer."

"I don't know. I find myself wondering if it's a con."

"How so?"

"If he's not the imbecile he wants us to take him for. True, all this interest in the rest of us, including you and me, the Stokes and Cobb and Whitaker gambits, are obvious red herrings. But I have the feeling Riggs has known that all along."

"He arrested us," rejoined Shelby irritably. "We each spent a night in jail. That's no laughing matter. You're saying that for him this is just part of the game?"

"Not a 'game' exactly, but part of a larger method to his madness, so to speak. And absent malice, what can be brought against him? He can claim in each case that he acted with honest intent."

"That could be questioned," rejoined Shelby cynically.

"Perhaps. But if it catches a murderer in the end, maybe that's a price Riggs is willing to pay."

"I wasn't willing for him to use *me* as a pawn in his charade."

"Nor was I. But no harm was done beyond our discomfort and inconvenience."

"I don't buy it."

"You're the psychologist," smiled Mike. "Maybe we'll never know."

"Oh, there's Melinda," said Shelby. "I need to sit with her through this. She's on the edge emotionally. But I do want to hear what you have to say about Ireland…after you hear *this*."

"We'll get together later, then…that is if Riggs lets us out of his sight," Mike added with a smile.

By 3:35, everyone was again gathered for what was to be a new disclosure of great import.

"All right then, everyone," said Riggs, calling the meeting to order. "Take seats somewhere and let's get moving. We've waited long enough. Miss Westbrook, you say you have compelling reasons why I should not arrest Miss Franks. I want to hear them. I presume you have good reason for asking everyone to assemble like this…some dramatic flair, I take it. Frankly, I don't much care for all that. I just want the information. So let's have it. Then I'll decide what's to be done."

"I appreciate your patience, Chief Inspector," said Maggie graciously. "I simply felt that everyone deserved to hear what Miss Franks has to say, since they have all been part of it together.—Go ahead, Melinda," she said, turning to Melinda who was seated on a couch with Shelby at her side.

Every eye turned toward Melinda. She drew in a deep breath. It was clear that tears were still close at hand. Slowly she began to speak in a soft and halting voice.

"I was born an orphan," she said, "or so I thought, in Ireland. I never knew anything but that I was the adopted daughter of Dave and Judith Franks of Belfast. They were good to me, as loving as a man and woman could be. But there was always a void in my life, a hole, an emptiness from not knowing who my real parents were. The only clue I had was this," she said, holding up the small book seen by Shelby at Nelson's Seat. "It is my mother's diary, left for me prior to her death, for my adoptive mother to give me when she judged the time was right. My mother's name was Fiona Kilcardy."

As he listened Mike St. John was filled with many thoughts. Things were beginning to fit into place.

"I was given every advantage my parents could afford," Melinda went on. "I was blessed with above average intelligence and an aptitude for literature and self-expression. My father, my adoptive father that is, was a joiner, a man skilled at what he did but certainly by no means wealthy. Dave Franks died when I was five. I scarcely remembered him. My mother met and married an American salesman from Minneapolis, where we moved when I was eight. That probably explains the somewhat ambiguous mix of tongues in my accent," she added with a smile. "People can never figure out where I am from. My stepfather, Harvey Ericksen, never managed to save more than a few hundred dollars. My upbringing was modest. I was fortunate enough to be given a grant to study at Cambridge, which otherwise would have been far beyond my parents' means. An education such as I have been fortunate to receive would not have been possible without the generosity of many whom I will never know.

"The moment the contest was announced for the inauguration of Barribault House, something within me leapt with the thrill, almost a premonition that I could not only enter the contest, I might be able to be one of the finalists. I had a feeling, a strange inner sense that...almost that I was *meant* to be one of the winners. I began to write feverishly, hundreds of poems. I studied the writings of Hugh Barribault to see what I could learn about the man, about his style, his interests, his method of writing. I wanted to give myself every advantage of doing well. I knew that he was not a poet. But the vision of the poet is to connect with universal human emotions and drives and longings and aspirations. I hoped to somehow be able to connect with this man I knew very little about and had never met.

"Eventually we did meet, of course. My dream was fulfilled, just like all of yours. I was selected to be among the Eight. I was humbled and honored. And that first night, when we all met one another and Hugh Barribault for the first time, I felt like he was no longer a stranger to me. From the moment my eyes looked into his there was a connection. It was more than my having studied his writings. There was a deep personal connection, a bond, a knowing that transcended anything I had ever experienced. Staring into his eyes, I was drawn into his very being. And I had the sense that, as he returned my gaze, that something similar was happening within him. When two people are drawn together like that, it is an irresistible pull of human magnetism that is overpowering. It cannot be prevented that they *will* come together. They are compelled to do so. They *will* discover what this mighty thing between them means, and where it is destined to take them.

"I went to bed that first night with the image of Hugh Barribault's eyes boring into me like probing hot lasers, though as yet I did not know why they were probing into my soul with such intensity, such question, such longing. I did not have to wait even twenty-four hours to find out. Mr. Barribault sought me out alone on our second day here—late that night, actually. After asking if I was comfortable and if I needed anything to make my stay more pleasant, he came straight to the point. Did I know a woman named Fiona Kilcardy, he asked. The question stunned me. I tried to hide the flood of emotions that surged through me like a tidal wave. I asked why he asked. He said he had once known someone by that name, that he had spent many years trying to find her without success. He said that the instant he had laid eyes on me I had reminded him of her. I blubbered some kind of non-descript answer that no, I had never met her, and made a quick exit to my room.

"When I was alone, hot, sweating, fighting back a turbulence of strange unsought tears, I lay down on my bed and cried and cried. Then I got up and went to the mirror. I didn't exactly say, *Mirror, mirror on the wall*, but something like it. For when I had been with Hugh Barribault I had seen something shocking in his expression, in the slant of his smile, in a certain peculiar wave of his hair, in the faint look of hesitation that passed his lips just before he asked a question. I had seen a reflection of *myself*. And as I stood before the mirror gazing into my own face, I now saw a reflection of *him*…and the conviction exploded within me that Hugh Barribault was my father."

Gasps of astonishment and murmurs of exclamation and wonder circulated through the room. Beside her, it was now Shelby Fitzpatrick rather than Melinda herself, whose eyes were flooding with tears. Even D.C.I. Riggs, where he stood at the side of the room, appeared moved.

"I was worthless the next day. I tried to keep the rest of you from noticing. I don't know if I was successful, but I was a complete basket case. Finally that night, knowing how it would look if I was seen, I crept out of my room and upstairs. I wasn't even sure which rooms were his. But I tried various doors until he answered my knock. The look that came over his face when his eyes came to rest on me standing there in the corridor confirmed my suspicion in an instant. I *knew*...and something told me that he knew as well.

"I asked if I could talk to him. In a hoarse voice, he nodded and invited me in. I told him that I hadn't been altogether truthful to him. I said, although I had never actually known her because she died when I was born, that Fiona Kilcardy was my mother. He stood staring at me in disbelief. Then he began to tremble. His eyes filled. Then he wept. The next second I was in his arms. We were both crying and shaking and holding one another as if our lives depended on it."

An outburst sounded. Eyes turned to see Jessica Stokes choking down a sob and grabbing for a handkerchief.

"We both knew it was true," Melinda went on, "what neither of us had ever dreamed. He knew that the lover of his young manhood, whom tragic circumstances had taken from him, had had a child he had never known about...*his* child. And I knew that I had found the father I had never even dared hope I might know. We talked and talked until late in the night. He was crushed, heartbroken, devastated to learn that my mother was dead and that I knew nothing about her. He told me of the years of his attempts to find some trace of her. But to discover that he had a daughter when he had not even known my mother was carrying his baby...that was a joy to him almost as great as the sorrow of her loss. In him I saw what the Prophet speaks of—that the joy was greater because the sorrow too had been great.

"The next days were ones of great happiness for me, and I hope for my father as well. We tried to go on with the schedule of presentations and discussions and keep our precious secret between ourselves until deciding what was best to be done. We were together as much as propriety would allow without raising too much comment. Obviously as you know, we were not entirely successful in that. My father planned to tell you all—tell you exactly what I am telling you now. But he wanted to find the right time and circumstance. He was a man of plans and precision. He wanted to think through the implications. There were matters about which he needed to speak with his solicitor, he said, though I knew nothing of what these things were. We were also discussing the suitability of my being one of the Eight, and whether my book of poems should be withdrawn so that there would be no appearance of impropriety in my selection. He said there was no question of publication. He would insure that. It was a question of whether a book authored by his daughter should be one of the contest winners. Of course, I was happy to step aside. I wanted to do whatever he felt best. But as the week progressed, he told me that issues were coming up with some of the rest of you that complicated his decision. It might even be best, he said, to postpone the entire contest and start anew. He didn't tell me why. I could tell more was weighing on him than simply the future of *my* book. Unfortunately, before everything could be resolved, and before he could talk to the rest of you...he was—"

Melinda glanced down as her hand went to her mouth. Beside her, Shelby handed her a tissue, and at last Melinda began to cry softly. It was obvious for the present that there was nothing more to say.

TWENTY-TWO

The Wrap Up

Maggie and Shelby escorted a tearful Melinda from the group and back to her room to recuperate from the ordeal. Within minutes she was sound asleep.

"I should probably go back," said Maggie. "The Chief Inspector will no doubt want to discuss where we go from here."

"I'll stay with her," said Shelby. "That is if Inspector Riggs trusts *me* not to try to make a getaway."

"I have a feeling his head is spinning just now trying to get a handle on all this. Anyway, *I* trust you."

Meanwhile downstairs, the four men had risen from their chairs and were milling around near D.C.I. Riggs in scattered conversation. Dame Meyerson sat staring straight ahead almost as if in a trance. Jessica Stokes was blowing her nose and doing her best to recover from an unexpectedly emotional reaction.

"What do you think, Chief Inspector?" Father Smythe was saying. "Is she telling the truth?"

"It's hard to say," replied Riggs slowly. He was thinking hard. Maggie had pinpointed his present mental condition with precision. "She seems sincere enough. But with women you never know."

"I always say, tears are a woman's most powerful weapon," mused Briscoe Cobb.

"Don't think that fact has escaped me," rejoined Riggs. "This could be an attempt to throw us off the scent. Even if it's true, she still could have killed him, especially if she knew about the will. It's all well and good to claim to be his daughter, but in fact that makes her's the strongest motive yet—namely, a fortune."

"Listen to you all!" said a woman's voice from behind. "You are unbelievable."

They turned to see Jessica Stokes staring at them. "The poor girl has just lost her father, and all you can do is pick it apart with cold calculating analysis. Do you care nothing about what she is going through?"

She turned and hurried from the room before a fresh onslaught of tears overwhelmed her.

The three men looked at one another in puzzled amazement.

"What brought that on?" said Cobb. "She's hardly one to talk. She's the coldest fish of the lot."

"I don't know, Dr. Cobb," said Graham Whitaker. "I think she has a point. I for one was moved by Melinda's story. I believe her entirely. There are some things I don't think you can fake."

"Come, come, Whitaker," chided Riggs, "don't tell me you're a sentimentalist."

Whitaker smiled oddly. "I know what it is to lose someone you love," was his only reply.

As the conversation between the men continued, Mike St. John sidled away and moved inconspicuously toward the door. Maggie Westbrook was just approaching from the stairs. Having a good idea what was on Mike's mind, she nodded imperceptibly. A significant look passed between them.

Mike continued up to the guest rooms. He stopped in front of Melinda Franks' door then knocked lightly.

A few seconds later Shelby Fitzpatrick appeared at the door. She held a book in one hand with a finger between the pages.

"Is she…?" whispered Mike.

"She's asleep," nodded Shelby. "She's been through a terrible ordeal."

"Can you talk?"

Shelby glanced behind her, then slipped into the hall and gently closed the door behind her.

"I've been reading Barribault's *Love's Dry Tears*," Mike began. "I think it may hold the key to this whole thing."

"Wait till I tell you what *I've* been reading," said Shelby, lifting the thin volume in her hand toward him, her finger still in place where she had been reading.

"What is it?" asked Mike.

"You'll hardly believe it—it's Melinda's mother's diary."

"Where did you get that!" exclaimed Mike, then caught himself and lowered his voice.

"From Melinda. She has had it all along."

"But she only just now realized she was Barribault's daughter?"

"He is never mentioned in the diary by name. From what I've read, Melinda could never have known. This was written before Barribault was famous, before he had written anything. He and Melinda's mother were never married. If it is true that Melinda was their daughter, they actually knew one another only briefly. One of those fleeting interludes of romance that are the staple of fiction, you know."

"Not in my book," said Mike.

"Nor in mine," smiled Shelby. "It just may be, however, that such a real life interlude fills in the gaps of Melinda's story, even though it would seem to be more tragedy than romance.— *Macbeth*, not *As You Like It*."

"Or more aptly *Romeo and Juliet*," said Mike.

"How so?"

"I am beginning to suspect that *Love's Dry Tears* was based more than incidentally on Hugh Barribault's life."

"Really!"

"I think it well may be," nodded Mike. "I don't know much about Barribault's early years. We need to do more digging. But I have the definite feeling that there's more autobiography in *Tears*, disguised as fiction, than people realize. If the two are connected, it may be the diary that will finally tell the true story behind the book."

"If you're right, then…" Shelby glanced away, her mind racing. "What about the film?" she said. "And, you know…Dame Meyerson, aka Jenny Swain…is there a chance…I mean, that…could she be involved after all?"

"I have no idea," replied Mike. "I never saw the movie. Until a day or two ago I'd never heard of the book or the movie. When it comes to old movies, I'm afraid you're our resident expert."

"I may be a motion picture buff, but I've never seen it either. The film version of *Tears* was gone with the wind as quickly as Jenny Swain's career. But that's Hollywood."

"Do you suppose that's what *we* as authors have to look forward to—fame one day, obscurity the next?"

"Neither of us are even published yet. Now I wonder if we ever will be."

"Maybe we've already had our five minutes of fame."

"The question I can't get out of my mind is why Barribault turned on Jennifer and set out to ruin her career—if her version of events is to be relied on. It's one of those Hollywood mysteries that has never been solved. If we could find a copy of the film. But we'll never get our hands on one here."

"That mystery may hold the missing clue."

"You know," said Shelby, "in the absence of the film itself, what we might use as a substitute is a copy of the screenplay. You don't suppose…"

"He was a consultant for the project. Why wouldn't he have a copy among his manuscripts?"

"A great idea. We need to get into his archives."

They looked at one another for a moment.

"Miss Gordon!" both said at once.

* * *

The two author-sleuths were just about to walk into Miss Gordon's office when suddenly Shelby grabbed Mike's arm and stopped abruptly.

"Wait," she exclaimed. "What are we thinking! As far as she knows, we're still suspects in her boss's murder. She's not going to tell *us* anything. If we explain what we're after, she'll go straight to Riggs."

"You're right. He'll put the kibosh on us."

"Maggie is our only chance of getting access to Barribault's records. Oops—that reminds me, I'm supposed to be watching Melinda! I'd better get back. Why don't you go downstairs and see if you can find a way to ask Maggie to come up and talk to us."

"I'm on my way," said Mike.

He made his way down the stairs as Shelby hurried back along the corridor toward the guest rooms.

Mike walked back into the Sitting Room to see D.C.I. Riggs and D.S. Westbrook in conversation at the end of the room. Jessica Stokes was nowhere to be seen. Dame Meyerson still sat alone and silent. Her male colleagues Smythe, Cobb, and Whitaker were standing near the two detectives engaged in soft conversation but also listening in on the dialog between Riggs and Westbrook.

"…want me to do, Chief Inspector?" Maggie was saying as he drew near.

"Get an early night, Miss Westbrook," replied Riggs. "It looks like we've got this thing wrapped up."

"How long will you be keeping the guard posted here?"

"I'll tell Sgt. Simmons to release his detail. We'll do a final check-off of the crime scene upstairs tomorrow. Then that will be us. Barribault's solicitor should be here by then and it will be up to him to sort everything out from here. We have our man. On our end, the D.A. will take it from here in building his case against Thompson."

"I take it, then, Chief Inspector," said Briscoe Cobb, inching toward the two, "that you have officially dropped the charges against me? In other words, am I again a free man?"

"I would be interested in the answer to that question," said Mike, approaching the small group, "as it applies to me?"

"Yes, yes, of course," replied Riggs. "A mere formality. I should have made that clear. With all the exicitement of the last few hours—the arrest of the Thompson fellow, then the Franks girl giving us a scare, it slipped my mind. But yes, the charges against you both are dropped."

"You will not mind if I ask you a question as well?" said Dame Meyerson, rising and walking with quiet dignity toward them.

"Not at all."

"And you will not arrest me on some ridiculous whim?"

"Of course not. What do you take me for?"

"I take you for a buffoon, Chief Inspector," retorted Dame Meyerson.

Riggs smiled, though did not strike back as some of the observers expected.

"You find that humorous?"

"Actually, I do, Dame Meyerson."

Dame Meyerson shook her head in disbelief. "You really are too much, Chief Inspector," she said. You never had an idea what was going on, running around helter skelter arresting people right and left."

Again Riggs smiled. "You simply misunderstood my strategy, Dame Meyerson."

"Your *strategy*!"

"It's all part of my method to keep people off guard. Nothing is more deadly than an underestimated detective. So I keep things stirred up. Perhaps occasionally I arrest someone who retaliates. But by mixing things up, no one knowing what I might do next, it shakes things loose. When people are together in a room, they talk. You never know what you may learn. People say things in the heat of the moment, in shock, in self-defense...yes, and also in anger, that they might not say otherwise. I learn things. It's all part of the game. You can't argue with my results. I always get my man. So what is your question?"

"Does your innocence verdict apply to me as well?" asked Dame Meyerson.

"Certainly."

She snorted and walked away.

"In any event, I take it then that we are free to go," said Father Smythe.

"You may take that as official," replied Riggs.

Smythe left him and walked after Dame Meyerson.

"So, good lady," he said, drawing up beside her. "Will you be ready to leave in the morning? We shall only be twenty-four hours later than originally planned."

"Actually, Dugan," she said, turning toward him. "I think I shall pass on your kind offer."

"Oh...ah—you are—"

"I am going to stay on a little longer...a day, two days—I don't know exactly. At least until some of the rest of it gets sorted out."

"What does any of it have to do with you now? Except your book of course. But if they decide to go ahead with publication, which I doubt, they will surely contact us by—"

"It's got nothing to do with my book. That's the last thing on my mind. It's just that I need to see this through."

"See what through...why?"

"It's personal. I need to know where I fit into Hugh Barribault's past."

Whatever Smythe may have thought about such a statement he kept to himself. He merely shrugged. He and Dame Meyerson parted without further discussion of his plans for departure.

As D.S. Westbrook drifted away from the others, Mike St. John sought to catch her eye. She saw the look and eased inconspicuously toward him.

"Shelby and I would like a few words with you," Mike whispered. "We are not convinced that the whole story has yet come out."

"There definitely remain too many questions for my comfort," she said in a low voice—the missing quill...*your* quill...the clock...how he was rendered unconscious...too many dangling threads. Do the two of you have ideas?"

"Nothing definite—only nagging questions about Barribault's past, the film made of his book...and maybe Dame Meyerson."

Maggie cocked an inquisitive eyebrow. "Dame Meyerson? *She* is still active in your minds?"

"I don't know. But we would like to talk to you."

"All right. I'll slip away when I can."

As Mike left the room, Maggie again approached D.C.I. Riggs.

"So, Chief Inspector," she said, "shall I be going, or would you like me to get started with the final check-list upstairs?"

"No, we'll take care of that tomorrow. Go on home, Miss Westbrook."

Maggie nodded and smiled.

"Another case solved, what?" said Riggs. "You did well. You're coming along, Westbrook."

"Thank you, sir. And tomorrow?"

"I'll see you at the station. We'll likely transfer the prisoner to Elgin and possibly have our first debriefing with the D.A."

Maggie nodded and sauntered away. Instead of going outside to her car, she climbed the stairs again to the second floor. After a brief stop by Mike St. John's room, she knocked lightly on the door of Melinda's Franks' room, then walked inside. There she found Melinda still asleep. Shelby was seated at the bedside absorbed in the diary of Melinda's mother. Mike entered a few moments later. The three slipped quietly to the far side of the room and sat down.

"Mike said you wanted to talk to me," said Maggie softly to Shelby.

"Yes," replied Shelby. "This is absolutely remarkable. It's the diary of Melinda's mother. She never divulges Hugh Barribault's name, but it is a dramatic story. He wasn't the only young man she was involved with.

"Mike said it was also connected to the best-seller Barribault wrote, and the movie Dame Meyerson played in."

"We're trying to figure out those connections. Mike is reading the book now."

Maggie turned toward Mike.

"How is Dame Meyerson involved?" she asked.

"I don't know that she is," Mike replied. "But why did Barribault do what he did? I am convinced it has something to do with what took place in Ireland with Melinda's mother."

"Dame Meyerson wasn't involved with him back then?"

"No, and there is no hint in the book of the love triangle with the other man named Hainn who is in the diary."

"A love triangle?" said Maggie.

"From Fiona's point of view," said Shelby. "That's Melinda's mother. But not from Hugh Barribault's—he apparently knew nothing of the other man."

"Did this...what's his name—Hainn...did he know about Barribault?"

Mike and Shelby looked at one another inquisitively.

"We don't know," replied Shelby. "The diary tells the story from Fiona's point of view. Then later in *Love's Dry Tears* Hugh Barribault fictionalized his side of the thing—is that how you see it, Mike?"

"That would be my take on it."

"But neither of them ever saw one another again?" asked Maggie.

"No. Melinda's mother died when Melinda was born. Melinda never knew anything about Hugh Barribault. Nor apparently did he know there had been a child."

"We thought that if we could get into Mr. Barribault's archives, there might be notes or manuscripts, possibly a copy of the original screenplay of *Tears*, something to tie in the book, the diary, and what happened between Hugh Barribault and Melinda's mother."

"You think Hugh Barribault's archives or old manuscripts might fill in some of these gaps?"

"There aren't very many other options."

"Could you arrange for us to search Barribault's files?"

"I'm not sure Chief Inspector Riggs would—"

"I wasn't actually thinking of inviting him along," said Shelby. "I was thinking more of just the three of us."

Maggie thought a moment.

"I will talk confidentially with Miss Gordon and see what I can learn. It may be that I could come back later tonight...after the Chief Inspector is gone. As far as I know, none of our other officers will be here either."

"None of the others can know," said Mike. "It might be best if we did not apprise Melinda of our plans either. She's been through enough for one day."

"All right," said Maggie. "I'll talk to Miss Gordon. I'll find some way to contact you later. In the meantime, it would be helpful if you finished reading the book and the diary."

* * *

Maggie slipped down the stairs and outside. Inspector Riggs' car was still in front of the house.

On her way through town Maggie parked at the square for a brief visit to The Paper Shoppe.

"Hello, Alan," she said to the tall man behind the counter. "Did my dad come in for's paper the day?"

"Nae, Maggie—I haena seen him."

"He's a wee under the weather. I told him I'd stop on my way hame an' check an' get it for him gien he hadna been in."

"Gien he got ane somewhaur else, bring it back. Ye dinna want twa papers."

Maggie handed him ninety pence.

"Funny thing, though," the shopkeeper added, "John Thompson bought twa identical papers a feow days syne—I mind because it was the day o' the incident in Glaisga, an' I thoucht it keerious."

"Ah, weel, ye ne'er ken foo fowk du some things."

As she drove home to Fordyce, however, Maggie could not rid the brief conversation from her mind. The terrorist incident in Glasgow had taken place on the same day as the Barribault murder. Now John Thompson was in jail. Why on *that* particular day had he purchased two newspapers?

TWENTY-THREE

The Private Investigation

Maggie Westbrook telephoned the Barribault offices from home a few minutes before 5:00. She hoped to find Miss Gordon still in her office but D.C.I. Riggs gone. He would not react kindly to discover her eleventh hour attempt to take the investigation in a new direction without him.

"Hello, Cynthia," she said when the Barribault assistant answered, "it is Maggie. Have you heard anything further from Mr. Barribault's solicitor?"

"Not since I spoke to him last?"

"Do you know when he will be here?"

"Hopefully tomorrow," answered Miss Gordon.

"Do you know if D.C.I. Riggs is still there, or has left for the day?"

"I talked to him briefly about an hour ago. I haven't seen him since."

"What I really need is from you anyway," said Maggie, inwardly relieved. "I would like to look into some of Mr. Barribault's past notes and manuscripts and files. I am particularly interested in research notes and early drafts of his book *Love's Dry Tears,* and the screenplay that was made of it. Where are such files kept?"

"In the Library on the third floor."

"Could I find it easily?"

"Oh, aye. The boxes of old files and manuscripts are in the storage room at the back of the north wall. Everything is clearly labeled. What are you looking for? Perhaps I can—"

"I need to see if there are notes he made as he was writing the book, and also for the screenplay...perhaps notes Mr. Barribault made during filming."

"I thought everything was completed. What are ye looking for, Maggie?"

"Jist a hunch o' my ain I want tae follow up on afore we steek the file o' the case."

"Wud ye like me tae bide a wee whilie jist the noo?" asked Miss Gordon, lapsing into the local dialect in response.

"That winna be necessar. I will edder come back this een, or luik intil it the morn. I still hae the key ye gae me."

"Gien ye're sure ye dinna need my help."

"I'm siccar. Thank ye, Cynthia."

Maggie hung up the phone. She would have supper and wait until later, when the evening had settled in. Hopefully everyone at Cullen House would by then be safely snug in their rooms.

* * *

Night fell over the Moray Firth.

Maggie Westbrook called to let Shelby know she was on her way, then left Fordyce about 9:45. She let herself through the front door of Cullen House a few minutes before ten o'clock. All was quiet.

Stealthily she crept to the second floor, glanced up and down the hall, then tiptoed to Shelby's room. She tried the latch. It opened, and she let herself in.

Mike and Shelby were waiting for her.

"How is Melinda?" asked Maggie softly.

"Exhausted but otherwise fine," replied Shelby. "We had a light supper with her and the others. She's in bed. I think the crisis has passed. *And*," she added with emphasis, "we think some of the pieces of her history may be starting to fit together."

Maggie looked back and forth between them. "I can tell that you two are bursting with news."

"What is it?" she said.

320

"I finished *Love's Dry Tears*," said Mike. "Shelby has read the diary from cover to cover. We've been on the internet most of the evening too, trying to research Hugh Barribault's past."

"I'm a' lug, as we say."

Shelby looked at her with question.

"I'm all ears," smiled Maggie, then sat down to listen.

"This is what we have deduced from the book." Mike began. "A protestant girl in Northern Ireland named Fiona Kilcardy grew into her teens as the terrorist violence in Northern Ireland reached its height in the 1970s. Her name in *Tears* was Mary Kenrick. Her father became a leader in the loyalitst paramilitary brigades after Bloody Sunday in Londonderry in 1972. Her older brothers were also drawn into the movement against the IRA. Though the violence began to diminish after 1976, the IRA and Sinn Féin continued active in the north, as did a few radical unionist protestant groups. Fiona's family was among them.

"In 1981 the British chief secretary of Ireland, Lord Frederick Cavendish, and his under secretary, T.H. Burke were stabbed to death in Phoenix Park in Dublin, where they had come for meetings with Irish leaders. The murderers belonged to a nationalist secret society called the Invincibles. These Phoenix Park murders are pivotal as this is the point where young Hugh Barribault enters the story, or as Barbault calls himself in his fictionalization of it—Gavin Stanley.

"British troops were a common sight on the streets of Belfast and Londonderry ever since 1969. As the son of a wealthy financier and uncertain what to do with his life, young Stanley, aka Barribault himself, joined the army at the late age of thirty-three. This part of *Tears* dovetails exactly with Barribault's actual biography. Stanley was sent to Northern Ireland in 1981. He was a low grade corporeal who happened to be on patrol in Belfast with another soldier when a minor incident broke out. The elder Selwyn Kilcardy—Barribault uses the actual name of Fiona's father in the book, calling him Selwyn Kenrick—had been instrumental in organizing an attack in Belfast in retaliation for the Phoenix Park murders in which several mid-ranking IRA operatives were killed. The IRA discovered Kilcardy's role in the incident. He went into hiding. They therefore made plans to kidnap his now twenty-six year old daughter Mary, or Fiona, and hold her for ransom. This is the role that Jenny Swain, our own Dame Meyerson, played in the film. That ransom would be Selwyn Kilcardy himself. Three hooded IRA terrorists burst into the Kilcardy home, killed two of Mary Kenrick's brothers on the spot and dragged Mary away at gunpoint.

"Outside, a block away, Corporal Stanley, aka Hugh Barribault, heard the shots. He and his partner ran toward the scene. Stanley reached the building just as the terrorists and their captive were coming out. Knowing nothing more than that a girl was in mortal danger, he dropped to the ground and pulled the pistol from his belt. In either a remarkable display of marksmanship or sheer luck, thirty seconds later the three IRA terrorists lay dead on the ground and he was carrying the girl away from danger. Relatives and friends arrived shortly. The girl was unharmed, though obviously the family was shellshocked by the death of her brothers.

"It is not difficult to predict what came next. Corporal Gavin Stanley and the girl he rescued became involved. He was dashing and heroic, and the fact that he had saved her life was the icing on the cake. What girl *wouldn't* fall in love?

"A whirlwind romance amid war-ravaged Belfast, both their lives in danger...no one could script it more perfectly, including its tragic end. The dramatic irony was increased in that Gavin Stanley had been raised Catholic, but he had not yet told Mary. He was certain it would make no difference to her. But how could it not create conflict if Mary's family found out?"

"Hugh Barribault wasn't Catholic, was he?" said Maggie. "I didn't think he was religious at all."

"We didn't either," said Shelby. "But remember when Mr, Whitaker was talking about the old man's endowments, how most of them went to Catholic hospitals and schools and other institutions. In researching it we found that the family was indeed traditionally Catholic."

"What young Gavin Stanley—and I must assume Hugh Barribault in real life—had not anticipated was the internal conflict that began to build within *him*. Without planning, yet neither avoiding it when the moment came, Gavin and Mary were intimate. Gavin Stanley's temporary elation was followed by a wave of unexpected guilt. His conscience had not bothered him with killing three men. But after crossing the line of sexual fidelity, his conscience and the Catholic teachings of his youth sprang awake like a roaring lion. He had been unfaithful, not merely to the Church of his fathers, but also toward Mary. He had not behaved honorably toward her. And being seven or eight years older added all the more to his guilt. He had seen himself as her protector. Now suddenly he had not behaved like a gentleman. For days he could not bring himself to face her. In despair, he sought the confessional where tearfully he poured out to a priest he never knew a detailed account of the facts that haunted him like a black cloud.

"At last, Gavin left a brief note through the door of the flat asking Mary to meet him the next day at a park in Belfast. He returned to his quarters. In a terrible twist of fate, a car bomb was set outside his barracks, and that same night Gavin was wounded badly in the leg and chest and did not regain consciousness for nearly a week. Several of his comrades were killed. When he woke up he found himself in a military hospital back in England. Beside himself to contact Mary, he wrote letter after letter but never received a word in return.

"The moment he was well enough to be released, Stanley returned to Belfast. Months had passed. A bombed out shell was all that remained of the row of houses where Mary had lived. A desperate search during the following months turned up not a trace of Mary or her family. At this point the fictionalized account drifts away from reality. The fictionalized Gavin Stanley continues to serve in the military, which Barribault did not do, turns to drink and becomes a James Bond sort of character specializing in espionage. But the internal struggles of the character, I believe, continued to be based on the author. Whatever relief was gained from the confessional was short-lived. If anything, the mental anguish grew worse as a result because of the impotence of the absolution to rid him of his guilt. Stanley, as Barribault's alter-ego, loses his faith and never sets foot inside a church again. This is one of the things that makes Gavin Stanley such a compelling character—he is no modernist. His loss of faith does not stem from skepticism or anger toward God or the Church, but from his own guilt. He actually *wants* to believe, and probably does believe, but laments the fact that he *can't* follow his beliefs any longer. He is torn in two directions, toward and away from faith. His own feelings of unworthiness follow him the rest of his life. The impotence of the confessional to remedy them is a silent plague of despair he cannot escape. The underlying theme, even more powerful than his love for Mary, is the ongoing guilt that he can find no way to make right—either with Mary or the Church. Even the hard cold life of the spy is infused with an undercurrent of a morality that he never resolves. He is the classic conflicted and complex character. The ending is actually very sad, and Gavin Stanley is eventually killed by the IRA."

The three were silent a few long seconds.

"In the larger picture of the Northern Ireland conflict," Mike went on, "the attempted abduction and rescue was minor. It was but one of a thousand such personal stories of tragedy that never make national news. But a story becomes immortal when someone has eyes to see in it a larger perspective. This Hugh Barribault did when he fictionalized his experience into Gavin Stanley's story. Barribault was somehow able to draw into his narrative a perceptive history of the Northern Ireland conflict. It is a page-turner, yet contains such pathos and depth, I understand why it received such accolades. And such a poignant romance doomed to tragedy was ideal for Hollywood. It was Romeo and Juliet meet the IRA. Though Hugh Barribault was unknown as an author, his father Winston Barribault was well-enough known that *Love's Dry Tears* received a major launch with endorsements from all across the spectrum of British society. Every Sunday supplement ran specials on Barribault and the book. It was a slam-dunk million copy seller the first year. Awards and best-sellerdom followed, then the film, and Hugh Barribault's career took off. It did not take long for his reputation to surpass that of his father."

"That is a remarkable chronology!" said Maggie when Mike had finished. "You're sure of the connections to Barribault's actual life?"

"We've been on the internet all evening,' said Shelby. "We've looked into every detail of his life."

"Obviously much in the book is fictionalized," added Mike, "but the basic gist, we believe, is substantially Hugh Barribault's own story. I cannot but wonder if Barribault somehow hoped the book would bring Fiona forward. Of course by then he could have no way of knowing whether she was married, or even still alive. In any event, he never saw the real Fiona Kilcardy again. But the *full* story doesn't begin to come clear until you add what Shelby discovered from Fiona's diary."

Maggie and Mike turned to Shelby.

"In its own way, the diary is just as remarkable," Shelby began. "The book and diary tell the same story as if from behind the wall of their separation—neither able to see the whole, and only able to perceive one side and not the other. After all this time, it is *we* who are able to see the whole. For the first time, the diary and the book are being read by the same eyes."

"Amazing."

"How curious, too, that so much fame and acclaim came to Hugh Barribault for his version of the tale...when in fact all his life he only knew a portion of it. It is only with Fiona's diary that the full facts come to light. In the same way that Fiona never knew of Hugh's Catholic past, or the guilt he felt for their sexual liason, she too had secrets she kept from him."

"You have definitely succeeded in getting my attention," laughed Maggie, then caught herself and again lowered her voice. They did not want the others aware of their late-night meeting. "So what was Fiona's secret?" she whispered.

"Fiona was engaged to a young man, a certain Fingall Hainn," Shelby went on softly. "For this, because the diary is our source, we know the real names. Interestingly, however, she never mentions Barribault by name. I have no idea why. Perhaps she had learned of his Catholicism and was afraid of her family's reaction if they knew his identity. But in the diary he is simply referred to as *the Corporal.*"

"It sounds like a love triangle."

"In a way. But at first only Fiona knew of both men. Neither of them knew about the other, and Barribault *never* knew there were three involved."

"All this took place so long ago, how can it have anything to do with our present case and Hugh Barribault's death?" said Maggie.

"Shelby's not through," said Mike. "The intrigue deepens."

Maggie turned again toward Shelby.

"The incident involving Hugh Barribault, and then their hasty and tumultuous love affair," Shelby went on, "came into Fiona's life so quickly that she had no fitting opportunity to tell either of her two young men about the other."

"Where was the other man...what was his name?"

"Fingall Hainn?"

"Where was he when the incident involving Barribault took place?"

"Away in the south—in Cork, I believe."

"So at first he knows nothing?"

"But Fiona realizes that she is suddenly involved with two men," Shelby went on. "Oh, how I would love to see the young Dame Meyerson's portrayal of this in the film! In any event, Fiona agonizes over her indecision in the diary. With sexual intimacy, which she passes over lightly, she realizes her choice has been made. Whatever love triangle may have existed in her mind, she knows that she must tell Fingall it is over between them and that her heart belongs to another. This quandary of how to tell him obviously intensifies when Hainn returns from Cork.

"Then the note from Hugh Barribault appears, the meeting is planned in the park, but inexplicably Hugh never comes, and disappears from her life as quickly as he came. She never knows of the car bomb. Recuperating in England, Hugh Barribault never knows that Fiona is pregnant with his child. Fiona never hears from him again, nor has any idea what has happened. She waits all day in the park, till darkness threatens to make the streets unsafe, then walks home weeping, assuming that he has deserted her?

"Fiona's writing turns dark. She falls into deep depression. In her despair, she allows Fingall Hainn to take advantage of her. Eventually she can hide her pregnancy no longer. Fingall thinks the child is his. She laughs at the suggestion, then tells him the truth, that the child belongs to the corporeal who saved her life. He is filled with rage. Fiona is terrified for her life. He makes wild threats against her unknown lover.

"Then she makes a curious statement in her diary—that she has the feeling that Fingall already knew, perhaps not that she was pregnant, but knew there was someone else, and suspected how far it had gone. It was as if he knew all, but had held his fury in check until she told him herself. His last words to her were—"

Shelby paused and flipped through the diary.

"Here is is...he said, *Weep for him now while you can. He will die before you lay eyes on him again. He will die at my hand.* As her baby grows within her, Fiona's depression deepens. She despairs of being able to give a child a life of happiness. She begins talking with herself in her diary of other possibilities. It gradually becomes obvious from her dark prayers and morose reflections that she has begun to consider taking her own life."

"And does she?" asked Maggie.

"How can we know?" answered Shelby. "The final entry, so poignant and sad—"

Again she opened the worn covers of the diary, and read.

"She writes, *If I never see you again, my precious little child, after you come into the world, forgive me for what I must do. But it is best, so that you may have a life free from the death and evil that is the terrible legacy of hatred that has torn this land apart—hatred between people who claim all to love the same God, but who hate their fellow man. I hope and pray that you will be able to escape it, though I have not been able to, for that hatred has consumed everything I once loved. For me to remain with you would place you in danger all your life. I will see you soon. Know that my love goes with you and will abide with you, even though I cannot share it. I love you..*"

"Is there no more?"

Shelby shook her head and turned the open book so that Maggie could see the final entry she had just read.

"And the daughter, I take it, is our own Melinda Franks?" said Maggie.

"We have no idea what were the circumstances," Shelby went on, "but as Melinda told it, she was adopted by Dave and Judith Franks of Belfast. Once she was old enough, they gave Melinda the diary left by her mother. Melinda said she always assumed, from what they told her, that her mother died in childbirth."

TWENTY-FOUR

The Screenplay

A ll of Cullen House was silent.

Shelby's room now quieted with an even deeper silence than that of the darkness outside. The detective and her two amateur assistants sat contemplating the intriguing tale from the two sources—the best-selling novel and the secret diary—brought together at last after the passing of decades. They were all thinking how like this was to a real-life Romeo and Juliet, two lovers whom circumstances conspired to prevent meeting again, both ultimately going to their deaths never knowing of the other's love.

"It is so sad," said Shelby at length.

"A modern Greek tragedy," nodded Mike.

Suddenly Maggie started upright in her chair and her eyes shot open.

"Did I hear you mention Cork!" she exclaimed, turning to Shelby. Then catching herself, she began whispering again. "In fact, I think I heard you say it twice!" she said softly.

"Right," said Mike. "The home of Fiona's Irish fiancé."

"We don't *know* that he was Irish," said Shelby. "Or that that was his home. We just know that he was there when the IRA tried to kidnap her."

"Wait here—I'll be right back!" exclaimed Maggie in an excited whisper. She jumped to her feet and ran for the door and disappeared.

Mike and Shelby chatted softly until they heard steps tiptoeing toward them along the hall. A moment later Maggie reentered the room, several manila files in her hands.

"Where have you been?" whispered Shelby eagerly.

"To Barribault's study," replied Maggie. "It's not only a crime scene, it is also where most of the information pertaining to this case is kept. I have here the detailed questionnaires you each had to fill out after your selection as finalists. By then your identities no longer needed be kept secret. So Mr. Barribault was asking for personal details. You will never guess what I discovered. A fourth of you were born—get this!—in Ireland."

"In other words...*two*," laughed Mike.

"Yes. But it could be significant."

"Why more than that two of us are American?" asked Shelby.

"Because if Fiona's fiancé was Irish," rejoined Maggie, "that establishes a connection to Barribault we didn't know about. Those kinds of links are the bread and butter of detective work, the hidden motives not obvious at first glance.—You said you were online earlier...is access available throughout the house?"

Shelby nodded.

"May I use your computer, then?" asked Maggie.

Shelby went to the writing table, brought over her laptop, and handed it to Maggie. "I'm going to access Scotland Yard's data base," said Maggie.

"Can you do that!" said Mike.

"If you have an access code and password."

"I want one!"

"Sorry, Mike. Not for the everyday citizen I'm afraid," Maggie laughed. "They only give you access when you make detective. Even Sgt. Simmons doesn't have a password."

Maggie began flailing away at the keyboard of Shelby's laptop.

"There, all right...I'm in! Now, let's see what we can find."

Mike and Shelby watched with fascination as she flew over the keys and scrolled down lists of dates and followed one trail after another with lighting speed.

"You've done this before!" laughed Mike.

"Once or twice," smiled Maggie. "I'm sort of the computer person at the Buckie station. Riggs is hopeless about high tech stuff. He still thinks it's cigar ash and blood stains and strange accents of mysterious Orientals and poison residue in glasses. He fancies himself a modern day Sherlock Holmes. But when there is no cigar ash or poison residue, he's not adverse to asking for my help…oh, my—you're not going to believe this!"

"Don't keep us in suspense," said Shelby.

"Neither of our two Irish-born authors show up by their birthdates. According to Scotland yard, they were never born…at least on those dates."

"You mean in Ireland?"

"In the entire U.K.!"

"Could their names have been changed?"

"That might explain it, but *why*? And if Barribault was such a stickler for forthrightness and honesty, a changed name it seems would have been of enormous interest to him. This may throw the whole question of motive into a new light."

Maggie paused, thinking hard.

"Do you remember what Inspector Riggs said about the murderer being left-handed?' she asked.

"Vaguely, now that you mention it," said Shelby.

"Our forensics team agreed," replied Maggie. "From bruise marks on Barribault's arm, the way he was held—though he was apparently unconscious at the time—while the quill tip was shoved into his arm, and the damage to the quill itself…the way it was gripped…everything confirms a left-handed thrust. I'm not sure whether we checked that with Mr. Thompson. Chief Inspector Riggs arrested him so fast we didn't look at all the details. However, both of our Irish born non-persons according to Scotland Yard, are lefties."

"So am I," added Mike.

"Yes," smiled Maggie. "I had not forgotten that fact. Should I put you back on the list of persons of interest?"

"That will have to be your call," replied Mike with a subtle smile of his own.

"Ireland is predominately Catholic, isn't it?" he asked after a brief pause.

"Absolutely," replied Maggie. "You should know that?"

"I do. I was just putting it on the record, so to speak."

"What are you thinking?"

"I was just recalling an interesting conversation we had shortly after our arrival. It was one of the few times religion came up. With two clergymen involved, you might think it would have been otherwise. But Father Smythe found me neither amusing nor my views particularly to his liking."

"Tell me about it," said Maggie.

"We were talking about beliefs in general terms. Father Smythe, I think, lumped me in with the whole side of the spiritual spectrum that he termed fundamentalist."

"And that offended you?"

"Oh, gosh…not in the least. I *am* fundamentalist in many things, and free-thinking and liberal in others. You can't categorize my beliefs into a box any more than you can anyone's. I do not care for religious labels in general…but offended, no. What I found interesting, however, was an aside comment Father Smythe made about his own religious training at seminary."

"Which was?"

"Well…" replied Mike, thoughtfully, still trying to lay hold of the thing, "he rattled off several authors whom I would assume are among the theologians who influenced him. Obscure names most people would not know."

"But you had heard of them?"

Mike nodded. "My reading is quite diverse. Yes, I have read their works. What I found interesting, however, is that all three were Catholic."

"What were their names?"

"Hans Urs von Balthasar, Karl Rahner, and Hans Kung."

"You're right," laughed Maggie. "Never heard of them."

"In what would be considered the more liberal circles of scholarly Catholicism they would be names most would recognize. But in the general population, even among devout Catholics, probably not."

"What did you find odd about Father Smythe's reference to them?"

"I don't know, he simply has not struck me as a man who would be widely read theologically. He's a thorough modernist, not what I would term a theological scholar."

"Everyone has to read theology in seminary, don't they?" said Shelby. "You did, and you're less Catholic than he is."

"I read none of those authors in seminary," rejoined Mike. "That was on my own. You would actually be surprised what a limited theological diet most clergymen receive. Seminaries are not geared to give aspiring priests and pastors a broad foundation of ideas so much as to stamp out clones to carry on the indoctrination of the masses according to the prescribed teaching of one or another religious tradition. I know it sounds callous, but that is my perspective. That is why so little fresh thinking comes from the professional pulpit. An odd thing too, perhaps, for a minister to say…but I say it."

"Are you an exception to that rule?" asked Shelby with a peculiar smile.

Mike returned her look with a curious expression. "We'll leave that discussion for another time," he said. "The point is, I doubt very much if Father Smythe read a word of Hans Urs von Balthasar in any Anglican seminary in England."

"Where *did* he attend seminary?" asked Shelby, turning to Maggie.

Maggie opened one of the files she was holding and flipped through the pages.

"His file doesn't say. The references to schooling are incomplete. The only listing noted here says, 'Graduate work, Kings College, London.'"

"Okay," said Shelby. "But what does this have to do with the problem at hand? The book and the diary link Hugh Barribault's past to Melinda. We're pretty sure she didn't kill him—at least I am. So there must be other links we haven't found. We know one of them—that's Dame Meyerson. I want to know what happened on the movie set that made him turn on her. That is, *if* her version of events is accurate. What if she was telling us all that to cover *her* tracks? I still think she has the best motive."

"I don't know," said Mike. "Dr. Cobb stood to lose everything. Dame Meyerson and Jessica were not going to have to give back their advance checks. I still want to know more about

Cobb. He's the only one Barribault accused of outright lying. What if he was in financial difficulty? The loss of that hundred thousand might be motive enough to have killed him."

He paused a moment.

"How's this for a wild thought," he went on. "Is there a possibility that Dame Meyerson, or Jenny Swain if you like, could be Melinda's mother?"

The two women did not register as much surprise as he had expected.

"What are you suggesting?" said Maggie.

"But according to Melinda her mother is dead," said Shelby.

"Do we absolutely *know* that?" rejoined Mike. "What if she was given up for adoption, then the mother disappeared, she becomes an actress, changes her name to Jenny Swain and unexpectedly becomes a star, she is cast for the lead in the movie, Barribault doesn't know who she is at first, then when he finds out, or perhaps he does know and is his obvious choice to play herself in the movie...then the lovers' quarrel...she waits for years for her revenge...somehow manages to win his writing contest—"

He began shaking his head. "No," he said. "Now that I try to explain it, it's too far-fetched."

"Stranger things have happened in Hollywood," said Shelby.

"It's as good as any other theory," said Maggie. "But if it were true, why wouldn't Barribault tell Melinda that her mother was here too. What a wonderful story that would make! The perfect family reunion. However, I see no evidence of a connection between Dame Meyerson and Melinda."

"And with their daughter found and all three suddenly together," said Shelby, "I cannot imagine any possibility of Jennifer killing him—not unless I badly misjudge her. I'm not saying I always get the right read on everyone, but I do not see her as doing anything but melting in light of such a discovery. Yes, she said she hated him at first. But I think everything would have changed instantly to discover she had a daughter."

"You're the movie buff," said Mike. "Is it possible Jenny Swain had an Irish past as Fiona Kilcardy?"

"Anything's possible, I suppose. But I have not a hint of information pointing in that direction. I have to think there was something else going on between she and Barribault."

"This should all be easy to check," said Maggie. She consulted Dame Meyerson's biographical questionnaire, then returned to the computer. "No," she said after a couple of minutes. "Everything is just as she represents it—birthdate checks, born Leicester as Jennifer Sarah Swain. Nothing suspicious there. No Irish connections whatever."

Maggie thought a moment.

"I spoke with Cynthia Gordon earlier," she said. "She told me where Barribault's files and old manuscripts and research notes are kept. It would be helpful, as you mentioned before, to check some of that material, especially a copy of the screenplay if we could find it."

"What are we waiting for, then!" said Shelby excitedly.

"The files are in the Library," said Maggie. "With three of us prowling the house so late…we'll have to walk very quietly."

* * *

An hour later, the three detectives were sitting on the Library floor perusing notes and folders and files and manuscripts, several boxes open, papers strewn about the carpet. They had located a copy of the screenplay for *Love's Dry Tears*. Shelby and Maggie were skimming alternate scenes in search of whatever handwritten notes might have been added by the book's author. Mike continued to pour through early drafts and research notes for the writing of the book.

"You two finding anything?" asked Mike.

"Only uninteresting bits of stagecrafting—you know, stage right, stage left kinds of notations."

"It is remarkable," said Shelby, "how the three versions of this story—the diary, the book, and the screenplay—tell the same story at so many points. In that Hugh Barribault was certainly successful, he kept the screenplay faithful to his interpretation of events."

"He must have had influence with the director to have achieved that."

"Oh, wow—here's something interesting—look at this," said Maggie, "it's where the scene opens with Mary and Gavin having dinner together, just before...you know, they sleep together and it all breaks apart. Here's a note in the margin: *Talk to Dir.—Jenny's portrayal far too suggestive...makes seem Fiona seduced me. Not true to events. No one to blame but me. Can't allow Fiona be turned into onscreen trollop. Won't tolerate such interpretation."*

"Strong language!" said Shelby. "I would definitely like to ask Jennifer how that turned out. Still," she added, turning to Maggie, "where in that is a motive for murder?"

"I don't know. He got mad at her, she got mad back. Then all these years later she killed him...it's thin—*unless* there is more to the story. You're right—we need to talk to Dame Meyerson."

"As I listened to her telling her side of the filming and her affair with Hugh Barribault," said Mike, "I did not get the impression I was listening to a murderer."

"Nor did I," added Maggie. "To my mind she was a lady who had been hurt, and though angry when she first saw Barribault again, was genuinely grieving for a man she had cared deeply for. When I talk like this Riggs calls me a sentimental sap. But you have to trust your instincts."

She turned toward Shelby. "You are the psychology professional...what do you think?"

"I tend to agree," replied Shelby. "But murder involves deeper motives than meet the eye. I may be in over my head here."

"Not really," said Mike. "Maggie is right. You have to trust your instincts. Okay, it's not scientific. But when the two of you, both shrewd and intelligent students of people, have the same response, I think that carries some weight."

"Maybe," laughed Shelby. "But remember my first reaction to you. I thought you were a religious dunce!"

"Ah, yes, the good old days. How quickly one forgets! I'm not talking about first impressions, but rather carefully thought-out responses born out over time. And returning to a point from earlier, if Ireland is somehow the missing link in this thing, there must be connections we haven't found to Barribault's interlude there that may have also been connected to Melinda's mother...if not connections to Dame Meyerson, then perhaps to someone else."

"What about Barribault's stint in the military?" suggested Maggie. "Is there a chance his army service produced relationships that continued later? What about the fellow who was with him when he killed the three terrorists? An experience like that would draw men together. If we're looking for motives going back many years, perhaps to Ireland, Fiona isn't the only person who may be linked to them."

"Remember that day when Ireland came up in conversation?" said Shelby. "Dame Meyerson was the only one who said she had been there."

"What was her business in Ireland?" asked Maggie

"She did a benefit in Dublin, after the peace talks got underway."

"Did Melinda say anything in the discussion?"

"Not at the time. But then later it came out about the story of her birth—you heard all that."

"And Father Smythe?" asked Maggie. "Had he been to Ireland?

"He said he'd never been."

"Then he's hiding something."

"You mean he *has* been?"

"He has indeed," replied Maggie. "He was born there."

"*He's* the other one you were talking about?"

"But you said the names and Irish birth records didn't match. Are you saying his name isn't Dugan Smythe?"

"I am not prepared to go that far yet, only that I have not yet found a Dugan Smythe in the birth records. The records going back that far are never one hundred percent reliable. We need to look into it further."

An odd look came over Mike's face. He was recalling something that had happened earlier. He turned toward Shelby. "Do you remember the morning of the murder, when he was late to the ten o'clock session?" he asked.

Shelby nodded.

"Mr. Barribault asked him if he had been to town early and he said that he had just been out for a stroll on the grounds. But he looked flushed, more so than a leisurely stroll in the gardens would account for. Now I remember what bothered me about the incident—a newspaper was folded and tucked into the pocket of his coat. I remembered seeing part of the headline. My subconscious has been working on that ever since. It was the headline of *that* morning's paper about the terrorist incident in Glasgow. I went into town later and picked up a *Telegraph* myself. The headline seemed familiar...now I know why—because I had seen that fragment of it sticking out of his coat."

"I don't understand the significance of it," said Maggie. "He went into town every day for a paper."

"Because when Mr. Barribault asked him if he had been to town that morning, he denied it. Why would he lie about so simple a thing? It's not big in itself, but *why* would he not be up front about having bought a paper?"

Suddenly the wheels of Maggie's brain began to spin. Could Alan Long's newspaper sales on the day of the murder hold the key to everything!

"I've had a loose thread gnawing at me all day too," said Maggie. "It's also about newspapers that day. Alan at the Paper Shoppe told me he sold *two Telegraphs* that day to John Thompson, Chief Inspector Riggs' current suspect. Now, Mike, you tell me that Father Smythe came into your meeting with a paper he denied buying. Something about the whole situation is weird."

She pulled out her mobile phone and punched in a number.

"Hello...yes, hi Keara, it's Maggie Westbrook. I'm dreadfu' wae for waukin' ye this gait, but I maul speik wi' Alan—tis rale important."

She waited a minute until the sleepy shopkeeper came on the line.

"I ken ye'll be gettin' up wi' yer papers in jist a feow oors, Alan, but I maun spier o' ye gien ye sold a paper the morn o' the murder, early like, afore ten, till ony o' the eight authors fae the muckle hoose."

It was silent a moment.

"Whilk o' them, Alan...Father Smythe, Dr. Cobb, Dame Meyerson...aye, I ken he cam til ye ilka day...aye...aye, he's the yoong meenister...ye're siccar...aye, thank ye, Alan."

She put the phone away and drew in a deep breath.

"Of those we are interested in," she said, "the only papers he sold that day were to Mr. Thompson and you, Mike. He is certain because the incident of John Thompson buying two papers was fresh in his mind. Also, the *Telegraph* is one of his least popular papers. Alan knows everybody in town and knows which of the eight or ten dailies they buy. He could tell you who bought every *Telegraph* on any given day. On that day, after selling Mr. Thompson his two, he saw no one from the muckle hoose—that's what they call Cullen House—except you, Mike. He remembers you specifically and thought it odd."

"Odd?"

"He remembers thinking that you were the wrong clergyman to be buying the day's *Telegraph*."

"But then Father Smythe showed up here with a *Telegraph* in his pocket."

"Something doesn't smell right," said Maggie. "If you two want to keep looking through Barribault's files, I'm going to take a run into Buckie."

"What for?" asked Mike.

"I want to have a word with John Thompson about those two papers."

TWENTY-FIVE

The Two Papers

Maggie drove through the deserted countryside to the station in Buckie. There she was admitted to see the prisoner. It was after midnight when she walked into the small block of cells. Waking up grumbling, Thompson sat up.

"If you don't let me out of this bloody place..." he began when he saw who had interrupted his restless and irritable sleep.

"Please, Mr. Thompson," said Maggie, "I am sorry. But at the moment there is nothing I can do. I am working on it. If you are innocent, I will get you out of here soon, I promise."

"*If* I'm innocent! You've known me half your life, Maggie—you can't really believe these charges. Your Chief Inspector is an idiot!"

"No, I don't believe them, Mr. Thompson," rejoined Maggie. "My father is almost as angry at me as you are. When he heard you had been arrested, he threatened to throw me out of the house. But I don't wear the biggest hat in this office. Please I just need to ask you a question...why did you buy two newspapers from Alan Long on the morning of the killing?"

"That's easy. One was for the priest."

"Why him?" asked Maggie.

"He came into my store early, just as I was opening. He was out early for a walk—needed to clear his head, he said. He seemed distracted. I asked him what was on his mind. All he said was that there was something from a long time ago that needed sorting. The price paid that a few rosaries would not atone for, he said, whatever that meant. I told him I was going to nip down to the Paper Shoppe for a *Telegraph*. He asked me to pick one up for him."

"Where was he in the meantime?"

"In my shop. I told him to have a look around and if anyone came in to tell them I would be right back."

"You trusted your shop in his care?"

"It was only for a few minutes. I thought nothing of it."

"When did you notice that your quill was missing?"

"Come to think of it, I don't think I saw it again that day. I was rather busy and never got back to my workroom. You don't suspect him of taking it."

"Why not?"

"He's a priest."

"Yes, and there's only one of the Eight whom I have once heard speak a word of profanity, and it's him. So what does that say about his holiness quotient?"

"You think he pinched it?"

"It seems it's a good possibility. You never saw it after that. Still…you don't recall seeing it the night before either, and the day prior you had visits from all eight authors. If your quill is involved, I suppose technically all eight remain suspects."

Thompson nodded and Maggie turned to go.

"Maggie, get me out of here," he said.

"Soon, Mr. Thompson," she said. "Very soon."

* * *

As Maggie returned to Cullen through the quiet darkness she realized it was time to bring in D.C.I. Riggs. Her boss would not be pleased to be awakened in the middle of the night. If she went any further without him, however, the repercussions would be even worse.

At the head of Grant Street she pulled to a stop at the gate into the grounds. She turned off her engine, bracing herself for Riggs' reaction, and pulled out her mobile phone.

When he came on the line she explained the situation as diplomatically as possible, that she had had one or two ideas she wanted to follow through on without bothering him so late, but that she had come to an impasse and did not know what to make of it. She needed his insight and knew that it was time for him to review the information. She was sorry and hadn't wanted to bother him unnecessarily, but she felt it urgent that they discuss the matter before anyone left in the morning. After the brief expected tongue lashing for taking matters into her own hands, he said he would be there as soon as he could dress and make himself a thermos of hot coffee.

Maggie said she would wait for him at the gate.

D.C.I. Riggs and D.S. Westbrook drove into the precincts of Cullen House about one o'clock A.M., parked a hundred meters away and covered the rest of the distance on foot. On the way through the grounds, Maggie explained that she had been working that evening with Mike St. John and Shelby Fitzpatrick.

"They are suspects!" Riggs exploded. "What are you thinking, Westbrook?"

"They have been very helpful, sir," said Maggie. "All I want is for you to hear what they have come up with."

A sigh of exasperation was Riggs' only reply.

Once inside the house, Maggie tip-toed up to the study. There she motioned to Mike and Shelby to follow. The three carried what files and other information they felt was pertinent. Five minutes later they were gathered in one of the ground floor lounges out of earshot of the rest of the house.

"Chief Inspector," Maggie began, "I know this is a dreadfully inconvenient time, but I am afraid several of the individuals are planning to leave in the morning, and I want Mr. St. John and Miss Fitzpatrick to tell you briefly what they told me. They have read Melinda's mother's diary and High Barribault's book *Love's Dry Tears*—the one, you recall, that Dame Barribault starred in the film of. They have made some striking discoveries."

Riggs took a sip of his coffee and nodded.

Mike and Shelby briefly recounted the parallel version of the story from the twin perspectives of Hugh Barribault and Melinda's mother.

"Here is where it gets interesting, sir," said Maggie. "On the questionnaires Mr. Barribault sent out after the selection of the Eight finalists had been made, there are some discrepancies—"

"What kind of discrepancies, Westbrook?" growled Riggs.

"Mostly to do with birthdates and names," replied Maggie.

"I don't follow you."

Maggie explained further. "We have two Irish born authors," she said, "as well as possible name changes involving more than merely Dame Meyerson. Scotland Yard's records only add to the confusion, as you will see."

She handed him several sheets she had printed from her research of the police data base in London.

"I see what you mean," he said, nodding as he looked it over. Yes...this one here," he added, pointing to the sheet he held on top, "—this certainly does raise questions of identity."

He rubbed his chin as he continued to peruse the information.

"Ghob...Ghobh...*Gh* and *bh*...how do those translate?" he said, mumbling to himself.

"What is it, sir?" asked Maggie.

"I'm just looking at this Gaelic name that matches with the birthdates you ran—*Ghobhainn*."

"Do you know Gaelic, Chief Inspector?"

"Not much...forgotten most of it. I put in a stint in Wales when I was young in the force, and a few months in Northern Ireland. Unless I am mistaken, the English of that name...no, I oughtn't to say anything without checking. What we need, Westbrook, are fingerprints. We need to know positively who everyone is, where they come from, where they were born...everything. Do we have everyone's prints?"

"There are none in Mr. Barribault's files. On our end of it, we only fingerprinted those individuals we had under suspicion."

"Right. We can't very well charge in now in the middle of the night and stick a fingerprint pad in the faces of the others. That wouldn't do much for the element of surprise. Let's see—who do we need...Whitaker, Smythe, Franks—did we get prints for Stokes? I think we got the other four. Is there anything they might have touched—something you could identify positively that would have their prints on it?"

Shelby and Mike looked at each other.

"The ink well and pen stand!" they said together.

Riggs eyed them inquisitively.

"I'm listening," he said.

"Where we met for our sessions with Mr. Barribault," began Shelby, "you know how it is...eventually everyone gravitates to the same place until, almost as an unspoken rule, everyone lays claim to their own little corner."

"Exactly as in church," added Mike. "It is the most fascinating thing to observe from the pulpit. When someone changes from their customary spot—"

"Yes, well never mind about all that," interrupted Riggs. "What were you getting at, Miss Fitzpatrick?"

"There is a green leather overstuffed chair in the room off to one side. Beside it sits an occasional table with various ornaments on it. One of those is a crystal ink well and pen stand, complete with a long fountain pen. It was obviously mainly for decoration. Mr. Barribault loved antique writing things. I noticed that often, sitting next to it, one of our colleagues fiddled with the ink well and pen and even occasionally took notes with the pen."

"And then put it back in the stand?"

Shelby nodded.

"Did anyone else use them?"

Mike and Shelby looked at each other, then slowly shook their heads.

"That's it, then," said Riggs. "Show me these things."

They rose and left the room. Climbing the main stairway to the Sitting Room they opened the door softly, went inside, and closed it after them.

"Where is this pen whatever it is?" asked Riggs.

"Over here," said Mike, leading him toward the green leather chair.

Riggs bent down to examine the items on the table next to the chair.

"The lab's closed, but I'll take these things in and see what prints I can lift myself and get them off to Scotland Yard. Westbrook, see if you can find me something to put them in."

Riggs took out his handkerchief and began carefully to gather the inkwell and pen and inkstand. "We might get something off the table too," he said, "if we need it later. Hopefully this will get us what we need. What about the others—where did the fellow Whitaker usually sit…and Stokes?"

More examination of the room followed. A few minutes later Riggs was ready to be off to the station.

"Will you need help emailing the fingerprints, Chief Inspector?" asked Maggie.

"I might at that, Westbrook. You know me with all your electronic mumbo-jumbo. Let me see if I can find any viable prints first. You stay here for now. Take a chair up to the landing. Position yourself there just in case. Someone may try to get an early start again. I want no one leaving until we clear up these questions. Put your mobile on vibration if I have to call you. If I can get the prints off to Scotland Yard, I'll wait until I have something definite. Otherwise, I will call you to come in and send someone else out to watch the place."

"I think we've done about all we can for now," said Maggie when Riggs was gone. "The two of you might want to get some sleep."

"I am too tired to argue," said Shelby. "I think I will take you up on your offer."

TWENTY-SIX

The Confirmation

By four in the morning, having heard nothing more from Chief Inspector Riggs, at her post on the second floor landing Maggie Westbrook began to doze. Positioned as her chair was, no one would be able to get past without waking her. Gradually she slumped in her chair and drifted off.

Some time later, a faint noise disturbed her. Maggie started awake and listened.

She glanced at her watch. Five-ten.

Whispering and movement was coming from the direction of the guest rooms. She shook herself awake. In two or three minutes soft footsteps came toward her. A moment later, from around the corner of the corridor Graham Whitaker came into view carrying two suitcases. He was followed by Jessica Stokes with a small bag over her shoulder. Maggie was as surprised to see them as they were to find her sitting at the landing blocking their way.

"Uh...Miss Westbrook," said Whitaker softly, astonishment obvious in his voice.

"Yes...hello, Mr. Whitaker," said Maggie in a loud whisper, rising from her chair to meet them, "—Ms Stokes," she added. "Where would the two of you be going, if you don't mind my asking?"

"I asked Jessica if she would like a ride to Manchester," replied Whitaker. "She agreed to accompany me. We decided to get an early start."

"I see. Well…I am sorry to interfere with your plans, but no one is to leave yet."

"I don't…why is that?" said Whitaker.

"I thought we were free to go?" added Jessica.

"Some new developments are being looked into," answered Maggie.

"What kind of developments?" asked Whitaker.

"Chief Inspector Riggs will explain everything."

"Let him explain, then," said Jessica, growing perturbed. "Where is he?"

"He is following up on a lead at the station in Buckie. In the meantime, I am going to have to ask the two of you to return to your rooms."

More surprised than irritated, Whitaker turned back toward their rooms. With a sigh of resignation, more irritated than surprised, Jessica Stokes joined him, mumbling her annoyance about the impossibility of getting back to sleep now, and the inconvenience of being harassed by such bumbling provincial flatfoots.

* * *

Maggie heard the two doors close, the one a little loudly. Whether those in the other rooms were sleeping after the disturbance was doubtful.

Again she glanced at her watch. It was now five-twenty. Morning was not far off, though the sun would not rise for another hour and a half. Quiet again descended. In the distance, however, Jessica Stokes made little attempt to moderate her movements as she made tea in her room.

About twenty minutes later, Maggie heard the turning of another latch, more softly this time. Obviously trying to move lightly on the carpet, feet stepped into the corridor. Gently a door closed.

Without analyzing her reasons, Maggie thought it best this time if she were not seen.

She rose noiselessly from the chair, tip-toed hurriedly along the adjacent corridor, and darted around the corner into the west wing. Ten seconds later, she heard a single set of footsteps walk past the chair where she had been sitting and begin descending the main staircase. In the distance outside, the faint sound of an automobile engine disturbed the early morning quiet. It stopped almost the moment she took note of it. All became silent again. Waiting another few seconds, Maggie crept from her hiding place and followed the shadow ahead to the ground floor in the dimness of the stair lights.

Below she heard the main door of the house, locked from the outside but passable from within, open.

* * *

From inside his room, Mike St. John was wide awake. He had managed a couple hours sleep since leaving Shelby and Maggie, but more was out of the question now.

He dressed hurriedly, then opened his door softly and crossed the hall. His light knock was answered as Shelby opened her door a crack.

"Are you awake?" Mike whispered.

"Duh! Who could sleep—what's up?"

"I'm not sure."

"I've been hearing noises for half an hour."

"Come on—let's find out."

Already dressed, Shelby stepped through the door and joined Mike in the corridor.

They crept along the hall to the landing.

"Maggie's gone," said Shelby, seeing the empty chair.

"I think the front door opened a minute ago," said Mike. He led the way down the main staircase.

* * *

A lone figure clad in thick overcoat, for the morning was cold, walked gingerly across the gravel entryway beside the looming black wall of Cullen House. He did not care for the crunch of his steps echoing in the stillness. But he had no idea he was being followed. The sound would not matter in a few minutes anyway, he thought. He would be away from this place, his vow of thirty years at last fulfilled.

The sound of feet across the gravel alerted Maggie Westbrook to the danger of herself being detected as she dogged the steps ahead. Slowly she eased her way toward the side of the drive. Feeling soft wet grass beneath her feet, she continued.

Arrived at the garages, the shadow Maggie had by now lost sight of set down a single suitcase. He walked to the latch behind which the hired Mercedes had been kept since his arrival.

He turned it and lifted the door.

An explosion of light filled the garage. The would-be traveler squinted to focus. A tall thin man in a shabby overcoat and hat stood in front of the Mercedes.

"Inspector Riggs!" he laughed nervously. "I did not expect you to see me off in person. I am honored by your consideration."

"Enough of all that," said Riggs. "I'm not here to honor you but to prevent your making a run for it."

"A run for it!" he laughed. "What are you talking about? I understood the case was solved, and that we had permission to leave."

"Yes, well the case *is* finally solved," said Riggs. "But you do *not* have permission to leave."

"I don't understand…why the devil not!"

"Because, Dugan Smythe, I am arresting you for the murder of Hugh Barribault."

"You've got to be kidding, Inspector!" laughed Smythe.

"Actually, *Mister* Smythe," said Riggs with emphasis. "I am not kidding at all. You are under arrest."

Just then Maggie walked into the light of the open door.

"Ah, Miss Westbrook," said Riggs, "I was just on my way in to see you when I saw our friend here in the window coming down the stairs. I decided to meet him here instead."

Maggie walked forward into the garage.

"Your hunch paid off," Riggs went on. "I discovered some very interesting information from Scotland Yard. On the drive in, my limited memory of Gaelic began to come back to me. At least enough to remember that the name Ghobhainn is Gaelic for Smith. I began to see why you turned up nothing in Ireland on

Father Smythe's birthday. Eleven people were born that day in Cork—one was stillborn, six were girls, two of the boys are now dead, a third is presently serving in the Irish parliament. That leaves the eleventh, a boy born as *Ghobhainn*, not Smythe at all—"

"Isn't that right, Smith?" added Riggs, turning to the man in front of him

"Yes," replied the man they knew as Father Smythe. "So I changed my name to English when I came to England. What of it? There's no crime in that."

"There is in murder," rejoined Riggs. "And therefore...Mr. Smythe, I am arresting you for the murder of Hugh Barribault. Or perhaps I should use your birth name, and say that I am arresting you, Fingall Ghobhainn, or as you changed it for the first time, Fingall Hainn, for the murder of Hugh Barribault, the man who stole your fiancé."

Fingall Ghobhainn, aka Fingall Hainn, aka Father Dugan Smythe, stood for a moment dumbfounded. Behind him Mike St. John and Shelby Fitzpatrick walked slowly out of the darkness into the brightness cast by the garage light.

Slowly a sneer of contempt came over Smythe's face.

"You meddling imbecile," he spat with disdain. "You still don't know the half of it. The evidence all points to suicide. Even without a suicide note...his old books, they contain clues. He was following a pattern, I tell you!"

"Take him into custody, Miss Westbrook."

"You will never make this stick, Riggs, you fool!" shouted Smythe. "You will be laughed out of court when the evidence comes out."

"We shall see about that, *Ghobhainn*," rejoined Riggs. "We shall see about it indeed."

TWENTY-SEVEN

The Tale Told

The mood in the Breakfast Room of Cullen House was electric.
Constance Fotheringay had put out the normal breakfast buffet of the past two weeks without knowing how many of the authors would still be at the house. There had been considerable discussion the day before about departure.

No one was talking about leaving now.

Mike St. John and Shelby Fitzpatrick came in from outside as Maggie and D.C.I. Riggs were leaving with what was presumably their final prisoner. They were soon joined by Graham Whitaker and Jessica Stokes, both of whom were still awake and had heard the commotion outside. Unable to resist making a spectacle, Riggs turned on his siren, completely unnecessary under the circumstances. That had awakened the rest of the house and most of the town as first light of day spread over the roofs of the village. Word quickly spread of the arrest. Soon everyone was wandering down to get the latest news.

By seven-thirty, those who remained of the Eight were all talking feverishly about the morning's events. Learning of their role in the night's developments, Mike and Shelby were fielding a barrage of questions. Gradually even butler Coombes, Miss Fotheringay, and Mr. and Mrs. Walton slipped unobtrusively through the door and stood silently listening. The cook and the housekeeper soon had to refill some of the platters and bring out

350

fresh tea and coffee. It was obviously going to be a busy day. Ever faithful Coombes had been on the phone early and Cynthia Gordon arrived shortly before eight.

At 8:10 Maggie returned with John Thompson at her side. Despite a miserable night's sleep, he too was curious about all that had happened. He was greeted almost with a hero's welcome for his fortitude in having endured incarceration with them. As they walked through the door, sporadic applause broke out, both in acknowledgment of Thompson's ordeal, for he was a man they all liked and had enjoyed talking to, and also out of respect for Maggie Westbrook, whom by now they considered the brains of the detective duo.

"Welcome back to the land of the living, Mr. Thompson!" said Dame Meyerson.

"Hear, hear!" assented Dr. Cobb, as Thompson began walking toward them and shaking the hand of each in turn. "I am glad to see that you survived the Riggs' inquisition, Mr. Thompson," he said.

"Thank you, Dr. Cobb," said Thompson. "I have to admit that coffee smells very good," he added with a glance toward the sideboard. "It was a long night!"

"We shall have to form a club—membership to include all those arrested by the fathead Riggs. By all means, come join us and tell us your tale!"

"What I want to know," said Graham Whitaker as the newcomers took chairs, Thompson with a bracing cup of strong coffee, "is who *is* Father Smythe if he is not who we thought he was."

"I have just been explaining it to Mr. Thompson on our drive in from Buckie," said Maggie. "I should really let Mike and Shelby tell you. They are the ones who connected the dots."

"Not really," said Mike. "One thing simply led to another. Gradually we learned more and more. Actually, in all fairness, it would seem to be Chief Inspector Riggs who put the final pieces together."

"Riggs is a moron," muttered Dame Meyerson.

"Perhaps not as much as he lets people think," rejoined Mike. "It was he who recognized the name Ghobhainn. That was the important clue that unraveled the rest. We must give credit where credit is due."

Mike turned to Maggie. "Why don't you give everyone a summary."

"All right," nodded Maggie. "Actually, I might pour myself a cup of that coffee before I start too. I've been up all night!"

A few minutes later, she returned to a chair.

"We owe our initial leads in the right direction," Maggie began, "to Mike's reading of Hugh Barribault's book *Love's Dry Tears*, whose screen star we have been privileged to have with us." She turned with a nod of acknowledgment in Dame Meyerson's direction. "Also to Melinda for allowing Shelby to read the very private and personal account of a young life in turmoil, her mother's diary which was intended for none but her own eyes. Thank you, Melinda," she said, turning to her with a smile. "These two books got us started—I should say got Mike and Shelby started...they were the real detectives. Then Chief Inspector Riggs made the connection with Ghobhainn."

Maggie paused a moment to take a drink of coffee, then resumed.

"A boy was born in Ireland as Fingall Ghobhainn. He dreamed of becoming a priest, for reasons we do not know, and at eighteen entered the Catholic Seminary of the Holy Family. Scandal, however, forced him to withdraw and in anger he discarded his Catholic upbringing and moved to Northern Ireland, where he called himself Fingall Hainn. In Belfast he came under the spell of Melinda's mother, Fiona Kilcardy. However, while Hainn was away for a visit to Cork, a young English corporeal by the name of Hugh Barribault saved Fiona from an IRA kidnap attempt. Hugh Barribault and Fiona Kilcardy fell in love. They were tragically separated when Barribault was wounded in his barracks by a car bomb and transported unconscious back to England to recover. By the time he returned to search for Fiona, who was pregnant with Melinda, he could find no trace of her. Terrorist activity had destroyed her home and most of those nearby. They never saw one another again.

"Fingall Hainn, however, had learned of the liason while Barribault was still in Northern Ireland and vowed revenge on the man he now viewed as his mortal enemy. Eventually Hainn moved from Northern Ireland to England, where he changed his name again, this time to Dugan Smythe. There he resumed his study for the priesthood, this time as an Anglican. When many years later, along with the rest of you, he was announced as one of the winners of Hugh Barribault's literary contest, he could hardly believe his good fortune. His thirst for vengeance sprang to life anew, and at last he saw his chance. But he was not content only to exact revenge, he wanted to make a statement, which he did with Mr. Thompson's handmade quill—"

In the distance a doorbell faintly sounded. Coombes, standing placidly along one wall listening to Maggie's account, left the room. He returned a minute later and whispered in Miss Gordon's ear. She also left the room.

While Maggie had been recounting developments, as had been the case since she left her room that morning, Melinda's mood remained subdued. It was, after all her father who had been killed. Less than twenty-four hours earlier, in despondency over reminders of her mother and the loss of her father, she had been standing on the edge of a bluff contemplating ending her own life. The exuberance of the others as they talked about the details and motives of the killing jarred dissonantly with the emotions with which she was struggling.

As Maggie now went on to describe what she and Riggs had pieced together of the sordid details of the fatal meeting between Smythe and her father after the breakup of the bridge game, she softly began to weep. Shelby was about to go to her when Dame Meyerson rose from her chair, walked around the table, and sat down at Melinda's side. She placed a tender hand on Melinda's arm, then offered her a handkerchief. Melinda glanced toward her, smiled, and continued to cry softly.

Melinda was noticeably relieved when Miss Gordon returned ten minutes later and walked immediately to where she sat with the others.

"Miss Franks," she said, "Mr. Barribault's solicitor has just arrived. He is upstairs in the office. He would like to speak with you."

Melinda nodded, then rose and left the room with her.

* * *

The six authors and D.S. Westbrook continued to discuss the strange turn of events. The four who had managed to sleep most of the night peppered Mike and Shelby with more questions about the diary and the book.

"I would like to ask you a question, Dame Meyerson, if you don't mind," said Shelby.

"Not at all."

"When we were looking through Mr. Barribault's files, we found a copy of the screenplay for *Tears*. It had a handwritten comment from Mr. Barribault about the scene between Hugh and Fiona on the fateful night when Melinda was conceived. If we are reading it accurately, it seems he was upset with how the scene was filmed."

Dame Meyerson sighed and nodded. "Upset is putting it mildly," she said. "That may be what turned him against me, or at least partially," she added wistfully.

"What happened?"

"Hugh was furious when he saw the first take of the scene. I admit, it was steamy. My cleavage was hanging out all over the place and the bedroom scene was pretty torrid. I played it exactly as the director told me to. But Hugh hated it. He yelled at the director, at me, at everyone. He demanded we change it."

"What happened?"

"We did change it...temporarily."

"How do you mean?"

"We shot it again, two or three times, in fact. I had more clothes on. The camera didn't get into bed with the young couple. Hugh was mollified and let it go. As it turned out, however, that was one of the last scenes to be shot. It came nearly at the end of the schedule. Hugh and I had already had our fling. But the director was not happy with Hugh's interference. He insisted privately that the movie would never get off the ground without sex. So unknown to Hugh, in the final cut he reinstalled the rated version of the scene. Hugh never knew it until opening night. He had to keep his cool publicly, but he was furious. He always blamed me along with the director. He thought that I had taken liberties with the scene and never forgave me. That was the beginning of it. I think too, by then, he resented that he had been intimate with me, almost as if I had usurped Fiona's place in his life by seducing him. That's not what happened, but in his mind that may have been the shape it took."

"It almost sounds like a redux of his original guilt-ridden liason with Melinda's mother," suggested Whitaker.

"A little weird, if you ask me," said Jessica.

"There may be some truth in that," said Dame Meyerson. "I think Hugh felt guilty for allowing someone—namely, *me*—to come between him and the memory of his first love. I suppose that's kinky psychological stuff. That's when he began to get strange toward me. Before I knew what was happening, it was as though I had become his enemy...and he destroyed me with everyone he knew in Hollywood."

She paused and looked toward Shelby with a sad sort of smile.

"What you say fits together," said Shelby. "Guilt is a powerful force. It may be that the guilt he felt over the affair with Fiona came rushing back upon him after you and he were involved, made all the worse by the fact that you were taking Fiona's place in the memory-gallery of his affections. It makes sense. Guilt is one of the strongest psychological forces I have to deal with regularly in my practice. Guilt can cause people to become seriously unhinged. When they do, they behave in very irrational ways. That sounds like what happened to Hugh Barribault. It's too bad you were caught in the middle."

"Why did Hugh Barribault's letters never reach Melinda's mother?" asked Jessica, addressing the question generally.

A few glances went round. At last Mike spoke.

"That is a mystery," he said. "In Barribault's book, the fictionalized character Gavin is as puzzled about it as we are. I take that as a reflection of Barribault's own frustration." He looked toward Shelby.

"In Fiona's diary she hints that she is being watched, but there is nothing conclusive. Perhaps the letters were intercepted by Hainn or by IRA operatives still surveiling Kilcardy and his family. Maybe the house had already been destroyed and their whereabouts lost track of...it's one of the uncertainties of this case we will probably never resolve...unless Smythe—that is Hainn—eventually tells more."

"You know there is one element in all this that I really have difficulty understanding," said Dr. Cobb. "I cannot harmonize Hugh Barribault's rigid insistence on what he called traditional values, and his insistence that everyone around him be squeaky clean, with the fact that he himself had two love affairs, killed three men, and then abandoned his religious faith as well as both the women he loved. It strikes me as the most blatant form of hypocrisy. His one man crusade was at odds with the reality of his own life."

"I see it differently, Dr. Cobb," said Shelby. "To me his conflicted motives make perfect sense. He was trying to make up for his own failure to adhere to the very values he held so strongly and felt compelled to press upon others."

"But it made him less tolerant of those around him. Why wouldn't his own failings have increased his sensitivity to the failings of others?"

"Guilt is not always rational, Dr. Cobb."

* * *

As they broke up briefly and wandered to the sideboard for provisions, Shelby eased toward Mike with a mischievous expression.

"You know, all this reminds me of one last thing I want to clear up with you," she said, "before I completely eliminate *you* from my list of suspects."

"What are you talking about!" Mike laughed. "After I helped get you sprung from the pokey as I believe you Yanks call it?"

"Surely you know the expression about loose ends, Mr. St. John. You wouldn't expect me to be less diligent in my analysis of your movements than anyone else's."

"*Mister* St. John…so we're back to that, are we? What loose end has my name on it?"

"Only that, going back to your staunch support of my innocence when Riggs first had *me* on the hook, it crossed my mind that all that could have been a ploy to win my confidence. Isn't that just the sort of thing a guilty person would do, to deflect attention from themselves—act sincere and sensitive?"

Mike looked at her questioningly. For the merest instant he wondered if she was serious. In vain he searched for the twinkle in her eye that would give her away.

"I told you," he said, gazing intently into her face, "that it was your expression that convinced me of your innocence." A slow but slightly perplexed smile spread over his lips. "I am looking for that expression again now, but am finding myself miffed."

Shelby stared back seriously, then gradually returned his smile.

"I had you going, didn't I?" she said.

"What a dirty trick!"

"But really, for a brief period, it did occur to me that you might be trying to take me in. I have to admit that I was already starting to see you in a different light than at first. Then I realized that I had seen the same look in *your* eyes that you said you saw in mine when we walked into the hall—utter surprise that could not be faked. I knew you were telling the truth for the same reason you knew I was.—But I do still have one question that bothered me at the time...on the night of the murder, when you and Graham went to investigate the falling tree during the storm, why were you gone so long? You said you went outside to investigate, but then you came back completely dry? I noticed it immediately. That's why I was suspicious of you. And you *were* away long enough to have gone up to Barribault's study."

"Very perceptive. However, did you not notice the umbrella stand by the main door? I knew it was raining so I grabbed an umbrella on my way out. The front door was locked from the inside. I unlocked it, and went out. I thought I saw something in one of the lit windows. I went round the corner of the building to look closer. But nothing resulted. I came back into the house, relocked the door, put away the umbrella, and rejoined the rest of you. If you had looked closely, you would have seen that the bottoms of my trousers and shoes were wet."

"You have convinced me," nodded Shelby. "You are officially removed from my list."

At the other sideboard, Whitaker and Thompson had fallen into conversation.

"I have a question for you, Mr. Thompson," said Graham as the two men refilled their cups and picked up a few buttered pieces of cold toast. "One of Inspector Riggs' most compelling arguments against you was learning that you had snuck into the grounds on the night of the storm. So...*were* you here that night?"

"I was," answered Thompson.

"Why?"

"There was nothing so sinister in it. It's just what I told— what's her name, your friend who works at the Co-op?" he asked, turning to Maggie.

"Jennie."

"Right—it's like I told her that evening...I was making a new key for one of the old locks at the big house. Stupid, I suppose, to have gone so late. But I reached home after closing the shop, then remembered I'd promised Hugh to have it taken care of by the next day. So I came back to try it."

"Why did you walk into the grounds?" asked Maggie. "It was already dark."

"I don't know, just a whim I suppose. I love a forest in a storm. It was a wild night—I just felt like walking. Obviously I was not trying to *sneak* in or I wouldn't have walked right past the Co-op in plain view. I tried to make that point with your Chief Inspector. I suppose it was too simple an explanation for him."

"Did the key work?" asked Dame Meyerson.

"Yes, that's what I went up to tell Hugh, and then Whitaker heard me in his study."

"How was he then?"

"Very sleepy...so much so he seemed drugged."

"What time was that?"

"Nine-thirty, ten. I don't know, what time did the tree go down? We both heard it. I said I ought to get going. Hugh said I shouldn't go out with the weather as it was. So I waited a while. We had a drink together and chatted. But he continued to act out of it. When the wind died down, I left."

"You didn't see Mr. St. John when you left?"

"No, I went out the same way I had come. I told Hugh I'd leave the key in the lock for the night. He didn't seem bothered by that. Which reminds me, I'd better tell Coombes."

He paused a moment.

"Actually, come to think of it I did hear steps in the corridor behind me as I was leaving, coming toward Hugh's study from the main staircase."

"You don't know who it was?"

"No, I didn't especially want to be seen, so I hurried on."

"And you were able to make it out?"

"A fallen tree or two didn't bother me. I had a torch. Though I did scratch my hand," he added, extending his palm.

"I suppose I should have been more persistent in trying to get out to notify the police," said Whitaker.

Twenty-Eight

The Evidence

A s they were talking, Detective Chief Inspector Riggs returned to Cullen House. He walked into the Breakfast Room gathering like a galleon under sail. With the triumphant flourish of a conquering warrior, he removed his coat and hat and approached the three tables where the six of the authors, John Thompson, and his own Detective Westbrook were sitting.

"Good morning, ladies and gentlemen," he said magisterially. "I am sure you know by now that your own Father Smythe, whose real name is Ghobhainn, is in custody for the murder of Hugh Barribault. It took most of the night, during which time I was in near constant contact with Scotland Yard, but in the end I was able to put the pieces together sufficient that it enabled me to make the arrest. I apologize for the inconvenience our investigation may have caused any of you, but sometimes police work is complicated. We must all do our parts, as it were, to see that justice prevails in the end."

A few humorous expressions were exchanged as they listened to the Chief Inspector's implication that he had solved the case single-handedly. But all were in good fettle and no one minded his bluster on this morning.

As he glanced about, for the first time he noticed that Melinda was not with them.

"Where's the Franks girl?" he asked.

"With Mr. Barribault's solicitor, sir," said Maggie. "He arrived a short time ago and wanted to see her."

"Right...did he want to speak with me about the case"

"He did not mention it."

"Ah, well...right." Riggs drew in a breath and again turned to the assembled authors. I don't know how much Detective Sergeant Westbrook has told you," he went on, 'but we have learned that this is not the good Mr. Ghobhainn-Smythe's first criminal activity. Two unsolved incidents in Ireland have apparently been following him for years. The first occurred when he was attending the seminary in Cork and was accused of questionable activity involving two young boys. He was suspended from the seminary pending investigation. Though nothing was ever proven, the evidence seemed incontrovertible. In outrage he abandoned his Catholic faith and fled to Northern Ireland. There, several years later and going by the name Hainn, his path crossed that of Hugh Barribault. After Barribault's killing of the three terrorists attempting to abduct Fiona Kilcardy, a Belfast priest was roughed up pretty seriously. The police report tells of a young English soldier coming to ask for confession. The priest told him to wait in the confessional. Almost immediately another young man appeared and without provocation beat the priest enough to require hospitalization. On the day of the incident, the priest regained consciousness an hour later, stripped of his robe. Both young men were gone but the confessional had obviously been used. We think Ghobhainn the young man responsible. The fact that he was unable to produce a passport when I asked for one also aroused my curiosity. It is being looked into at this moment. I have a feeling that we will find that no passport has been issued to Dugan Smythe, but that an Irish passport is still valid in the name of Fingall Ghobhainn.

"And this," said Riggs, reaching into his coat where he had draped it over a chair, "I believe belongs to you, Mr. St. John." He pulled something from a stiff hollow cardboard tube that had been protruding from the pocket, and to everyone's amazement produced the inscrutable quill Mike had purchased from Thompson's shop.

"Where did you find it!" exclaimed Mike.

"In Smythe's car. Along with this…yours I believe, Miss Fitzpatrick," said Riggs, taking a book from the other pocket and holding it out to Shelby.

Shelby took it, though obviously confused. "No, Inspector," she said. "I've never seen this—what is it?"

"I am not talking about the book itself. To answer your question, however, it is one of Hugh Barribault's obscure novels."

"Time Runs Out," Shelby read from the cover. "What does it have to do with me?"

"If you will just look at the folded paper there…between the pages, as a bookmark."

Shelby turned to the page where the paper had been inserted. "It's the page torn out of my journal!" she said in surprise.

"Kept by Smythe in this book that he brought with him for the occasion. Why don't you read the highlighted portion," said Riggs.

Shelby looked again at the page in the book.

"The antique clock that had been in the family for generations," she read aloud, *"crashed to the floor, glass shattering, its dials and weights exploding off their moorings, the huge oak cabinet coming to rest next to the body lying dead with a hypodermic needle protruding from its arm.*

"'Time has finally run out on you, Campbell,' said the killer, then walked from the room.—"

She glanced up at Riggs.

"What's it all about, Chief Inspector?" she asked.

"This book was also found in Smythe's car, locked in the boot in a small case, along with a hypodermic needle filled with a lethal quantity of highly concentrated nicotine, a portion of which he mixed into the ink for the quill. Smythe obviously came here planning to kill Hugh Barribault after the fashion of Barribault's own fictional killer. Poetic justice I suppose you literary types would call it—by using Barribault's own props to stage his death. What he hadn't planned on was finding an antique dealer specializing in handmade quills that imitated a hypodermic needle in design. It was too delicious for him to pass up. Of course, he couldn't buy your quill, Mr. Thompson. That would have been too obvious. But he did get you to give him a thorough demonstration. And when you, Mr. St. John, purchased the first quill, that left him no alternative but to steal the second, which he did the morning you, Mr. Thompson, left him alone in your shop for a few minutes. He then appeared at your meeting, obviously out of breath from the long walk into town, but denying he had been so that he could not be connected to the missing quill. There was also a Swiss army knife, which he used to file down the top of the quill to make a razor sharp point. It's being analyzed right now to see if the metal fragments on it match the tip of the quill. With his fingerprints all over it, it's incriminating enough to convict him straightaway. Smythe hoped we would take Barribault's death for suicide. He assumed we would eventually find the link to the book. He had even apparently planned for there to be a suicide note," Riggs went on. "Along with his other effects in the small travel bag in the boot of the car we found these."

He pulled from his trouser pocket several sheets of paper. He opened them and passed them among his listeners.

Exclamations of astonishment spread among them.

"He was obviously practicing a suicide note—as you can see, attempting to mimic Hugh Barribault's handwriting. On the other sheet, you especially, Miss Fitzpatrick, will see his practicing of *yours*."

"This is amazing," said Shelby, shaking her head. "No wonder he was able to fool us. It looks exactly like mine!"

"It may look like it, but he would not have been able to fool us indefinitely. You recall that I took your journal for a day to have the ink analyzed. The report came back and indicated the presence of two very distinct types of ink. You said you were running out of ink. What was written in your journal after that, the forged part, matches the ink in the lethal quill, which is very different from the ink used in the rest of the journal."

"But there was not a suicide note," said Cobb.

"No—that is puzzling," nodded Riggs. "Perhaps on the night of your bridge game he saw his opportunity and decided to go ahead without writing up a final version of the note. Perhaps in the heat of the moment he simply forgot. Then this final incriminating nail in his own coffin—the Swiss army knife."

"Why would he keep all these things to implicate himself?" asked Whitaker. "The page from Shelby's journal, the book, the practice sheets of handwriting, the knife. It seems unbelievably idiotic."

"All he would have had to do is dump it all into a bin. It might have incriminated any of us," added Cobb.

"The mind of the criminal is beyond understanding," said Riggs. "Believe me, I have seen stranger things than this in my time."

"Why was the clock knocked over?"

"I don't know. I see no connection between it and the murder, other than the highlighted page in the book. Poetic justice again."

"Didn't you say that he was already dead an hour or more when we found him?"

"That's right," said Cobb. "Some of the blood was already dry when we walked in."

"The blood mixed with ink and nicotine," added Riggs, "accounting for its color and gooey consistency."

"Yet it was the crash of the clock that awakened us. He must have died a good hour before that."

"I'm sure Smythe planned it so, though for what reason I have no idea," said Riggs. "He knocked over the clock, then hurried down the back stairway from the study in his nightclothes so that he could come up behind the rest of you and walk upstairs and act shocked along with you all."

"The old Wooster ploy, eh. St. John," said Whitaker.

"So is this what we're left with, Chief Inspector?" said Mike. "Let me see if I can put it all together. Smythe came here with the intent of killing Hugh Barribault with the hypodermic needle filled with concentrated nicotine, which he would make look like suicide. Late that night he came to Barribault's study bringing wine, drugged Barribault with more valerian from what Coombes had brought earlier, then after he was unconscious he plunged the quill tip into his arm, released the ink he had laced with nicotine after stealing the quill, then either left or waited there for an hour, returned, knocked over the clock to wake us all up hoping that eventually you would find it as a clue from his book along with the quill indicating suicide, then rushed back down the back staircase, joined us nonchalantly from behind, then came up with the rest of us to find the body, already growing cold."

"That's how it looks," nodded Riggs.

"But why did he take my quill?" said Mike. "Why steal it from my room when he already had the second quill to do the job?"

"That we may never know. Maybe a souvenir of his long awaited triumph over Hugh Barribault. As I said, who can know how a criminal mind thinks? In any event, that appears to be about it. At last you are officially all free to go."

TWENTY-NINE

The Will

Meanwhile, in Hugh Barribault's study Melinda's tears were flowing afresh. She was listening to a tape recording of her father's voice as he dictated a new will on tape while speaking on the telephone to Mr. Forsythe in France from a week earlier, leaving everything to his daughter.

Behind them, the door of the safe, whose combination Forsythe had retrieved from the sealed envelope in the safe in his own office, stood open.

Cynthia Gordon, present at Mr. Forsythe's request as a witness to the proceedings, also sat dabbing at her eyes to hear her employer's voice again.

"So you see, Miss Franks," said Forsythe when the recording was complete, "everything is perfectly legal. This handwritten copy I found in his safe corresponds word for word to what you just heard. There is no possible doubt of its legality. Except for the minor provisions noted, the entire Barribault estate and its business and philanthropic endeavors is now in your hands."

Melinda continued to cry for another minute or two.

At length Forsythe turned to Barribault's secretary.

"If you do not mind, Miss Gordon," he said, "I would like some time with Miss Franks in private."

"Of course," she replied, then rose to go.

"We will come to your office shortly," said Forsythe. "Once we settle a few formalities here, I presume you and Miss Franks, along perhaps with some of your senior staff, will want to begin talking over your plans. I understand things have been in limbo. You might want to begin notifying your people how things stand."

Gordon nodded and left the study.

"You will be joining us for those discussions, won't you, Mr. Forsythe?" asked Melinda.

"Of course. There will be a host of legal complexities. I want to meet with your staff solicitors later today. Once you make some preliminary decisions about the publishing company and foundation, then we can all begin getting things moving again...but no more rapidly than you are comfortable with."

"I understand," Melinda nodded. "One thing I am already sure of, Mr. Forsythe," she added, "and I know you will be able to help me with the legalities of it...what is involvded in changing my name to Barribault?"

"A few legal forms, nothing more," he replied. "Especially in a case such as yours, where there has been an adoption, and now with your discovery of the identity of your birth parents, it is a relatively simple process."

Melinda nodded. "If you don't mind," she added after a moment, "I would like to go down and see the others briefly. I want to ask them to stay until we get everything sorted out—at least insofar as they are involved in decisions that must be made."

"Surely," said Mr. Forsythe. "I will wait for you here."

* * *

When Melinda descended from the study, she had mostly regained control of her emotions.

She met D.C.I. Riggs as he was leaving the house.

"Ah, Miss Franks," he said, glancing up to see her coming down the stairs.

"Hello, Chief Inspector," smiled Melinda. "Thank you for your persistence in bringing all this to closure."

367

"That's what I do, Miss Franks. Is there...do you need to speak to me about anything?"

"I don't think so, Mr. Riggs. I have just been with my father's solicitor. It will take some time to get used to everything, but it will sort itself out."

"You know where to contact me if I can be of further assistance. I will keep you apprised of further events, the trial, and all that."

"Thank you, Chief Inspector."

Melinda left him then turned toward the Breakfast Room. As the eyes of the others fell on her, they already saw a change in her countenance. One by one, they rose to greet her with smiles and hugs which even included the stoic Jessica Stokes and Briscoe Cobb.

"I will probably start crying again," said Melinda, "but I do want to talk to you all. I have been speaking with Mr. Forsythe and Miss Gordon. I want you to know where things stand. I know some of you had planned to leave today. I hope you will be willing to postpone your plans until we can talk. I would like to suggest we meet in the Sitting Room at two o'clock this afternoon. That will give us a chance to eat, clean up, rest for those who need it...and give me a chance to organize my thoughts."

She drew in a breath, as if to reassure herself.

"Mr. Forsythe is expecting me again upstairs," she went on. "There are many things to resolve—the will, the foundation, all the legalities...I don't even know what all. But he is a considerate and patient man and is walking me through it."

She glanced about at her fellow authors. All were smiling broadly to see her, though tearful, speaking with such poise.

"Oh...and, Mr. Thompson," Melinda added, "I realize you are probably exhausted, but if it is not too great an inconvenience with your shop, I would appreciate it very much if you could join us this afternoon. For better or worse, after the events of these days, you are one of us now. I will explain everything more fully this afternoon."

Thompson nodded and said he would be there.

THIRTY

The Future

A gain the Barribault authors and John Thompson gathered in the Sitting Room at 2:00 P.M. By then D.S. Westbrook had left for home to get a few hours sleep.

Coffee, tea, and trimmings had been set out by Constance Fotheringay. New life had been breathed into the whole house. With Melinda's permission being told by Miss Gordon in general terms about the will, the staff was anxious to serve their new mistress, most confessing that they had liked her from the beginning, in spite of the rumors, a few adding that they had known there to be something special about her the moment they laid eyes on her.

A feeling of optimism was obvious the moment Melinda walked in to greet her fellow authors who were gathered with John Thompson of Abra Bits and Collectables.

"Here we are together again," she said. "I am still overwhelmed by all that has happened. Heartbroken, of course, but overwhelmed by my father's generosity and faith in me."

She smiled sadly. "Just when I found him, he was taken from me," she said. "It doesn't seem fair, does it? But they say life isn't fair, so why should I be an exception?"

She sighed deeply. "All I know," she went on, "is that I am happy to be alive, and I am more thankful than I can say for you all. Though I have known you only a short time, I know you will be lifelong friends. I am so appreciative to have had you to share this difficult time with. Especially for you, Shelby," she added with a smile. "You really did save my life. I know it was because you believed in me. Now that I see that my father believed in me too, I am going to try to learn to believe in myself again, and do the best I can to be faithful to carry out my father's legacy and vision.

"In that light, I would like to ask you all to stay on for a few days. It is my hope that we can pick up where we left off before my father's death—with plans for Barribault House. I realize that for any enterprise of this nature, the energy and vision of a founding presence and strength is what embues an organization with its essential life. Without my father's vision and energy…can a major new publishing house get off the ground? I don't know. But I would rather try and fail than simply give up without trying. I have been in conference with Mr. Forsythe and Miss Gordon and several others most of the morning. They see no reason why we should not go ahead with plans as my father put them in place. He hired the most expert staff he could find. Those people are still willing and excited about the prospects. So that is my intent.

"I know that there were issues with a few of you. What I propose is that we start with a clean slate. At the time he envisioned Barribault House and the Barribault Foundation, my father did not know he had a daughter. There was talk about some of the authors eventually being on the board for the organization. I think that was the source of some of the friction, if I understand it correctly from my talks with Miss Gordon who was privy to my father's concerns. With the change in his will, at least for the present, that contingency will not exist. It will simply be a matter of publishing your books as the initial line in the Barribault House launch. Therefore, I plan to publish the books selected in his contest exactly according to his original intent— *your* books. There are two exceptions. We will obviously not be publishing the erstwhile Father Smythe's manuscript. And this morning Dr. Cobb came to me in private to withdraw his manuscript and return his advance check. I am convinced in discussing the matter with him that he did not intend to deceive my father. Whether *honest mistake* is the proper term, I cannot say.

Perhaps there was a little duplicity involved. But I am not one to point the finger and Dr. Cobb's conscience is his affair, not mine. Despite the water that has gone under the bridge, Dr. Cobb is one of us. I therefore proposed that we delay publication of his book and include it in our next year's list of titles, to which he agreed.

"That leaves us with six manuscripts. I would still like to publish eight books per my father's intent, and to market our launch as 'the Eight,' as we have been called. Therefore, I have already spoken with my father's chief editor upstairs and asked him to look at the manuscript you submitted to the contest, Mr. Thompson, which I have learned about from your talks with Miss Westbrook.

"Finally, as the eighth title for our initial launch, as the new book he was working on was not completed, I have decided to publish a new edition of my father's first novel, *Love's Dry Tears*. I am hoping, Dame Meyerson, that you will join me in writing an introductory tribute to my father, and I to my mother."

Dame Meyerson smiled and nodded, blinking back tears, then looked away and sought the handkerchief she had earlier shared with Melinda.

"For now, that is all I have to say," concluded Melinda. "We have had many ups and downs in a short time. I know some of you had planned to leave, and even have your bags packed upstairs. If you need to go and would like to come back another time, I will understand. But as we will be resuming plans for the publication of your books, there remains much work to be done. Those of you who can stay, therefore, I propose that we jump back into it where we left off, with consultations with the editorial and marketing staff upstairs, and that we get to work on the final preparations for your books...and mine.

"Finally, let me say again how much I appreciate your kindness to me through what has been a very trying personal ordeal and tragedy. I will never forget any of you. You have become dear friends."

* * *

It was obvious within a day or two that Cynthia Gordon and Melinda were going to hit it off and work well together. It did not take long for Cynthia to realize that Melinda had inherited many of her father's gifts. Soon the atmosphere in the offices of Cullen House were not merely back to normal but invigorated and motivated even to higher heights. If anything the staff was more committed to Melinda than they had been to her father in the knowledge that they had to work all the harder as a team to make their group effort work—their futures depended on it.

Though many aspects concerning the future of the estate would take a year or more to sort out, with death taxes sure to take their substantial bite from the Barribault fortune, once the straightforward provisions of the will were formalized, Melinda was enabled access to enough of her father's assets to keep the organization moving freely.

Several days after meeting with her fellow authors, Melinda announced her plans to call a major press conference. She had already been in touch with her adoptive mother and step-father in Minneapolis. Arrangements were being made to fly them over for the occasion.

Three days after the announcement, news teams from all over the U.K., including a large contingent from the B.B.C., began descending on Cullen at daybreak. Kept at bay for so long by Riggs' guard detail, most had given up their coverage of the Barribault murder days earlier. Now they were back, not only in Cullen but invited into the grounds. Those journalists who had been at the Seafield Arms all this time were treated like celebrities by the newcomers. By nine o'clock the front of Cullen House was swarming with journalists and photographers to such an extent that cars and vans lined the narrow drive a third of the way back to the village.

At eleven o'clock sharp, the front doors of the majestic house swung open and a beautiful young twenty-nine year old woman walked through the door, followed by about a dozen men and women. Her cornflower blue eyes reflected depths of both sky and sea, indicating seriousness, intelligence, and also bearing traces of secret sorrow. Her hair down to her shoulders, naturally curly and abundant, was a dark ginger, which might have indicated Celtic roots. In fact, half her heritage was Irish, the land of her birth.

She walked to the bank of microphones with a poise and confidence far in advance of her years.

"Good morning, ladies and gentlemen," she began. "I am Melinda Franks, one of those whom you of the press has for the past several months been referring to as the Barribault Eight. I came here as a graduate student from Cambridge, thinking only how fortunate I was to be selected to have my book of poetry published. With my colleagues, I soon discovered that more coincidences than could be imagined were at work among us. It is a long and complex story which will no doubt all come out in time. So I will cut straight to the punch line and tell you that within a few days of my arrival, I learned that Hugh Barribault was my father."

Astonished exclamations buzzed through the press corp like a jolt of electric current. Where she stood waiting, Melinda was flanked on one side by her six authorial colleagues, and on the other by her adoptive mother and stepfather, Mr. Forsythe and Cynthia Gordon, and D.C.I. Riggs and D.S. Westbrook.

"This revelation was as great a surprise to him as to me," Melinda went on after a moment. "Actually greater, in that being adopted I knew I had a biological father though had no expectation of ever discovering his identity. My father, on the other hand, did not know he had a daughter until the events of these past two weeks uncovered that fact.

"As you all know, of course...my father was killed a week ago—"

Melinda paused and glanced away, struggling to keep her emotions in control. She took a deep breath, then another, then looked up with a smile.

"Obviously," she said, "I do not want to go into that end of it. The two detectives who worked on the case are here with me. In a moment I will let them tell you about the case itself and the series of events which led to the arrest of our colleague, the man known to you as Dugan Smythe. They will answer all your questions. After that, I would like to tell you briefly what are my plans insofar as my father's publishing company are concerned. I would also like to introduce you personally to each of my colleagues who have shared the ordeal of recent days with me, and give them a chance to say a few words.

373

"The long and the short of it is that Barribault House and the Barribault Foundation will both go forward exactly according to my father's vision. There will of course be a few changes. Otherwise I am working with my father's expert staff to get everything back on track as smoothly and as quickly as possible. Two of those changes which I will just note briefly are that the book authored under the name Father Dugan Smythe will for obvious reasons be withdrawn from our list. In its place we will republish my father's first novel, *Love's Dry Tears*, which, though fiction, substantially tells the story of my father's and mother's brief time together in Ireland and which has therefore become very meaningful to me. Rounding out the eight titles in our initial launch will be a novel of early Scotland, *Heirs of the Ancients*, by Cullen's own John Thompson, who has been awarded an equal prize sum with the other winners, and who is replacing among 'the Eight' Dr. Briscoe Cobb, who, though he is still with us here, has withdrawn his book for consideration until a later time.

"I will introduce Mr. Thompson and the others in a few minutes. But now I would like to invite Detective Chief Inspector Richard Riggs of the Buckie Police Force to come forward, give a brief statement about the investigation, and then answer whatever questions you may have."

THIRTY-ONE

The Parting

A week had passed. A brief Indian summer basked the Moray coastline in Mediterannean like temperatures.

Melinda Barribault, as she was now calling herself, had stepped into the role left her by her father Hugh Barribault more quickly and competently than anyone had expected. Yet to the few who had come to know her well, she was still the young woman who had come to Cullen with hopes of having her first book published. More often now than before she sought the open spaces of the shoreline where she might be alone with a constant flood of new thoughts and feelings.

As she was returning from a pensive walk to Nelson's Seat and back late in the morning, she saw Shelby walking toward her.

"Out with your notebook I see?" said Shelby, smiling as they met.

"You never know when inspiration might strike," said Melinda, returning her smile. "I am feeling something bubbling inside."

"A new poem?"

"Probably. Something peaceful, serene, maybe a little melancholy, something about this place, about the changes that have come over me since I arrived. It gets into you, doesn't it—the sea, the sky, the smells of the ocean, the solitude."

"It does," rejoined Shelby as they began walking back through the village toward Cullen House.

"I have never been so at peace in my life. A strange thing to say so soon after losing my father and almost throwing myself onto the cliffs. But it is what I feel."

"Not so strange, really," said Shelby. "Sometimes it takes a major emotional event to open new places inside us. I am happy for you."

"I wouldn't be feeling what I am today had it not been for you. You reached out to me. I don't know if any of the others would have."

"I think each in our own way, we all found ways to reach out to one another. It was an amazing thing as I look back on it.— Have you had any success locating your mother's family in Ireland?"

"A few leads are surfacing. Some of my internet people are working on it. If I have relatives still living, I want to find them and know who they are, and make sure they are financially provided for. My father was a rich man. Even after taxes I will have far more than I need. If there are family members to be found, they deserve to share in my good fortune. I've also talked to my mum about finding where my mother is buried. She thinks she was cremated. We have someone looking into the records of Belfast's crematoriums. I know it's not very pleasant. But I have to try to make every possible connection with the past."

They walked for a while in silence.

"Everyone is nearly ready to go," said Shelby at length.

"I know," smiled Melinda sadly. "I am not looking forward to it. But this day had to come. I know I will cry buckets."

"We all will," said Shelby.

"Not Dr. Cobb or Jessica."

Shelby laughed. "You may be right, though they will be crying on the inside. Have you decided about school?"

"Not entirely. I am certainly not going to return just now. I've written to Cambridge explaining everything. I will have to see how things work out. What about you?"

"Back to the hectic pace of southern California. Part of me isn't looking forward to it. I will miss it here. But we all have lives to get back to, though your life is now here."

"You fly home from Glasgow?"

Shelby nodded.

"When is your flight?"

"In two days. Mike's going to drive me down to the airport in Glasgow. We'll follow each other into Aberdeen, I'll drop off my rental car, spend the night with him—in separate quarters!—then we'll go down to Glasgow tomorrow."

"All that way in his clunking VW bug!"

"It will be an adventure!" laughed Shelby.

* * *

A light farewell lunch behind them and bags brought down and sitting outside the front door, the men walked together to the garages to bring their three cars around to load up.

"Well, Rev. Pinker," said Graham Whitaker, "what will be your next Wodehouse?"

"I've been trying some of the standalones," replied St. John. "But they don't have the magic of Blandings and the Wooster Chronicles."

"By the way, I have a bone to pick with you," added Whitaker. "Do you remember that evening early on when you nailed me for calling it Anatole's steak and kidney pie...I have been thinking about it. I realize I wasn't wrong at all."

"It *was* Emerald Stoker's pie that Gussie went for."

"Granted. But you will similarly recall the hunger strike episode which caused Anatole to give notice. That also led to a midnight raid on the larder for steak and kidney pie—this time Aunt Dahlia and Tuppy tucking in, not Gussie...*Anatole's* steak and kidney pie."

"Of course, you're right! I concede you as the Wodehouse master!"

Graham laughed and the two men shook hands warmly.

On the other side of Whitaker's car, Jessica Stokes stood at the open door, then looked toward Melinda beside her. She smiled a little awkwardly.

"I've been trying to find a way to say this," said Jessica. "I'm sorry. I don't think I treated you very well at first."

"It was hard for us all. We were in an unfamiliar setting."

"I thought you were a flirt. I feel bad for that. Now I see how wrong I was."

Melinda laughed. "We all have own ways of interacting with people," she said, "our defense mechanisms, the little games we play. You had yours, I had mine. Please, don't worry about it. I am not offended in the least. Besides, I *was* a flirt—what can I say!"

"Good bye, Melinda," said Jessica. "Thank you for how kind you have been to me. I wish you the very best."

As Graham Whitaker and Jessica Stokes drove off, Briscoe Cobb walked up to Mike with his hand outstretched. "Well, St. John, we shall have to continue our theological musings someday—see if we can't figure out the meaning of the universe and all that."

"Right, Cobb," laughed Mike. "Perhaps we shall at that."

"What are you going to do with your quill...after all the time it was missing?"

"That's easy. I'm going to write another mystery with it!"

"An entire book with a quill! That will be tedious work."

"But a new experience, thus an adventure. Don't forget, it is no ordinary quill."

"Have it your way, St. John!" laughed Cobb.

He turned to Melinda.

"Well, Melinda, my dear, it looks like it's all yours now. I want again to express my gratitude for giving me a second chance. I will do my very best not to disappoint you."

"Everyone deserves a second chance, Dr. Cobb. I've needed a few in my life too."

Cobb walked to his car and opened the left side door of his Jaguar for Dame Meyerson. His passenger, however, had paused and walked slowly toward Melinda. Both women opened their arms and embraced. A bond of affection neither could explain had drawn them into a unique and wonderful relationship during the past days, almost as a mother and daughter, yet so much *more* than a mother and daughter. They held one another for several long seconds.

"I am sorry," whispered Melinda, "for what you had to go through...you know, with my father."

"Sorry, how do you mean," asked Jennifer softly. "You weren't to blame."

"I know. I'm just sorry for the pain you had to endure. It must have been very hard."

"No more than what you went through. I feel bad for you too. That's something we will always share. We both loved him, yet we both felt the pain of that love. He wasn't a saint...but we both loved him."

"You will come back, won't you, Jennifer?" said Melinda. "Like we talked about—just the two of us. We need to spend time together, away from the hubbub."

"I would like that. I would like that very much. Yes, I definitely will. Good bye, Melinda."

Dame Meyerson turned and walked to the car where Dr. Cobb was holding the door. She glanced back one last time. Melinda smiled radiantly. Dame Meyerson wiped at her eyes, returned the smile, then climbed in and Cobb closed the door behind her.

Only three of the Eight were left.

Melinda and Shelby had said their tearful goodbyes the night before. Nothing more needed be said between such friends as they had become. Mike St. John walked slowly to Melinda and opened his arms. She fell into his embrace.

"You are an amazing young woman, Melinda Barribault," said Mike. "I am proud to be your friend. The world doesn't know what it has in store from you!"

Melinda stepped back, her ginger-orange hair a mass of curls and disarray, her bright blue eyes swimming in liquid gratitude.

"Thank you, Mike," she said. "I have you to thank for much of how this has turned out."

"Don't forget what I said, as I am the closest of the Seven now, other than Mr. Thompson, if you need help or moral support in *anything* at all...please call. I am less than two hours away. It may get overwhelming at times. Please call."

"I will, I promise."

Two minutes later Mike's VW sputtered away out of sight with Shelby in her rental following.

Now there was only one.

* * *

Melinda watched them go, suddenly feeling very alone.

When the last of the cars had disappeared, she went inside for her jacket, her notebook, and her mother's diary, then set out for a long walk to the shore. From there she made her way to the bluff overlooking Bow Fiddle Rock.

An hour later sitting on the thick springy sea grass of the bluff, she opened her mother's diary. She flipped randomly through it, reading here and there the words that now carried such poignant meaning. At length she turned to the last page and read her mother's final words—written to her before she was born.

She thought a moment, then took out her pen and set it to the page below her mother's final entry.

Hello, Mummy, she wrote. *It is Melinda. I am now twenty-nine. I am finally beginning to know who I am. I want you to know that I intend to make you proud of me. I only knew Daddy for a week, but in that time I learned to love him. I am going to make something of my life, now that I know who you and Daddy are, and the love you had for each other. I will do my best to continue Daddy's work, and make you both proud of me.*

She closed the book and drew in deeply of the fresh sea air. How long she sat she could not say. When feelings turned themselves into words within her, time stood still. After several seconds, or perhaps an hour, she picked up the other book beside her, this time her own notebook. She opened to a fresh page, then took her pen and began to write.

COMING HOME

I have always felt a calling to something simple, yet deep,
personal…
the essential me.
A distant voice, a whispered word,
a pull from within and without.
Indistinct, sometimes its only names were longing and discontent,
A desire for solitude,

silence,
belonging.

That longing met one my heart had ached for without knowing it.
He too went alone to the sea,
to the fields,
to the mountain top.
Even in the midst of pressing crowds,
a garden of solitude grew in his heart.
He possessed the secret to plumb the silence.
He knew his Origin of belonging.

How does one discover that heart-garden of solitude
where grow flowers of peace?
Was it mere aloneness, this serenity I sought?
Was it being able to detach from the world's pace,
to withdraw,
observe,
reflect,
To separate from the hectic life while still participating in it?

Yet the answer is right in front of me.
Surely it is no dream that life can be informed by simplicity,
That an oasis exists where the heart's desire can be fulfilled,
Where simple solitude dwells in harmony with hurry,
stress,
crowds,
expectations...
even grief.

Is such hope a mere fancy spun from my imagination?
Surely no. I was meant to be here—
to discover my origin of being.
I was drawn to this place to learn of that simplicity
wherein dwells true reality.
In the garden of inner solitude,
I have at last come home.

THIRTY-TWO

The Farewell

Two months later, on a chilly afternoon of early December, as dusk settled in over a bright clear day of approaching winter, Melinda sent all the publishing staff home early. She also requested the household staff to take the afternoon and evening off and away from the house.

She wanted several hours alone, the entire place empty, no one anywhere nearby. Only herself.

The moment she had planned, since being given the idea by the title of her father's book, had come at last.

From where she had been keeping them for this occasion, she removed two urns, one that had been sealed twenty-nine years ago, the other but two months, from a shelf in the storage room which had served as their temporary private home.

Carrying one in each hand, with solemn reverence in her heart, Melinda descended the stairs and went outside. She walked to the private and secluded place in the garden. There she sat down on the stone bench where she and her father had had their last talk alone the last afternoon of his life. He had called this his favorite place on the entire grounds.

Behind the bench, with a simple stone engraving marking the spot, would be a fit final burial site for her father and mother.

With the shovel she had brought out earlier, she methodically dug a hole two feet deep at the place she had selected, then set the two urns beside it. Slowly she went to her knees.

Tears filling her eyes, she placed the urn of her mother's remains into the bottom of the hole, then set her father's beside it. She touched the one, then the other, allowing her fingers to linger on each several seconds. Slowly, and with a sigh of contented sad finality, she stood.

She drew in a deep breath, hesitated a moment, then took up the shovel from where it lay against the bench. Gently, almost reverently, recognizing, even in the covering of dirt, the last element in this sacred rite of passage, she began to fill the hole until its contents were no longer visible.

Good bye, Mummy...good bye, Daddy, Melinda whispered. *You are both now home at last. You will be at peace here, and we will all three be together...until I see you again.*

CPSIA information can be obtained at www.ICGtesting.com
Printed in the USA
LVOW08s1443210115

423772LV00020B/786/P